I0690134

The

inaldi

egacy

By Courtney Cole

LOVE IS DANGEROUS.

Lakehouse Press, Inc, 2014

Cover design by The Cover Lure (Matthew Phillips)

Library of Congress Cataloging-in-Publication Data

Cole, Courtney
    Minaldi Legacy, The/Courtney Cole/Lakehouse Press Inc/Trade

pbk,ed
ISBN 13: 978-0615960395 (Lakehouse Press Inc)
ISBN 10: 0615960391

Printed in the United States of America

Part One:

Of Blood

And

Bone

By Courtney Cole

"Nothing makes us so lonely as our secrets."
--Paul Tournier

Prologue

Luca is gone.

I know it before I open my eyes. The weight of his body next to me is absent, the scent of him gone from the air. I sigh, reluctant to begin this day because I know what it holds for me. I know that if Luca is truly gone, I will spend every hour frantically searching for him.

Gazing around, I find my large suite empty. Everything is neat and tidy and exactly in place. Each lavish piece of furniture is polished with lemon oil, each extravagant painting on the wall carefully dusted. Each expensive vase, each crystal lamp, each woven rug is perfectly aligned and exactly how I left it. Something is different, though, somehow changed in this room that I fell asleep in last night.

My sleepy eyes do another quick sweep, and this time I notice the balcony doors standing wide open while the bright morning sun streams onto the mahogany floor and the white sheer curtains on either side flutter in the sea breeze.

This is the difference and it slams into me like a concrete wall. I didn't fall asleep with those doors open. I would never do that now, not since I know what dangers lurk in the world, the darkness that can find me.

Immediately after I notice this inconsistency, I also see that across the room, my bedroom door is tightly closed and the bolt is still slid firmly in place.

Just as I left it last night.

My heart stutters as I realize what this means.

While I slept, Luca must have climbed from my balcony ledge to escape. But the drop is well over thirty feet and there are sharp rocks at the base of the house. There are gardens directly behind, but beyond that, there is a cliff with a hundred foot drop to the sea below.

I leap naked from bed and rush to the balcony's edge. My bare breasts press against the cold railing as I peer down at both the gardens and what I can see of the pristine sand beyond that. Luca is not lying broken and bleeding there, so I try to still my racing heart. I search the beaches and craggy landscape on both sides of my periphery and I still do not see him.

He somehow survived the fall.

A hundred different things run through my mind, but the one that stands out in the forefront is the image, the possibility, that he managed to drag himself, broken and bleeding, to a different location, somewhere where he is even now waiting for me to help him.

Because I promised.

I promised him that I would help him, that I would keep him from the darkness that plagues him, that I would heal him.

That I would save him.

I swallow hard and as I do, I realize that my throat is tender from Luca's hands last night. I know that if I look into a mirror, there will be a bruise in the perfect formation of his long fingers around my neck.

As I softly touch it, I remember his face from the night before. It was shadowed in the moonlight and like always, he was beautiful. Luca is handsome in a very classic and beautiful way, dark hair and cut cheekbones. His bangs are long and almost hide his magnificent dark eyes until he shakes his hair away. And when he does, the sadness that dwells there is apparent to anyone who knows him.

But last night, I didn't need to look into his eyes to see that his darkness had returned. I knew it from the moment he stepped into my room.

I can always see it. It changes everything about him, even the way he walks and moves. The way he stands. The way he speaks. The way he feels.

He is an entirely different person when the darkness comes.

These are the moments that he dreads with every breath when he is himself; the moments when he is no longer Luca. In these moments, he is filled with thoughts that are no longer his own.

He cannot help it, he cannot control it, he cannot stop it.

But I promised him that I would.

And I have failed him.

I scramble to my wardrobe and pull on clothing, choosing a shirt with a collar, hoping to somewhat hide the bruise on my neck. The only other people here at Chessarae are servants, except for Luca's mother in her lonely wing. But she is locked in so she never comes into the main part of the house. No one will see me but the staff. And they are used to seeing strange things.

I rush through the house, through the extravagant corridors and over the marble floors, the rich and polished surroundings that I would never have dreamed I would find myself in. I don't notice it now though. It has faded into an insignificant corner of my mind. All that matters now is Luca.

I make my way out the back of the house, through the gardens, through the English maze that is perfectly manicured and challenging to maneuver. I manage it with ease, however. I memorized its twists and turns on a happier day.

The weather is stormy today and the normally cheerful and bright Maltese sky is gray and thunderous. I can feel the electricity in the air, snapping the ends of my long hair with static. This day looks as foreboding as I feel, which I hope is not a sign.

I search through the maze. I search the beaches as my feet sink into the cool sand. I search the gardens with their exotic and sweet-smelling blooms and then I search the garage. His car, a shiny black Jaguar, is still in its slot and its hood is cool to the touch. Luca has not driven it today. I search the front lawns and the back. And just when I begin to panic, to fear that he has not returned to Chessarae after all, I search the stables.

As I walk through the heavy wooden doors, the smells of the horses and the hay and the saddle-soap and leather assail my nose and I breathe them in. I've always loved this place. It is peaceful here. And I suddenly know, because I can feel it, that Luca is here.

I walk quietly down the main corridor, staring into each stall as I pass.

And finally, finally, when I come to the very last stall on the left, Luca is there and my breath hitches in my chest, freezing on my lips.

Luca is slumped on the ground, in the corner, his expression desolate. He is beautiful even here, even in this condition, and I cannot help but stare down at him as tears fill my eyes.

He is dirty and his clothing is torn. There are smears of blood on his shirt, dried now to a rusty dark brown. I swallow hard, trying not to imagine where the blood has come from.

Luca's face is tortured as he stares up at me, his head in his hands. There is blood on his fingers.

"It happened again."

His words are low and husky and rough, yet elegant at the same time. He is always refined, always perfect, always Luca.

His self-loathe is apparent and it breaks my heart.

I nod mutely because there are no words for this moment. I bend to help him to his feet. At 6'3", he towers above me. He is slender and strong and masculine. He is lithe and powerful, beautiful and graceful.

And sometimes, on his very darkest days, he is a depraved killer.

But I have gotten ahead of myself. I should begin at the beginning.

If I don't, you will never understand.

Chapter One
From the Beginning

Eva

As I step from the ferry onto the pier, the first thing I notice about Malta is the smell in the air. It smells of sand and sea. Everything about this small island nation revolves around the shimmering blue water surrounding it. Fishermen have been born and bred and lived and died for thousands of years here. The sea is everything.

As a testament to that, ships and boats and dinghies are everywhere around me. There are fishermen, sailors and dockhands. There are fish mongers, there are fish markets and there are crusty old Maltese men who creep out to the piers at the crack of dawn to fish just for the pure enjoyment of it. The saltiness of the sea is in their blood.

Romans used to call Malta the Land of Honey. And as I stand here in the early evening light, I can see why. The sun is just starting to sink over the horizon, over the edge of the sea, and everything here is bathed in radiant gold. The buildings created from sandstone and ancient rock appear to glow in the light. And even though the name truly stems from Malta's ancient history of honey production, I prefer to think it is because Malta is continually bathed in a honey-colored glow from the sun.

I make my way down the wooden planked pier, taking care not to trip over the uneven boards. After thirty hours of traveling, mere walking is a difficult feat. I can't remember when I've ever been so exhausted.

"Dr. Talbot!"

A voice with a Maltese accent calls for me and I turn my head to find a stooped older man in a white floppy fishing hat making his way to me through the throng on the pier.

I smile and hold out my hand.

"You must be Tomas."

The man shakes his head. "No, my name is Alanzo. Tomas was detained, but he sent me to drive you to your summer cottage."

I nod. "Thank you. I appreciate that very much."

Immediately and unbidden, I form an opinion about this man.

Loyal, Kind. Trusting and open. An inherent need to please.

I can see all of these things in his eyes. Since my doctoral dissertation involves studying the decisiveness of the first meeting while assessing the personality traits of strangers, I can't help but do it myself whenever I meet anyone. It can grow annoying. But it is why I am here; to continue my research over the summer and wrap up my project so that I can begin a Psychiatry practice.

The old man stoops to pick up my suitcase. I put my hand on his. "Please, there must be someone I can hire to bring my bags. I have quite a few more."

I motion behind me at a large stack of bags and sealed plastic crates. Alanzo's eyes widen and I can't help but smile.

"My research," I explain. "It takes up a lot of space."

"I see that," he agrees. "It's no matter. Come with me, bella mia, and we will arrange for your bags to be delivered to your flat."

Alanzo leads me to a small rickety counter where he speaks fast and fluent Maltese to the girl standing there. He scribbles something on a paper and hands it to her with his gnarled fingers and she nods. Then he pays her. I try to hand him US Dollars, which is all I have at this point, but Alanzo shakes his head and clucks.

"No, no," he waves his hands. "Tomas instructed me to care for you. It's all right."

I'm too tired to argue.

He whistles and holds his hand in the air and hails a taxi.

I am surprised for just a moment. I guess I thought that Valletta was small enough to walk from place to place. Yet even now, I realize the silliness of that notion. There are 400,000 people on Malta and half of them live in Valletta. To be fair, the only memories I have from this place are from when I was small, when I spent a summer here with my gypsy-like father. The memories from my ten-year old self are probably distorted as hell.

I remember Italian ices, shell-hunting by the sea and long periods of boredom during which I entertained myself as my father played poker. Poker is, and always has been, Eric Talbot's life's blood. It's how he makes his living, how he gets his blood flowing. It also allows him to be very, very mobile. Each summer that I spent with him was in a different place, from Portland to Taiwan. But I remember Malta as being my favorite, because of its easy way of life and happy people. It's why I am here now.

Alanzo and I slip inside the air-conditioned interior of the car. I lean my head against the seat for a moment. I'm so tired. Tired enough, actually, that I find myself waking up as the taxi comes to a stop outside of a little bungalow.

I blink the sleep from my eyes and open the door.

"It's perfect," I breathe as I step from the car.

Alanzo beams. "You like it?"

"Of course," I nod.

The small flat is made from stucco and is situated on a bluff overlooking the sea. I can see for miles and miles here and the beach below us beckons to me. The sand is pristine and perfect, the sun beautiful and cheerful and there doesn't appear to be anyone else for at least a mile. I have surely found paradise. I will have to watch myself to make sure that I don't succumb to the temptation of lying on the beach all day. I have work to do.

"Come, Dr. Talbot," Alanzo beckons.

"Please," I call from behind him. "Call me Eva. Everyone else does."

He smiles. "Alright. Come, Eva."

I follow him up the winding path to the door. Green vines and fragrant white flowers are tangled on each side of the little walk and I pass a motorized scooter leaning against the house in the shade. I raise my eyebrows.

"It's for your use," Alanzo explains. "You can ride it almost anywhere that is too far for you to walk and for other needs, you can ride the bus." I nod as I file the information away.

He unlocks the door and hands me the key, then steps aside so that I can enter.

"One bedroom, one bath, kitchenette," he says. "Just as you asked for."

It is clean, cozy and efficient.

I nod. "It's perfect."

"Linens and towels are included. You will have a cleaning lady come once a week. You will not need to care for the house. If you require something or if something breaks, call Tomas and he will contact your land lord."

I nod again.

I don't bother insisting that I can take care of it myself. Malta is a very patriarchal society. The men enjoy being caretakers. I don't wish to intrude on that. I only wish to study their behavior when I meet them.

I walk through the small flat, taking note of the cozy furnishings, the open back doors that lead to a little patio area surrounded by a garden and the very small bed. I cringe.

"Not what you are used to?" Alanzo guesses.

I shake my head. "I haven't slept in a twin bed since I was a kid," I tell him. "But it's okay. I'll make do."

Because I definitely don't want to sound like a spoiled, self-entitled American.

Alanzo looks at me kindly.

"You seem very tired, Eva," he observes. "You should rest. Tomas will be along in the morning to welcome you."

I nod again. "You're right. I am tired. Thank you so much, Alanzo. It has been a pleasure meeting you."

He smiles, a wizened old grin, and then he is gone and I am alone.

I look around at the quiet little cottage with the dusk settling in and I know that I won't be able to hold my eyes open for much longer.

I curl onto the skinny little bed and close my eyes. I have a scant few minutes to appreciate the ocean crashing outside of my open window before I drift into a dreamless sleep.

***

It is dark when I wake.

I lie still for a moment because I know that something has woken me, but I don't hear anything out of the ordinary in this unfamiliar house. Shadows fall in angular slants against my wall but nothing is moving. The silence is still.

And then I feel it again, a tickling on my arm. My stomach sinks with dread as I brush at my skin and come into contact with something moving; something thin and fleshy.

I scream and leap from the bed, fumbling for the light switch on the wall.

There, sitting on my bed atop twisted sheets, is the largest, most terrifying spider I have ever seen in my life. Its hairy leg-span must be four or five inches. It is black and white striped and has a huge bulbous abdomen with some bright yellow stripes thrown in. I scream again just looking at it. It is so horrifying that I hesitate to even squash it with a shoe. I don't want to get my hand that close.

I stand still, breathing harshly as I try to decide what to do. There's no way that something that terrifying isn't poisonous. *Oh, god. Oh, god. Oh, god.* I hate spiders. I'm not thinking clearly now. I've barely woken up and I'm faced with this spawn of Satan sitting on my bed. I'm all alone in a strange and foreign place and there is a killer on my bed.

And then there's a voice.

"Miss, is everything alright?"

A deep voice is calling from outside of my house. And before I can think about it and remember that I don't know anyone here and that a stranger really shouldn't be outside of my house, particularly in the middle of the night, I answer.

"No. I'm not."

In a scant moment, a man bursts into my bedroom.

He looks startled to see that I am alone.

And I am startled because he's alarmingly handsome.

So it appears that we are both startled as we stare at each other.

He's dark haired, tanned, and has dark eyes. His bangs are hanging artfully in his eyes, although the hair on the back of his head is a little shorter. It's a style that works for him. He's got broad shoulders, slim hips, chiseled yet graceful features and Sweet Merciful Mary, he's beautiful. He's dressed in jogging shorts and running shoes and a bead of sweat trickles down his temple. I don't even have time to wonder why he's out for a run in the middle of the night before I notice that he's also got that sexy, day-old stubble that I so love on a man.

I swallow and realize that my mouth has gone dry.

"Are you alright?" he asks, his eyes skimming over me, assessing the situation. It's a valid question. I *had* been screaming bloody hell, after all.

I nod. Then shake my head.

"Spider," I whisper.

His dark eyes widen and he follows my pointing finger with his gaze.

Then he laughs, husky and rich.

"Spider," he confirms with a nod, his dark eyes sparkling in amusement. "It looks like you've got yourself a perfect specimen of the Writing Spider."

"Writing Spider?" I repeat, watching it nervously, making sure it doesn't try to run across the bedroom floor and up my leg. "Is it poisonous?"

Handsome Running Guy nods solemnly.

"Oh, it's a known killer, alright."

I gasp and lurch even further away from the hairy creature on my bed and Handsome Running Guy laughs.

"I'm sorry. I'm only joking. I couldn't resist. It's not poisonous. I think its scientific name is Black and Yellow Argiope, or something like that. They are all over here. But you wouldn't know that because you're not from here, are you?"

I shake my head again, trying not to be overly enthralled with his charming accent.

"Is it that obvious?"

He smiles and suddenly it seems like all natural sources of light are pouring into my room, originating from this man. He's got such a strong presence that it makes my spine tingle. And my stomach is fluttering in a way that it hasn't fluttered since high school. Interesting.

He shakes his head and then holds out his hand.

"Luca Minaldi," he tells me and his fingers are cool as he shakes my hand.

"Evangeline Talbot," I answer. "But my friends call me Eva."

"It's nice to meet you," and his eyes agree with him as he stares at me. "The question now is would you like for me to kill your uninvited guest or should I release him into the wilds?"

"Kill it," I say firmly. Slight disapproval passes over Luca's face like a shadow.

"Are you certain?" he asks. "It's an amazing specimen and they do eat bugs. Bugs can get pesky here in Malta, Evangeline."

"You can call me Eva," I answer. "And if we release it into the outdoors, he might come back in."

I shudder again at that thought.

"True," Luca agrees. "And so might anyone else. Your door wasn't locked. And I can't call you Eva. We're not yet friends."

There is disapproval on his face again and I find his manner of speaking intriguing.

Rich, formal, gentleman, I list in my head as I stare at his manicured hands. Then I add *jaded* to the list. There's also something else about him, something that I can't put my finger on yet. I make a note of that. It's a little discouraging since my thesis is based on the notion that an intuitive person can peg someone on the first meeting. However, our first meeting isn't over yet and I return my attention to him.

"I was so tired when I got here that I barely remember walking through the house," I admit to him. "It doesn't surprise me that I left the door open."

"Well, that's understandable," Luca answers. "Jet lag is miserable. But do be more careful. You are in a strange place."

"So you've said," I nod, slightly impatient with the safety lecture. I'm a grown woman. I know how to take care of myself. "Now will you kill the spider or do I need to call my landlord?"

Luca smiles and the room brightens once again.

Interesting, both that this man's mood can change the atmosphere in my entire bedroom and that his mood changes so quickly. Should I add *mercurial* to the list?

I hold off on that one as he raises an eyebrow at me.

"You'd really call your landlord this late after business hours for an insect?"

I eye the spider. "That is not an insect," I tell him. "That's a monster. I've been told that I'm always welcome to call him in an emergency. I'd say this qualifies."

Luca chuckles and shakes his head.

"I hate to kill something that isn't hurting us," he tells me. "Let's find a jar. A large jar."

I shake my head and slip out to the kitchen, bringing him back a large canning jar that I found beneath the sink. I hand it to him and he quickly scoops the large spider into the jar, then covers it with his hand, unafraid.

I shudder on his behalf as I watch the long hairy legs twitching against his palm.

"How do you stand that?" I demand as I trail him to the back door. He walks a few feet into the night and releases the spider into the grass. It quickly scurries away into the darkness although I'm sure it will find its way back into my house soon enough.

"It wasn't going to hurt me," he told me. "Because I wasn't hurting *it*. That's usually how nature works."

"Not so," I counter. "Not always. I'm sure that a gazelle hunted by a lion would beg to differ with you."

Luca's lip twitches. "Lucky for us, this isn't the Serengeti. If you don't provoke something here, you will generally be left alone."

I smile. "Well, good. I'm not in the habit of provoking people. Unless they are lying on my couch, anyway."

Luca's eyebrows raise again. "Pardon?"

I laugh when I realize what I must have sounded like. "I'm a psychiatrist. Almost. I'm here for the summer to finish my dissertation. People pay me to probe at their secrets."

Luca seems interested now. I add *unafraid* to his list. People are generally a little put off when I tell them what I do which is why I like to get it out of the way right off the bat. It's like they are afraid that I will dissect their brains during casual conversation. And in all honesty, I sort of do. It's an occupational hazard. I can't turn it on and off.

"You're a psychiatrist?"

I nod. "Are you afraid?"

It was a joke. But he pauses for a moment before he smiles.

"Very, very afraid."

There is electricity between us. And I'm not sure if it is because he's so very handsome or if it is simply because he is a strange man standing in my bedroom. Either way, I can feel it and I smile.

"You should be."

He smiles back, a guarded smile. "Noted."

Luca hands me the jar back and when he does, his hand brushes mine. His touch is feather light but I can feel exactly where our skin comes into contact and it feels as though I will have a permanent impression of his fingers on my own. My eyes dart up and meet his, which are a turbulent black, full of charged energy.

Our gazes lock and I am speechless, utterly engrossed in the power of this moment. I've never been so instantly attracted to a man. I don't know if it is simply a by-product of my jetlag or if it is real.

However, I don't get a chance to ponder it. Out of my periphery, I notice a movement out of the corner of my eye and glancing down, I find that the spider, probably disoriented from this whole ordeal, is scurrying back across the lawn and is aimed directly at my feet.

It is moving fast and I barely have time to gasp or scream before Luca's foot slams down upon it with a sickening crunch.

Its long broken legs stick out from under the sole of his running shoe as I stare at him uncertainly.

"I thought you said it wasn't going to hurt me? That we shouldn't kill it because it meant no harm?"

Luca shrugs. "I changed my mind."

And something about this moment and his words and his nonchalant attitude sends goose bumps forming up and down my arms, although I don't know why. I'm shocked that he killed it, but it was just a spider. An insect. But it somehow seems strange. Five minutes ago, he was dead set against hurting it and then he turned around and killed it without a second thought.

I think I should add *mercurial* after all.

I glance at his face and now it seems as though shadows have passed over it, thunderous and dark. I inhale sharply as I watch him gracefully wipe his shoe off in the grass. He's lithe and muscular, like a lion, and I suddenly realize that a jungle cat is exactly what he reminds me of. He is sleek and powerful and masculine.

Dangerous.

The word pops unbidden into my mind and I try to shake it off.

He killed a spider, not a person or a puppy. I have no basis for thinking that he is dangerous. But as he turns his eyes toward me, there is something there, something in the dark depths that I can't define, something *dangerous.*

And so I reluctantly add it to his list. This is just my first impression after all. It remains to be seen if my instinct has any validity whatsoever. I can just as easily take it off the list as I put it on. I look up to find him staring at me with his dark and fathomless eyes. Those are eyes that a person could lose themselves in.

Why does it seem like everything has turned tense? I didn't mean for that at all. I was just surprised by the turn of events. So I tell him that. And then I hold out my hand.

"It was really nice to meet you, Luca. Thank you so much for taking care of the spawn of Satan. I really appreciate it."

He nods, relaxed once again. "Anytime. I'm a spawn of Satan specialist. I'm just happy that I was nearby and heard you scream."

"Yes," I agree. "That was very lucky for me."

"Hmm," Luca says, drawing out the sound. "Let's leave that verdict out for now, shall we?"

I stare at him, wondering what that means and why he seems so mysterious when he suddenly turns and walks out. I trail weakly behind him, trying to figure out what I had missed.

And then he's gone.

He's such a commanding presence that his absence is noticed immediately. The air around me lightens and the charged atmosphere is gone, like a thunderstorm that has abruptly moved on. I stand at the front door, watching him jog lightly down to the beach where he continues running in the wet sand. I watch his broad shoulders ripple as he moves until he is gone from my sight.

And I'm holding my breath. I realize it in an instant and inhale deeply.

Luca Minaldi, whoever he is, is intense.

I add that to the list and then examine it in my head.

Rich
Formal
Gentleman
Jaded

Unafraid
Intense
Mercurial
Dangerous

I have no way of telling at this point if these descriptors are accurate. In order to know for sure, I'll have to interact with Luca Minaldi again. Luckily, as part of my research, I have vowed that if I have meaningful interaction with anyone this summer, I must follow-up with them in a second or third meeting so that I can ascertain if my initial theory on his or her character was correct. It's the only way I can test my hypothesis in a practical sense.

But something deep inside of me tells me that my hypothesis should be damned in relation to Luca. I shouldn't pursue another meeting with him. There's something about him, something secretive and troubling, that I know I should steer clear of. My trained intuition is shouting at me.

And although I don't have any basis other than my own intuition for it, I add *secretive* to the list. Because one thing is clear. Luca Minaldi is an enigma. I shake my head and lock my door before going back to bed.

Chapter Two

The Beast

My vision tunnels as it always does when I lose myself.

I only have a split second, a moment, really; before I am overtaken by the basest of instincts, by the blurs of reds and blacks. I can't fight it. I have tried before and it is useless.

My periphery is vanished now, absorbed by the darkness. I can focus only on what is in front of me. My subconscious is gone, my guilt is gone, my logic is gone.

There is nothing left.

Except for a driving need.

As always, I succumb to it.

I can do nothing else.

My feet thump onto the twisted path to the beach and my head snaps to attention in the breeze. Someone in the near distance is cooking dinner.

Oregano, oil, beef.

I pivot and move into the shadows where I belong.

My nerve-endings are standing at attention. I can smell everything, see everything. I can feel *everything*. It is exhilarating and smothering at once. I breathe deeply and attempt to harness it. And then I charge ahead into the night, through the trees.

A house comes into focus. Small and neat. I pad lightly up the path and the ocean crashes behind me as I linger at the door. Dinner smells drift from the window and I inhale, allowing the breeze to wash over my skin as I stand still.

I am only hungry for one thing.

There is not the bustle of family from within these walls. There is no noise at all.

I don't knock.

I move silently through the rooms until I find what I am looking for.

She turns, startled.

But she doesn't scream. She looks curious; wondering why I am here, what I want from her. I don't hesitate to show her.

I cross the room in two strides.

Her throat is in my hands.

My tongue is in her mouth, her teeth scrape against mine.

She is screaming now because she can see what I want, but my mouth quickly muffles the noise.

I enjoy the vibration of the sound against my lips, the heat of her breath against mine. Everything is visceral now, an explosion of sensations and my vision blurs.

She is soft and I am hard and I rage against her, taking her over and over until her eyes glaze and her screaming stops.

Her heart is pounding against my chest and her body is so very fragile.

So I break it.

Chapter Three

Eva

A knock on my cottage door wakes me from sleep. I lie still for a moment longer, clearing my mind from sleep-induced fog. There is another knock and I climb from the bed, only just now remembering that I am still fully dressed, as I answer the door.

An elderly man is on my stoop with grayed hair and warm brown eyes.

He looks at me and grins.

"Dr. Talbot! You look just like your papa! But for your eyes and red hair."

I shake my head. This is something that I've heard my entire life. I do resemble my father with my straight Roman nose and delicate features. My father has dark eyes though, and I have inherited my mother's instead, as well as her pale skin and red hair.

"You must be Tomas," I observe. He grasps my hand and squeezes it while he nods.

"Yes, bella mia. I'm so sorry that I was unable to meet you yesterday. I'm an old man and I had a doctor's appointment to keep. I do hope that my friend Alanzo didn't ramble too much with his stories."

I laugh and shake my head. "No, Alanzo was charming. Thank you for sending him."

Tomas smiles. "I'm so happy to finally see you again. You probably don't remember me, but I knew your papa very well when you and he lived here so many years ago."

I laugh. "I don't remember much from that long ago, Tomas. But I'm very happy to meet you now."

Loyal, friendly, open.

I begin my mental list of Tomas' traits.

"Your bags arrived," he tells me, motioning to a stack of luggage outside of the door. "You must have been sleeping."

"I was very tired," I explain as we begin lugging the bags through the door. He clucks as he hands me a heavily loaded crate.

"I know," he tells me. "I was here earlier and saw you sleeping through the window. I didn't want to wake you because you seemed very tired. You will have to take care of yourself, bella," Tomas says as he eyes me. "Your papa wants me to look after you. I promised him that I would make sure that you slept enough and that I would keep all of the boys away so that you could finish your research project."

I laugh again. I'm still tired enough that everything seems funny, particular when he refers to men my age as 'boys'. At twenty-nine, I'm just a minute away from thirty. If boys aren't men by this point, they never will be.

"I'm not too worried about the boys, Tomas," I tell him. "I'm not here to find a husband."

I decide to get that out of the way right off the bat. Like their close neighbors, the Italians, family is very important to the Maltese. I know that I will be prodded the entire summer by well-wishing people who want to see me married off and happy.

I sigh at the thought because right now my only wish is to finish my dissertation and start my career. I've worked long and hard for it and I'm right at the cusp. Just this summer and I will be done with all of the academic red tape. It's almost surreal.

Tomas shakes his head.

"You're a pretty girl, bella. You will not have a problem finding a husband. I don't worry about that one bit."

I refrain from telling him that I'm not worried, either.

My stomach growls loudly, rudely interrupting our conversation, and I suddenly realize that it has been hours and hours since I have eaten. I look at Tomas.

"Tomas, where is the closest place to eat?"

"Now you're talking," he beams. "Your father also made me swear that I would make you eat this summer. He's afraid you are growing too skinny."

I self-consciously wrap my arms around my waist. It's true. While I was finishing up my residency this year, I worked many, many twelve and sixteen hour shifts in the Psych unit at the Oregon Health and Science University in Portland. There were times that food just wasn't that high on my priority list. Sleeping became the most important thing in the world, second only to breathing.

"If you walk down the road about one and a half kilometers, you'll find a little bistro on the beach. You will love it. Marianne owns the place. Just tell her that I sent you and she'll take special care of you, because she holds a special place in her heart for me." His faded eyes are twinkling now. "Would you like for me to take you right now?"

He looks at me with kind eyes and I would love to go and eat with him because I get the feeling that he is lonely. But I'm still so tired.

"Tomas, I'll take a rain-check on that. I still feel pretty exhausted and I want to unpack a little and shower before I eat, but I would love to have dinner with you sometime soon."

He nods understandingly. "Of course, Eva. I'll get out of your hair now and let you settle in. But I'll check in on your from time to time. And of course, you will owe me a dinner date. I'll come around to collect on that. Don't hesitate to call me if you need anything."

I smile and agree and walk him to the door where he kisses both of my cheeks in the European fashion before he leaves.

Regardless of my rumbling tummy, I find that I am simply too tired to be of much good. The jet-lag has gotten to me. I grab a crocheted blanket from the back of the couch and curl up for a nap. To my complete surprise, I don't wake up for six hours, when it is once again evening.

Jet lag has truly wiped me out, I decide as I sit up and stretch, then drag myself from the small couch.

I make my way into the tiny bathroom to shower and brush my teeth. Traveling around the world does tend to make a person happy for the small things in life. I have decided that clean teeth and clean underwear are two of the most important things in the world. Without them, I feel less than human.

I put my clothing away in the little dresser in the bedroom and then set up an office area in the little kitchenette. It is dark outside but my stomach is rumbling louder than ever and I find myself wondering how long the little bistro that Tomas told me about will stay open tonight. Since I am famished and don't have any food in the house yet, I decide to find out.

Despite my long nap, I'm too weary to walk so I examine the little scooter. Figuring out how to work it is a challenging feat in the dark, especially since there isn't a porch light. But once I figure out the various buttons, I roll down the curving road in the direction that Tomas had pointed earlier. At just around the kilometer and a half mark, just like Tomas said, I find a small path that leads down to the beach and I nose the little scooter downward.

When I get to the sand, I park it and walk since I know there is no way that the wheels would make it on the beach. As I walk along, a scream emanates from the dark.

I stop still in my tracks and glance around nervously, as the hair raises on my neck.

There's no one here but me. The only movement is the sea sliding back and forth along the foamy lip of the shore, and the trees rustling quietly along the craggy cliffs above.

It's quiet now. And I wonder if perhaps someone was playing. Maybe a child? It sounded like a woman, but I can't really be sure. And it's gone now. So it must've been nothing. If it were something, she'd still be screaming. And like usual, I am over-analyzing the situation. I smile to myself because that's an occupational hazard and keep walking because I can see a little café a hundred yards or so away. Its welcoming light shines onto the beach around it like a beacon, drawing me to it.

I step inside and find that it is empty. There is not a soul seated among the little tables and cozy booths. A candle flickers at each table, creating a warm and inviting atmosphere and I am instantly in love with this place. I already know that I will spend many evenings here because I am not much one for cooking.

I walk to the front and stand by the cash register, waiting for someone to notice me. It doesn't take long for a tiny woman to emerge from a swinging door. She can't be any taller than five feet tall, her white hair cut into a fashionable bob. Her ice blue eyes meet mine and she smiles welcomingly.

"Welcome. Table for one?" She looks past me questioningly.

I nod. "Yes. Table for one. How late are you open?"

"Oh, we're open until midnight," she answers warmly. "Don't worry about that."

I glance at my watch, an expensive medical school graduation gift from my father. Its silver hands tell me that it is 11:00 pm. I slept all day and evening, which is very unlike me.

Marianne leads me to a little booth and sits me down, fussing over me as she does.

"What is a pretty thing like you doing out in the dark alone?" she asks as she hands me a menu. But then she just as quickly takes it away. "I know just what you need," she winks. "Our special of the day is just what the doctor ordered for you, bella. You need some meat on your bones."

She doesn't give me a chance to argue, instead she is gone before I even know it. And I love how everyone refers to women as 'bella' here. *Beautiful*. It is endearing.

Marianne is back within a minute with a glass of red wine and a basket of fragrant bread.

"Eat, eat," she waves her hands. And then she promptly sits down in the empty seat across from me. "You don't mind, do you?" she raises an eyebrow.

"Of course not," I answer. "Please sit."

She smiles, because she knows as well as I do that she was planning to sit regardless of what I said. She watches as I make short work of a breadstick and half of my glass of wine. She looks satisfied by that and only then does she try to engage me in conversation, asking where I'm from, why I'm here, and what my plans are. I answer her and she is visibly impressed.

"A psychiatrist?" she repeats. "You must be a smart girl. Beautiful *and* smart. Your parents must be proud."

Someone from the kitchen brings out a steaming bowl of fettuccine and the smells make my mouth instantly water. Yes, I will be spending quite a few evenings here. I already know it.

Marianne watches me eat, a small smile on her face.

"Do you know a Luca Minaldi?" I ask curiously in between bites. She looks instantly intrigued.

"Why do you ask?" she inquires.

I shake my head. "Just curious. I met him last night. He was out jogging and heard me screaming about a spider." I tell her about the incident and she laughs.

"Yes, those are nasty little creatures," she agrees. "And I'm from here. I've never gotten used to them. It surprises me, however, that Luca Minaldi would approach you. He tends to stay to himself."

And that intrigues *me*.

"What do you mean?" I ask. Marianne shrugs.

"You'd think someone in his standing would come to all of the important social functions, but he seldom does. His family has been here in Valletta for generations. They own Minaldi Shipping and their ships can be seen all over the world. Yet, he doesn't seem to be much of a people person. It's too bad, really. With his looks and money, he truly is Malta's most eligible bachelor."

"He's single?"

I ask the question before I even think about it. Shit.

Marianne smiles. "Yes, my dear. He's single. He would have to come out and meet people in order to become married and he doesn't do much of that. He lives outside of town on the coast on an estate called Chessarae. It's a beautiful property, really. Although he never hosts any functions there anymore. Not since his mother is no longer well. She used to be quite the socialite. But no more… not since Nicolas died."

"Nicolas was Luca's father?" I take a guess. She nods.

"Yes. Nicolas died some years ago. Melina became a recluse of sorts after that. She stays on the property now. No one has seen her in a year or two."

"She lives with Luca?" I ask. For some reason, this surprises me. He seemed so self-sufficient. Power practically emanates from his pores, not the kind of person you would think lives with his mother.

Marianne smiles again.

"Eva, you are no longer in America. Things are done differently here. Families often live together because family is very important to us. When all is said and gone, family is what will remain. And besides, Chessarae is so large that there is room for five families to live there comfortably. But as it was, for years, it was just the three Minaldi boys and their parents. But then Nicolas died, and Christoph and Damien moved away, working in other Minaldi Shipping locations. Luca is the only one still at the house."

"Does he also work for the family business?" I don't know why I'm curious. I just am.

Marianne nods again. "Yes, he does."

Interesting.

I'm too interested. And I know that I'm not going to let it go. I need a follow-up meeting with him. His personality is just too interesting. There are too many facets to it that I can't put my finger on. And the things that I can pinpoint are fascinating. I tell myself that I am only interested in his mind, his personality, and definitely only in the medical sense, but I'm not sure that I believe it.

"How can I go about setting up a meeting with him?" I ask Marianne. She grins.

"I thought you'd never ask!" she laughs and refills my wine glass.

"You can either show up at their home unannounced," she tells me. "Or you can finagle a meeting at the library in town. His family is a patron of

34

the library and one of the few things that he comes into town for are the board meetings. As it happens, I also am on the board, so I can tell you when to come 'bump' into him."

I feel slightly lecherous in trying to plan a chance meeting with the town's most eligible bachelor in such a way. And I tell Marianne so. She just laughs.

"My sweet, a girl's got to do what a girl's got to do. If he isn't coming to you, go to him. Make it happen."

I don't bother to explain why I want to meet with him again. This is a cultural thing, I know. She assumes that I am fascinated with him as potential husband material. And so I let her believe that. And honestly, her notion is only half false. I'm not in the market for a husband, but I am certainly fascinated by him.

But the conversation topic changes and before I know it, I find that I have made a new friend and we have chatted until well past midnight. After I have finished six breadsticks and we have split two bottles of wine, I finally have to insist that I am going home. I promise Marianne that I will be back very soon and she promises me that she will come by the cottage with the library board meeting schedule.

The trail home is dark and breezy and I ride quickly. It feels eerie out here in the dark, borderline spooky, although I don't know why. I almost miss the trail that leads back up to the road, but I see it just in time and make my way back to my little cottage.

And even though I had slept all day, I find that I am still tired enough to sleep. In an effort to thwart a little of my jet-lag, however, I decide that I should stay up for a little while longer, just to make sure that I sleep through the night. I've got to get my body back in sync with the clock.

So, I try to stay awake and read, but my thoughts keep drifting to Luca Minaldi.

I truly have never met someone like him before and so I can't shake the thoughts that keep passing through my mind. The dark, dark energy that seemed to surround him, commanding the room. The way his thigh seemed so strong when it brushed against mine, the way the muscle moved in his arm, the way he seemed so lithe and powerful. I could practically see the individual muscles rippling in his shoulders through his shirt as he bent outside of my house. It was apparent that he is very, very fit. His stomach is rock hard, perfectly flat. As I wonder what it would feel like to run my hands across that flat expanse of muscle, my breath quickens at the thought.

His face was so, so handsome and the way the moonlight slanted against it only enhanced that and made him seem even more mysterious. Even now, the mere memory of it, of *him*, stirs fluttery feelings in my belly. I place my hand there, as if to suppress those stirrings, but the feeling of my fingers on my bare skin gives me a better idea.

I slide my hand downward.

In my head, my hand transforms into Luca's, sliding down my stomach, then along my leg, whispering into my ear as his fingers grasp the tender flesh of my inner thigh.

Eva, you are so beautiful. Let me touch you.

His hand continues moving, until it glides to a stop when he reaches *there*, a place that hasn't been touched in far too long.

The breath catches in my throat as his fingers gently massage the most sensitive part of me. He moves in a circle, his fingers as skilled as I thought they would be.

He looks into my eyes and his are as black and dangerous as they were last night. His body is naked and hard as it slides against mine.

I want you, Eva. His lips are perfect and full as they mouth the words to me. I nod, giving my consent and he slips his fingers into me, moving them at just the right speed. He moves faster just when I need him to, and I hold my breath and close my eyes, picturing his other hand cupping my breast before he bends his dark head and sucks my nipple.

It is my undoing and my head throws back as I come against my own fingers.

I fall limply back against my pillows and calm my ragged breathing.

As I do, I remind myself that this was just a fantasy. A far-fetched fantasy, at that. Luca wouldn't even call me Eva...because we aren't yet friends. I roll my eyes in the dark and curl onto my side. I don't know why he has fascinated me to the point of sexual fantasy. There's no way he would be in my bed. Even still, the last things I think about before I sleep are Luca's strong hands and his dark and mysterious eyes.

Chapter Four

Luca

I see her.

I know I am dreaming, but it is as real as anything I've ever seen. She's standing in front of me, her red hair gleaming in the moonlight. She turns her face and her skin is creamy white in the dark. She seems too beautiful to be real, ethereal almost. I take a step toward her and then stop.

Because I know I must.

Her intriguing eyes, not quite gray but not quite green, stare into mine and I can't help but to walk toward her. She's drawing me to her and she's doing it on purpose. She senses the danger, I can tell. But she doesn't care. I swallow hard. If she doesn't care, it makes it more difficult for me to do so.

"Luca, it's okay. Come to me," she pleads.

I know better, but I go anyway.

I touch her hand and she grabs mine, pulling me to her with desperation and need. She clutches my hair, covering my mouth with hers until we are kissing in a way that should light the nearby shrubbery on fire. She tastes like wine and her lips are full and swollen. She is the most tantalizing thing I've ever seen.

She rocks against me, and I am instantly hard. She slides against my body, pushing ever closer. I press my erection against her, nudging it firmly between her thighs. She smiles knowingly, her lips moving against my neck, as she grabs my hand and places it directly between her thighs. She is wet. She wants me.

And I want her.

She knows that I want her.

"Fuck me, Luca," she whispers, as her eyes meet mine.

I start to pull her closer to me, to pull her clothing off of her body, when her eyes widen as she stares at something behind me.

And then she begins to scream.

Her scream is terrified and horrified and the breath lodges in my throat. I am frozen and I don't want to look.

But I do.

I turn, hesitant because I am afraid of what I will find. And it is worse than I feared.

Stacks of bodies, of bloodied and bruised women, are piled behind me on the darkened beach and I clench my jaw in horror. I know I did that. I hurt them. But I don't remember any of it. And that is the worst nightmare of all.

She is staring at me in horror as she backs away, her eyes condemning me for being what I am.

A monster.

And then I'm awake.

I sit straight up in my bed and my sheets are damp from a terror-induced sweat. My fingers are curled around my pillow, clutching it for dear life. This is a familiar dream. I dream it often, almost every night, which is one of the reasons that I dread the night. Tonight, however, there was an addition to my dream.

Her.

Evangeline.

Her name is soft on my tongue and I say it aloud, quietly in the darkness of my suite. Shadows fall around me, against my walls and my bed, but that's fine. I enjoy it that way. I belong in shadows. I have known that since I was small and as long as I am awake, I feel comfortable there.

I reach for a glass on my bed stand and take a big gulp of water, allowing the sleep to fade away so that I can think more clearly.

I am intrigued by this new woman, by her open and curious face, by her interesting eyes, by her beauty.

I want her. This dream was a testament to that. And I haven't wanted anything for a very long time.

The knowledge is startling.

I can't fool myself into thinking that her beauty does not play a part in my fascination. Of course it does. She is breathtaking. But it isn't just that. She's smart and confident in a way that I haven't quite seen before. She's a very capable person. Except when she's dealing with a spider.

I smile at the memory and realize that I'm once again gripping my pillow. I release it, tossing it to the other side of the bed. I flex my fingers and as I do I see that there is blood beneath my fingernails.

I cringe, the familiar horror lodged in my chest, surrounding my heart. I numbly rise from bed and walk quietly into my bathroom, scrubbing my hands as vigorously as I can. I'm surprised I don't take the skin from the bone, but it remains firmly attached to my hand. It wouldn't matter to me either way at this point.

I stare into the mirror and like always, I don't like what I see. I saw my reflection in Evangeline's horrified stare. She saw me for what I am. I don't give a fuck if it was a dream. She can see through me.

I look away and dry my hands, then slide down the tiled wall until I am resting against the cool stone. I lay my head back and close my eyes. I'm very weary. Not tired, but weary. And there is a difference.

But as I sit with my eyes closed, her face passes through my mind yet again. Her smile flashes in my memory and I suddenly find myself wanting to meet with her again, even though I shouldn't.

I know where she lives. I could swing by unannounced and bring her a bottle of wine as a welcome to Malta gift. I could check to see if she has had any more uninvited spider guests. I could… do nothing.

I can't endanger her in such a way.

Suddenly, my reality crushes upon me in a way that I haven't felt in years. I have long since reconciled myself with my life. But now, tonight, it seems too great a burden to bear.

And try as I might not to think of her, I fall asleep sprawled on the bathroom floor thinking of her gray-green eyes.

Chapter Five

Eva

I decide to take the bus into town. I'm not sure why, but I know that if I don't expose myself to people from the very beginning, I might be inclined to become a hermit in my little shore-side cottage. And the entire reason I am here is to finish up my research, an endeavor that will involve people.

On the trip to town, I sit next to an older woman and as we chat, I compile my list of her traits in my head. *Beaten down by life, tired, negative.*

I decide that I don't like her energy. She's very jaded and worn-out, and I know that nothing in this life will make her happy. I have already decided that I won't be following up with her by the time she gets off at the next stop. By this time, I also realize that I don't much like the bus. There are babies crying, people coughing and an overwhelming stench of body odor. I fight the urge to pull my shirt up over my nose.

I feel like a witch, but I haven't eaten anything for breakfast and the smell is threatening to turn my stomach. I'm headed to the market to buy supplies for my kitchen, but I'm going to have to eat something first. So when the bus reaches the downtown area, I disembark and hunt for a café.

It doesn't take long to find since there's practically one on every corner.

I duck into one, a quaint little coffee shop with little bistro tables clustered on the sidewalk, and stand in line to order a coffee and a Danish. I never feel quite human until I've had a cup of coffee in the morning and so while I stand in line, I tide myself over by inhaling the rich aroma of the freshly ground beans.

As I wait, I hear a couple of women murmuring behind me in the line. They sound surprised and interested in something. And I accidently pick out the words "Luca Minaldi" in their conversation. This immediately snags my attention and I turn, only to find them watching the sidewalk. I follow their stares and find Luca himself standing outside.

My breath catches for a moment.

After my imaginary romantic interlude with him, I dreamed about him for most of the night. So it seems strange and a little startling to find myself staring at him in person for the second time in as many days. He's standing in the morning sun, looking chic and rich and sophisticated in black slacks and a gray striped dress shirt, open at the neck. He's every bit as beautiful as he was in my head last night. I don't know what he is doing here now, but he appears to be waiting for something. Or maybe someone.

I can't decide what to do. Should I approach him? Thank him once again for killing the spider? Thank him for his 'participation' last night? I silently laugh at that one, imagining the look that would result on his face from that conversation. I am surprised by how much I'd like to talk with him again.

As I'm pondering how to go about it, he turns and his dark, dark eyes meet mine.

His head is slightly ducked as he looks at me from under his bangs and his face is expressionless, almost hard. But his eyes….they are smoldering like nothing I've ever seen, like he knows something intimate about me, like he knows what I'm thinking.

Like he knows what I was thinking last night.

My heart takes off like helicopter blades. My lips part and I can't decide whether to smile or call out, but then he turns away. And he's gone.

I pay for my coffee and hurry to the door, but by this time, he is long gone, swallowed by the crowds that are milling about on the sidewalks. I have no idea where he went but it is obvious that he didn't want to stop and talk to me, regardless of what I saw in his eyes.

I don't know what I did to offend him and I try not to allow my feelings to become ruffled because I don't think I did anything at all. He seemed fine when he left my house yesterday. Perhaps he's just having a bad day.

I decide to sit at a little table rather than become jostled through the crowds, which would likely result in spilled coffee. So, I sit and try to forget about Luca Minaldi snubbing me. I try and forget about the burning expression in his eyes. I try to forget about my own traitorous and naughty thoughts about him. It's difficult, but I focus and eventually, I am distracted by watching the people around me.

And I remember why I love Malta.

The people are so happy here, so laid-back and carefree. They have a true southern European attitude, one that repels stress and embraces life. I love it. It is one of the reasons why I have such great memories of being here when I was a child. Even as a kid, I felt the absence of worry and stress here in this beautiful place.

I sip at my coffee, which is delicious. It is strong and perfect, with just the right amount of cream and sugar. I rifle through my little notebook, the one that I carry everywhere to make notes about people's personalities. I'm not in the mood to speak with random strangers today but it must be done. So I sigh and get up and start introducing myself to these happy Europeans.

It doesn't end up being as difficult as I'd thought it would be.

I end up with a couple of offers for coffee with potential new friends and a couple of requests for my phone number from men, along with several pages of notes about these very same people. I need to return home and transcribe my notes into typewritten pages but first I have to navigate the market. I don't cook but I still need to eat.

I wind my way through the streets, hunting for a market. I don't see one.

So, I stop and ask a kind looking elderly woman. She's very friendly, but I quickly realize that she doesn't understand English. Her frail-looking husband doesn't either. I am saved by a kind younger man who sees me struggling to understand.

"Miss, I couldn't help but overhear," he tells me in perfect English with a charming Maltese accent. His blue eyes sparkle and I can't help but notice that he is handsome. "Do you need directions to the market?"

I nod gratefully.

"I do. Thank you so much. I'm afraid I'm a little turned around. I don't know where to go to hail a taxi."

The stranger laughs and he doesn't seem so strange now. Something about him immediately feels familiar and friendly and he puts me at ease.

"You won't need a taxi," he tells me. "Once you reach the heart of the city, which is where we are now, you can walk anywhere you need to go."

Ah. That must be why I remembered it being so.

"Come, "he tells me. "My name is Adrian and I will just show you the way."

"I'm Eva Talbot," I tell him. "Thank you so much."

"Adrian Leopoldo," he answers. "You are most welcome. It is a pleasure meeting you." He is charming and friendly and we chat the entire way to the market and I decide that it *is* a pleasure to meet him. I can certainly use a friend here. And the fact that he is handsome is certainly not a detriment.

"Do you live here in town?" I ask him as we approach the busy marketplace. He shakes his head.

"No, I live outside of town. You?"

I shake my head. "No. I live outside of town, too."

Adrian grins. "Well, that's a coincidence. Perhaps we'll bump into each other outside of town sometime." I can't help but gravitate towards his grin. He's impossibly cheerful and I find that I quite like it.

Open.

Honest.

Cheerful.

I make my silent list of his personality traits. I'm fairly certain that I'm spot on with him.

"Eva?"

Adrian is looking at me and I realize that he's probably said my name more than once.

"I'm sorry," I tell him. "I was thinking about something else."

"It's okay," he smiles. "I was just wondering if you'd like to have dinner tonight? You're new here and far too beautiful to sit in your house alone."

He's flirting. It occurs to me in a rush and I don't mind it at all. He's handsome and funny and nice. Why would I mind?

"Of course. And how very kind of you to think about my welfare," I tell him with a smile. "I found this charming little bistro on the beach last night. Marianne's. Do you know it?"

He nods. "Of course. Everyone knows Marianne. Shall I pick you up at 7:00?"

I smile again. "It's not very far from my house. I can meet you there if you prefer."

But Adrian is already shaking his head.

"Haven't you heard? A young woman was killed last night, not too far from Marianne's. She is the second one in a month. The polizia haven't determined if it is foul play or a wild animal of some sort. Either way, it's best that you not wander around after dark by yourself, Eva."

My gaze is frozen to his as I remember the shrill scream that I had heard last night on the beach. Could that have been the girl? If so, I was mere yards from her as she was killed. That seems impossible. But then, as I remember the spooky feeling in the air on my way home, I shiver.

"A wild animal?" I ask quietly, in horror. "What kind of wild animal does Malta have that could kill a person?"

Adrian is subdued. "Apparently, both girls had injuries that were indicative of a wolf attack, although Malta doesn't have indigenous wolves. A few years back, a handful of wolves escaped from a zoo. It is speculated that they have bred and their pack has grown. There are stories of farmers who have lost cows to these wolves. So we know that they are still out there."

"Rogue wolves?" I am horrified at the notion but it is slightly intriguing too. I always find myself rooting for the underdog. And wolves that were contained in a zoo and then escape to find a life of freedom are certainly underdogs. But are they killers?

"I don't know," Adrian answers. "It seems far-fetched to me. From what I've always heard, wolves don't attack humans unless they are cornered. But what do I know? I'm not a wild-life expert. But they say that both of the girls had their throats ripped out which is apparently what a wolf will do. It's horrifying. So, in the meantime, until they figure this out, you should keep your doors locked and don't travel by yourself after dark. Okay?"

I nod.

"And I'll be around to pick you up at 7:00," he confirms.

I nod again, then tell him where my cottage is and he waves and is off. I find myself looking forward to our little date tonight, which is slightly surprising since I've been utterly fascinated with Luca Minaldi ever since I laid eyes upon him yesterday and Adrian is a far cry from Luca.

But as I walk through the aisles of the busy open air market, I put Luca out of my mind. He clearly doesn't want anything to do with me. I'll make a point to arrange a follow-up meeting with him later for research reasons, but only for that. I just need to see if he is as intriguing as I previously thought. And if my evaluation of his personality is correct.

But even now, if I'm honest, the mere thought of meeting with him again is exciting. His dark good looks are a night and day difference from Adrian's cheerful demeanor. And that dark thread in Luca, the darkness that I see passing over his face... it draws me in. And I know that my research is not the reason that I want to see him again.

Chapter Six

Luca

I stare out the window of the car, idly watching the green landscape blur past.

"Do you want to go straight home?"

Adrian is looking at me in the rear-view mirror and I nod.

"Yes, please."

I return my attention to the outdoors, to the farms and wildlife and beaches that fly past us; the stone and sand and greenery. Adrian always drives too quickly when he chauffeurs for me but I don't mind. I'm a fast driver myself and I'm distracted today anyway.

I seldom allow myself to become bothered by things like emotions and sentiment. I can't. Not if I want to remain sane, if that's what I am. And I suppose that notion is debatable. But regardless, whether I am sane or not, I cannot become wrapped up in worrying about the reactions of those around me.

But the look on Evangeline's face as I turned away in the street… it bothers me. It's nagging at me. I wanted nothing more than to approach her, to draw her to me like she drew me to her last night in my dream. But I can't do that. And I have no way of telling her so without sounding like a deranged lunatic. I can just hear that conversation right now.

I'm sorry, Dr. Talbot, I'd really like to get to know you better, maybe even fuck you, but I'm a monster and can't get near you.

Yes. I can see where that would go over well. And why have I been reduced to feeling such base instincts around this woman? I can't seem to control my thoughts.

But it doesn't look like she's faring any better.

For a psychiatrist, Evangeline Talbot isn't good at concealing her feelings. She wears them on her face for the whole world to see. I recognized that trait in her yesterday. And today, I could see that she wanted to talk to me, she wants to get to know me better. I can tell that she feels the same attraction for me that I feel for her. I can't explain it, but it is certainly there. The electricity between us is almost a tangible thing. It is that strong.

In fact, it has almost taken on a life of its own.

"Luca, are you alright?"

Adrian interrupts my thoughts and as I glance at him, I find his forehead is wrinkled with concern. I smile. He has known me since we were boys and his family has worked for mine for generations. He certainly knows me well.

"I'm fine," I tell him. "Just distracted. What are your plans for the day?"

Adrian turns the wheel fluidly as he guides the Mercedes along the winding coastal road. He drives with ease, just like he does everything else. Everything is easy for him. People, love, life. I've been envious of that more times than I can count.

"Unless you need me for something else, I am planning on servicing your Jag this morning, then I am helping Tegan repair a broken stall in the stables this afternoon. If you don't think you'll have a late night tonight, I have plans to keep."

"And miles to go before you sleep?" I smile as I recite a line from a favorite poem. Adrian shakes his head and laughs. He has never been an academic, so he probably has no idea who I am quoting. "Robert Frost," I tell him. He rolls his eyes.

To be fair, Adrian has never needed to be academic. His charm got him through school and when his charm couldn't accomplish something, I tutored him. He always knew that his plan in life was to work for my family, like his father before him. He is never serious and usually has plans in town on the weekends. It is nothing new. He loves the bustle and life of the city. I do not.

"That's fine," I tell him absently, answering his question. "I don't intend to have a late night."

Adrian noses the car through the massive iron gates leading to Chessarae and up the long manicured drive. The difference as we pass onto the property is immediate. It is quiet here, as though the property itself recognizes my need for serenity. I know it is a silly thought, but it is entertaining to believe that the land itself recognizes something within me, a need for peace and solitude.

"Will you be visiting your mother this morning?"

Adrian asks this seriously as the car draws to a stop and I open my door. I grit my teeth. It's Friday again. Already.

I nod curtly and he shakes his head.

"You don't have to, you know," he tells me. "I don't know anyone else in their right mind who would. It's not like she would know the difference anyway."

"*I* would," I tell him. And I leave him with the car as I turn and make my way into the house.

As I walk through the doors, an instant feeling of reverence passes through my body, as it always does when I return home. This home, this mansion, is a thousand years old. It was built by the Knights of Malta back when they first occupied the country, when their strength was at its peak. The interior, of course, has been redecorated many times throughout the years, but the exterior has remained the same. Heavy stone blocks create a formidable presence. It is ancient and permanent.

And it is mine.

I wind my way through the house and push through the heavy mahogany doors to my study. Each door is carved with the dignified crest of the Knights. Although my family has never belonged to the order, we have left their imprint on Chessarae in homage to their rich history. It gives the house character.

I walk straight to the bar that sits behind my desk. If I am visiting my mother today, as I always do on Fridays, I will require sustenance. My particular brand of sustenance comes in the form of forty-year old Scotch. I pour a glass, neat. I down it in one gulp. I savor the familiar burn in my mouth and then pour another.

"Don't," Adrian says from the door. He is uncharacteristically somber as he watches me drink. "Don't do this to yourself, Luca. She doesn't have the right."

"Leave me," I instruct him. "You know I have to go. I'd just as soon do it alone."

"But you don't have to do it at all," he insists. "You don't have to allow her to treat you as she does. It isn't right. You don't deserve it."

"Ah," I answer, as I swirl the amber liquid in the glass. "But therein lies the problem. You know that I do."

I gulp it down, then thump my glass down on the antique wooden sidebar. It makes a satisfactory clang in the silence and I turn to Adrian.

"Don't you have a car to service?"

I am being an ass and he doesn't deserve it. I know that, so I smile at my oldest friend.

"I'll be fine. Thank you for your concern."

Adrian nods and reluctantly leaves the room. He knows me well enough to know not to push it, particularly on Fridays.

Even still, I find that I don't want to leave. This study is my solace, my own fortress. The ceilings are extraordinarily tall in here, the walls paneled with cherry and framed with stone. It is dark, it is quiet and it feels like the safest place in the world. It was my father's before it was mine and his father's before his and so on. The idea of what these walls have seen, the secrets they must be keeping, is intriguing. And there are days, such as today, that I would just as soon never leave here.

But there are days, such as today, when I have unpleasant tasks to attend to.

I stride quickly out and down the halls to get this particular thing over with.

It takes almost five full minutes to walk from my study doors to my mother's wing. She has an entire wing of the house all to herself, and many nights, I can see the lights flickering on and off in the various rooms as she is up throughout the night.

Ever since my father died, since he committed suicide, my mother has not been well. Not that she was ever *well* to begin with. Not truly. But she is worse now than she has ever been. Now, to put it less than eloquently, she is fucking insane.

I stand for a moment outside of her doors, and I take a deep breath as I pull the key from my pocket and turn it in the lock. I am scared of nothing in this life. But I am not fond of my mother.

I push the doors open and find her rooms dark. Very dark. Her drapes are drawn and it takes a moment for my eyes to adjust to the absence of light. But once they do, once I can see the silhouettes and shapes from within, I still don't see her.

"Sophia?" I call out. My mother's personal attendant has been with us for years. She has tolerated more than any one person should ever tolerate, years of verbal and physical abuse from my mother, yet she still remains. I can't imagine why. I would have left long ago. "Sophia?"

"Yes, Mr. Minaldi?" She appears from nowhere, from the door leading to my mother's sitting room. She looks tired, as though she hasn't slept in a week. Her graying hair is disheveled and her clothing is rumpled, which is very unlike her. Sophia is not a pretty woman but she is always perfectly groomed, perfectly professional.

"Where is my mother?" I ask. Something passes over Sophia's face and I can't read it so I ask. "What's wrong?"

She shakes her head. "Nothing, sir. I just don't know that today is a good day for you to visit. Mrs. Minaldi has not had a good week."

"How so?"

I look around and everything in the suite seems to be in place. There have been times when my mother has completely thrashed the place during violent tantrums. Nothing appears to be broken now, which is a good sign.

Sophia sighs.

"She is hallucinating again," she tells me tiredly. "She thinks that she sees your father. It's all I can do to keep her contained in this wing."

"But you keep the doors locked," I pointed out. "Even my mother cannot escape a locked door."

"There are windows," Sophia answers grimly.

I startle as I stare at the walls of windows that line this room. Every room in the suite has similar windows. My mother insisted upon it when she was moved to this wing. Although her wing is located on the ground floor, the windows are still too high up to climb through. She would probably break every bone in her body if she attempted it. She is frail in her older age.

"What do you suggest?" I ask. "Bars on them?"

Sophia shrugs. "I don't know," she answers. "But she is desperate at times to escape, to find your father. She wants to save him."

"Her medication isn't working?"

Sophia shrugs again. "It is more effective at times than others. There are moments when nothing can touch her hysteria. I don't know what the answer is."

"Dr. Bianchi is on vacation," I tell her. "He won't return for two weeks. But we'll call him when he gets back and see if there is anything we can do."

"Perhaps a change of environment would be good for her," Sophia suggests. "There are homes in town where she can receive twenty-four hour care. Perhaps if she is in a place where Nicolas never was, it will ease her mind. Dr. Bianchi has already recommended this."

I'm already shaking my head. "No. My mother would never want strangers to see her in such a way."

She would rather be dead than that.

"You are a good son, Mr. Minaldi," Sophia tells me. I can see the admiration on her face but I don't deserve it. And since I don't deserve it, I don't acknowledge it.

"You never said where she was."

Sophia is hesitant. "She is resting in her sitting room."

"Sleeping?" I am hopeful. But Sophia shakes her head.

"No."

"Sedated?"

"Yes."

"Well, thank God for small favors."

Sophia smiles at me.

"You can take a break," I tell her. "I'll sit with her for a bit."

"Are you certain?" she asks and her hesitation is back. "You might need me."

"If I do, I'll call you," I assure her. "Go. You deserve a break."

She nods and slips away and I decide to just get this over with.

I find my mother curled on her side on a sofa. She is partially covered with a cashmere throw and her dark eyes are fixed in front of her, staring at nothing. She is small and slight, and the only things I have inherited from her are her dark eyes. My father's were green.

I sit down in the chair next to her.

"Mother, how are you feeling today?"

I have to force the words. I honestly have no wish to speak with her.

She doesn't answer and at first, I am hopeful that I can simply sit here in silence with her and then slip out unnoticed.

I have no such luck.

Her dark eyes turn toward me, slowly and eerily. I fight the shivers that ripple up my spine. She is a small woman, this woman who gave birth to me. There is no need to feel such trepidation around her. Yet, I do. When she looks at me, she sees through me, to the very depths of me. No one else can do that and it shakes the hell out of me.

"You came back."

Her words are throaty and simple.

"I always do, mother," I tell her. I start to reach for her hand, but change my mind. I am safer over here. I don't want to feel her skin. She will feel like ice, as she always does.

She turns her head more and now she is looking at me squarely. Her eyes are lucid and clear today and I wonder at what she is thinking.

I do not have to wonder for long.

"You left me here with that bitch. You don't love me."

I sigh. My mother doesn't have Alzheimer's. But she does have a wretched form of dementia that causes her to be cruel.

"She's not a bitch, mother. Sophia is good to you. You should be nicer to her."

My mother sniffs and then delicately sits up, her dark hair tumbling over her shoulders. I eye her warily. She could fly into motion at any time.

She watches my hesitation and her mouth stretches into a grotesque smile.

"You are afraid of me?" she asks. And her voice is ragged and edgy in this quiet room, this giant room that feels so much like a mausoleum. "Little Lukey, are you afraid of your mother?"

I steel myself against her and I can't help but resent her. She sometimes called me Lukey as a boy. Sometimes it was lovingly and sometimes it was mockingly. Even back then, you never knew what you were going to get with her. One moment she was kind and the very next, she was bitter and cold. The constant was that she was always detached. She never wanted to get that close to me, which might be exactly the reason why I do not feel close to her now.

"No. I'm not afraid of you, mother. Is there a reason why I should be?"

As soon as I ask the question, as soon as the words pass my lips, I know it was a mistake. A light ignites in her eyes, an eerie, unnatural light, and I unconsciously lean away from her.

"Why, yes," she answers. "Yes, there is, Lukey. You should always fear me because I know what you are."

And then she opens her mouth and begins to scream and twist and rock in her seat and I grit my teeth. This is the mother that I know now, the one who may or may not be feigning insanity. This is my life and she is but a piece of it. I close my eyes and let her scream.

Chapter Seven
Eva

What should I wear?

I ask myself this question as I look into my small closet. It's not that big of a question, because it's not that big of a closet. I didn't bring a lot of clothing. I choose a simple pair of khaki shorts, a black button up shirt and a pair of black slip-ons. I pull my hair into a low ponytail and slide on some lip-gloss. When in doubt, always go with a classic look. It's something my mother taught me and it's always held true.

I check the time. 6:55. Adrian should be here any moment.

For some reason, I feel a little nervous. It's silly, but true. I haven't had time for dates in so long, first because of medical school, then because of my residency. My personal life took a hard hit, I'll be the first to admit it. And even though I'm not truly interested in Adrian, at least not long term, it will still be nice to sit down with someone charming for a dinner. And that makes me nervous because I'm out of practice. I'll have to make an effort not to psycho-analyze him. Men tend to dislike that, if my memory serves me correctly.

There is a knock at the door and I glance at the clock. 6:59. He's right on time, early in fact.

I open the door and Adrian is smiling at me already.

"Hi," he says easily. And he hands me a bouquet of wildflowers. I laugh, because I recognize them from my own lawn.

"These look familiar," I tell him. "So you have good taste."

He laughs too because he knows he's been caught. "It's the thought that counts, right?" he tells me. "I'm sorry. I just left work. I wanted to stop and get you flowers, but I didn't want to be late."

"Now that *is* a quandary," I agree. "Just a second, let me put these in water."

"You look lovely," he calls from behind me as I turn and leave the room.

"Thank you," I call back over my shoulder.

I grab a tall glass because I can't find a vase and I fill it with water, then set the flowers on the table.

"I'm ready," I tell him as I grab my purse.

"After you," he bows low at the door, exaggerated and gentlemanly. I have to laugh again. There is something about Adrian's easy manner that is just so likeable. We laugh and chat all the way to Marianne's and when we walk through the door, she greets us with a warm smile.

"Mia bella," she says as she kisses my cheeks. "I see you've met our resident rogue!" And then she kisses Adrian's cheeks too.

"Don't listen to Marianne," Adrian tells me in an exaggerated stage-like whisper. "It's all unfounded rumor. I am no such thing."

"Pish," she tells him. "You've left more broken hearts behind you than a street-sweeper. You had better not hurt my new little friend."

"Me?" And Adrian looks completely offended and puzzled. "I would never. And besides. Since when does a street-sweeper break hearts?"

Marianne leans up and smacks Adrian on the shoulder.

"You know what I mean, you rascal. A street-sweeper bowls over everything in its path, much like you do." And she smiles again. "Let me show you to a table. I'm happy that you will be here to keep Eva company. As long as you behave yourself, that is."

And she turns to show us to our table and Adrian leans toward me.

"I see you have a fan club already."

I shrug. "People like me."

He grins and I grin back.

"I'm kidding. She's a very nice lady. She felt sorry for me last night since I was in here alone. She doesn't realize that where I'm from, that's very normal. A woman can eat alone and it's not a tragedy."

Adrian shakes his head. "Not true. Anytime you are eating alone, it is a tragedy for mankind. You should never be alone. There should always be someone with you to appreciate your beauty."

I have to shake my head again at his blatant and sugary flirting and I can see what Marianne means. I'm quite positive that Adrian has broken more hearts than he knows what to do with and probably completely by accident. Thankfully, I know that I'm not interested in a relationship with him. I know that because when I'm ready, it will be with someone who turns my heart inside out.

Someone like Luca Minaldi.

The thought pops unbidden into my head, just as thoughts of him have been springing up right and left since I met him. I shake them away. This is ridiculous. I'm here with a handsome and charming man. I'm going to enjoy it, not spend it thinking of Luca Minaldi.

So I do.

We talk and sip at wine for hours.

I eat more breadsticks than I know what to do with. Adrian laughs because I'm so skinny but can apparently eat my weight in bread.

"I don't know where you put it all, Eve," he tells me, his eyes sparkling.

"My name isn't Eve," I tell him. "It's Eva."

"I know," he answers. "But you are beautiful enough that you could tempt me into anything, even eating from the Tree of Life. So to me, you will always be Eve."

"I don't know if that's a compliment," I tell him and I know my cheeks are flushed from the wine. "You're comparing me to someone who was the fall of mankind."

He laughs and lifts his wineglass. "Here's to temptation."

I laugh and toast with him, but honestly, this conversation makes me a little uneasy. I feel a strange pressure now to return the admiration that he feels for me. And honestly, I just don't.

It's not that I don't think he's attractive. Clearly, he is attractive. And he's charming and sweet. And I like him. But when I think of him, I think of a golden retriever. Happy, loyal, not too deep. I think I need a man with substance.

Like Luca Minaldi.

Ugh. There he is again. My thoughts are not safe from him, night or day. I dreamed of him last night and today he has been running rampant in there. I once again put him out of my mind as I make polite small talk with Adrian.

I feel suddenly rude, suddenly fake.

I hope that Adrian hasn't noticed that I am not as engaged in our conversation now as I was. I can't help it. I can't help what I feel, but I can help how I act. So I smile brightly as Adrian tells me about growing up in Malta.

"It was a lovely childhood," he tells me. "I grew up on an estate outside of town. It was peaceful and very quiet and I had the full run of the place. But it was a little *too* quiet, you know? I like city life."

"See, I'm just the opposite," I answer. "I love the country and the quiet. I love people, but I like to return to my empty house at the end of the night and re-charge. I guess I'm an introvert in that way. You're an extrovert through and through. Being with people feeds your energy."

"You are right on the money with that," Adrian laughs. "I do love to be with people. My boss, who happens to have been a childhood friend, is just the opposite. He would never come out if he can help it, a total introvert. I don't really understand it."

Marianne comes back to our table with another bottle of wine, but I stop her before she can open it.

"I can't," I tell her, as I look at my watch. "I've still got work to do tonight and I need to get up early tomorrow. I really should go."

She smiles. "Will I see you tomorrow, sweet one? I'll save you a table."

I nod. "Of course. I can't eat my own cooking, trust me. I'll be here for dinner."

She kisses me and I marvel in the fact that she has accepted me so quickly. It's refreshing. People back home are slightly more suspicious and hardened toward strangers and I know that that is a cultural thing on both counts.

Adrian picks up the check, even though I try to insist that I would like to buy my own. But he is insistent, so I allow it this time. Once he pays it, we are once again out in the night breeze.

"I love this," I say as I sniff at the brisk and salty sea air. "I could breathe this for the rest of my life. It makes for such a good night's sleep."

"True," Adrian answers as he slips an arm around my shoulders. "And it makes for intimate date nights, too."

I look at him and shake my head, but I don't remove his arm. The breeze *is* chilly and his arm *is* warm.

"You're not getting into my pants tonight," I tell him bluntly. "Just so you know."

He laughs. "You Americans. You're always right to the point."

I smile. "I suppose. You should just know that my heart isn't going to be broken by you and left behind your steam-roller."

He laughs again. "I think you mean street-*sweeper.*"

"That too."

We round the corner and step onto my drive and I stop short. A shiny black Jaguar is parked in front of my cottage. And Luca Minaldi is sitting on my porch steps. His dark eyes briefly flicker over my face, over Adrian's arm that is wrapped loosely around my shoulders, over the entire scene. I wonder what it looks like to him, but don't take the time to dwell on it.

"Luca," I say as we approach. "What a nice surprise."

And it is. I'm surprised by the jolting thrill that shoots through me when I see him.

What is even more surprising though, is Adrian's reaction. He's standing at attention, ever-alert, staring at Luca anxiously.

"Luca, what are you doing here?" Adrian asks. "Is everything alright?"

I glance sharply at Adrian and then our conversation from Marianne's comes back to me. He grew up on an estate outside of town with a boss who doesn't like people.

He works for Luca.

Luca looks at him. "I'm fine," he tells him. "It's my mother."

And then he shifts his attention to me.

"Dr. Talbot, I realize that this is an imposition, but could you possibly take a look at her? She's been despondent all day and we cannot calm her down. Her doctor is out of town for the next two weeks. I'm not sure what to do with her."

"You could take her to the hospital," I suggest. But Adrian is already shaking his head.

"No, we can't do that. She would hate the publicity. Would you mind coming to look?"

It is Adrian who is asking me now and I find it sweet that he is so loyal to his employer. He said *we*, as if the problem is also his. I add *loyal* to his list and then look back to Luca.

Luca's expression is unreadable and as dark as always. But his eyes, there is something deep within his eyes, something vulnerable and sad, that does me in and I find myself nodding.

"Okay. I'm not licensed to practice medicine in Malta, so I can't prescribe her any medication, but I can come take a look at her."

"Thank you," Luca tells me and his voice is sincere. "I appreciate it more than you know."

I only just now notice that he is holding a bag. He sees me notice it and he holds it out. "I didn't come empty handed," he tells me. For the first time, I see the hint of a smile on his lips. "I brought you a house-warming gift."

I eye it curiously as he hands it to me. I peer into the bag and can't help but laugh.

There are two cans of aerosol insecticide nestled within tissue paper. The black and red labels on them announce that they are guaranteed to rid a house of common and pesky spiders. I look up at Luca and grin.

"Practical, yet thoughtful. Thank you."

He smiles back, and for the first time, it seems to really reach his eyes and warm them. They seem like milk chocolate now.

"You're welcome. I won't always be in the neighborhood when Spawns of Satan come calling. I thought you should be protected."

I smile and shake my head, embarrassed once again at how terrified I had been of that spider.

"Thank you. I'll just run this inside and grab a bag and then I'll be ready."

I brush past him to get inside and I know the instant I touch him. He's hard and masculine and he smells like spicy musk. I inhale slightly as I pass and his eyes meet mine. There is a connection there, a charged and potent connection. It's like he doesn't see anyone or anything else in the world but me, as though I have his complete and undivided attention. But the moment quickly passes when he turns away to speak with Adrian.

I drop the spider spray in the kitchen and then hurry to stuff a stethoscope and various other things that I might need into a small bag before I join them back outside.

"I'm ready," I announce. Both men nod and both men gesture toward their cars.

I stop and look at them.

Adrian looks expectant. I was, after all, just on a date with him. It would be perfectly normal for me to ride with him. He's standing next to a dark blue Mercedes, waiting for me to join him.

Luca stands still, completely quiet, next to his black Jaguar. He looks at me, but doesn't say anything, his face still expressionless. He doesn't ask me, implore me or expect anything from me. He just waits for me to choose him. And honestly, I know there is nothing else I can do. He draws me to him like a magnet.

I walk straight to him and he opens his car door for me. Although he doesn't say anything, and I might be mistaken, I think that I see a slight smile as I duck into his car.

He closes the door behind me and as he does, I catch a glimpse of Adrian's face in the side mirror. He isn't happy about my decision and I find that silly. I just chose a car to drive in after all. But as Luca slides into the driver's seat and the car engine roars to life, he brings with him his intense energy and I am once again mesmerized by his unique presence.

And I wonder if the decision that I just made is as inconsequential as it would seem.

The night speeds past us as Luca drives. He's a fast driver, but I see in the side mirror that Adrian is right behind us. He hugs our tail as we curve through the country roads.

"What are your mother's symptoms?" I ask Luca. He doesn't take his eyes from the road as he answers.

"My mother has had dementia for years. It has gotten progressively worse and although she is medicated, some days are worse than others. She hallucinates quite a bit, even when she is taking no medication at all."

"So her hallucinations stem from her own mind, rather than a side effect of medication," I answer. He nods.

"How old is your mother?"

"Sixty four."

"Is she in good health otherwise?"

"Yes. Physically, she's in perfect condition."

"What is she doing right now that is causing you such alarm?"

He glances at me.

"I'm not alarmed. It's just a new behavior. She's been screaming all day. She won't stop."

I look at him.

"Screaming?"

He nods.

"You said that she is medicated. Does she have sedatives?"

He nods again. "Yes. And she has been sedated today. Heavily. It does no good."

He glances at me once again, his gaze dark in the night, before he returns his attention to the road.

"I apologize if I interrupted a date."

I am startled by the fact that I don't want him to believe that it was, even if it is the truth. I'm not going to make excuses, however. I'm a grown woman and I don't need to explain myself to anyone.

"I met Adrian in town today," I answer instead. "He was kind enough to stop and talk to me, then invite me to dinner."

I am pointedly reminding Luca that he ignored me earlier. And he gets my point.

And then he smiles about my point.

"Yes, Adrian is good like that. He loves people, women in particular. I would have been surprised and disappointed in him had he not tried to date you. It would have been ever so out of his character."

Somehow, I feel like I've been pushed back into my place, as though Luca is telling me that I'm just one of many. That Adrian simply loves women. Which may or may not be the case and it doesn't really matter to me.

"He's good company," I answer simply. "Very friendly."

"Oh, he is that," Luca agrees. *"Very* friendly."

He turns the car onto a drive and passes beneath large gates. The name Chessarae is scrawled in the iron above us and the mansion itself looms on the horizon, rising out of the dark and clouds like something out of a movie. I can't help but stare because it is magnificent.

"Welcome to my home," Luca says as he pulls the car up front. He quickly gets out and walks around to open my door. He has impeccable manners. I add that to his list.

Adrian has pulled past us and disappeared around the side of the house. I can only assume that he is putting the car away. Luca leads the way to the front door, where he holds the door open for me and gestures for me to pass.

As I do, as I cross the threshold of his home, I wonder just what exactly I am getting myself into.

Chapter Eight

Chessarae is majestic and enormous.

It takes several minutes to wind our way through the front doors and the sparkling, perfectly decorated house before we find ourselves standing in front of Melina Minaldi's bedroom doors.

Luca is slightly in front of me, Adrian is to my right and we're all three staring at each other as we listen to the wailing coming from within. It's horrific and filled with angst; and it causes chills to run up my spine.

I don't hesitate. I push at the doors, but they won't open. Luca quickly pulls out a key.

"You keep them locked?" I am surprised by this.

He nods. "We have to."

He inserts it, turns it and opens the door for me, holding it as I pass.

"Wait," he tells me. "Let's see where she is."

He's hesitant and that surprises me. Luca is so strong and confident, yet he is leery of his mother? I once again wonder what I've gotten myself into as we tread quietly through her rooms, following the sounds of her screams.

We find her perched like a bird on a window sill, staring out over the estate. Her white filmy dressing gown hangs over the ledge and I can see from here that there is a beautiful view of the sea and the moon from where she is sitting. But she isn't enjoying it. Her face, which is normally lovely I am sure, is twisted at the moment into something unrecognizable as human. I can't help but suck in my breath at the eeriness of this situation.

Luca hears it and turns to me.

"Are you alright?" he asks. "Would you like to leave?"

And his face is softer in this moment than I have seen it yet. He sounds concerned and even a little bit protective, but then it is gone just as soon as it was there. He politely waits for my answer.

"I'm fine," I tell him. "This is what I do. Nothing surprises me anymore."

I approach Melina quietly and calmly. And instead of trying to talk to her, I sit on the opposite side of the window ledge and watch her.

She screams for a few minutes more and then she stops, staring at me.

In her agitation, her eyes are as black as night and I can see where Luca inherited his. Hers are as fathomless as his.

"Who are you?" she asks me. I can hear in her voice that she is lucid, and I can see it in her eyes, as well. She knows exactly what she is doing. So the question remaining is: why is she doing it?

"My name is Evangeline Talbot," I tell her. "I'm American and I'm here on your beautiful island for the summer. Who are you?"

She looks surprised by my question. I'm sure that she certainly isn't used to it. Everyone knows the Minaldis on this island. She probably hasn't had to introduce herself in years and years. But she looks at me squarely in the eye and extends her hand, her chin raised regally in the air.

"I'm Melina Minaldi," she says gracefully. I can see that she is proud of that fact. She is proud of who she is. But most importantly, she knows her name. This is an important gauge of her sanity.

"It's very nice to meet you," I tell her. "You have absolutely lovely skin, Mrs. Minaldi. Whatever do you use on it?"

As I speak, I slide my fingers along her wrist, along her pulsepoint. I pretend to feel the softness of her skin, but truly I am checking her pulse. It is steady and slow, not erratic and fluttery as I would expect from someone in a psychotic episode.

"I use a cream that my mother used," she tells me. "It's made from crushed pearls."

"Well, you can tell," I answer her. "Your skin is glowing. You don't look a day over thirty-five."

"Ha!" she crows. "I'm sixty-four and I've earned every line on my face."

So she knows her age. I'm secretly probing her, trying to gauge how much of reality she is still living in. Someone with advanced dementia doesn't remember details like their age.

"Well," I answer. "Your pearl moisturizer must be doing its job. You barely have even one line."

She sticks her chin higher in the air and I see the light reflected from her eyes. They are slightly glassy, a tell-tale sign of the sedatives that she has taken today. I'm surprised she's not sound asleep by now.

"My mother always insisted that I get eight hours of sleep per night," I tell her. "She said if I don't, I'll age well before my time. She says it is the fastest way to get wrinkles."

Melina looks dismayed and she drops her legs from her curled up position, allowing them to swing from the ledge as she looks at me. She trusts me now that we are sharing beauty secrets. Her body language tells me so.

"Does your mother have skin like yours?"

I nod. "Yes, she does."

"Then your mother must be very wise."

I smile at her, trying to instill confidence in her. She won't listen to me if she doesn't continue to trust me.

"Have you slept today, Mrs. Minaldi? You look a little tired. You should make sure you get your eight hours in."

She looks pensive. She doesn't even glance at Adrian or Luca. It's like they aren't even in the room. Finally, after she thinks about it a moment, she nods.

"I am quite tired," she tells me in a conspiratorial whisper. "I haven't been sleeping well lately."

She starts to get up and I take her elbow, helping her from the ledge. She barely weighs more than a feather, her arms strikingly thin.

"Oh?" I ask. "We should do something about that. It's not good to not sleep well. Women like us need our beauty sleep."

She looks pleased by that as she walks toward what I hope is her bedroom. I continue to hold her elbow.

"Yes," she agrees. "Beautiful women like us deserve beauty sleep. We aren't like the others, you know. We're special. My Nicolas always tells me so."

I look at her face now and it is open and honest. This doesn't seem to be an act. She truly does believe that Nicolas is here in the present tense. She was faking her psychotic episode but she's not faking her belief that Nicolas is alive.

"Well," I tell her as I ease her into her giant bed and pull her downy comforter up to her chin. "Nicolas must be very wise for a man. They don't usually know so much about women."

We laugh together like we know a secret and I know that I have won her over. She curls onto her side and closes her eyes. I am just turning away when I hear her whisper.

I turn back.

"What was that, Mrs. Minaldi?"

Her eyes are open, black as night, and she looks into mine. Her gaze is fierce now.

"You should leave now, Evangeline."

I startle at the harsh tone of her voice. It is a night and day difference from her laughter a moment ago.

"Why?" I ask.

"Because Chessarae is dangerous for you. My son is evil."

She closes her eyes again and doesn't reopen them. I feel frozen as I turn and find Luca. His gaze is dark and mine is tied to it. I can't look away from the pained expression that he is wearing. But he closes his eyes briefly, then turns away. He's not going to acknowledge what she said. I know that right now.

He motions toward the door and the three of us leave. As we do, Luca locks the door behind us.

"You were very good with her," he tells me as we walk away. "I've never seen her take to someone like that before."

"It's just something I've learned," I tell him. "People are much more inclined to be cooperative if they don't know that you're probing them for information."

"That's probably true in all levels of life," Luca agrees.

His eyes! His eyes draw me to him. They are filled with so many things, dark things, pained things; and the psychiatrist and woman in me wants to discover what has hurt him. Because clearly, even though he is strong and confident on the outside, there is trauma lurking on the inside. The average person probably wouldn't see it, but I can.

Luca looks at Adrian.

"Adrian, I won't be requiring anything further tonight. Thank you very much for staying late."

Adrian looks surprised, because it is clear that Luca is dismissing him and he wasn't expecting it. It's also clear that he isn't used to being dismissed. He looks almost confused as he looks to me, but what can I say? Adrian doesn't work for me. Finally, he nods and turns to me.

"I had a very nice time tonight, Eve," he tells me, his charming tone back in full swing. "We'll have to do it again soon."

I smile and he hugs me quickly before he leaves us. Luca doesn't miss a moment of the exchange and I can feel his dark gaze on my skin.

"Would you come with me for a few minutes?" he asks politely. "I'd like to speak to you about my mother."

"Of course," I tell him. He leads the way through the massive house and I soon find myself in a dark and masculine study. Luca gestures toward a leather seat.

"Please sit," he tells me. "Make yourself comfortable. Would you like a drink?"

"I would love one," I tell him.

He crosses the room in three strides and pours two glasses of what looks to be Scotch. He walks back and hands me a glass half-filled with the amber liquid.

While I am standing next to him, I can practically feel the power emanating from him. He's the type of person who has been born into it. It has been cultivated in him from the time he was an infant and it shows. Power and money are in every molecular strand in his body.

He's definitely a force to be reckoned with.

"To sanity," Luca says, tipping his glass toward mine. And then he downs his in one gulp.

I take a tentative sip and realize quickly that I was correct. It's Scotch. Neat. Without one ounce of tonic or even an ice cube to dilute it. It burns my mouth and warms my chest as it slides smoothly down. But for some reason, I don't want him to know that it makes me want to gag and cough. I want to seem unfazed, so I drink the rest in two gulps and hand Luca back the empty glass.

It is worth my numb lips because there is approval in his eyes as he takes it.

"Aren't you going to ask?" he says as he sets the glasses down on a heavy wooden side table. He is still staring at me and his gaze makes me feel like my skin will be ablaze soon.

"Ask what?" I feel slightly woozy already from the Scotch. To be honest, I'm also woozy from being so near to Luca Minaldi. For several different reasons, he has an interesting effect on me.

"Wouldn't you like to ask me if you're safe here with me?"

I look at him, remembering his mother's startling words. *My son is evil.*

"Am I?" I ask and my voice is barely a murmur.

"Probably not."

Luca's voice is quiet in the study, as dark as the night surrounding us, and I suddenly feel like I should run, somewhere far away from here. But at the same time, I know that I won't. I am ridiculously drawn to this man and the more I find out about him, the more I want to know. So I shake my head.

"I'm not afraid."

Luca looks at me again and I don't see one ounce of the vulnerability that I have seen there before. Instead, he is expressionless once more and darkly handsome.

"Well, that's the rub," he answers. "You should be."

Chapter Nine

Luca

I watch her absorb my words, drawing them into her body as she thinks about them. Her face, for once, is impassive. Evangeline isn't showing her hand.

"Why should I fear you?" she finally asks. She is trying to act unruffled. But I can see that she is nervous. Her slender hands fidget in her lap as she tries to sit still.

"Oh, we don't really have the time to get into that this evening," I tell her. "There will be other nights, I'm sure. I don't want to scare you away so soon, Dr. Talbot."

"I've told you," she says. "Call me Eva."

I look at her long and hard and she fidgets under my gaze. On some base level, I find satisfaction in that. She is very unflappable. The fact that I have gotten beneath her skin says something.

"Ah, we've already gone over that, haven't we?" I ask. "We aren't yet friends."

She lifts her chin and I can see her cheeks are flushed. Have I offended her or is it the effects of the Scotch? She downed hers like a sailor, something that I wasn't expecting. I could tell she didn't like it. Women usually don't, but she certainly hid it well.

"As you like," she answers. I almost smile, but don't. I offended her. The capable, no-nonsense Dr. Talbot might be more sensitive than she seems.

"Why does Adrian call you Eve?" I ask. The question is out before I think about it. I hadn't meant to ask, but ever since I heard him do it, I've wanted to know.

Her eyes meet mine quickly. She is surprised. And flustered. She shakes her head.

"It's silly. It's a private joke, I guess."

"Why is it private?" I ask. "You just met him this morning. How private can it be?"

The idea that Adrian would share anything private with her is instantly annoying.

She shakes her head again. "I don't know. I just don't feel like explaining it. It sounds silly out loud."

"You're embarrassed?" And now I'm the one who is surprised. "I wouldn't have thought that you embarrass easily, Dr. Talbot."

"I don't."

But that's a lie. I can tell by the flush lining her graceful cheekbones. I resist the urge to run my thumbs over the color, to trace the way the delicate color curls over her cheeks and illuminates her face. It's becoming on her. So, I tell her that. She flushes even deeper and I have to smile.

"Maybe you just embarrass easily with *me*," I muse, watching her lips press together until they turn white at the corners.

"You don't like me much, do you?" I ask her. She's once again the one who is surprised as she turns her face toward mine.

"Why ever would you think that?" she asks.

"It's just an observation," I answer. "You seem on edge around me."

"That might be because you told me that I'm not safe around you," she replies, her chin lifted in the air. I smile wider and she sucks in a breath. I do affect her. And I like that. It only seems fair since she affects me in a very similar way. The fact that the crotch of my pants shrinks two sizes whenever she is near is evidence of that.

"Valid point," I concede. "But you haven't asked why."

She shrugs, her shoulders thin and elegant. "Does it matter? Unsafe is unsafe whatever the reason."

I nod. "Very true. You're very astute."

She nods too, cool now. "Yes, I am. Now, what were you wanting to discuss about your mother?"

"To the point. I like that," I tell her. I pour another scotch and hand it to her, taking one for myself. She doesn't refuse it. I'm impressed once again.

I sit down in the chair facing her.

"I would like to hire you," I say simply. She is impassive as she stares at me, the scotch glass in her lap.

"I'm not licensed to practice medicine here," she answers calmly. Her eyes, such a unique color, are glued to mine. Her stare is unwavering and once again, I'm impressed with her. She has such poise. I briefly wonder if it is a result of her training.

"That is no matter," I answer. "My mother can continue to have her medications prescribed by her current physician. You can work hand in hand with him. She reacts differently with you, far better than she reacts with him. She was calmer in a matter of minutes with you than I have seen her in months. If you had that effect on her every day, it would make my life much, much easier. Even though my mother and I have a...tenuous relationship, I want her to be comfortable. I will pay you handsomely, Dr. Talbot."

She is quiet for a moment as she looks down at her hands, at the scotch glass, then back up to me.

"I'm here to finish my dissertation, Luca. I don't have the time to be a round-the-clock attendant. I don't wish to sound rude, but I am here in Malta for a reason and I only have the summer to complete it."

"Fair enough," I tell her. "But I don't want you to be a round-the-clock attendant. You're a doctor, not a nurse aide. I would simply like to pay you to visit with her once a day or so. And if she has episodes like she had today, then I could call you and you could come and talk her down like you did this evening. It shouldn't be too taxing for you and I would compensate you very well for your time. Surely you would like to pay your student loans off early."

She stares at me, once again impassive, although I had expected her to be surprised or impressed by the implication that I would pay her quite so well.

"Perhaps. I'll consider it. But first, I need for you to tell me why Mrs. Minaldi feels that Chessarae is dangerous. Why does she think that you are evil?"

I take a moment, studying Evangeline's face as she waits for my answer. She's calm, cool and very collected. She doesn't seem to believe my mother's words. If she did, she wouldn't be here right now. Instead, she is waiting for me to refute them.

I don't.

I say, "My mother is suffering from dementia, Dr. Talbot. It is hard to imagine why she says the things that she does."

"Yes," Evangeline answers slowly. "About that. Your mother's presence of mind is not as altered as I would have thought. She knows her name and her age. Her pulse is slow and steady. I don't believe her psychosis is as advanced as she would have you think. It is there, to be sure. She does believe that your father is still alive. However, I've seen cases like this before. A person's grief is so overwhelming that in order to protect themselves, they concoct a new world, one in which their loved one still remains. That could be why your mother is so focused on you. Perhaps she is making you a villain in order to somehow shield herself from some internal guilt, rather than taking it onto herself."

I am impressed that she gathered all of this from ten minutes with my mother. So I tell her that. I don't hand out compliments easily, although there is no way she could know that.

She smiles. "It's what I do, Luca. I think your mother has the presence of mind to manipulate you. She's faking psychotic episodes in order to control you."

I stare at her. "You gathered this from one meeting?"

Evangeline nods, confident in her assessment. "My thesis project revolves around studying the personality traits of a person based on the initial meeting. It's a skill I've gotten quite good at. Why would you mother want to manipulate you?"

I shrug and take another drink. "I have no idea."

Evangeline stares at me. "You're lying."

"Does it matter?" I meet her gaze and she is trying to figure me out, to take me apart mentally, thought by thought. I almost laugh. That will never happen. No one on the planet will be able to figure me out. It's a feat that I haven't accomplished myself.

"It matters," she answers. "If you want me to help your mother, you have to help me. You can't lie to me. That would just hinder the process."

"So I'm a process now?"

I set my glass down purposefully on the table, then lean toward her. The space between us is narrowing by the moment, charged with the energy that we create. I rest my hand on her slender knee, very lightly, as if to emphasize my point. She sucks in her breath.

"I'm many things, Evangeline. But a process isn't one of them."

She shakes her head, flustered, ignoring the fact that I am touching her.

"You're not a process," she answers. "You're a mystery, an enigma. If I could figure you out, I'm sure I could help your mother."

"I think you've got that backward," I tell her bluntly, removing my hand and easing back in my seat, breaking the spell. And then I wish I hadn't said a thing because her eyes light up and widen with a revelation.

"You think I could help *you* if I figure out your mother? Do you need help, Luca?"

I smile at her question and I can feel the taste of grim reality on my lips.

"Evangeline, I need more help than you will ever know. But I'm a lost cause."

"I don't believe in lost causes, Luca." Her words are soft, her tone even softer. She reaches over and puts her hand over mine and hers is pale against my darker skin. It is slender and small, and although something urges me to grasp it with my own, I remain motionless. It is one thing to touch her when I am in control, but it is quite another when she is trying to comfort me. I can hardly trust myself to remain aloof.

"There's a first time for everything," I answer. She starts to say something, but I interrupt her. "But let's focus on my mother for the time being. Will you help her?"

Evangeline is silent as she considers it, but it only takes her a moment before she nods.

"All right. I'll do what I can."

Her voice is whisper soft in the silence of my study.

"When can you start?"

"Immediately."

It's the right answer.

Chapter Ten

Eva

I can't figure Luca out.

One moment he seems vulnerable and the very next, he is once again the powerful Luca Minaldi that the rest of the world sees. It's frustrating and I feel as though I need to take my internal list of his character traits and tear it into pieces. I'm never going to get it right.

"I can't figure you out," I tell him. "I don't know what to make of you."

He is standing at the windows of his study, looking out over the property. In the light of the moon, he is slender and masculine, a striking figure against the window panes. He turns and I swear that my heart begins to race. He has a profound and unexplainable effect on me.

"I don't know that you are supposed to," he replies. His voice is husky and deep. "My family is complex, Evangeline. Am I correct to assume that everything that you learn here is protected by doctor-patient confidentiality?"

I nod, not gracing that with an answer. A small smile tugs at the corners of Luca's lips.

"Good. I should also mention that I prefer that my employees don't involve themselves with each other romantically. Will that be a problem?"

He's staring at me again with those inky eyes and I know he's talking about Adrian. I should be furious that he would try to control me in such a way, because I know that's exactly what he's doing.

I *am* annoyed. But more than that, I am fascinated. He's intrigued enough with me to want to interfere? My heart races once more. I know it shouldn't. I know I should be overwhelmingly offended at this maneuver. But on the same token, I'm a strong enough woman that I can handle him. I can handle anything.

"I seldom date at all, Luca. So while generally I would tell you that you don't have the right to tell me who I can or cannot see romantically, it probably won't be an issue. If it does become one, I'll let you know." I keep my voice cool.

Luca looks surprised and satisfied at once, but he doesn't comment. He simply nods.

"My mother seems to be at her worst in the evening hours. If you could schedule your daily visit with her during that time, I would sincerely appreciate it," he tells me.

I nod. "Fine. I'll begin tomorrow after dinner."

"Perfect." Luca is curt now as he adjusts one of his cufflinks. "I'll be happy to drive you home. I'm sure you are tired. I do thank you for coming out here so late."

"You're quite welcome." I raise an eyebrow. "You're going to drive me yourself? Don't you have staff for that?"

The corner of his mouth twitches again.

"Yes. But Adrian is finished with his duties for the night. I'm not a slave-driver. My staff members receive time off. I'll take you myself."

"Thank you," I answer simply. He gestures toward the door and I walk ahead of him. I pause at the door and he opens it, then leads the way through the rest of the house. The house is quiet and darkened and I don't see any signs of other staff members. However, I decide that it isn't that odd. It is late, after all. They have probably turned in for the night.

We step into the fragrant Maltese night and Luca opens the car door. I slide inside, enveloped by the luxurious leather seat. I am once again reminded of Luca's lifestyle. He is surrounded by luxury. And I'm sure that he has seldom heard the word no, or been refused anything.

The engine roars to life and we are once more on the road.

"Are you enjoying Malta so far?" Luca asks politely, making small talk after a few minutes of silence.

"So far," I answer. "I haven't been here long, but it is truly a beautiful place."

"That it is," he agrees. "But like anywhere, it has its downfalls."

"Such as?" I ask doubtfully. "I find it difficult to believe that Malta has any. It is so lovely."

Luca steers the car fluidly around a sharp curve. "Well, Dr. Talbot, as I'm sure you are aware, beauty can often be deceiving."

I stare at him. "Are you saying that Malta is deceiving?"

He glances at me.

"No. I'm saying that like anywhere else, Malta isn't perfect. It has secrets and issues of its own."

"Issues of its own," I repeat. "Just like anyone. Even you, Mr. Minaldi."

He smiles now, his teeth white in the night. I am struck once again by his masculine beauty. I decide that his car suits him. He is like a jaguar himself. Lean, sleek and muscular.

"So I'm Mr. Minaldi now?"

I nod.

"Until we're friends."

He smiles again and I smile back. I can't help it.

Unlocking Luca's personality will be a challenge, but it will be an enjoyable one. I suddenly realize that I like making him smile. It's like the clouds suddenly lift from his face and the sun shines once again. It is a silly thought, but it is the most fitting I can think of. Luca is such a commanding presence that his mood has a tangible and noticeable effect on the atmosphere around us. It is like nothing I've ever seen.

He pulls into my driveway and I find that I wish the drive had been longer.

"Here you are, Dr. Talbot," he tells me. He opens his door, walks around the car and then opens mine. "Thank you again for coming this evening."

"You're welcome," I tell him. "I am glad I could help."

He starts to get into his car, then stops.

"Dr. Talbot."

I look back over my shoulder at him. He is staring at me with a strange light in his eyes, something I haven't yet seen in him.

"Yes?"

"Make sure you lock your doors. There are a few less than beautiful things in Malta."

He ducks into his car and is gone. His dark car slides past me back out into the road and I am alone in the night. I walk inside and click the door closed, locking it behind me.

When I wake the next morning, I find that another girl is missing from Valetta.

Chapter Eleven

The Beast

The darkness caves in around me and there is a loud roar in my ears. I try to fight it, to shake it off, at least until I return home. Even as I do, I know that I will fail. I resist it for as long as I can but I cannot make it home. It is of no use and before I know it, my vision blurs and I have no control.

I am not myself.

I scan the horizon, searching for a light, searching for signs of life.

I search until I find it.

And then I do.

I move forward, light on my feet. I am quiet and stealthy and I am only thinking of one thing.

One thing.

She is walking along the road in the dark, her white shorts far too short. Her tanned legs are long, her blonde hair is short. She has a butterfly tattoo on her shoulder.

None of those things matter.

It wouldn't matter at all if they were different than they are.

I am not myself.

She hears me and turns.   At first she isn't afraid, but then she recognizes me for what I am. She can see it on my face and then I see terror on hers.

She screams, but there is no one to hear.

She tries to run, but I am faster.

She tries to fight, but I am stronger.

Her hands are like a child's as they beat against me, but it is of no matter. It is as though she is not fighting at all.

I bend my head and her blood runs down my chin, into my neck and onto shirt.

It doesn't matter.

Nothing matters.

Fiercely fragile, her heart is beating wildly against mine.

And then it isn't.

Chapter Twelve

Eva

Sunlight shines into the windows of my cottage as I eat a cup of yogurt, granola and Maltese honey.

I have the television turned on for the first time since I have been here and I am glued to the local news as I sit curled up in a living room chair.

The girl that disappeared last night, Annica Rossi, will make the third woman in a month's time. Two are known to be dead, but this one, this Annica Rossi, is just gone. She is only twenty-three and had been walking home from her job at a local bar last night. She is only six years younger than I am.

I stare at the collage of pictures of her on the television; of her young eyes, her slightly rough appearance, the tattoo on her shoulder and I have a feeling that wherever she is, she isn't alive. She shouldn't have been out so late by herself, she should have known better. But she shouldn't have had to pay for such a small transgression with her life. She was young. Youth are known to make mistakes born of ignorance.

Something isn't right in Valetta and I remember Luca's words.

There are a few less than beautiful things in Malta.

That's one way to put it, I guess.

I eat the last bite of my breakfast and then venture to my makeshift office. I sort through notes from this week and transfer them into typewritten files. I am very neat and orderly when it comes to research because I have to be. If I'm not, it will all fall apart and I won't be able to pull it together into something workably intelligent. I'm rather like that in real life, too. Everything has its place, its file, its slot. My thoughts, my feelings, my memories. My emotions are usually filed away in Tupperware-like mental containers.

I guess it's why I make a good doctor. I'm very matter of fact and always have been. My mother and father both like to tell me stories of from when I was a kid. I was the same even then. Other girls were crying because there were mean kids on the playground. I was too busy trying to determine what made them that way to let their mean behavior personally affect me. I'm like that to this day. I have a distinct ability to remove myself from any given situation and analyze it.

I'm compartmentalized.

Except with Luca.

I hate the thought that I allow him to get to me, but I have to admit that he does. But truly, even at the same time as I hate it, I know that I like it a little bit too. It means that I am human. I have strong emotions after all, emotions that I'm not able to control or dampen. There for a few years, I was starting to wonder.

I wrap up my busy work and then wind my hair into a knot at my neck. I need to go into town and mingle with the locals so that I can gather some more initial meeting data. Some friendly conversation will be a nice break from the quiet solitude of my cottage. So after changing my clothes, I'm out the door.

The day is beautiful and the sun shines onto my shoulders. I decide it's the best feeling in the world. I can smell the salt in the air and I know that I will forever associate that smell with this place, with the beautiful Maltese landscapes.

Even though I hate it, I ride the bus into town and then after I grab a coffee, I walk down to the wharfs, taking my time as I wind through the throngs of people in the marketplace. I know that the crusty old fishermen who frequent the piers will be excellent subjects for research.

I am not wrong.

I spend several hours on the faded wooden piers, talking and laughing with the fishermen who linger here. They look rough and cantankerous, but each one of them is willing to chat with me about life in Malta and their love of fishing. It is very apparent that fishing is not a hobby for them, it's a way of life. They take it very seriously. Many of them are retired commercial fishermen and it is in them to the bone.

As I speak with the last fisherman of the day, Tobias, the conversation suddenly and unexpected takes a turn toward the recent killings. Tobias looks at me with cloudy blue eyes.

"Miss, you'll want to make sure that you stay safe, you hear?"

I nod. "Of course. I always do."

He nods back, this stranger who I only met an hour ago. "Be sure that you do. A pretty thing like you shouldn't be out and about on your own right now. Maybe even during the day. There's no sense in taking chances."

"Oh, I'm sure I'm safe in the daylight," I tell him. "Wolves usually come out at night, don't they?"

His gnarled hands cast out his line again and he reels it slowly back in. He stares at it thoughtfully for a moment before he speaks.

"I'm not sure that it is wolves. I know that's what they're saying. But I've lived here my entire life, for eighty-four years, and I've never encountered a wolf here. I've fished at every source of water in this area. Streams, rivers and the sea. I've been in the woods, on the beach, on the roads. And never once have I seen a wolf or even any signs of a wolf."

"Never?" I ask him, raising an eyebrow. "Not even a paw print?"

He shakes his gray head. "Not even a paw print."

Chills roll up my spine at his words and their meaning. If he's been out and about in the countryside for so long and has never seen a wolf, then odds are, there aren't any wolves to be seen. The hair rises on the back of my neck as I think of the alternative.

"You think there's a serial killer on the loose."

My words feel stilted in my mouth and Tobias looks grim as he slowly nods.

"I guess that's what it would make him."

"Him?" I look at Tobias. "How do you know it's a man?"

He shakes his head and then re-casts his line. We both watch it sink into the swirling sea.

"Because it must be. A woman isn't violent enough to do what was done to those women."

I swallow hard.

"I heard their throats were ripped out."

Tobias nods. "That's what I hear, as well. A woman wouldn't do that."

I think about that. "Well, women are far less likely, historically speaking, to commit murders of a violent nature. And serial killers are sixty times more likely to be a man than a woman. But there's always the remote chance that it is a woman."

Tobias is shaking his head. "I don't believe it. My gut says it's a man. Keep your doors locked, Dr. Talbot."

That's exactly what Luca told me and I know that it is good advice.

I wish Tobias a good afternoon fishing and I venture from the pier and onto the beach below. I look back over my shoulder and Tobias' face is grim, which one again causes goose bumps to form on my arms. I wipe them away. This is silly. I'm in broad daylight. I'm fine.

The sea is active today and the waves that crash against the shore are at least three feet tall, maybe four. I can see several small boats getting tossed about in the current and I am happy that I am standing on dry land. Although my feet are killing me. Three-inch wedges weren't the best idea. I slip them off and carry them, allowing my aching feet to sink into the damp, cool sand.

I try to put troubling thoughts out of my head and choose to look for shells along the beach as I walk instead. It's a mindless and calming activity. I know it is a couple of miles from here to the shore outside of my cottage, but I decide that I can stop at Marianne's for a late lunch/early dinner.

I step around stones and seaweed and driftwood that have washed ashore and find myself continually looking at the water. The view is beautiful here, the horizon endless. It is impossible not to put troubling thoughts to bed when the scenery is so beautiful and tranquil.

And then I see him.

Walking toward me, strolling quietly, is Luca Minaldi. He's calm and quiet and an enormous brindle-colored dog is walking slightly ahead of him.

Luca is dressed in Khaki shorts and a button-up chambray shirt with the sleeves rolled up. The breeze ruffles his dark hair and I can feel the penetrating heat of his gaze even from here.

Why does it seem that I bump into him everywhere that I go? Marianne said that he seldom leaves his home, yet I've seen him everywhere.

He's within speaking distance now, so I call out a hello. His dog, an enormous monster of an animal, growls softly. Luca murmurs something to it and it instantly falls silent, although now it drops back to walk next to Luca's side, perfectly in sync with his step.

There's a hint of smile on Luca's face, but then it is gone and he waves.

"That's quite a guard dog," I say as I stay a respectable distance away. I glance at it, at its enormous yet aerodynamic body and slightly shaggy fur. "What is it?"

Luca's hand rests on the great dog's back for a mere second and the dog sits at his side, still at attention. "This is Grendel. He's an Irish Wolfhound."

"Ah," I answer. "I remember hearing bits and pieces about that breed over the years. They're gentle giants, right?"

Luca looks doubtful. "Perhaps some are. Grendel was trained to be a guard dog as a pup. It made my mother feel more comfortable to have one. He gravitated toward me, though, and now I have a constant companion."

"Nice name," I reply. "I loved Beowulf when I was in college."

"It seemed fitting," he answers. Looking down at his guard, whose eyes are ever alert and fierce, I have to agree.

"He *does* seem like a Grendel," I nod.

Luca glances at the notebook in my hands. "Have you been out working?"

I laugh. "If you can call it that. I've been chatting with talkative old fishermen out on the wharf."

"Did you get a lot of material for your project?" Luca is polite, although he does seem genuinely interested.

"Yes, I did," I answer. "I love the people here in Malta. They are so friendly and easy to read."

He smiles now and I suck in my breath. Because he usually seems so dark and commanding, it is a breathtaking difference when he smiles.

"Most of them, anyway," I add. Luca looks amused.

"Not all of them?" And now his dark eyebrow is raised and his bangs are hanging just slightly over his eye. He looks like a fully-clothed underwear model and I swallow.

"No. Not all of them."

He's amused again and he takes a step closer to me. Grendel stays where Luca told him to stay, evidence of his training.

"Is there anyone in particular you're having trouble with?"

He's near me now, clearly inside my personal space. I can smell his subtle spicy cologne, something unique to him. I've never smelled that scent before. He steps one more step toward me and now I can feel the warmth coming from his body. I swallow hard again.

"You know there is. I can't read you."

Luca is still now, watching me with his intense gaze. I feel it brushing along my skin as potently as though he were touching me with his fingers.

"Dr. Talbot, you don't have enough time to figure me out. It would take all the time in the world. And the last I checked, you only have the summer."

He's so close to me now that my wits are addled, something that very rarely happens. I struggle with my composure, struggle to seem unfazed. As he looks at me though, I feel like he can see my thoughts. He *knows* the effect he's having on me. I'm sure of it.

"Yes," I confirm. "I'm only here for the summer."

His chest is broad. I'm staring at it now since it is eye-level for me. His shirt is tailored and stretches perfectly across his shoulders and I'm staring at him so intently that I startle when he speaks.

With his head ducked close to mine, he murmurs, "Pity."

Then he steps away from me.

And the intense mood is lifted. The electricity between us is alleviated for the time being, although I know that won't last long. There is an attraction between us, something dark and fierce and I would be a fool to not acknowledge it. And I'd probably be a fool to give in to it, as well.

"What time will you be visiting with my mother this evening?"

He's polite and casual now and his posture is relaxed. Yes, the charged atmosphere is gone. I can breathe again.

"I think around 8:00 pm. Will that work for you?"

He nods. "That will be fine. Please stop by my study afterward. I'd like a report."

I nod. "Of course."

And he turns and walks away without another word. Grendel walks with him, once again perfectly attuned to his master's movements. I watch them until they are quite a ways away before I take another step.

Luca never looks back.

Chapter Thirteen

Luca

I feel her watching. Evangeline's gaze is firmly implanted between my shoulder blades and I fight the urge to turn, to return to her side and continue speaking with her, to continue breathing her in. She smells of fresh air and flowers and I have been taken off guard by the connection that I feel with this woman.

All I can do is wish I wasn't feeling it.

There's no way I can tell her to stay away from me, that I'm dangerous for her. It would sound ridiculous, like stuff that fiction and legend are made of. I am not Heathcliff and she is not Catherine. The reasons that separate us are different from those of that fabled pair. Heathcliff was tortured because he could not have his Love. I will be tortured regardless, but I refuse to drag anyone else into it, which might be my single redeeming quality.

And so I walk away.

Grendel and I make our way over the damp beach back to Chessarae and as I do, a familiar feeling begins to grow from within me and with it, I feel a heavy weight on my chest. My vision blurs, then focuses and I want to punch a wall as immediate and profound rage explodes inside of me.

I am surprised, taken aback, aghast.

It's back. Already.

I swallow hard as the light begins to pull away from the corners of my eyes and the blackness threatens to overtake me. It is imminent. I don't have much time. This onset was sudden, more so than most times.

I feel the same sense of comfort that I always feel as I pass through my property gates, but it is dimmed this time. Many things are dimmed right now, my emotions are dulled even while some of my senses are heightened. My feet sink into Chessarae soil and I sigh. Chessarae is my refuge. I draw strength from the solitude. It will keep me safe.

But rather than going into the house, into the stone bricks and mortar that I call home, I quickly follow the trails into the garden that lead me through the English Maze. The flowering bushes are fragrant, but I bear them no mind, even though my sense of smell has been awakened, as if from a long slumber. I can smell everything right now, the lilies, the lavender, the roses.

I wind my way to the center of the maze and when I reach it, I find myself in a familiar oasis. There is a small bubbling pond here with a fountain, benches and a circle of white marble statues. The twelve Greek Olympians stare at me with lifeless marble eyes. They know the secret that is contained here in this oasis. They have watched me come and go many times before.

My vision blurs once more and I focus hard on holding off the blackness. It is coming, but I am almost there. My stomach muscles strain as I hold them tensely, my entire body coiled as I fight this internal battle.

I stride quickly around the pond and approach a large statue of Hades on the other side. That the god of the Underworld guards this particular secret is an irony not lost on me. On his platform base, there is a small bronze plaque. It is very old yet still in pristine condition and I press it firmly, until I hear a click. It slides to the side and reveals a thumb pad. I place my thumb upon it and an infrared reader slides over it, reading my identity. A green light flashes, granting approval to enter.

Hades stares down at me knowingly as the statue raises slightly, exposing rollers from beneath. It rolls smoothly and noiselessly backward, revealing a hidden staircase below. I can see the marble steps descending into darkness and I step inside with Grendel at my heels.

There are only two living people in the world who know that this exists. I am one of them.

I punch at a button on the wall on the way down and simultaneously, lights come on in the tunnel and Hades slides back into place above me. I am hidden from the world now. And that is the sole purpose of this secret place. I begin to feel a coming sense of relief. I will make it. I am so close.

One hundred and twenty four marble steps later, we have reached the bottom. This landing leads to a hallway branching off into both directions. One direction leads to underground tunnels that go straight to the house and emerge in my study and in the basement. The other leads in the opposite direction to a small living area. It is soundproof from the world above.

No one from above would ever guess that this underground fortress is here. It was built by my great-great-grandfather, back when this type of technology was cutting edge; at least, it was cutting edge here in

Malta. The ancient Egyptians were utilizing hidden rooms and tunnels and sliding, trick doorways a couple of thousand years ago for their tombs. But then again, ancient Egyptians were ahead of their time in many ways. They created their underground fortresses to protect their dead, to keep them safe from grave-robbers. Mine was created for an entirely different purpose.

To keep me in.

I continue down the hall into a luxurious living space and gaze around. Recessed lights provide a soft, ambient glow. We refer to this place as 'the cave'. It is clean, modern and fully-stocked. Adrian sees to that.

One wall houses an entire rack of wine. The other consists of shelves and shelves of books and has a couple of leather reading chairs situated in front of it. A third wall is covered in expensive, original art; as well as several television screens. Each of them reflects the center of the English Maze from a different angle as reflected by the hidden cameras there. We always know if someone approaches.

The fourth wall is different.

A large bed is pushed against it, secured tightly to the floor so that it cannot be moved.

Chains protrude from the wall, heavy and metal, winding through the iron headboard. Thick padded handcuffs are attached to the chains and are resting right now on the thick pillows.

I know that if anyone happened upon this place, they might draw the conclusion that I am a depraved sex fiend, that this is my sex nest and that I bring women here to commit freakish sexual acts upon them.

That couldn't be farther from the truth and I know that no one will ever 'happen' upon this place. This cave was designed for me, for my great-great-great-grandfather who was just like me. It was designed to be perfectly hidden, completely impenetrable, and to protect the women of Malta from me, from the Minaldi men.

The chains are archaic and painful to wear, but I wear them because I deserve them.

Because I'm a monster, like my father before me and his father before him, and so on.

There is no help for me.

What I told Evangeline was true. She cannot help me.

No one can.

There is a sudden noise behind me and I turn, only to find Adrian approaching with a large box in his hands. He looks as surprised to see me as I am to see him. His blue eyes are at first shocked, then narrow in caution. He's careful now. He knows what my presence here means.

"Luca," he says, his eyes skimming over me. I know he's checking for my presence of mind. "What are you doing here? Are you feeling alright?"

I shake my head in short staccato movements.

"No," I rasp. "It's coming."

Adrian is alarmed and he sets his box down, approaching me cautiously, staring into my eyes. "It's too soon," he says.

I know and I grimly agree with him.

"I don't know why," I tell him as I stride quickly toward the bed, toward safety. "Nothing is different. I'm the same as I ever was. I'm not doing anything differently."

I am just a few moments away from the precipice, from losing it. I know this, so I move faster. I grasp a metal manacle and wrap it around my wrist until I hear a click. I have enough slack in the chain to reach my other wrist and do the same.

I take a deep breath and try to relax, slumping against the headboard onto the bed. I made it. Everything will be fine.

But it won't. This shouldn't be happening, not so soon. I say that again to Adrian, although even now, my words are starting to slur and my thoughts are beginning to run together. Soon, everything will become visceral and I won't think anything logical at all.

Adrian stares at me thoughtfully. "I haven't wanted to say anything," he begins uncertainly and then he pauses.

I stare at him through the thickening mental fog. "But?"

My lips are heavy and numb. It's coming. My breathing quickens.

"But this is the way it usually happens, according to everything my father taught me."

Maddeningly, he trails off and I wait for him to continue, but he doesn't. He picks up his box and carries it to the cabinets next to the wine and begins to put supplies away. I don't have time for this. Within minutes, I won't be cognizant.

"Adrian," I growl. "Tell me what your father told you."

"I'm sorry," he turns around apologetically. "I just hate to upset you. It might be nothing, so I don't know whether I should worry you with it."

"Worry me," I growl again. Adrian looks pained.

"My father told me that the Minaldi curse continues to worsen with age. You have passed your thirty-year mark. You will continue to become more active, the curse more violent with each year. It will become worse when you reach thirty-five, worse still when you reach forty and so on."

I feel suddenly and nauseatingly numb.

"My father," I begin. Then I clear my throat. "How often was my father contained here at the end of his life?"

It's difficult to speak now. I lick my lips.

"Before your father died, my father spent the majority of each month down here with him," Adrian admits. "Nicolas was down here more than he wasn't."

It is a sobering thought. Before my father committed suicide, I had known that he was becoming more and more despondent. I knew the reason, obviously, since we share the same blood. But he didn't speak of it. Not ever. Not to me, not to anyone, except for Adrian's father, Benjamin.

Benjamin was the only one who knew the extent of my father's illness, of the darkness that lived within him. Just as Adrian is the only one who knows the same of me. Our families are intertwined. They have been for generations. The Leopoldos have been our loyal companions for hundreds of years.

"I will not allow it to get to that point," I say bluntly. Adrian knows exactly what I mean and he nods grimly.

"But we aren't at that point yet," he says. "We don't need to consider anything right now."

"Not yet," I concede. "But when we are…" I trail off and Adrian nods.

"I know."

I feel empty inside, although to be honest, I feel empty most of the time. It is a defense mechanism, something I perfected long ago.

My 'curse', as we refer to it, is undefined and undiagnosed by medical professionals. It is a genetic anomaly that has plagued the Minaldi men for hundreds of years. It is inescapable, it is dark, it is crushing.

I believe that is why Evangeline has intrigued me so. For the first time in as long as I can remember, I have felt something besides the dark void that lives within me. Evangeline is a hopeful person, full of light. And being around her is invigorating. The attraction between us is undeniable.

If only I could pursue her as a normal man would.

But I'm not normal, so I cannot.

I strain unconsciously at the chains, pulling as hard as I can away from the wall. The padded manacles bite into my skin, even through the thick cushion that they contain. Even now, my mind is breaking away, doing what it wills, not what *I* will. The black clouds spill into my brain and I can no longer think as myself.

I am not myself.

I am not myself.

I am not myself.

I bellow like the beast that I am and Adrian closes his eyes. He will stay with me as he always does, but he can't bring himself to watch the animal that I will become. The blackness closes in and then I know nothing more.

Chapter Fourteen

Eva

I should be working, but I'm researching instead. And I'm not researching anything work-related. I should feel guilty, but I don't.

I can't remember a life before the internet and search engines. It has truly revolutionized everything. Back in my mother's day, you couldn't simply plug a man's name into the computer and pull up his history. And honestly, I can't believe that I waited until today to do this.

After Luca told me that he wanted to see me the other night after my visit with his mother, he wasn't there. He simply wasn't in his study and none of the servants knew where to find him. It was so strange. He made a point to ask me to stop and give him a report, and then he wasn't there. It's true, he could have simply been called away on a business matter, but if that were the case, wouldn't his staff have known? Wouldn't he have been handling the matter in his study? Something felt very odd, very wrong.

I type Luca Minaldi and push "Search" and a multitude of hits are returned. I sift through them with interest, staring at the various pictures of him. Luca is an intense figure, even through a camera lens. Always handsome and elegant, he poses in formal dress for various pictures at various events. There are also random and candid pictures of him captured by tourists and bloggers and posted online on gossip sites. But there aren't as many as I would have guessed, not from someone from a family as affluent as his. And I know the reason.

Marianne told me that he is practically a recluse. He ventures into the city for only a few things, for library board meetings, for his company board meetings, and to sign documents at the bank. That is pretty much it, except for when he runs. He is pictured several times jogging along Maltese roads, his running shoes well worn, a testament to his dedication to the sport. He doesn't compete, so it must just be a hobby for him, an outlet for stress, I would guess.

I do learn a few things that I hadn't known, though.

Luca Minaldi is thirty-two years old. His birthday is October 15. He has two brothers, Christoph and Damien. He has never been romantically linked to anyone in particular, although he has been photographed with various dates at social functions, and never with the same woman twice. He attended Cambridge and graduated Magna cum Laude with a degree in business, then continued on to earn an MBA.

He is currently the Senior Vice President of Operations at Minaldi Shipping. His younger brother Christoph is the Senior VP of Marketing and his other brother, Damien, is the President and CEO. His brothers moved away to other Minaldi Shipping global locations years ago, while Luca stayed here because Valetta is where their main operations (shipyards and warehouses) are located. Damien is located at their corporate headquarters in London and Christoph works in their Abu Dhabi offices.

These things are the cut and dried facts that are easily accessible on the web.

I dig a little deeper and read through a handful of gossipy social Maltese websites. It seems that Luca has been the subject of fascination for years. He is considered mysterious, handsome and the most eligible bachelor of Malta, a title that doesn't seem to affect him at all. He is unfazed by the attention and ventures into town as little as possible. He is gossiped about frequently, with speculations on whether he stashes mistresses around the world unbeknownst to the Maltese public or whether he is homosexual.

I can sense the latter is not the case. The dark, fiery stares that he gives me can attest to that. Sexual energy churns between us, something that warms my belly just thinking about.

Luca is certainly a mystery. I've known that from the beginning, and he only grows more fascinating as I learn more about him.

I stare at his picture, which stares back blankly from the computer screen. This is the only time I've been able to stare at him without feeling that intense energy that he brings when he is with me in person. Even now, his gaze is intense, even though I am safe through a computer screen.

Safe.

I am startled at that word and I ponder it for a moment. Why would that thought occur to me? Do I subconsciously feel that I'm not safe around Luca?

As a psychiatrist, I am a firm believer that we should listen to our subconscious, to our instincts. It is interesting that I should feel, even for a second, that I am unsafe around Luca. I think about it for a few more moments, turning it over and over in my head. I finally decide that I have simply been swayed by the fact that both Melina and Luca himself told me that I should feel that way.

But Melina is unbalanced and Luca is... tortured. That is the best way I can sum him up in one word. Something about Luca—something in his past probably, is torturing him. I can see it in his eyes, I can sense it in his presence. And the woman in me, the maternal side that wants to fix little children, aches to fix whatever it is that is hurting him.

The depth of my emotion concerning this is startling. I have very strong feelings about it. I want to help him and I don't even know why. I barely know him. And certainly, I can't help him until I know what it is that troubles him. So I decide to make it my mission to find out, a feat that will not be easy since it is widely known that Luca Minaldi is a secretive mystery. I smile to myself. Fortunately, I am very good at what I do.

I solve emotional puzzles.

I pull out my research and work for a while, before I realize that I haven't eaten lunch. I glance at my watch and find that it is 3:00. Well past lunchtime. I put my work away and make my way to Marianne's. She is happy to see me and we chat for at least an hour and a half while I eat lunch. She laughs and talks about Adrian, inquires about Luca and is surprised when I tell her that I've seen him again. I can't divulge the capacity

116

of our meeting, so instead I downplay it and make it sound as though we just bumped into each other.

Technically, it isn't a lie. When Luca came to my house to ask me to visit with his mother, we did bump into each other.

"Well, bella," Marianne laughs. "I won't worry about you being alone quite so much. It appears that you've got that under control." She lifts her wine glass and clinks it with mine.

I feel slightly warm and flushed, a by-product of the wine. I decide that I need some fresh air or all I'll want to do is curl up into a ball and take a cozy nap for the remainder of the day. So I wish Marianne a good day, promise that I'll be back tomorrow and make my way back out to the beach.

I take my shoes off and decide to walk for a little bit before I get back on my scooter and ride home. As I sink my toes into the soft sand, the breeze is cool and crisp on my face and it does wonders to perk me back up. I inhale the salt, the brine in the air and I know that I love it here. I may never want to return to the States.

I love this time of day, too, just when the late afternoon begins the slow turn into dusk. I have to laugh at myself. I'm feeling so content right now, with my belly full of pasta and wine, that pretty much anything would make me happy. There is still enough light that I feel safe out here since I am on my way home. And also, I promised Marianne that I would call when I reached my cottage safely. If I don't call soon, she will send out search parties. Of that, I am certain.

I smile and hum a nameless, tuneless song as I walk. My feet sink into the foam lip of the sea as it slides to and fro against the beach. Life is good right now.

I walk a good mile and a half probably before I decide that I'd better turn around. I glance regretfully ahead of me, at the tree-lined coast, before I turn. I realize that I'm regretful only because that is the direction that Luca always goes into, the direction that houses Chessarae. I had been subconsciously walking toward it, *toward him*, hoping to see him.

This is getting ridiculous.

I turn and start my walk back to my scooter.

After a half mile or so, something in the water ahead catches my eye. Something silvery white in the late afternoon sun. I stare at it as I walk closer, and then as I approach it, a heavy feeling forms in my chest.

Whatever it is looks fleshy.

Oh my god.

I can't help the ominous feeling of panic that rises in me and smothers the air trying to rise from my lungs. Visions from long ago flit through my head, of another time and place when I found something floating in the water. *Someone.*

My breathing comes in pants and I know that something isn't right here today. Just like something wasn't right twenty-two years ago when I found my little brother floating face down in the lake behind our house.

I can't breathe and I have to force myself to move. I take a tentative step toward the thing in the water and I'm terrified to look even though I know I have to. Chills run down my spine and I glance around for signs that someone else might be near in case I need help with *this thing*. But there is no one. Only me.

My legs feel numb as I take another step toward it, then another.

Whatever it is has washed up onto the rocks that line the shore and it is covered in tattered fabric. I gulp, swallow hard, and then walk the remaining twenty yards.

It's a person, just as my instincts already knew.

I force myself to wade through the shallow water and stand over it, staring down, fighting the waves of nausea that are welling up in me.

It's a partial person. Something... sharks, crabs, *something*, has eaten half of it. Of *her*. I know it is a *her* because there is a butterfly tattoo still on her shoulder. Her shoulder is one of the only things that I can see that is still intact and I am suddenly so very thankful that she is face down. She has no legs or arms left and there is seaweed matted into her short blonde hair.

I know, beyond any doubt, that this is Annica Rossi.

Chapter Fifteen

I don't even realize that I am screaming until Marianne is pulling at my shoulders, pulling me away from this battered corpse. She sits me down on a piece of driftwood a short distance away, turns me in the opposite direction of the body and then pulls out her cell phone. The polizia arrive in less than five minutes.

By the time they arrive, I have calmed myself down. I take deep breaths and stare at the sand by my feet until I no longer feel panicky. I am slightly ashamed that I lost it in such a way. I'm a doctor. I shouldn't fall apart simply because I see a dead, half-eaten body. But to be fair, I'm a psychiatrist. I'm not accustomed to coming into surprise contact with a mutilated corpse. I doubt anyone is, particularly someone who lost her own brother to a drowning.

Marianne holds my hand as we wait for the lead detective to come speak with me. As the person who found *her*, they have to take my statement. That's fine with me, although I don't have much to tell them. I was walking along, minding my own business and there she was. The end. And that's what I'll tell them.

There's a team of them here now, all poking around her in a very official way, poking around the beach and then finally, the coroner comes and they remove her from the water and place her onto a stretcher, covering her up with a sheet. I feel a sense of relief for her. She deserves some privacy, some sort of dignity.

We wait forever. The polizia certainly aren't in a hurry to question me and allow me on my way. It's agonizingly frustrating. I just want to leave. My nerves and the cool evening breeze are causing me to shiver and I haven't brought a jacket. But still they let us sit. They don't even look in our direction.

Marianne and I chat and I am ever grateful to her for staying with me. I tell her that and she waves away my gratitude.

"It's what anyone would do," she insists. It's not, but I let it go.

We talk for a while longer and then she looks up and stares.

"Honey, look," she instructs.

I look up and am startled to find Luca jogging down the beach toward us. Grendel is at his side and I don't know why I am surprised at their presence. I was half-expecting (half-wishing) to see them earlier and now here they are.

Luca is clearly concerned as he stares at the scene in front of him before his gaze brushes over me. He is surprised, I can see it. And very curious. He jogs up to me and stops. Grendel stands at attention by his side. The dog's gold eyes appraise me sharply, but he doesn't growl this time. We're apparently making progress.

"What's going on?" Luca asks. He's as handsome as ever, even with the light sheen of perspiration gleaming on his brow. His dark hair is damp as he brushes it out of his eyes. His shirt is soaked through at the top. From the looks of it, he's been running for a while but he's not even breathing hard.

Marianne answers before I do.

"They found the third girl. We think," she adds. "Eva found her. The polizia won't confirm it, but Eva saw a tattoo on her shoulder. It's the girl."

Luca looks appalled. "She's dead?"

I nod. "Very. It looks like sharks got her."

"Oh. So she wasn't murdered?" Luca is surprised now. I shrug.

"I don't know. They aren't saying what they think. She could've drowned, I guess, and the sharks ate her remains. Or maybe she was murdered, then dumped into the sea."

Luca is somber again, shaking his head. He is a handsome and polished, even here.

"Either way, you shouldn't be here, Evangeline. This isn't a place for you."

His concern for my wellbeing makes my heart quicken.

"I have to be," I tell him quietly. "I found her and they want my statement."

He stares at me for a scant moment before he turns on his heel and walks to the lead detective. They speak for a moment in words that I can't hear before they both return to me. The detective is wearing rumpled clothing and is distracted, but he pulls out a little notebook and pen and turns his attention to me.

He says, in a very thick Maltese accent, "I apologize for your wait, Miss Talbot."

"Dr. Talbot," Luca corrects him. The detective nods.

"*Dr.* Talbot," the detective amends. "Can you tell me how you found the body?"

"Is it Annica Rossi?" I ask. The detective shakes his head.

"We can't confirm that yet," he says. "But it is a possibility."

I inhale shakily and then tell him how I found her. It only takes a minute because there isn't much to tell. He writes down what I say and then tells me that they will get back to me if they have any further questions. He thanks me and then leaves. Our interaction only took five minutes, after I waited forty-five for him to get to me.

I turn to Luca. "Thank you for expediting that process."

He shrugs. "It was nothing. You didn't deserve to wait out here in the dark. Come. I'll walk you home."

Marianne looks at me. "I'll see you tomorrow, bella," she says. "Lock your doors and use common sense, alright?"

I nod. It's clear that she doesn't think Annica Rossi drowned. I don't either.

I watch her retreat toward her restaurant before I look back at Luca.

"You don't need to walk me home," I tell him. "It's unnecessary."

"Perhaps," he answers. "But I want to. It would make me feel more comfortable. You've had a rough evening. It's the least I can do."

"Okay," I reply. "Thank you."

He touches my elbow lightly as I get up from the driftwood. His touch is electric and I can still feel the imprint of his fingers long after he removes them from my skin. For some reason, I ache to lean back into it, into his warmth. I decide it must be the emotional toll that this evening has taken on me.

Luca walks me to my scooter and then he pushes it as we walk. It doesn't take us very long to reach my cottage and we don't talk very much along the way. The night has been sobering, the events of it thoroughly quenching my good mood.

"Would you like a cup of tea?" I ask as Luca delivers me to my door. He looks at me. I can feel him examining me, studying my motives. His gaze practically burns my skin and I struggle to not fidget beneath it as I wait for his decision.

Finally, he asks, "Do you have Scotch?"

I have to laugh as I shake my head. "Um, no. I don't. But I have wine."

"That will do," he answers. He waits while I unlock the door and he tells Grendel to stay on the porch. The dog immediately sits and watches the perimeter with alert eyes.

Luca sits on my patio as I dig around for a corkscrew. I finally locate one, open the wine and bring it along with two glasses to the small table on the patio.

"Where were you the other night?" I ask him. "You said you wanted a report and then you weren't there."

He stares back at me calmly. "I had a matter to attend to. I apologize for not seeing you. Evangeline, are you all right?" he asks me as I pour him a glass of wine.

I notice that my fingers are shaking, sloshing the blood red liquid onto the sides of the glass. This is probably why he asked. I grip the crystal glass tighter.

I nod. "I'm fine. I just hadn't been expecting to find a murder victim today."

Luca looks grim. "I'm sure. But it is possible that she wasn't murdered. She could have simply gone into water that she shouldn't have."

I stare at him, at the way his mouth is pressed into a line.

"You don't believe that," I observe.

"No," he admits. "But I didn't want to alarm you."

"I'm already alarmed," I tell him. "I'm trying not to be, but I'm here alone in a tiny cottage not even half of mile from this latest victim. I would be a fool if I wasn't afraid."

"You're not a fool," Luca answers. "It's clear that you're anything but that."

His dark eyes are so dark that they are almost black as he stares at me. The sky above us is just as black and with his dark hair, he seems to melt into it. He smells like some exotic blend of masculine spices. I want to lean forward ever so slightly and inhale his neck. And then I am startled by my own impulse. It is so unlike me.

"No, I'm not," I answer. But my thoughts conflict with that notion.

I don't know if it is the emotion of the evening, but I find that all I want him to do is lean forward and kiss me, to wrap his strong arms around me and hold me there, against the safety of his chest. But of course he doesn't, so I take a slow sip of my wine. He watches me.

"Are you going to be alright?" he asks. "You're still shaking. Do you need a jacket?"

"I'm not cold," I tell him, although the breeze is slightly chilly. "I'm just rattled. But yes, I will be fine."

His wine glass is empty so I fill it up and then top mine off, as well. My hand is still shaking and I sigh.

"Maybe I'm not fine," I admit. "I've never seen anything like that before. And even though my brain knows that I'm safe as long as my doors and windows are locked, my body apparently doesn't believe it."

Luca smiles sympathetically. "That's completely normal," he answers. "I don't know anyone in their right mind who wouldn't be upset. Honestly, I'd wonder about you if you weren't."

"*You* aren't upset," I point out. He smiles again and I can see that he is tired.

"I wasn't the one who found her," he answers. "It's easy for me to remain calm. And although I'm calm, I *am* upset by the situation. It's unnerving. In fact, I have an idea. Why don't I stay here tonight? That might put you at ease and you can get some rest. I'll sleep on the couch."

I glance at his face and find that it is a serious offer, but I automatically reject the idea.

"No, no. I could never impose on you in such a way. I'm sure you have a king-sized luxurious bed waiting for you at Chessarae. I'd never put you on my couch. Or even in my tiny little bed. But thank you very much for offering. It's very gentlemanly of you."

He stares at me again, his gaze as black as night. The moonlight brushes softly against the chiseled features of his face and I inhale sharply at the expression I find there.

"Oh, make no mistake," he tells me softly. "I'm not much of a gentleman."

My breath hitches in my throat and I stare at him, into his stormy gaze before he laughs.

"Evangeline, truly. I want to stay. It will make me feel better. I won't sleep well knowing that you are frightened and alone. In fact, if you'd like, we could both return to Chessarae and you could sleep there. In your own room, of course," he adds.

"I couldn't impose on you in that way, either," I tell him.

"So, I'll stay here. No problem," he replies, as though he knew that I wouldn't come to Chessarae. "Just give me a blanket and I'll be fine on the sofa."

I look at him doubtfully. "Are you sure?"

He nods. "Quite sure. Trust me, no harm will come to you while I am standing watch."

His words actually comfort me and I feel a sense of relief that I won't be alone tonight. He sees the acceptance on my face.

"Wonderful," he says as he takes the last gulp of his wine and stands up. "All I'll need is a blanket."

I smile at him in gratitude. "I can't believe I'm letting you do this. But thank you. Very much."

He shakes his head. "Don't mention it. You came out to Chessarae and calmed my mother down when you didn't have to. I am in your debt."

We return into the house and Luca locks the door. I find him an extra blanket and then pause at my bedroom door.

"Thank you," I say again. "Really."

He settles onto the couch, with his legs hanging off the end. "It's not a problem."

He looks horribly uncomfortable on the small little sofa, but I smile at him anyway and close the door to my bedroom.

I am so weary that I don't remember even changing into pajamas before I fall into a heavy sleep.

Dreams instantly plague me.

Nightmares.

I see Annica washing up over and over on the beach, but this time, she is right below my cottage. She rolls in the surf, her skin gray and cold and dead. Her arms and legs are still torn off, but she is facing upward this time. Her eyes are glued to mine and her mouth is speaking. I bend to hear her. *Help me, Eva.*

And then she starts to scream and snakes slither from her mouth; huge black snakes with red eyes. There are so many of them and they all head straight for me, moving quickly through the sand. And behind them, my brother Christopher replaces Annica. And more and more snakes slither from his decomposing body and glide through the sand toward me.

I scream.

And hands are restraining me.

I open my eyes and Luca is with me.

I grow still as I look at him.

He stares back at me in concern and he is not wearing a shirt. His skin is warm against my arm and my eyes meet his.

"You were screaming," he says uncertainly.

I don't say anything.

Instead, without thinking, I grab him and clutch him to me, hiding my face in his bare, warm shoulder. He startles, then wraps his arms around me, holding me close. I don't even realize that I am crying until his skin beneath my cheek turns wet.

"Shh," he soothes me, stroking my hair with his smooth hand. "You're all right, Evangeline. I'm here. You're safe."

I sniff, trying to choke back the tears, trying to hide my distress. But emotions that I keep well-hidden are erupting and there is nothing I can do but let them come.

Luca holds me for the longest time, waiting until I have cried myself out, holding me closely and not asking any questions. His voice is soothing and low in the dark and honestly, it is the sound of it that brings me back from the edge of hysteria.

When I am finally quiet and still, Luca pulls away from me and stares into my eyes. He lifts a thumb and wipes an errant tear from my cheekbone.

"Are you going to tell me what is making you so upset?"

I sit still for a moment.

"I'm sorry," I tell him and my voice is so quiet in the stillness, in the night that wraps around us. "My brother died years ago, when I was seven and he was four. I found him. He was floating in the lake behind my parents' house. Finding Annica like I did brought the memories back and I had a horrible nightmare about both of them."

Luca pulls me to him again, but not before I see the sympathy on his face, tender and gentle.

"That must have been horrible for you," he murmurs as he strokes my back with his fingers. "You were too young to have seen something so horrible."

"It *was* horrible," I agree, burying my face once again in his chest. "For so many reasons. It was the downfall of my parents' marriage. My father, who has always been a little irresponsible, was supposed to have been watching Christopher while my mother worked the night shift at the hospital. Sometime in the night, Christopher got up and ventured outside. We don't know why he went into the lake. I found him in the morning."

I'm all cried out now. I have no tears left, but I remain ensconced in Luca's arms. He is a comforting presence right now and even through my distress, I marvel at how his personality can change in an instant. He can go from impassive to commanding to sympathetic and comforting in the space of one moment. *Mercurial.*

"I'm sorry that happened to you," he says softly, ducking his head to look into my eyes. "I really am. I can't imagine what I would do if that had happened to one of my brothers. You must be a very strong person. You were a very strong little girl, too, I'm sure."

I shake my head. "I don't feel like it right now," I admit to him. "I don't feel strong at all."

His dark eyes are understanding, so fathomless and black. They seem like such deep pools that I might fall into and drown in.

"It's okay to be vulnerable sometimes," he tells me. "You're only human."

"You're very kind," I answer. I push the hair out of my eyes and try to ignore the warmth that being near him generates, the fluttery feelings in my belly. I want him and try as I might, there is no ignoring that. I have to recognize and admit that I want this man.

On impulse, before I can think the better of it, I lean forward and kiss him. I wrap my arms around his neck and pull him to me; inhaling, feeling, touching, absorbing. I am lost tonight, sad on a very basal level, and Luca can fill the void in my heart.

If only for tonight.

His mouth is soft, yet masculine. His day-old stubble grazes the softness of my cheek and he tastes like warm wine. He is hesitant at first, holding his body very still as I press myself into him. My softness meets his firmness and I sigh into his mouth. At the sound, his hands grip at my back, sliding and moving until they are running along my spine and up into my hair. His fingers are strong and he deepens the kiss, pushing his tongue into my mouth as he pulls me tightly to him.

His chest is rock hard and his biceps are wiry bands of muscle wrapped around my back. The air hangs heavy around us, charged with sexual energy. It threads over and under, weaving between us, pulling us closer. We are enmeshed now and I don't know where I end and he begins; that is how closely we are tangled.

Luca's breathing is ragged and his smell is intoxicating. I inhale as deeply as I can with his tongue wrapped around mine.

It is everything that I thought kissing him would be.

And then he stops.

The air around us is charged and hot and magnetic, but Luca is motionless as he stares down at me, his beautiful eyes fixed upon mine.

My heart is racing as I stare back at him.

"I can't, Evangeline," he tells me regretfully. "You're distraught, not yourself. This isn't right."

I take a second to catch my breath, to bring myself under control. I know my cheeks are flushed. I can feel the heat staining them, evidence of the rejection that I feel.

But he's right and I know it, so I nod.

"Okay," I whisper. "But I thought you weren't a gentleman."

Luca smiles in the dark and starts to get up, to return to the living room couch, but that thought makes anxiety shoot through me and I tug on his arm.

"Please stay," I tell him. "I can't get the nightmares out of my head and I know they're going to come back. I keep seeing her face. And Christopher's."

My voice breaks off in the dark and Luca looks down at me gently. And then, without even complaining or commenting on the size of the bed, he sits back down and curls behind me, wrapping his strong arms around my waist. His scent curls around me like a blanket and I inhale, feeling calm for the first time all evening.

"Sleep," he tells me. "I'm right here."
He stays with me all night.

Chapter Sixteen

Luca

When I wake, I am hard.

While it is not uncommon for a man to wake with an erection in the morning, I know it's not a by-product of Mother Nature, but because I am pressed against Evangeline's very lovely backside. I mentally groan. Why did I do this to myself?

The memory of her frightened and sad face from last night flits through my mind in answer.

That's why.

I disentangle myself from the covers as gently as I can so that I don't wake her. Her hair is spread over her pillow like a cloud of deep red silk. In sleep, she is vulnerable and soft. I bend down, without thinking, and kiss her forehead. She doesn't stir and I don't know why I did that.

I make my way out to the living room and pull my shirt on, then hunt for coffee in her kitchen. After I find it, I put some on to brew, then check on Grendel. He's still lying right where I left him.

"Good boy," I tell him through the door. He looks at me and his tail thumps twice on the ground, but he won't get up until I tell him that he can.

"You're up," a soft voice says from behind me.

I turn to find Evangeline standing in the doorway of her bedroom. Her hair is still sleep-tousled and she's still in her pajamas. She's as sexy as anything I've ever seen and I swallow hard. Her pajama shorts are very, very short. I suck in my breath.

I cannot allow myself to be affected by this woman.

I nod.

"Yes. And there's coffee on."

Gratitude shimmers in her eyes and I can see that she is like me. Coffee is the first thing she thinks about. She patters out to the kitchen and pours a cup before it is even finished brewing. She blows on it, then sips at it. She looks at me.

"You don't have any yet. Here, take mine." She shoves it into my hands and I can't resist but to sip from where her lips had just been. The idea of it makes me hard again, as well as the memory of her kiss from the night before.

I hand her the cup back. "I can wait," I tell her. "You go ahead."

She stares at me for a moment, her grayish eyes pensive.

"I'm sorry I kissed you last night," she says apologetically. I stare at her and can't help but smile. She does look sorry.

"I'm not," I assure her.

She smiles a soft, sleepy smile and I find it endearing.

"Evangeline," I begin. "I think you should come stay at Chessarae. You're out here all alone and you're not going to rest easy that way. I've got dozens of guest rooms. You can have your pick. It would make me feel better."

She looks doubtful and starts to shake her head, but I can see the temptation on her face. She does want to, which means that she is really afraid here. She's a very independent person so I know that she must be incredibly nervous to even consider it.

"It's not an imposition at all," I tell her. "Truly."

She's quiet for a moment and then she nods.

"Thank you. Maybe I will take you up on that, for just a little while, until they find whoever is doing this. This whole thing has shaken me more than I thought."

"It would shake up anyone," I tell her again and she nods.

"Thank you."

She leaves to get dressed and I assume to pack a bag and I am left with doubts and trepidation of my own. Why did I do that? It's going to make my life so much more difficult as I worry about her safety in my home.

I'll have to be even more careful, more so than I've ever been.

But it seems to be time for that, anyway.

Chapter Seventeen

Eva

I wasn't going to accept.

But just as I was ready to say the words, *No, thank you*, visions of my nightmares came back to me, the horrible snakes coming from Annica's rotting mouth and then Christopher's and I was saying yes instead.

It was as much of a surprise to me as it was to Luca, but it was a relief to me as well. That was surprising too. I hadn't realized how scared I had been. The idea of being at Chessarae, behind the stone walls that look so impenetrable and strong, is comforting.

I pack a bag and emerge back out into the living room.

Luca is casually waiting for me, sipping a cup of coffee and browsing on his phone.

"Adrian will be here momentarily with the car," he tells me. "Chessarae is within jogging distance, but I thought it would be easier to drive with your bag."

He smiles now, a gracious host and I smile back.

"Thank you again," I tell him. "I feel a little silly."

He frowns. "Never feel silly," he tells me. "You're being smart, not silly."

"Okay."

The crunch of tires on gravel outside distracts me, followed by a soft knock on the door. I answer it, to find

Adrian standing on my stoop. He is surprised to be picking Luca up from my house, I know. His expression is polite, but curious. Perhaps even slightly dismayed. I almost want to explain, to tell him that Luca and I didn't do anything inappropriate together, but I don't. Luca and I are adults. Even if we had done something, it wouldn't be inappropriate. So instead, I smile.

"Good morning, Adrian. Thank you for coming to pick us up."

He nods, still studying me curiously. "You're welcome. It's my job."

He takes my bag and puts it in the trunk, then returns to the house.

"Luca? Are you coming as well?"

Luca turns from where he is standing at the back windows, his face back to being impassive and curt. The gentleness that I'd seen last night is gone. I find that I miss it already, but I intend to not show it. He can do what he wishes.

"Of course," Luca answers.

We all slide into the Mercedes and are on our way to Chessarae before I even know it.

A bit later, as we pull through the gates and up the drive, Luca turns to me.

"You, of course, will have full use of the property while you are here. Do you ride?"

I look at him. "Horses? I used to when I was a child."

He smiles. "We have a stable, if you'd like to take it up again. We also have a private beach. Feel free to use it. If you need anything at all, just ask a staff member. Or me."

We walk into the house and he instructs a maid to take me to a bedroom. He tells her the one that he wants me to use, then turns to me.

"I must excuse myself. I have a conference call. But do settle in and make yourself at home. Would you join me in the dining room for dinner? I eat at 7:00."

I nod. "Of course."

He smiles and the room is brightened.

"I'll see you then."

And he's gone. I'm left staring at the maid, who stares back at me. It is clear that she is shocked by this turn of events and I'm left to assume that Chessarae doesn't receive many guests.

The maid leads me through the twists and turns of the enormous house, up a grand staircase and through a long hallway. She glances sideways at me.

"This is the family's wing," she tells me. "Mr. Minaldi and his brothers have bedrooms down this hall. Yours will be just up the hall from his."

I gulp. It's clear she thinks that I will enjoy that fact, maybe even find it convenient. She clearly thinks that he and I have a more than friendly relationship. I suppose that's an understandable assumption, since he rarely has company.

"It's kind of him to do this," I tell her. "He took pity on me last night. I was afraid to be alone after these killings."

The maid nods solemnly. "Yes. It's horrible. I can't believe it's happening, actually. Not here in Malta."

She comes to a stop outside of a closed door and then opens it, gesturing me inside. I am amazed at the luxury contained within. It's not just a bedroom. It appears to be a suite.

The maid turns to me. "There's a living room, sitting room, bathroom and dressing room in here. Mr. Minaldi is just three doors down. If you need anything at all, please just let one of us know."

And she turns around and leaves. She isn't quick to warm up to people, I decide. But I am too distracted by my lavish quarters to be bothered. The bed is enormous and cushiony, covered in a fluffy pillows and a soft duvet. The furniture is expensive and heavy and the art hanging on the walls is priceless. In contrast to the heavy, dark furniture, the lamps have crystal accents and there are ornate and feminine chandeliers hanging throughout the rooms, even over the sunken marble bathtub. It's beautiful.

I venture back out into the bedroom and find that I have a balcony there. I stand at the rail, staring at the sea below.

I can't believe the view. It is beautiful, as well.

There is nothing but sea for miles and miles.

It is apparent to me once again how secluded and quiet Chessarae is. It's near enough to town that Luca can jog, but it feels like it is in its own universe.

From the balcony, I have a beautiful view of the gardens, as well. There is an intricate English Maze below and English gardens to the left and right. A gardener is hard at work pruning one of the many rose bushes and I watch him humming to the music in his earbuds.

To my far right, I can see where the jagged horizon forms into cliffs. The cliffs rise dramatically above the seascape, some one hundred feet or so. Below that, the sea crashes with fierce ferocity against the rocks. This is a place of both incredible beauty and grace, but also natural danger. It's a beautiful and delicate balance, something that I will forever associate with Chessarae.

As I stare absently out to sea, a movement from below, from the corner of my periphery, catches my attention. I look, only to find Melina running through the gardens. She is in her customary white dressing gown and it is streaming behind her in the breeze, along with her long dark hair. She doesn't have a gray hair on her head. And she should not be out of her rooms.

I turn at once and run for the ground floor. It takes me several minutes to burst out from the back of the house and to spill out into the gardens. I look around, but there is no sign of her. So I take off for in the direction I last saw her running in.

Toward the cliffs.

It doesn't take me long to weave through the gardens and to emerge on the rocky hillscape. As I do, I find Sophia pleading with Melina as she backs ever closer to the edge of the dangerous cliff. My pulse is racing and I can't breathe, but I rocket to where Sophia is standing.

Melina is having a bad day, that much is apparent. Her eyes are crazed, her hair is unkempt and she is babbling in crazy gibberish.

"Melina?" I call. "What are you doing?" I hold onto Sophia's arm to prevent her from inadvertently pushing Melina even further toward the edge.

Melina narrows her eyes.

"Who are you?" she calls back suspiciously. I'm not surprised. Even though I've met with her four times thus far, she doesn't know me now. But that is normal for her particular stage of psychosis. Some days she has known me, others she has not.

"My name is Evangeline Talbot," I tell her, as though we're meeting for the first time. "I couldn't help but see you running and I was wondering if I could be of any assistance?"

I hear Sophia on her cell phone behind me, but I don't take the time to listen.

Melina's eyes are still crazily out of focus.

"I don't think you can," she answers back, her voice thin and frail. "I don't want to be here anymore."

"Here at Chessarae?" I ask. "This is your home and it is very, very beautiful. You're so fortunate to have such a beautiful home."

Melina glares at me. "You have no idea," she spits. "Chessarae is evil, just like everyone who lives here."

I take one step toward her, but as I do, she takes one step back. She is only a few dangerous feet from the edge now. I freeze, my hand reaching out to her. The wind is strong up here and it whips violently around us. Melina's gown is wrapped around her legs and our hair is blown into our faces.

"Come in to me," I urge her. "I'd love to talk with you about why you think Chessarae is evil, Mrs. Minaldi."

"I can't tell you," she whimpers. "I can't tell anyone. But I can end my involvement in it. And I will. I'm going to end it today."

She backs toward the cliff, one more step.

My heart stops because I know that she wants to jump.

"Don't," I call out. "Please, Melina."

She sinks down to her heels, rocking back and forth. Her dressing gown is spread around her, but her eyes are focused on me. I know she will lunge backward if I move at all.

"You don't understand," she whispers. "You don't understand."

"Then tell me," I urge. "Make me understand, Melina. I can help."

She laughs now, a haunting and horrible laugh. I know I will never forget the sound. "You have no idea," she tells me. "You can't help. No one can."

I hear rustling from behind and I turn to see Luca and Adrian approaching us cautiously. Luca looks stricken, Adrian is resigned. They are accustomed to this behavior. But they can see, right now, the very real danger Melina Minaldi is in. In an altered psychotic state, she has no logical bearing on where she is.

"How did she get out?" I hear Luca asking Sophia.

"She attacked me," Sophia answered. "While I was unlocking the door. She ran out and I couldn't stop her. I can't believe how fast she is."

"Adrian," I call. He approaches.

"Yes?"

"Can you run into her rooms and bring me back a syringe and the sedative bottle in her medicine cabinet?"

"Absolutely."

And he's gone. Melina looks at me suspiciously.

"What are you talking about? Where is the handsome one going?"

If this was any other time, I would have smiled at her description. Adrian is handsome, but not nearly as handsome as Luca.

"Adrian is going back to the house, Melina," I tell her. "It's dangerous out here on the cliffs. You don't want anyone to get hurt, do you?"

She studies me for a moment, then shrugs.

"I didn't invite anyone out here with me," she says matter-of-factly. "You all followed me. I can't control your behavior."

She is laughably logical even in the middle of her lunacy.

We are silent for a moment as I wait for Adrian to return. I don't want to startle her until we are ready to act.

"Why are you here?" Melina asks. "Why are you with *him*?"

The malice in her tone as she refers to Luca is astounding and I can't wrap my mind around it. I can't fathom why she hates her own son as much as she appears to. So I ask. She looks surprised by my question.

"My son is evil," she tells me. "He is the devil's, not mine. I should have had his nurse drown him when he was an infant."

Luca inhales sharply from behind me and I ache to comfort him. The way she speaks of him is horrible, but dementia is often this way. The affected turn on those who they love. It is a tragic disease.

144

"I hardly believe your son is evil," I told her. "Surely you're mistaken."

She laughs again.

"If you believe that, you'll soon be dead with the others."

My heart seems to freeze.

I look at her face and she is so convinced of her words. I glance back at Luca and he is impassive once again. He is so very good at covering up his emotions, but I've decided that it might just be the way he copes. It is a defense mechanism.

Adrian is back and running up behind us. He hands me the sedative and I turn, concealing my hands as I draw the liquid into the syringe. I tap it, then put it behind my back as I face Melina once more.

"Luca," I murmur quietly. "Go to the right."

He looks, then nods, then tells Adrian to go to the left. I focus on keeping Melina's attention on me. I speak to her soothingly, making her focus on my face and my words.

Within a minute, Luca and Adrian rush her from each side.

She struggles within their arms, but I am there within a few seconds, administering a strong sedative to calm her. Her eyes flutter closed as they keep her restrained.

Luca scoops her into his arms and I accompany him as he carries her back to her suite. Her limp feet dangle over the side of his arm and she looks as small as a child.

He puts her on her bed, where we leave her with Sophia.

As Luca locks the door behind us, he thanks me.

"She could've died today," he says. "You stopped her. Thank you."

"You're welcome," I answer, staring him in the eye.

He shows no sign of distress about the incident, about the way his mother feels about him. It breaks my heart that he buries his feelings in such a way. I know that if I were able to help him deal with the feelings, he would feel so much better. So I tell him that.

He smiles a grim smile and for a flickering, fleeting moment, I see something in his eyes, something vulnerable. And then it is gone.

"I think I owe you an explanation," he tells me instead of agreeing. "I have an engagement tonight, but I'd like to sit down with you tomorrow. It's the least I can do, since you are living in my home."

I am surprised at his sudden willingness to talk to me, but I don't question it. I nod instead.

"Of course."

He smiles and my heart flutters. He is more handsome than any one man has the right to be.

"Until tomorrow."

And he walks away. His spicy cologne lingers in the hall behind him.

Chapter Eighteen

At 7:00 p.m., I find myself alone in the large formal dining room.

After a moment, Adrian enters. I startle, thinking for a moment that he is Luca. I try to hide my disappointment when I realize that he's not.

"Eve, Luca has been detained on a conference call. He wants you to go ahead and dine without him."

I glance at the long, daunting table. Alone.

"Do you want to join me? I could use some company."

But Adrian is already shaking his head. "I cannot, bella mia. I'm sorry. But it is tradition. Staff cannot eat in here."

I find it strange that as close as Luca and Adrian are, he hasn't bucked this tradition. But it *is* tradition here, and I must respect that. So I smile and Adrian ducks back out of the room.

When I am alone again, the quiet in this enormous room is smothering.

My fingers drum restlessly on the gleaming mahogany tabletop as I wait for the first course, a chilled cucumber bisque. It is garnished with shaved cucumber rinds and looks almost too beautiful to eat. I thank the butler who delivers it, then lift a spoonful to my lips. It is as delicious as it is beautiful.

I wish that Luca was here so that I could talk to him about the things that his mother said earlier, the hurtful things that I know must have crushed him. It worries me that he has continually borne the brunt of her delusions and anger without ever having an outlet to process those feelings. I know we'll discuss it tomorrow, but I'm impatient to try and help him. In my head, I see the little boy that Luca must have been at one time and it saddens me. This is not a good atmosphere to have grown up in.

I finish the next four courses then retreat into my room, comfortably full and just slightly tipsy from wine. The solitude in my room is startling at first; the quiet is so still that it almost roars in my ears, although I should be growing used to it in this large, lonely house.

I open the balcony doors and the crash of the sea against the shore provides a quiet and rhythmic background noise as I answer emails from my mother and my father, then work for a bit on my thesis project. My dissertation is coming along nicely, although I know that I need a few more subjects for research material. I make a note to go into Valetta sometime this week.

When I'm finally tired, I cover my bare legs with a cashmere throw while I read a book to relax. I know I'll never sleep until my mind is calmed. The wine didn't help with that, which is unusual.

I read for several chapters before I sigh and set it aside.

I can't focus on the book. Normally, I would find it incredibly interesting, but not so tonight. Tonight, all I can see in my head is a pair of dark eyes; dark eyes that are churning with so much unspoken emotion. Dark eyes that are an enigma that I can't solve. They are at first hard and calculating, then impassive, then soft and gentle. I want to uncover what they really are, but I can't get close enough. It's frustrating.

I finally sigh and give up, putting the book away and turning off the crystal-encrusted light. I can hear the sea through the open doors and I focus on that, trying to allow it to lull me to sleep. I visualize the clean sea air covering my body and then focus on relaxing every single body part, attempting to will myself into sleep.

No such luck.

I am wide awake and staring at the ceiling, watching the moonlight glimmer off of the crystal in the chandelier above me. Each perfectly cut piece of glass sparkles with the light of the moon. It is fascinating.

And then my door opens.

I hear the heavy wood swinging quietly over the thick, plush rug covering the stone floor. I gasp, the small noise loud in the quiet, but I look up to find Luca. I exhale a sigh of relief before a rush of excitement thrills through me.

He's here. In my bedroom.

He is standing in the dark shadows of my room, his face somber. He is rigid and alert, not the picture of casual elegance that I have come to expect from him. I look into his eyes and there is an expression there that I haven't seen before. The light is gone from them and he's staring woodenly at me. I instantly decide he must be drunk.

"Luca, are you alright?"

I sit up in bed and pull the covers around me. The nightgown I'm wearing tonight is barely-there silk, practically indecent. A person can see right through it.

Luca doesn't answer. He's still leaning against the door, staring at me with the strangest expression and his eyes are so flat that they don't even glitter. A chill runs down my spine and my heart thuds against my ribcage.

My son is evil.

Melina's words spring unbidden into my mind. I'm being foolish. Luca is many things, but evil isn't one of them.

"Luca?"

He strides across the room and is next to the bed in six steps.

I stare up at him. His eyes meet mine but I don't see anything familiar there. He's not himself; he's not anyone I know. His chiseled features are taut, his expression so empty. It's startling and causes my heart to thunder against my ribs.

"Luca," I whisper. But he still doesn't answer.

And then he moves and is everywhere. He is above me and around me on the bed, his spicy scent enveloping me in the night. His strong legs straddle me and his mouth is suddenly on mine, rough and hot. He tastes of Scotch and man and his teeth bite into my lip.

What the hell?

I am braced against him, as my heart pounds loudly against his, as his hard thigh slides along mine. This is so unexpected and shocking. I can't wrap my mind around what is happening, even though time seems to be passing in slow motion.

Luca's hands clench me tightly and I am sure that I will have bruises in the form of his fingers tomorrow on my arms. But before I can pry them away, he moves them, ravaging my breasts.

At first he is much too hard, too harsh and strong. But then he relents, his fingertips sliding into gentleness as he palms my nipples, then moves in a circle around them. His fingers are long and strong. Sensations shoot through me, stemming between my legs and spreading through my belly. I can feel him, hard against me, as his erection lodges against me, tucked into the juncture of my thighs. He is rock hard.

I swallow and I can practically feel my heart in my throat.

Luca is breathing harshly now, loud in my ear.

"Luca!" I cry out, finally finding my voice. "What are you doing? This isn't like you."

"Don't you like it?" he asks thickly, and his words are almost slurred. He looks up at me and the expression is almost lucid, but not quite. It's still hazy and empty. I don't understand it.

"Are you drunk?" I ask, trying to assess him. He doesn't smell like alcohol, however, even though he vaguely tastes of it. He also doesn't move.

Instead, he leans forward and kisses my neck, his teeth nipping at the skin beneath my earlobe. His touch gentles, then firms; gentles, then firms. It's a rhythmic rush and against my better judgment, I find myself leaning into it. His hands grip the sensitive tissue of my inner thigh, hard, then harder.

He is rough and this isn't how I pictured this scenario with him. I pictured it as sweet and sensual, like when I kissed him in my cottage or when I fantasized about him during those first nights here in Malta. This is very much not that. This is charged and electric and violent.

He laughs, but doesn't answer my question.

Of course he's drunk, I answer myself silently. He has to be. This is not the Luca that I know.

He yanks me to him, ripping my nightgown from my body before he drops the delicate silk into a twisted heap on the floor by the bed. I'm pushed naked backward onto the bed and his fingers are inside of me, sliding in and out, while his arm creates a fascinating friction on the delicate skin of my belly. I can feel the moisture from my body dripping onto his hands. In this moment, I have to admit that I like it. He's being rough and I like it.

What is wrong with me?

I moan as he sucks on my nipple, as he slides it in and out of his mouth at the same speed that his hands are moving.

Sweet Jesus.

He gets rougher, sucking harder and moving faster. His hands are everywhere and I arch up toward him, bucking my hips to get closer. I have no excuse for enjoying this. I'm not drunk. But I want him anyway.

Things that I should care about seem to fall away.

I don't care that he isn't answering me. I don't care that theoretically, he is my employer. I don't care if this isn't my dream scenario. All I care about are the sensations that are overwhelming me.

The moments are coming in flashes now. His lips against my neck, his mouth on my breast, his hot breath on my skin. His hand brushes my thigh, his fingers grip my side. His fingernails cut into me and I gasp. He glances at me, but doesn't truly see me. His gaze is unfocused.

Luca steps backward, away from me. The cool breeze blows over my skin as I watch him, causing goose bumps to form. I wait, my breath frozen and my cheeks flushed, for him to come back to me.

His strips his slacks off and kicks them to the floor. His penis is long and hard and curved against his belly, an impressive sight. I eye it and then him. It's been awhile since I have been intimate with anyone but he doesn't give me time to be nervous.

He pushes against me again and he is not gentle. His bare chest slides over mine as he thrusts hard and fills me up, sliding with an exquisite friction. I whimper and clutch at his back. I should be angry, I should be resisting, but I don't want to. I want him here. I want him inside of me. I can't lie. The truth is that I've fantasized about this from the day I met him.

The flashes come back, instead of logical thought.

He thrusts.

I arch.

My leg curves around his hip.

His hands are in my hair.

He pulls.

I moan.

He bites my lip.

I taste blood.

As he thrusts into me, hard and rhythmic, I force myself to focus. Because when I stare into his eyes, they are flat and black. The thunderclouds that I sometimes see in them are markedly absent. The milk chocolate gaze that I sometimes see there is gone. There is nothing there right now, just an empty void and it startles me. I grip him tighter at the same time as I pull him closer with my legs. He is filling me, filling an emptiness that I didn't even know that I had. I find myself wishing that I could do the same for him.

"Luca?" I whisper.

But he doesn't answer and his handsome face is twisted into something angry. But then, I'm distracted by the overwhelming sensations that threaten to carry me to a place that I hadn't expected to go tonight, not like this.

Luca thrusts harder and harder and finally I'm screaming his name as intense pleasure wracks my body in waves and leaves me shaking on the sheets. He throws his head back and groans and I feel his hot seed pouring into me, completely filling me and then he falls limply to the side.

"Luca?" My voice is quiet in this large room, tentative.

He doesn't say anything and he doesn't stay. He simply picks up his slacks, puts them on and walks away without a word. The door closes once again behind him and I'm left alone.

Did that just happen?

The wet ejaculate running down my thighs tells me that it did.

I lie in a motionless heap, my legs still quivering, as I think about what just happened.

Was I just raped?

That's absurd. You can't rape the willing, I tell myself.

And I did want it. I was willing and I wanted Luca more than I've wanted anything in quite a while. But if I'm honest, I know that it wouldn't have mattered if I'd submitted willingly or not. Luca would have taken me with or without my consent. The look in his eyes told me that.

My son is evil.

I can't shake the words. He's not evil. I know it. I know it in my bones and in my heart. He's not evil. But he's... *something.* I just don't know what it is. He was right earlier. I deserve an explanation, especially now, and I can't wait to get it from him tomorrow. But it will definitely have to wait until tomorrow. I'm not leaving this room tonight.

I get up and clean off, then lock the door.

Then I go back to bed and replay every moment of the intimate exchange.

It had been primal and intense and electrifying, even as it was puzzling. And as I think about where his lips had been, the way he thrust into me, the way he bit at my neck, thrills shoot through me. My lips are swollen from his kiss, my body aching from the rough sex. Everything about it seems so forbidden, so erotic. It was dark and electrifying, yet puzzling and mysterious.

Just like Luca.

Chapter Nineteen

Luca

I wake on my bed, fully clothed. I don't remember going to bed at all. In fact, I remember very little from the time that I finished up a conference call and had a nightcap in my study until now. My heart beats fast although I'm no stranger to a foggy memory.

I lie still for a bit, trying to clear my thoughts, to let the sleep fall away. As I do, I catch a whiff of sex.

What the fuck? I lift my hands to my face and inhale. *Sex.*

This jerks me wide awake and I quickly sit up, trying to remember the events from last night. But my memories are a frustrating fog.

I vaguely remember walking from the study down the hall toward my bedroom, but it's a blur from there. When my curse comes, I usually remember everything up until the moment that the darkness overtakes me. I don't remember anything of the sort from last night.

Nothing at all.

Something isn't right. Am I changing? Is this what happens as I get older? The frequency of my episodes becomes higher and I don't remember anything?

My head drops into my hands.

What did I do last night? What the fuck did I do?

There's no way of knowing. My heart sinks as I come to that realization. I won't know unless I've done something and gotten caught. And at this point, being captured would almost be a relief, a welcome end to the constant anxiety and stress surrounding me for so long.

For years, my curse has been controlled. It is only now, this year, that episodes have come on so quickly and without warning that I'm not able to get home in time. And that is why I have recently made the decision that I simply won't leave Chessarae. Not unless it is very, very necessary. The people in Valletta thought I was a recluse before. They'll surely think so now.

I swing my legs out of bed and make my way into the shower, allowing the hot, steamy water to run over me for at least a half hour. It feels as though I'm washing away the unknown and to be honest, it is a very good feeling.

I convince myself that if I don't remember anything, then there probably isn't anything to remember. I more than likely finished my nightcap and fell immediately to sleep. I turn off the water and grab a towel, running it over my hair and stepping back into my bedroom.

As I do, I am startled to find that I am not alone.

Evangeline sits on my bed, fully dressed. She looks pensive, as though she isn't sure what to think. And then she turns to meet my gaze. She doesn't seem embarrassed at all that to find that I am stark naked. I quickly wrap the towel around my waist.

"Yes?" I ask her. I try to appear unnerved, as though it is completely normal to find a beautiful woman in my bedroom. "Can I help you with something, Evangeline?"

She was expecting me to say something else. I can tell. Her face is expectant, then it clouds over with my words. She opens her mouth and then closes it.

"Evangeline?" I prompt. "Do you need something from me?"

I cross the room quickly, pulling out a shirt from my wardrobe. I pull it on over my head and as I do, the towel drops to the ground exposing every bit of my manhood to her.

"Shit," I mutter, turning away. Instead of picking up the towel, I pull on a pair of underwear and then a pair of slacks. When I am dressed, I turn back to Evangeline and smile.

"Okay. This should make things more comfortable." I sit on the edge of the bed next to her and she almost flinches away. I narrow my eyes. "Dr. Talbot?"

She looks at me calmly, her gray-green eyes unflinching.

"Yes. To answer your earlier question, yes. I do need something from you, Luca. Yesterday, you said that you owed me an explanation. And after last night, I think I deserve one more than ever."

I am frozen and can barely breathe.

"Last night?" I repeat and then stop, remembering the smell of sex on my hands. *Surely not.* Surely if I'd done something with Eva, I would remember it.

I meet her eyes, though, and I know it is true. The beautiful, delicate woman sitting before me is calm and quiet and strong. But I can see it in her eyes. I assaulted her. My head drops into my hands.

Chapter Twenty

Eva

"An explanation," I remind Luca, as calmly as I can.

He seems upset, distraught even. I am puzzled. I'm the one who should be distraught. Whatever is making him so upset? I ask him that and he looks up at me with tortured eyes, the dark and pained expression that has caused my heart to melt more times than I can count lately. It's particularly angst-filled today.

"I'm sorry," he says, his voice pained. "For anything that I might have done last night. I'm very sorry."

He stares at the floor as if he can't meet my gaze.

I stare at him. "You don't remember it?" I ask, struggling to keep my voice steady. *He doesn't remember being with me at all? How insulting.* "Were you drunk?"

Luca shakes his head curtly, just one movement. He stares out his windows, his eyes so distant, as though he is wishing that he were anywhere but here. I should be furious with him, but I am intrigued instead. There is something here, something about Luca that I don't know. I can feel it. I have felt it all along and it is time for him to share it.

Right now.

"You had sex with me," I announce. "You came into my room and you had sex with me. It was rough and you didn't talk to me, either before or after. After it was over, you left without a word. "

I wait for a response.

Luca stares at the floor and I notice that his fists are clenched at his sides. His knuckles are white.

"Luca?"

He doesn't immediately answer, but after a moment, he raises his head and his dark eyes are tortured.

"Did I hurt you?" he asks. He sounds like he is forcing the words from his lips, as though they are abrasive and painful in his throat.

"You bruised my arms," I tell him. He immediately moves closer to me and picks up an arm to examine it. I allow him, my heart twisting for the pain I see on his face. I wish I understood what was going on with him. So I tell him that.

"What is going on?" I ask. "I know things aren't what they seem. Last night you were a different person, someone cold and distant and borderline violent. But that's not the person that I know. That's not the *Luca* that I know."

I'm pleading with him. I can hear it in my voice and he can, too. I don't want to believe it of him. And I know that he can hear that, as well.

He lets my arm fall back to my side and he closes his eyes for just a moment before he opens them again and looks me in the eye.

"Evangeline, you don't know me at all. There are many things about me that you don't know. But there's one thing about me that you should. I owe that to you."

I nod. "Okay. Tell me. I won't judge you."

He almost smiles, the corners of his mouth curving ever so slightly. But it isn't a smile of humor. It's a dark, cryptic smile. As though he knows far better than I do that I am wrong.

"I'm sorry I hurt you," he tells me again. "Very, very sorry. I wish it hadn't happened."

I smile now. "I'm not sorry that it happened," I tell him honestly. "A twisted side of me enjoyed it."

His head snaps up now, his surprised gaze locked with mine.

"You enjoyed it?" he croaks. I have to smile at his expression. I shrug.

"It's been a long time for me," I admit. "And you're a very handsome man, Luca. In all honesty, I've been attracted to you since the moment we met. Was it an ideal encounter? No. But I can't lie and say that I'm sorry it happened."

He's quiet now as he assesses me. He's probably trying to determine just how much of a freak I am. Clearly, only a freak would enjoy what happened last night. Right?

"I'm drawn to you, too," he tells me quietly, finally. "You're refreshingly honest. You're such a light in the world and I am exactly the opposite. I shouldn't be near you, I should stay far away. But I haven't. And for that, I'm truly sorry."

I roll my eyes.

"Oh, God. Please tell me that you're not going to say that you're dangerous for me and that you need to stay away from me for my own good. Please tell me those words aren't going to come from your mouth. That's the stuff that movies are made from. That's not reality."

Luca is silent, every muscle still.

"It's *my* reality," he tells me soberly and I can see that he is completely serious. "I'm dangerous, Evangeline. I really am. And while I would like nothing more than to explore this attraction that I feel for you, I simply can't. And after I'm finished explaining everything, you will understand why."

I'm uncertain now, hesitant.

"Okay," I answer slowly. "Explain. Do you have a drug problem? Is that why you can't remember last night?"

"Jesus, Evangeline!" he snaps. "Of course I don't have a drug problem. Although I wish that was the case. It would be such an easy fix."

I'm taken aback by the brusque tone to his voice, then dumbfounded to hear that he thinks a drug addiction would be easier to overcome than whatever his problem actually is.

"I'm sorry. But a spotty memory and out of control actions can signal a drug problem. Tell me what it is, Luca. Maybe I can help."

"You can't help," he says quietly, his expression dark. "No one can. And I don't want to discuss it here. Do you trust me enough to come with me? I need to show you something so that you'll believe me."

I ponder that for a moment and to my surprise, I do find that I trust him. He might have secrets, but I can see in his eyes that he would never knowingly hurt me. Whatever last night was, it wasn't something that he purposely did. He was out of control. He wasn't himself.

He wasn't himself.

I nod. "Yes. I trust you."

He stares at me, long and hard and regretful. "I hope you don't live to regret that."

He stands and offers me his hand, and to my surprise, I take it. His fingers are long and strong and warm as they wrap around mine. I expect him to release it after he helps me from the bed, but he doesn't. He holds my hand tucked inside of his as we make our way through the house, out the back doors and into the English Maze.

Chapter Twenty-One

Luca

I lead Evangeline down the secret steps into my cave. Her expression is contained and guarded. She meant what she said. She's desperately trying to withhold judgment. I respect that about her even though I know that after I am finished explaining, she will contact the authorities and I will be arrested. Surprisingly, I am numb to that. I don't dread it at all.

I almost welcome it.

As we round the corner into the suite, Evangeline's eyes widen.

"What the hell?" she murmurs as she takes everything in. When her gaze passes over the bed with the chains protruding from the wall, her eyes narrow.

"What the hell, Luca? You're into kinky shit and you thought you would bring me here because you think I'm kinky, too? I've got news for you. I'm not. I enjoyed last night, but I'm not a sexual freak."

She spins on her heel and starts to walk for the door, but I grab her elbow gently.

"Please wait," I ask her. "You don't understand. This place is for me, those chains are for me. I needed for you to see it before I tell you my story. See how elaborate this hideout is? Do you see the expense that has gone into making it safe and secluded from the rest of the world?"

Eva keeps her eyes narrowed as she nods. "I do. But I don't see how it is relevant, Luca."

I take a deep breath. "Can we sit? I want to explain. Would you like a glass of wine?"

She rolls her eyes. "It's 9:00 a.m., Luca."

I shrug. "Do you?"

She levels her gaze at me. "Yes."

I have to laugh and I get a bottle of wine and two glasses, and we sit on the couch facing each other.

"You need to talk now," she instructs me as I hand her a glass.

I nod. I'm not sure where to begin, but I decide to just start speaking. The words begin pouring from my mouth, beginning with when I was small and first realized that I was different.

"My mother would lock me in my room," I remember aloud. "She would bind my hands and lock me in my room until the darkness passed."

There is horror on Evangeline's face. "She locked you in your room? Alone?"

I nod. "She didn't know what else to do."

"There are many other things that she *could* have done," Eva says drily. "What do you mean when you say 'the darkness'?"

"The only way I can describe it is to say that everything becomes blurry and then shortly after that, I enter oblivion. I don't know what happens or what I do. When I wake, I can remember feeling blurry and entering the blackness, but nothing after that."

"How long has this been going on?" Evangeline asks, her voice no-nonsense and medical. She's trying to tap into her psychiatrist self, to remain impassive and detached, but I can hear a thin strain of horror in her voice.

"All of my life," I answer simply. "I don't remember a time when it didn't happen."

"Is this why your mother thinks you are evil?" Eva asks. "Because you have blackouts? Perhaps they are seizures. Have you been examined by a doctor?"

"Yes, this is why my mother thinks that I am evil," I tell her. "And no. I personally have not been examined. My mother would never hear of it when I was small. It would have been devastating for the family name for this to get out. You see, it doesn't just affect me. It affects Minaldi men. My father was afflicted. His father, his father's father and so on. My father once told me that my grandfather had gone to a doctor in desperation, but they could find nothing wrong with him. It is a medical mystery, a genetic anomaly."

"What do you do when you become 'afflicted'?" Evangeline's voice is small now, as though she is afraid of the answer. She is gripping her wine glass with white fingers. I'm not sure what is paler, her fingers or her face. The blood seems to have leached from her entire body.

"I think I'm violent," I tell her. "It's been getting worse. And I fear that I might be responsible for the deaths of the girls in Valletta."

She gasps and her wine glass tumbles to the floor and shatters, spattering the couch and the rugs and our legs with crimson wine.

Evangeline leaps to her feet, hunting for things to clean up the mess. "I'm sorry," she tells me. "I'm sorry. I was just…. this is surprising. This isn't what I was expecting to hear. I'm sorry."

She is keeping her distance now and I don't blame her. She flutters about like a hummingbird, finding paper towels and a broom and dust pan. I take the broom from her and when my fingers brush against hers, she cringes away. And then she apologizes. When I look into her eyes, I see fear there.

And it is crushing.

I hadn't realized that I would care so much about what she would think. But the fear in her eyes practically reaches in and crumbles my spirit into twisted up bits. More than anything else, I don't want her to fear me. I would never purposely harm her, so I tell her that.

"Not purposely," she agrees. "I know you would never purposely harm me, Luca. I know you well enough to know that."

She is still keeping her distance as she throws the broken glass into a trashcan. I notice that she stays a small distance away, leaning against the marble counter in the kitchenette.

"I know when it is coming," I tell her. "You're safe. If I begin to get an episode, I'll let you know and you can stay away from me."

She sticks her chin out, an attempt at pluckiness.

"I don't want to stay away from you," she tells me firmly. "I want to help you. I know that I can, Luca. This is the twenty-first century. Medicine has come a long way since your great-great grandfather tried to get help. Back then, they were still using leeches to suck toxins out, for God's sake. I can help you. I promise."

I stare at her.

"You should never make a promise that you can't keep, Evangeline," I finally answer. I can hear the hopelessness in my voice and I'm sure she can, as well.

"I don't," she answers.

I know that she believes it. Evangeline Talbot has spirit. I have to give her that. It never occurs to her that perhaps something is impossible, that something just can't be done. That *she* can't do something. It's a trait I admire about her. It's something similar to what lives in me.

I finally nod.

"Okay. I'll let you try. What should we do first?"

Evangeline thinks on that for a moment. "We'll have an initial session. We'll just talk. I need to get a feel for things. And I'll want to have a blood panel run on you; just to make sure your blood levels are all normal."

"Fine," I agree. "We can start tonight after dinner."

"Fine," she answers. She smiles and there is no fear there now. And for a scant moment, just one, I feel hope. I feel like perhaps, just maybe, Evangeline can help me. But then reality comes immediately crashing back down because I know she can't. There's no reason for false hope. No one can help me.

But I smile back at her anyway.

"It's a date."

Chapter Twenty-Two

Eva

Luca doesn't show for dinner.

He sends a handwritten note excusing himself. Apparently, there was an urgent matter at Minaldi Shipping and he had to leave unexpectedly. He won't be home for at least another day and so he promises me a rain check.

I can do nothing but think about what happened last night, about the things that he told me this morning...about his theory that he is the one killing the girls in Valletta. The mere thought causes chills to race down my back, standing the hair up on my neck.

It can't be him.

I don't know if that's what I really believe or what I *want* to think. Either way, I sit on my balcony with my laptop and throw myself into research. I uncover everything I can possibly find about the murders in the newspapers online. I research disorders that could possibly explain Luca's symptoms. I try to piece everything together.

More importantly, I focus on my own feelings about him. I'm angry with him; for scaring me, for confusing me, for practically accosting me. I say *practically* because I really did want it. I'm so conflicted by the events and my own emotions that I consider leaving.

Chessarae is dangerous for you.

Melina's words play in a loop in my head. Maybe I'm really not safe here. It's only a coincidence that I wanted Luca. It wouldn't have mattered if I didn't, he would have taken me against my will. I am under no delusions about that. The cold and dark look on his face as he hovered above me in the night can attest to that.

But then I remember the tortured look that was there after I told him what he'd done and it threatens to rip my heart out of my chest. Especially when I remember what else Melina said. *I should've had his nurse drown him when he was an infant.*

What kind of mother says such a thing? My heart breaks for the childhood he must have had. He grew up knowing that his own mother wished that he'd never been born. I can only begin to imagine what kind of issues that would give him. And yet he still takes care of her, still gives her top of the line medical treatment. I think that goes a long way to show what kind of person that he really is.

I swallow hard.

I can't abandon him. For reasons unknown to me, he's chosen to let me in and expose everything that he is. Probably for the first time since he was a child, he's made himself vulnerable to someone. To *me*. Against his better judgment, he'd like to hope that I can help him. I can sense that. I just can't bring myself to crush that fragile hope. I can't do it.

So instead, I'll stay. I'll stay and try everything I can think of to help him.

Luca touches me in a place where I haven't ever been touched. He pulls at my heart; his vulnerability, his darkness. He needs me. It appeals to the psychiatrist in me, but more than that, it appeals to the woman in me. The feeling is as strong as anything I've ever felt.

It's as though I'm getting sucked out to sea in a dark current, the waves swelling above me and pulling me under... and I can't swim away from it. I can't leave him.

I can't abandon him like his mother did. She didn't physically leave, although that would probably have been healthier for him. No, she tore his heart apart by rejecting him when he needed her the most. I won't do that. I won't.

I walk restlessly on the beaches and in the gardens. I turn the situation over and over in my head and even though I have theories, I can't make much progress in analyzing it until I have spoken with Luca in depth.

On the third day, my phone rings.

"Evangeline, it's Luca."

As if I wouldn't recognize his voice.

"Hi," I say softly. "Are you planning on coming home or have you made a run for it?"

He laughs.

"I'm so sorry," he tells me. "It was a supply chain emergency that I had to handle in person. I'll be home tonight so I'm calling to reschedule our date. I should arrive after dinner. Will that work for you? You could meet me in my study after you eat."

"Of course," I tell him. "It's a date."

We hang up and I take a walk in the fresh air and then put my notes together, organizing my thoughts as well. As much as I'm looking forward to it, hearing what Luca might tell me frightens me as well. I only hope I'm ready for it.

Chapter Twenty-Three

Luca isn't back in time for dinner. He said that he wouldn't arrive until afterward, but I guess I was still a little hopeful that he might be early. Instead, I'm alone once again in this huge room.

I pick at my food, pushing it around on my plate. I'm not hungry. I'm anxious. I'm scared about what Luca might tell me, about how I should process hearing un-hearable things.

I'm also anxious because I've never encountered a disorder like his and I have to wonder how much of it is as he thinks. Schizophrenia sometimes presents itself as paranoia. The patient gets crazy ideas and fully believes them. But Luca doesn't seem Schizophrenic. He seems calm, lucid, intelligent. And dangerous.

I suck in my breath at the thought, at the memory of his eyes from the other morning. So dark, so pained, so full of emotions that I can't even name. It wrenched something inside of me loose, something that I had hidden long ago.

The ability to care.

When my brother died, I lost the ability to care. Not because I wanted to, but because it was so very painful that I had to find a way to cope. My parents weren't themselves during that time; they were so engrossed in their own grief and anger and devastation, that they didn't really have it in them to help me through my own ordeal. I was left to deal with it alone. And the way I eventually handled it, the way that I was able to come through it intact, was to compartmentalize my emotions, to learn to step back from anything that might be painful. It's why I've never been in a serious relationship.

I've been in sexual relationships. I've had casual relationships. But I've never had a lasting, deeply emotional relationship. I would never take that risk. I unconsciously made the decision long ago that nothing would ever hurt me again.

I know that drawing closer to Luca is taking a chance. I feel him pulling me to him, closer every day. Every time I see him, I want to be even closer. And he's damaged. I don't know to what extent yet, but my heart doesn't seem to care.

I push my plate away and glance at the giant clock on the far end of the wall.

It's time.

I pad through the quiet, darkened halls that lead to Luca's study. But before I get there, I hear faint music.

I stop.

Music?

I strain my ears and listen.

In this house, this large and silent house, the piano music that drifts down the empty hall is haunting and desolate. It causes chills to run up my spine and goose bumps to form on my arms. I don't know why.

Without thinking, I turn into the direction that it is coming from.

I am led into a large open room that overlooks that sea through a wall of glistening windows. A grand piano is situated next to the windows and Luca sits at it, bathed in silvery moonlight as his slender hands deftly and gracefully play the ivory keys. His dress shirt is unbuttoned at the collar, his tie untied. He is immersed in the music that he is creating, oblivious to everything but the haunting melody that is flowing through the beautiful instrument beneath him and into the salty air around him.

Each breath I take is saturated with the haunting melody and the sea and I am frozen in the doorway, unable to move. Luca's beauty in this moment is greater than anything I've ever seen. His face, so chiseled and perfect, is dark and shadowed now. His glossy dark hair slants across his forehead but he is distracted by nothing. He is intense as he leans into the music.

I watch his hands, so slender and graceful and long. They lightly urge the music from the ivory beneath them and I know in this instant that this man, this beautiful man, cannot be a killer. It is impossible. This is why I haven't gone straight to the polizia with his claims. He cannot be the person that he thinks he is.

I slump against the doorway, unable to move away from him or the beautiful music that he is creating. I close my eyes and let it waft over me, inhaling it, imagining that his fingers are flowing over me as softly as they move over the piano keys. Somehow, watching Luca play the piano is erotic. I don't know how or why. But it is eternally and achingly sexy.

175

The melancholy music flows to a haunting stop and I open my eyes.

Luca is turned to me now, his exquisite hands in his lap. His eyes meet mine and I don't know what his are saying. The expression is unreadable.

"Your hands are not those of a killer," I tell him softly, barely above a whisper. "It's impossible, Luca."

He closes his eyes briefly, then reopens them. And I find that I am thankful. I need to see into his eyes.

"You don't want to think so," he answers and he sounds weary. "I don't either. But all indications point to the contrary, Dr. Talbot."

I ignore his words.

"I could listen to your music forever," I tell him instead. He smiles and the room brightens.

"I didn't write it," he says with a small grin. "Ludovico Einaudi did. It's beautiful, isn't it? I've always loved his work, but this is my favorite. It's called *I Giorni*. It has a haunting quality that I can't get away from."

"I agree," I tell him. "If I could hear that every night before bed, I think I would sleep better."

He looks at me thoughtfully. "Do you have trouble sleeping?"

I nod. "I'm an insufferable insomniac. I have been since I was a kid. Since..." My voice trails off.

"Since your brother died?" Luca guesses.

I nod.

Emotion bubbles up in my throat, but I push it back down. I swallow hard, then swallow again. Luca is staring at me, his expression still unreadable.

"Perhaps I can make you a CD," he tells me and his tone is kind. Very kind. "You can listen to it as you ready for bed, and it might soothe you into sleep. I personally find the piano soothing, both playing it and listening to it."

"How long have you played?" I ask.

"Since I was old enough to reach the pedals," he answers. "Doesn't every rich boy learn to play the piano?" He is wry now, almost sarcastic. "My mother insisted upon it. But I am glad now that she did."

He rises from the piano bench and approaches me.

"Shall we, Dr. Talbot? I'd like to get this over with."

I take his offered elbow. "You're not looking forward to speaking with me?" I ask, feigning hurt feelings. The corners of his mouth lift into a very small smile.

"Not particularly," he answers truthfully.

I smile back. "I promise, it won't hurt," I tell him.

"Never make promises that you can't keep," he reminds me as he holds his study doors open for me. I enter first, then turn to him.

"Where would you like to sit?" I ask.

He sits in one of the leather armchairs that we sat in when I was first here. I take the other one.

"Can you start at the beginning?" I ask. He nods.

And so he tells me of life at Chessarae. Of being a child here, with a mother who was distant and detached and a father who was never home. Luca knows why now, because Nicolas was increasingly confined to the cave in the maze, more and more as his life progressed. But since the Minaldis do not speak of their curse, not even to each other, he didn't understand as a boy. He felt abandoned and alone.

Luca Minaldi may be confident and powerful on the outside, but on the inside he is a broken little boy. And with each word that comes from his mouth, from his perfectly formed lips, I feel my heart constrict just a little more until it is difficult for me to speak, to ask him questions.

"When did you understand what was happening to you?" I ask. It's hard to formulate sound around the lump that has swelled in my throat.

"I always knew," he answers, quiet in this large room. He gets up and pours us each a glass of Scotch, moving fluidly. He takes a gulp of his and I grip my cold glass tightly.

"I always knew. My mother told me at a very young age that there was something wrong with me, that I was a monster like my father. My brothers and I had a nurse who stayed with us in our wing. If we showed signs of sleepwalking or something similar, she was instructed to tie our hands to our bed and not allow us to leave until it had passed. As time went on, it was clear that it only afflicted me. My brothers were normal."

A tear slips from the corner of my eye now as I picture Luca as a boy, terrified and alone in the darkness of his room, tied to his enormous bed.

"Luca... I..."

I can't speak any more. The words won't come. And another tear slips down my cheek. My eyes are hot and burning, so I close them.

"Don't cry for me, Evangeline," Luca tells me. "I came to terms with this long ago. Life is, at times, a malevolent bitch. We must deal with our burdens. Everyone has one, including you. You still struggle with your brother's death. You know it as well as I do. You've built a wall around yourself. Don't think I haven't seen it. It's invisible, but it is there."

I nod. I can't lie. It is true.

"But no one ever tied me to a bed," I say softly.

"Perhaps not," he answers. "But they might as well have. You're tied to what happened, just the same."

He's right. I know he is right. But we're not here to talk about me. We're here for him, so I tell him that and he nods.

"You're right," he answers. "You're here because you want to save the un-savable."

I shake my head.

"Don't say that," I almost plead, surprising myself with my emotion. "You're not un-savable."

He chuckles mirthlessly. "Okay."

"Please. Tell me what you remember of your episodes. How have they gotten worse? What do you remember of each one? What exactly makes you think that you are violent, that you could be behind the murders in town?"

Luca speaks and his voice is husky in the night, like velvet. As he tells me what he remembers, I ache to reach over and draw him into my arms and hold him there, protecting him from everything the world might do to him.

"There was blood on my hands."

He finishes up with these words and the hair stands up on the back of my neck.

"Blood on your hands," I repeat slowly, my heart frozen in my chest. I feel suddenly numb.

He nods.

"I washed it away and I have no idea how it got there but it was the morning after the second girl, Sophia Romano, was killed. Then again after the third."

I swallow.

I had really wanted to believe that he is wrong, that he isn't a violent killer. But how can blood on his hands be explained?

I shake my head silently as I realize that it can't.

Chapter Twenty-Four

"I don't want to be this way," Luca tells me. I can hear the sincerity in his voice. It is aching and raw and I can do nothing but believe him. The truth is in his eyes. He is not lying.

"I know," I tell him. "There has to be a medical answer. There is something... a chemical imbalance maybe. We'll find it and fix it. I promise."

He grins, his smile both a little wicked and a little sad. "Don't forget what I said about promises."

"I won't," I whisper. Luca hasn't taken his eyes from mine and we seem to be attached by an invisible tether. The energy between us right now is palpable, I can practically reach out with shaking hands and touch it.

"Evangeline," he says softly, his dark eyes glued to mine. "I'm so sorry about the other night. I wish I could remember. I wish I could take it back."

"I don't," I tell him honestly. "I really don't."

He gazes out the window for a scant moment more, seemingly deep in thought, before he crosses the room to me. He kneels in front of me and looks into my eyes. In this moment, he is as vulnerable as I've ever seen him, as

I've ever seen anyone. He's completely open to me, hiding nothing.

I want so desperately to kiss him.

"I can't," I tell his dark eyes, praying that I don't fall into them. "I want to kiss you right now. But I can't. You're my patient. There are ethics..."

Luca shakes his head, his hands on my knees and his gaze upon mine. "You aren't my doctor, Evangeline. You're my friend. I'm simply talking to a friend who wants to help me tonight. You're not licensed to practice medicine in Malta, remember? So where does that leave your ethics?"

He smiles wolfishly and waits without moving. He's offering himself to me. I know that. And it is against his better judgment. He has told me that, as well. Yet here he is, on his knees in front of me.

I suck in a breath and inhale the air that is so charged with everything that Luca is.

Whatever that is.

It's dangerous on many levels. I know that.

I reach out unsure fingers and trace the top of his shoulders, moving over the contours. They are so broad, yet so slender at once. He's perfectly built. Strong, lithe and powerful. I drop my head. I know that I don't want to resist him anymore. For the first time in my life, I'm going to do something that my heart wants to do, not what my head tells me to do.

I grip him tighter with my fingers and pull him to me. He folds in between my knees, pressing me to his chest. I can hear his heart thumping rhythmically against mine as my fingers linger on his warm back.

He dips his head and presses his forehead to mine, staring into my eyes. His are a smoldering and stormy black.

"I'm afraid to get close to you," he tells me. "I'm afraid for you."

"I'm not," I whisper. "I'm not afraid of you. Kiss me, Luca."

Even I can hear the thick desire in my voice and Luca hears it too.

He groans and covers my mouth with his own, muffling the sound with my lips. He is pressed so close that he seems to absorb me. Every plane of his body is against every plane of mine. I don't know where he stops and where I start, but it doesn't matter. All that matters is him and me and *this*.

I can't breathe as his fingers run along my arms, down over my back and further to my hips and then he pulls me up, into him. He grips me tightly, his hands cupping my behind before lifts me, laying me on the thick rug on the stone floor. He hovers above me, brushing the hair from my eyes before he is once again in my mouth, my tongue mingling with his. We both taste of Scotch, but his taste is exquisite. So hot and primal and Luca.

I don't care what the future brings. As long as there is this.

So I tell him that and he groans again, into the side of my neck. He kisses me there, brushing his lips along my skin, inhaling me as though I am the most fragrant thing that has ever existed. His breath is warm on my neck.

I arch into him and he melts into me. He is hard. Every bit of him is hard. I can feel it, can feel *him*. The tip of his erection pushes against the juncture of my thighs, against my damp panties. He pulls off my skirt, then my panties and I am exposed to him as his hand slides against the softness of my thigh. The cool air brushes against my hot flesh and I almost shiver. I can feel the rigidity of his penis pressing against me, but he withdraws it and I want to whimper.

But it is replaced by his fingers. Long and strong, he plays me as deftly as he played the ivory keys of the piano. An ache spreads through me, radiating from the lowest depths of my belly. I suck in my breath and push against his hand, my hips moving in an age old rhythm that comes as naturally to me as breathing.

"I want to see you," I murmur against his neck, before I nip at his earlobe, pulling that delicate skin lightly in my teeth. Luca sucks in his breath and takes a step away, staring down at me as he purposefully removes his shirt and tosses it onto the floor.

His biceps are lean, yet bulging and muscular. His chest is perfectly chiseled. Each muscle rippling into a perfect V that points to his crotch. My heart is pounding and I watch his long fingers as they unbuckle his belt and then he steps out of his slacks. Then his underwear.

His hard erection is standing at full attention, curved against him, evidence that he definitely wants me. He is magnificent.

My breath is frozen now, while his is harsh and ragged.

Holy hell. His is the most beautiful male body I've ever seen, absolutely perfect in every way.

The energy between us is intense, like nothing I've ever felt before. I can't help but to reach down and grasp his hardness, sliding my fingers along it, listening to his sharp intake of breath as I touch him. I can't help but smile.

He's hard for *me*.

This is for *me*.

With my grasp firm, I slide my hand up and down his shaft, smiling a little as I feel the tremors in his abdomen. He likes my touch and he leans into it as I move my hand. I decide to take it a step further and with my eyes still joined with his, I lick a trail from his abdomen to his nipple. When I arrive, I trace a little circle around it with my tongue before I slip it into my mouth and suck.

He almost gasps as he grabs my shoulders and moves me away.

"If you don't want me to come in your hand right now, you need to stop," he rasps.

I can't help but smirk. He smiles at that, wolfish and wicked, and I know that I am in trouble.

He bends in front of me yet again, rocking me backward until I am once again lying in front of him. He hovers above me, his stare still frozen to mine as he slides first one finger into me, then two. I feel tremors rippling through my belly and I can't breathe again. The friction is exquisite and I never want it to stop.

And then he withdraws his fingers, and very, very purposefully puts one in his mouth. Still staring me in the eye, he slides his finger in and sucks the taste of me off.

Oh, holy hell. I've never seen anything sexier than that.

Luca's eyes are a stormy, stormy black as he looks into mine. His gaze is on fire and it sets me ablaze as he bends until his face is mere centimeters from mine.

"I want to be inside you, Eva."

I look at him.

"You called me Eva," I state simply.

He smiles against my lips.

"I think we're friends now."

He laughs softly, his chest rumbling against my own as he lifts my leg around his naked hip.

Finally.

He moves gracefully above me then slips into the moist depths of me and I push into him with all of my strength. *Oh my god.* I wanted this. But I never knew it would feel so good.

I am emotional now and I feel tears slipping down my cheeks once again, but Luca kisses them away as he rocks against me. He seems to instinctively know that I'm not sad, I'm just filled with every emotion that I think I've ever had.

Luca thrusts and I quiver, my thighs shaking against him. His chest is damp and my mind is a blur now. I can only think of him. I can only see him. Everything else fades away.

Except for Luca.

He is the only thing that matters in this moment and I focus on his face.

He moves slowly, easing in and out of me and I clutch his shoulders. When he lowers his hand, swirling his fingers around the most sensitive part of me, I cry out. He silences me with his mouth, his lips soft against mine. His fingers move in time with his thrusts and I feel myself coming undone, building toward a precipice that I know I will fall from.

I don't even breathe as I rock toward it, clutching Luca for dear life as he brings me higher and closer to the edge. And then without warning, the room explodes with color and light and sensations too strong to even name. I have never experienced such a thing in my life. It wasn't a simple orgasm. It was unnameable. Indefinable. It was amazing, but so much more than that.

"Say my name," he instructs me, his voice hot and low in my ear.

"Luca," I breathe.

"Again," he says.

"Luca." I can hardly speak at this point, can hardly breathe.

I hang on to him limply as he thrusts harder and faster.

"Tell me what you want," he demands hotly. "Tell me, Eva."

He slows and slides all the way out, hovering there. Waiting.

"Tell me," he says again; still waiting. Unmoving.

"Come in me," I whisper, and I don't know where the words come from. I just know that I want to feel him. I want to absorb his sadness and his need and everything that he has to give me.

And then he buries himself sharply into me again. I gasp and clutch at him, the delicious friction pushing me upward yet again. He is kissing my shoulders and my neck and finally, he causes me to come undone. I am all but whimpering from it when he shudders.

I feel him throbbing and pulsing inside of me as he empties everything that he is into me. And then we are quiet and still in this emotionally charged moment. He is balancing his weight above me and I can still feel every bit of him. Still inside of me, he leans his forehead once again to mine and then kisses me, his lips brushing the dampness of my brow.

He pulls out and rolls to the side and I feel immediately empty, as though I am missing something.

Because I am.

I never want to be without Luca again and that thought, that emotion, startles me. It scares the hell out of me.

I sit up.

Luca is sitting up too, gazing at me with his dark stare. It's the stare that has haunted my dreams from the moment that I met him.

"You're beautiful," he tells me. "Just so you know."

"Thank you," I murmur. "You're beautiful, too."

He laughs.

"Men aren't beautiful, Eva."

"You are," I insist. "Inside and out."

His breath catches and his gaze is stormy again.

"I wish that were true."

"It is," I say. And I mean it. "There is a part of you that needs my help. But Luca, I can help you. I really can."

He stares at me, then smiles slightly, sardonically.

"I'm a monster, Eva. There is no saving a monster. But I love that you want to try."

My heart constricts at the expression on his face. He has no hope for himself, so I have to hope for him.

"You're not a monster," I argue softly. "You're a man, Luca. A man like any other, you're made of blood and bone. You're not a monster. You have a good heart. I can see it in your eyes and I can feel it when you're inside of me. Whatever this is, this darkness that plagues you…. We'll figure it out. Together. I promise."

He sighs raggedly and I know that he won't argue with me tonight. But he won't believe simple words, either. I know that, too. So I will simply have to show him. I have to help him. I have to. I will be as lost as he is if I don't.

Chapter Twenty-Five

My phone rings and wakes me from a delicious sleep filled with sensuous dreams and dark eyes.

I fumble for the offending noisemaker, find it and growl an intelligible greeting into it.

"Good morning. Are you hungry?" The voice on the other end is husky and smooth.

It's Luca.

That fact makes me instantly happy and I smile, remembering last night. Luca had spent most of the night with me and it was delicious. I run my fingers along my arms and then my neck, remembering how his lips had touched the same places.; how his fingers had caressed every inch of my body. It gives me pleasant shivers.

"Yes," I tell him honestly. "I'm starving."

"You should be," he laughs. "I'm in the mood for pizza," he continues, and I can hear him smiling through the phone. I picture his perfect white teeth.

"Luca," I point out. "It's 8:00 a.m."

He laughs.

"Well, to get good pizza, it will be a bit of a jaunt. Are you up for it?"

"Of course," I tell him. "I love good Italian. I'll go to great lengths to get it. I'll meet you downstairs shortly." I throw some clothes on, yank a brush through my hair and rush down the stairs.

He meets me in the foyer downstairs and asks if I have my passport.

"In my room," I tell him. He smiles.

"You should go get it," he tells me. I raise an eyebrow, but do as he asks.

A short time later, we have flown to Italy on a Minaldi jet and are sitting on the patio of his favorite Italian restaurant.

In Italy.

Our conversation is light and friendly. We don't talk about anything heavy or ugly or deep. It is simply a lovely day in the sun; something that two friends or two people on a date would do.

I stare at him over a piece of hot, perfectly greasy pizza, winding a piece of cheese around my finger. Luca, in his expensive slacks and tailored shirt, should look out of place with a slice of pizza in his hand. But he doesn't. He looks casual and at ease. I smile.

"Do you do this often?" I ask, one eyebrow cocked. He looks innocent.

"Do what? Have lunch?" he takes a bite, chews it and looks at me then grins. "In Italy?"

He laughs and I have to laugh with him.

"Well, Italy isn't that far from Malta, really," he defends himself. "Only a few hundred miles."

"Uh-huh," I nod my head, humoring him in an exaggerated way. "Yes, I always take a private jet to lunch too. Definitely."

He laughs again and flicks a rolled up straw wrapper at me. I duck and it sails past me. I've never seen the light-hearted side of Luca Minaldi. I like it. So I tell him that.

"What?" he asks. "You think I'm always gloom and doom?"

But after I point it out, he doesn't seem as light-hearted as he was and I regret bringing it up.

His phone rings and since it is an important business call, he has to take it. He excuses himself and takes it outside of the dining area. I eat another slice of pizza and drain the rest of my soda. And then I sit and enjoy the sun on my shoulders while I wait for him to return.

After a few minutes, he is back.

"Are you ready for the best Tiramisu you've ever had?"

I grin. "You will never have to ask me that question twice."

He tosses some bills on the table and we go right around the corner to a little bakery where he orders one piece of the decadent dessert. We sit at a bistro table in the corner and he feeds me bites.

This cannot possibly be the same Luca Minaldi that I have come to know. This Luca Minaldi is relaxed and casual. I immensely enjoy it. Although we know that shadows linger around us in the form of his family's 'affliction', it feels wonderfully amazing to simply enjoy a normal, fun day.

"What would you like to do now?" he asks me after we've all but licked the little dessert plate. His question surprises me.

"I thought this was just a lunch date," I tell him. "We have time to look around?"

He smiles again.

"I thought we could turn it into a day trip. That is, if you don't mind."

I pretend to think on that.

"Hmm. Spend a day in Naples, Italy with a dashing tall, dark and handsome man? I guess I could do that."

He laughs and before I know it, we are hailing at taxi and on our way to the Capella Sansevero.

"If you see nothing else in Naples in your entire life," Luca tells me during the short drive, "You need to see *The Veiled Christ*. It's breathtaking."

"*The Veiled Christ*?" I am doubtful that this is as breathtaking as he claims. But he is already shaking his head.

"You'll see," he says knowingly. "It's a statue carved by **Giuseppe Sanmartino** back in the 1700's. It's amazing."

I am both amused and impressed. Normal men might have simply taken me for a walk in the Historic Centre and let me wander aimlessly around. But true to form, Luca has definite opinions about what is entertaining or worthy of our time. I would expect nothing less from him.

And as it turns out, he is correct.

I find myself sucking in my breath at the detail on the statue, which is in the center of the Sansevero Chapel. The depiction of Christ, thinly covered by a sheet of marble, looks as though Christ Himself is lying on the stone in front of us. He looks though he is getting ready to rise from the marble and speak to us. His facial features, his crucifixion wounds, everything… are perfectly detailed.

"Did I tell you?" Luca asks quietly from beside me. I nod. This chapel seems so reverent that we shouldn't even speak. To speak would mar the serenity that this place holds.

After I soak in the beauty for several minutes more, Luca turns to me.

"Would you like to go beneath the city?"

I nod. "Definitely. I've heard about the underside of Naples. It's supposed to be like stepping into ancient Rome."

"And it is," Luca assures me. "Come. You will love it."

He steers my elbow through the throngs of people waiting to see *The Veiled Christ*. A short time later, we find ourselves deep under the city of Naples in a place where time seemed to rewind and stand still.

"Oh, my word," I breathe as we make our way through the sand-stone brick tunnels. We descend into first century B.C., into a Greco-Roman theatre which has the seating capacity of six thousand. Our tour guide tells us that Nero sung through an earthquake here.

I am spellbound by the history surrounding us. It's amazing and awe-inspiring. Luca reaches over and picks up my hand, holding it within his as we wind our way deeper and deeper through the catacombs.

My favorite part is the section beneath the San Lorenzo Maggiore church. In other parts of the tunnels, we had to use our imaginations to picture what life must have been like. But here in this part, we are surrounded by ancient Roman storefronts; by a Roman laundry and bakery. By the street that ran below. It is absolutely incredible. So I turn and tell Luca that.

He smiles at me graciously, looking pleased by my joy.

"*You're* incredible," he tells me. He lifts my hand to his lips and kisses it and my stomach flutters. Even in the dim lights of the tunnel, he is strikingly handsome. He bends and presses a kiss to my forehead, then holds my hand for the rest of the tour.

It's a magical day.

We fly back to Valletta in the evening, quietly enjoying each other's company. I lay in his lap on the leather sofa on the plane, staring up at him. He absently twirls a piece of my hair as we chat.

"Did you always want to be a doctor?" he asks, making conversation. I nod, my neck scraping against his zipper.

"Yes. Ever since my brother died. I became fascinated with how people handle different situations and why everyone does so differently. Have you always wanted to work in the family business?"

He thinks on that for a second.

"It was never really a choice. I never considered what I wanted to do, because my brothers and I always knew this was our path in life."

"That makes me a little sad," I tell him. "People should always have a choice."

He stirs a little, then rests his arm over my hip.

"I had a choice, Eva. This is what I chose. To be complacent and take my place within the family. I'm not as excited about it as my brother Damien...he always wanted to run the company. But I'm fine with it. I would probably choose it again, if I needed to."

"Well, that's the important thing," I answer. I find myself sleepy, so I tell him that. He smiles.

"Go ahead and sleep then. We have a while until we get home."

Home.

Oddly enough, it feels good to think of Chessarae as home. I close my eyes. I wake some time later to feel Luca's lips on my forehead, then my neck.

I open my eyes and look into his. I see a delicious storm brewing there.

"Did I ever tell you thank you for lunch?" I ask. He smiles, his grin full of something delightfully wicked.

"Nope. But I know a way you can show me."

I smile back. "Is that so?"

He nods seriously. "Absolutely."

"And how is that?"

He grins wickedly now. "Well, first you put your hand here." And he lifts my hand, settling in onto his crotch, which grows instantly hard beneath my fingers. I quirk an eyebrow, then grin.

"And then what?"

"Use your imagination," he whispers into my ear as he nips at my earlobe.

"I'm a doctor," I remind him. "I don't have much imagination. I'm left-brained." But the entire time I am speaking, my hands are moving. Before he even knows it, his pants are unfastened and my tongue is circling the tip of his penis, while my fingers are sliding up and down the shaft.

"You're doing fine," he growls, his hands cupping my behind and pulling me closer as his breath comes in pants. "You seem to have the mechanics down."

I smile, my lips curving against his erection, before I close my mouth and begin to suck, all the while still moving my hands.

I can hear the breath catching in his chest as I move faster and faster. Finally, he speaks, although it sounds almost pained.

"Eva, if you don't stop, I'm going to come in your mouth."

I don't stop.

* * *

I'm weary by the time we reach Chessarae. The sun has already set and it is late as we glide into the driveway.

"Are you hungry?" Luca asks me. "I can have the staff prepare dinner."

I shake my head.

"No. I'm fine."

He nods, then comes around to open my door and we enter the quiet house. The servants have all retired for the evening. It's empty and dark. I find that I'm not ready for the day to be over, and apparently, Luca isn't either. We are both reluctant to part ways and return to our separate rooms.

"Let's have wine on the terrace," Luca suggests. And I agree.

"That sounds lovely," I tell him.

I take a seat in the gardens while Luca brings the wine.

I am amazed at how serene and happy I feel right now, after the angst I felt last night on Luca's behalf. I start to bring it up, but Luca shakes his head.

"Let's have a day where we don't discuss ugliness, shall we?" he suggests. "This has been a good day. I'd like to keep enjoying it."

I nod. "Okay. I understand that." He smiles in appreciation and sips his wine.

"You know what I'm in the mood for?" he asks me. I shake my head.

"No, what? I know what you were in the mood for earlier, but I think you've been indulged on every level…" my voice trails off and he laughs.

"Let's go for a ride."

"A ride?"

He nods. "A ride."

Luca sets his wine glass down and holds out his hand. I take it and I find myself being led to the stables.

"By yourself or with me?" he asks as we enter the building. The sweet smells of hay surround us and I murmur, "With you."

"Good answer," he says approvingly, and he only saddles one horse. He lifts me up, then swings up behind me. I lean back against him, against his warmth and strength. I can feel his heart beating against my back and I enjoy the feeling very much.

By now it is dusk and we are on the beach, the large horse easily carrying us through the sand. The sea crashes to our left and I stare at the moon.

"It's beautiful here," I say drowsily, my back absorbing the heat from his chest. "I love it here at Chessarae."

"It can be very beautiful," Luca answers. "Especially when *you* are here."

His strong arms tighten up around me and warmth fills me up. I'm treading a dangerous line here and I know that. The line is about to blur to a place where I will no longer be able to be objective where Luca is concerned. Tonight, however, I am having a hard time caring about that. We ride for at least an hour more.

When we finally return to the stable, it is very dark and I am very tired.

However, when I slide to the ground and turn, only to find myself face to face with Luca, I suddenly realize that I'm not *too* tired. He ducks his head and covers my mouth with his, still hungry. We make love again, here in the stable against the wall. He picks me up easily and holds me as my legs encircle his hips. I don't even feel it as my back slides against the stable wall. I lick the side of his neck and I decide that I love the taste of him. I tell him that, whispering it into his ear.

"I love the taste of *you*," he says, and his eyes get a wicked gleam.

He pulls out of me and slides to the ground to his knees and then fills me with his tongue. My knees instantly grow weak. My hands grasp first at his hair and then at the wooden beams of the wall behind me and my eyes glaze over with pleasure. It's all I can do not to whimper. By the time he is finished, however, I am doing more than whimpering. I am screaming his name, then falling limply to his chest as he moans mine.

By the time we finally return to the house, I have decided that it has been a very good day.

Chapter Twenty-Six

Luca

I don't know why I have done this. I have no excuse. My behavior is as reprehensible as I am myself. To have drawn Eva to me like I have, to have acted on what I know we shouldn't have... it's unforgiveable.

Yet even still, I tighten my grip on her. She is sleeping now, deep and still and peaceful, her crimson hair spread around her on the pillow. The moonlight drifts in through her balcony doors and I wonder why we didn't open them before we collapsed into the bed.

But we weren't thinking about the balcony doors when we came into this room.

We were exhausted by how much we had 'indulged' ourselves today.

And after we came into this room, and my intentions were only to tuck her in, I couldn't help myself. She was so soft and beautiful, I couldn't resist but to stay. I drew her to me and she came so easily, sleeping in my arms. Her soul is so beautiful and I know that I will break it. Against every lingering shred of my will, I know that I will break it. I sigh raggedly in the dark room.

She's beautiful and gentle and God would never give me someone like her and allow it to work. He wouldn't.

Yet still I clutch her.

She is soft beneath my fingers and I know that I should let go. That I should get up from this bed and never come back.

But I can't.

The selfish part of me can't do it.

Eva moves slightly and I adjust my hold on her, allowing her to turn. She settles in, turning her face into my chest and I wrap my arm around her. She is vulnerable in sleep and I feel an inherent need to protect her.

Against myself.

I sigh, a ragged sound in the night. I carefully get up, taking care to not disturb her. I'm restless now. If I stay in bed, I know I will disturb her. I first cross to the balcony doors and open them, allowing the fresh sea breeze to come in. Then I make my way down the halls to the great room where I play the piano, trying to play the restless energy out of myself. But an hour passes and I am still wide awake.

I move to the outdoors for a walk in the fresh air.

The gardens are lit with the silvery light of the moon. I can smell the earth, moist with evening dew, as I walk through the dimly lit paths. I move quietly through the fragrant blooms to the terrace. I sit on a nearby marble bench, staring absently at a bubbling fountain in front of me, trying to allow the soft blue light in the water to lull me to a sleepier place.

It doesn't work.

"You couldn't sleep, either?"

Adrian's low voice interrupts my solitude and I turn to find him standing behind me. He's dressed casually, in sweats and a t-shirt and it looks like he has been in bed. His hair is slightly rumpled. I shake my head.

"No. You?"

Adrian shakes his head. "Nah. Fucking full moon."

He rolls his eyes and I lift mine to the sky. There *is* a full moon tonight. I hadn't noticed it until now. Huge and yellow, it hangs low in the sky, barely visible on the edge of the horizon. It's a beautiful sight, Mother Nature at her finest.

"So the moon's at fault for your shitty sleep patterns now?" I scoff.

Adrian shrugs. "Why not? Everything else is blamed on it. Child birth, bad behavior, crimes, epileptic seizures. Why not my insomnia?"

I shrug. "As you like."

He sits next to me and hands me a flask.

"Night cap?"

I take it from him wordlessly and take a gulp.

Scotch. Adrian always knows what I like. Of course, I hooked him on the stuff years ago. I wouldn't be surprised if he kept this flask in the glove compartment of the Mercedes. I mention that and he smiles without incriminating himself.

"What's going on with Eva?" Adrian asks instead, his blue eyes focused on me. He doesn't beat around any bush. He never has. I sigh.

"Is it that obvious?"

"Luca, you've moved her into your estate. You disappeared with her on the jet all day. And since you didn't fill me in, I know that you're doing something that you know I wouldn't approve of; something you know that you shouldn't. For all I know, she's in your bed right now."

I don't confirm or deny that.

"She is," Adrian says, his eyes widening as he watches my face.

"No, she's not," I answer. Because she's not. I was in hers. And Adrian correctly guesses that next.

"Then you were in hers," he says firmly. I stare at my hands, my jaw clenched so tightly that I can feel it twitch. Adrian rolls his eyes.

"Luca. I don't want to rain on any parade, but you know this isn't a good idea. And you know why."

I take another slog from the flask and set it on the table, then turn a hard gaze to my friend.

"I'm not a child, Adrian. And the last I knew, you worked for me, not the other way around."

A stain of red flashes on Adrian's cheeks and I feel instantly guilty.

"I'm sorry," I tell him. "That wasn't called for. I'm sorry, Adrian. I'm on edge."

"It's alright," Adrian says, laughing it off as he always does. "I get it, Luca. She's gorgeous. And smart. And has it all pulled together. She is the total package. But it's not a good time for you."

"It will never be a good time for me," I point out, dejected. Adrian stares at me, his thoughts hidden. I arch an eyebrow at his expression. "What? It won't."

I'm grumbling now like a spoiled child, but I can't help it. This is my life we're talking about. And at this particular moment when there is a beautiful woman sleeping in the house who by all logic is unattainable to me, I'm feeling like life is a little unfair. In fact, life is sometimes a raging bitch whom I would like to punch in the face.

"It is what it is, Luca," Adrian says quietly.

"I know."

I reach for the flask on the table one more time and take a gulp. I'm finally starting to feel sleepy.

"Thanks for the drink," I tell him.

"Thanks for the shitty company," he tosses back. I smile.

"You're welcome."

Adrian shakes his head and tucks his flask back into his pocket. I nod at him.

"Good night."

"'Night."

He goes in one direction for his room and I go in the other to Eva's. I find myself once more thankful for him. He's been there for me since I was a kid. We grew up together and he's talked me into as many things as I've talked him into. I know that he means well. And more importantly, I know that he's right.

And I hate that.

As I make my way through the quiet house, I feel significantly sleepier and I silently praise the effects of the Scotch. But as I enter Eva's rooms and latch the door behind me, my mind starts to fog and cloud and I curse.

Fuck.

Not now. Please not now.

But the inky black fog still curls around my conscious thought, threatening to eradicate it, blurring the edges of logic, quickly absorbing any cognizant thought. My shoulders slump.

Fucking full moon. If the situation weren't so dire, I would laugh that I had just blamed my darkness on the full moon like Adrian. I'm not a werewolf. But I *am* cursed and it *is* coming.

Right now.

I lean against the wall for a moment, trying to breathe deeply and stave it off.

I feel different than normal. My mind is a blur, but not blackness. I'm puzzled and confused, but remain still for a moment, trying to breathe through it, to figure it out. I should be slipping away at any moment, but instead, I am remaining in a static foggy state.

What the hell? Why are things changing?

"Luca? Is everything alright?"

I glance up to find Eva sitting up in bed, her sheets pulled tightly around her shoulders. Her face is anxious and beautiful in the moonlight.

"It's coming," I tell her brusquely. "Now."

She leaps from the bed and rushes to me, naked. Her hands are on my flushed face, her cool fingers brushing the hair away from my forehead.

"It will be okay, Luca," she tells me calmly. "Focus on my face. Look into my eyes. We can do this."

"You don't understand," I growl. "I've got to get out of here. Now."

I start to leave, to turn away, but she clings to my elbow. "Do you trust me?" she asks. "You won't hurt me. I know it. Trust me now, Luca. Don't leave."

I'm still able to think logical thoughts, although the clouds are building in my mind. Perhaps I can remain sane tonight. Perhaps she can help me. It's a possibility. All things are possible, right? I know that I'm beginning to think like a lunatic, but I don't care. All I know is that I want to stay with Eva. I don't want to leave this room.

I don't want to hurt anyone.

I turn to her and fold into her waiting arms. But even as I do, the fog begins to overtake me and turn to red. My vision tunnels and I gasp. I can see through the fog, but my thoughts are sluggish and growing slower by the moment. I suddenly feel sexuality raging through me; a fierce and aggressive need and I am hard against her.

"I'm sorry."

"For what?" Her gray-green eyes are turned toward me, confused and anxious.

"I don't know, I don't know," I mutter, trying to turn away, but she holds me fast and my thoughts aren't coming as they should.

"This isn't right," I tell her helplessly. "This isn't right. I'm not myself."

The light fades away and the blackness comes, as it always does.

The last I remember, I am pulling her back to the bed and my hands are on her neck, her eyes closing.

Then nothing.

When I open my eyes again, it is light. And I am in the stable. I sit for a moment, alone, trying to remember what happened, what I have done.

But nothing is there.

I catch glimpses of things; of Eva's frightened face, of my fingers around her neck, my tongue on her body, my hard thrusts into her.

I raped her.

I am aghast, appalled; filled with hatred and repulsion. Of myself. I'm a monster. I don't deserve to remain alive. This has to end. I can't do this anymore. The desolation of it all has finally pulled me under. I cannot continue to exist in such a way.

I sit with my head in my hands until I feel Eva's presence. I feel her before I see her, but when I look up, she is here.

She found me.

And then I realize that there is blood on my hands and my stomach turns over.

"It happened again," I tell her needlessly.

Her face is tortured and sad as she nods silently.

There is no need for words.

Chapter Twenty-Seven

Eva

Luca doesn't remember anything that happened last night, but he insists that his episode came on differently than before. He was cognizant for longer than normal, then there was absolutely nothing but fog. No memory whatsoever. He's insistent that his curse is changing, that he will not live in such a way. He wants to go to town and turn himself in to the polizia, but I was able to talk him out of that for the time being.

I don't know why.

The ethical side of me knows that that is the right thing to do.

But the side of me that is in love with Luca can't bear it.

I'm in love with Luca.

I swallow hard as I label the vial of his blood that I took from him this morning. I love him. He has broken through the barriers that I have surrounded myself with and he stole my heart. He holds it unwillingly in his hands, because he doesn't want me involved with him. But I cannot do anything else. I love him.

I write his name on the label and wrap it around the tube of crimson blood, dropping it into a padded envelope. I give the envelope to a maid to send out with a courier. Luca relented so easily this morning, allowing me to take his blood even though he is certain it won't reveal his problem. He truly feels that he cannot be helped and that breaks my heart.

He is secluded now, closed away in his cave. He doesn't want me there. He wants to remain there alone until he sees that his curse isn't returning today, until I can try and figure out how to help him. The bruises that he left on my neck filled him with such anger and self-loathing that he couldn't even look at me. I tried to tell him that he didn't rape me, that I could have stopped him.

But truthfully, if I had wanted to stop him, I don't know that I could have. But I didn't tell him that part. I didn't have to. He already knows and it is tearing him apart. I picture him, alone and chained in his cave and my heart splits into two. I cringe and my eyes grow hot. But I push that away. I can't help him if I fall apart. And I know that in order to help him, I need to speak with someone who has been there all along, even longer than Adrian.

I have to speak with Melina.

I find myself at her door, a tiny tape recorder in my hand.

I knock and Sophia answers, her face surprised.

"I'm sorry, Dr. Talbot," she tells me politely, her body blocking the entrance to Melina's rooms. "But we weren't expecting you until tomorrow. She's not even dressed."

"That's fine," I tell her. "I've just had to rearrange my schedule. I'd like to see her now."

I practically push past her. Nothing will deter me.

"Very well," Sophia says, allowing me to pass. "She more lucid in the mornings, anyway. You will probably be able to help her more this way."

Her words don't surprise me. Most people with dementia are this way. But since Luca wanted me here in the evenings with her, to help diffuse difficult situations, that is what I did. Someone with dementia truly can't be helped, their disorder can't be healed. It can only be controlled as well as possible with medication and therapy. There was no way that I could heal her by meeting with her during lucid mornings. But I can glean information that I can possibly use to heal her son.

I find Melina seated at her dining room table, an elegant shawl wrapped around her thin shoulders. She looks up in surprise.

"Dr. Talbot," she greets me. I am surprised that she remembers me. She hasn't yet done so in any of our other sessions. "Please sit, have breakfast with me. You are here quite early today."

She is acting as though nothing is out of the ordinary, even though she seems as lucid as I am. I am flabbergasted as I sit across the table from her and inconspicuously push the button on my digital recorder to "Record."

"Mrs. Minaldi, you seem bright eyed and bushy-tailed this morning," I tell her with a polite smile. She looks up at me, intrigued.

"Is that an American saying, dear?" she asks, as she butters an English muffin. She offers one to me, but I shake my head.

"Yes, it is," I answer. "It's an idiom that means you are full of energy and ready to face your day."

She smiles at that.

"Of course I am," she tells me. "Why wouldn't I be?"

She proceeds to eat her breakfast, oblivious to the fact that I am astounded by her clear state of mind. It is normal for a person with dementia to be clearer in the morning. It is not, however, normal for that person to be completely lucid, a night and day difference. That is not normal at all.

I don't point that out. Instead, I observe her and plan how to get crucial information from her. The woman that Luca had described from his childhood would most likely not offer that much up voluntarily. I watch her eat for a moment more before I speak.

"Mrs. Minaldi, do you remember much from Luca's childhood?"

She stops what she is doing and lowers her hands to the table. "Of course. Why do you ask?"

I consider my next words carefully as she watches me with a hawk-like gaze. Gone are the clouds of delirium. I'm sitting in front of a person who is as sharp as they come. I feel slightly like I've fallen down a rabbit hole.

"When did you know that he was different?"

Melina stares at me.

"Different? You mean, when did I realize that he walks in his sleep?"

She isn't going to tell me anything. I can see that from the determined set to her jaw.

"Yes," I reply limply. "When did Luca first start walking in his sleep?"

Melina picks back up her roll and takes a delicate bite. After she has chewed and swallowed, she answers, "From the time he was small."

"How small?" I choke out. I'm finding this situation a little overwhelming.

"Very small," she levels a gaze at me. "Why are you asking me these questions?"

"Because I'm trying to help him with his sleepwalking problem," I answer, still playing by her rules. If she wants to call it sleepwalking, so be it.

"You can't," she answers calmly. "There's nothing to be done."

But we're interrupted by Sophia now, as she enters with a tray.

"It's time for your tea, ma'am," she says to Melina. Melina smiles at her.

"Thank you, dear." She takes the delicate china cup and pulls the bag from the steaming liquid, placing it on a fragile saucer. She takes a sip, closing her eyes. "It's perfect. Thank you."

Sophia nods, then backs quietly away.

Melina is a perfect lady now, with exquisite manners and I know that I'm getting a glimpse of the dignified person that she used to be.

"Did you really used to tie him to his bed?" I ask, unable to stop myself. The images of Luca as a little boy, scared and alone, have tormented me since I first heard of it. Melina's gaze practically stabs me now, impaling me through the heart.

"Of course," she answers simply. "How else could I keep him from hurting himself?...or someone else?"

I suck in my breath because her voice has changed now. It's not the pleasant, normal voice from a bit ago. It's now the icy, strange voice that I have grown accustomed to from her. I look up quickly to find her slightly unfocused gaze upon me, inky black.

"Don't poke around where you shouldn't," she tells me eerily. "You can't help my son. No one can. And you can't help me, either."

She pauses, one bony finger pointed at me. "Unless you *want* to help me," she adds. "Do you?"

I am frozen, my eyes on hers as I nod. "Of course I want to help you," I tell her. My heart is pounding hard now.

"Then help me end it," she says. "Just help me end it."

She slumps against the back of her chair and I am appalled at the sudden change in her demeanor, of her mental state. How can she go from completely and utterly lucid to completely and utterly out of it in one moment? It defies logic and medical explanation. Does the curse somehow affect her, as well?

I am somewhat sheepish that I am referring to it as a curse. I know that there is no such thing. But I am unsure what to call it. *The affliction*, I guess. That's what I should call it.

"Are you afflicted too?" I ask her. She looks at me as if I'm foolish.

"Of course not," she answers croakily. "Am I a Minaldi man? I am afflicted only in that I've had to watch these goings-on for years. And I'm weary of it. End it for me, Dr. Talbot. You can end it for me. Just give me a triple dose of my evening medication. That should do it. End. It. For. Me."

She is lucid, yet insane now as she spits the words at me. I have chills running down my back as I push away from the table.

"I can't do that," I whisper, shaking my head. Her eyes are glued to mine.

"This won't end unless it ends with us," she tells me. "Luca and his brothers and me. We're the only ones left. It must end with us. The Minaldi line must end. It has to."

Her words are chilling, the meaning of them even more so.

She wants to die. She wants her sons to die. She believes so strongly in a curse that she wants to die to end it. And she is willing to sacrifice her children. It is unfathomable.

Her eyes are burning into mine and I find that I have to turn away. I can't take it anymore. As I leave the suite, she is still calling from behind me.

"It has to end!"

I'll never get the sound of her voice out of my head. It is embedded there forever.

I head out to the English Maze, to the heart of it where the entrance to the cave lies. I knock against the statue of Hades, knowing that the hidden cameras around it will reveal my presence to Adrian, who I am sure is keeping Luca company below.

I am correct, because it isn't long before the statue slides backward and Adrian steps out.

"Is Luca alright?" I ask him.

Adrian's face is filled with sympathy as he nods.

"He's fine. He's calmer now."

I nod. "I'd like to see him."

Adrian shakes his head, regret pooling in his blue eyes.

"I'm sorry. He doesn't want to see you yet. He doesn't trust himself. I have to agree with him, Eva. He's fine right now, but as you saw for yourself last night, that can change in one instant. The frequency of the episodes is increasing. The onset is coming more quickly. Luca is a danger to himself and to everyone around him until we get this under control. He understands this. You need to understand it, as well."

Adrian is stern now, watching me for signs of agreement.

"I can help him," I tell him limply. "I just need a chance to try."

Adrian shakes his head again, his big body filling up the entrance of the passageway.

"You can't," he tells me softly. "I know you want to. But you don't understand what you're dealing with. It's not anything that medical books have seen before. It's unexplainable. What you can do right now to help him is to do what he asks. Give him some space. Allow him to calm himself down and hopefully bring himself back under control. That's what you can do."

I'm numb as I slowly nod.

"Alright," my traitorous lips say. I want to scream and shout and demand to see Luca, but I know that Adrian will never let me pass. He is loyal to Luca. He will never go against Luca's orders. "I'll give him space. When does he think he will return to the house?"

Adrian softens now, staring at my face. "I don't know, Eva. Hopefully soon. We don't have cable out here."

He's attempting to joke, to lighten the situation. But it doesn't help. I'm in no mood. I nod.

"Please let me know the second that you are back. And please, tell Luca that I came."

Adrian nods. "He knows."

"Okay," I whisper, as I turn to leave. There's nothing else to do. Luca controls everything that happens on Chessarae. If he doesn't want me to see him, I won't be seeing him.

I choke back tears as I make my way back to the house.

Chapter Twenty-Eight

Luca

"She's gone?" I ask Adrian as he returns from the passage.

He nods, not saying a word.

"Was she upset?" I ask, although I know the answer.

Adrian nods again.

"Luca, you know you have to do this. You don't want to harm her."

I flex my wrists, straining them against the manacles that restrain them. I slump against the headboard.

"No, I don't want to harm her."

Adrian returns to his book, and I return to thinking about a life that I can never have. Both of us are waiting for me to snap, to re-enter the darkness that has consumed me of late. So far, it hasn't come. But it will, because it always does.

I am more alone than I have ever been.

I bow my head and close my eyes.

I would pray, but I know that God doesn't want to hear from monsters.

Chapter Twenty-Nine

Eva

I have dubbed Luca's affliction Dr.Jekyll/Mr.Hyde's disease.

I cannot bring myself to continue calling it a curse or even an affliction. It is a medical condition because there is no such thing as a curse. As a physician, I know that. And as a medical condition, there has to be a cure somewhere. We just have to find it. Depression, schizophrenia, polio, measles, mumps... they all started out as incurable diseases and now they all have treatment. Luca's disease will be the same. This thought is what is keeping me going.

It has been two weeks since Luca secluded himself in the cave.

The darkness of Chessarae has closed in around me and for these two weeks, I have been a woman obsessed. I have had one singular thought and that is to help Luca. I have spent my time creating endless notebooks filled with notes and more sessions with his mother. I have scoured the internet and medical research books looking for any indication of similar diseases reported by others.

So far, there is nothing.

I am utterly dejected and I feel like I haven't slept in days.

I sent an email to a mentor of mine, a renowned psychiatrist, asking his input. I am anxiously waiting for his reply. I didn't include all of the details, of course. Only the sketchy basics and obviously, I didn't include the part where Luca has acted on his violent tendencies.

At the thought, my hands automatically flutter to my throat, although the bruises from Luca's hands have long faded. That night flashes through my memory like lightning in a storm. His face was so dark and troubled as he clutched me to him, then thrust me away. He turned me over and entered me from behind, pulling me to him, closer and closer, as he thrust harder and harder. Then he wrapped his fingers around my throat and squeezed, whispering words that I couldn't hear or understand.

My words, my pleas for him to stop, grew louder until he finally listened. He turned me around and looked into my eyes and I begged for him to focus, to focus on my face. His eyes grew slightly clearer and filled with distress before he curled up and fell asleep. I had stroked his hair until I fell asleep myself, hunched over him.

When I woke, he was gone.

He had climbed from my balcony and somehow survived the fall. To this day, I don't know how.

My eyes fill with tears now at the memory. The thought that he is confined to the cave, a self-imposed exile, is tearing me apart. Adrian comes out from time to time but there is no news. Luca hasn't had another episode, but he wants to be cautious and wait longer. I want to see him, but he refuses.

And I feel like a shell of myself. I know I need sleep, that I will feel better if I do. Yet whenever I try, all I see are Luca's tortured dark eyes and I can't.

I push the mountain of research on undefined psychological disorders to the side and stand up, stretching. I haven't even showered today. I've been up since the crack of dawn, sifting through page after page of research reports. I have a crick in my lower back, so I stand in the shower for quite a while, allowing the hot water to work out the muscle cramps. Finally, I step from the shower, into the steam-filled bathroom and towel off. I pull on jeans and a soft shirt, and towel-dry my hair.

Instead of taking my daily walk through the maze to beg information from Adrian, I decide to walk along the beach instead. The beauty of the sea will do me good.

I slip my shoes from my feet and allow my toes to sink in the sand as I absorb the morning's beauty. Sea gulls scream overhead and the foam lip of the water slides toward me and then away, over and over in a rhythmic cadence that soothes me. I am staring at the horizon absently as I walk back toward the house when I hear my name.

I look up to find Adrian walking toward me. He is freshly showered and in clean clothing and most importantly, he has emerged from the cave. That can only mean one thing: That Luca has too. Adrian wouldn't leave him there.

I run toward him, drawing to a stop when I reach him.

"He's out?" I ask breathlessly.

"Yes," Adrian nods. "He never had an episode and so he finally decided it was safe to return to the house. For now, anyway. But we'll need to keep a close eye. He says he doesn't feel like himself, that he hasn't for weeks. I don't know what to make of it."

I see the pain on Adrian's face now, something that I haven't noticed before because I was so immersed in my own.

"This must be hard for you," I observe, reaching out to touch his arm. "You love him, too."

Adrian nods. "He's like my brother," he answers. "I don't know what to do for him."

"I don't either," I admit. "And it's killing me."

He looks at me now, really examines me, and he looks surprised.

"Eva, you look horrible. You've got to get some rest. You can't help him if you run yourself into the ground."

He is stern now, so unlike Adrian. Adrian is always laughing, always easy-going and relaxed. But not today. "You need to go take a nap. And get something to eat. You look like you've lost weight and you didn't have it to lose in the first place."

I nod. I know that. I'm not taking good care of myself. I know.

Adrian starts to say something, then closes his mouth. I lean closer.

"What is it?" I ask. He shakes his head, not wanting to say. "Adrian, please."

He looks at me thoughtfully, then relents. "Eva, Luca doesn't want to see you because he knows he is dangerous for you. He's right. He doesn't want something to happen to you and neither do I. You really should go. For your own good."

He's pained now and I'm speechless. I can't go. Adrian has no idea what Luca means to me. And I know that Luca feels the same about me. He hasn't said the words, but I have seen it on his face. I have felt it in the air between us.

"I can't," I whisper. Adrian nods wordlessly.

"Adrian," I say quietly. "When I was with Melina a couple of weeks ago, she begged me to help her 'end it all'. She thinks that the Minaldi line should end with her and her sons. She is insistent. I tell you this because I know that she will try to end it if she can. She will continue to try."

He nods. "I know."

There is a pregnant pause and then he continues.

"She's right, though, Eva. The line should end with them. It really should. This horrible thing has been going on for generations. It is time for it to end."

A lump forms in my throat. "Surely you mean that Luca and his brothers should remain childless and allow the family name to die out. Surely you don't mean...."

My voice trails off. I can't say the words. I can't say, *Surely you don't mean they should die.* My tongue refuses to form the words.

"Of course," Adrian agrees. "Of course that's what I meant."

But from his tone, from his face, I can tell that it wasn't what he meant at all. Luca is getting to him, years of watching his friend deteriorate. Or perhaps it is from years of being around Melina. But whatever it is, whatever he means, Adrian is finished talking about it and has turned toward the house. I struggle to keep up, one step of his for every three of mine.

I grab at his elbow. "Adrian, stop."

He slows and turns to me.

"Adrian, I have to help him. I'm desperate to help him."

I can hear the desperation in my voice and I know he can too. His eyes soften as he stares into mine.

"Sweet Eve," he murmurs and tucks a stray piece of my hair behind my ear. "I hate to see you so upset. Please, listen to me. You can't help. You can't. And I don't want you to get hurt. You're far too precious."

And to my shock and horror, he bends and kisses my lips. I don't kiss him back and as soon as I regain my senses, I push him away.

"Adrian!" I snap. "What the hell are you doing?"

He is apologetic now, chagrined.

"I'm sorry, Eve. I haven't had much sleep either. That was out of line. I'm so sorry."

I stare at him for a moment and then accept his apology. Of all people, I know what it is like to be sleep deprived. I've been a walking zombie for two weeks.

"It's okay," I assure him. "Just don't do it again."

He nods and I turn and as I do, I see Luca standing on his bedroom balcony. From his stricken face, I know that he saw the entire thing. And before I can lift a hand or shout to him, he turns his back and walks back into the house.

Chapter Thirty

I make it to Luca's bedroom in record time, practically running over anything that stands in my way.

"Luca!" I cry out as I burst into his rooms.

He is standing at the windows, beautiful and slender and refined. The breath catches in my throat as I realize just how much I missed him, just how beautiful I had forgotten that he is. Power exudes from him, power and beauty. He's wearing black slacks and a blue pull-over that hugs his chest perfectly. He turns to look at me.

"Luca," I whisper. "It wasn't what it looked like. I didn't kiss Adrian. I don't *want* to kiss Adrian. I only want you."

Luca stares at me thoughtfully, quietly. And he nods.

"I know," he says simply.

I rush across the room and throw myself into his arms.

"Please don't do this again," I tell him helplessly. "Ever. You can't lock yourself away like that. I missed you so much. I was so worried and there wasn't anything I could do. Adrian wouldn't let me see you."

Luca's strong arms finally close around me, as though he tried to resist but couldn't. He pulls me to him and I bury my face against the softness of his shirt, inhaling his smell. I am crying and didn't realize it. I really am an emotional wreck and I know that I need to pull it together.

I clutch him to me and he pulls away. But I won't let him. He has kept himself from me for two weeks. He isn't going to pull away from me now. I won't allow it.

Finally he acquiesces and I feel the moment he gives in, as he clutches me to him as well. He inhales my hair and buries his face in my neck and I sigh.

"Please don't do this again," I beg him. "I can't stand it."

I feel weak and helpless, but this situation has been so emotionally charged that it has taken a toll. It would take a toll on anyone.

Luca doesn't say anything, he just lifts me into his arms and carries me to his bed. His lips are on mine and his body is wrapped around me.

Words cease to matter.

Luca kisses every part of my body, every plane, every curve. His lips are soft, his breath warm as he moves from place to place on my body. He even kisses my fingertips and by the time he is done kissing me, he is hard against me and I am breathless.

"Please," I say quietly, into his ear as I lean up against him. "Please, Luca."

I need him to fill me, to convince me that everything will be alright, that he will never leave me again and that we will figure out what is wrong with him. That we will fix it. That we will have a future. In my head, which is clouded by unreasonable thoughts, making love with him will convince me. It's what I need.

Luca knows that and he gives it to me. Slowly, gently, lovingly.

He loves every part of my body, worshipping my arms and my legs and my lips. He looks into my eyes as he enters me slowly, filling me with everything that he is. I am crying now, crying from the satisfaction that I am with him again. He kisses my tears away and moves faster, pulling me to his chest and rocking with me. I clutch his back and whisper into his ear, whisper words that I don't even know I am saying.

It is an emotional experience and I am limp when it is over, after he arches against me and shudders; after he empties everything that he has into me. He is hot and throbbing, then he lays against me, careful not to crush me.

"I love you," I tell him softly against his strong shoulder.

He is silent, but I feel his muscles tighten.

"I know you love me too," I tell him. "I know you do. Whether or not you feel that you should doesn't matter. Because I know that you do."

Luca rolls to the side and looks at me, his dark hair damp on his forehead, his eyes stormy and troubled.

"I love you," he tells me, as though he is admitting a secret. "Of course I love you, Evangeline. How can I not?"

But he turns away now, hiding his expression from me. I touch his shoulder.

"What is it?"

And he doesn't answer and his silence is frightening. An ominous feeling shudders through me, laying heavily on my heart and I shake his shoulder again.

"Luca, you're scaring me. What is it? What's wrong?"

He sits up, pulling his shirt back over his head, not looking at me. He gets up to find his pants and he puts them back on before he says anything. But finally, when my heart is firmly lodged in my throat, he speaks.

"I can't be with you anymore," he tells me. His voice is flat and expressionless and I know he is purposely trying to distance himself. It's why he's not looking at me. I turn his chin toward me, trying to force him to look at me.

"Look at me," I insist. "Luca!"

My voice is something that I have never heard. It is desperate and anxious and sad.

Scared, terrified, alone.

"Please, Luca. You're not making sense. I'm an adult. You can't make these decisions for me, for the both of us. You can't protect me. I will protect myself. I will help you, Luca. Everything will be alright. I promise."

But my voice is thin, as though I'm trying to convince myself too, because I am. He knows that and he looks at me sadly, his hands limp in his lap.

"Eva, you deserve someone like Adrian. Someone with no secrets or darkness. Someone who can make you laugh like there's nothing wrong in the world; because in your world with him, there won't be. Please. You deserve a normal life. And you won't get that from me. While you are with me, you are going against everything you've been trained to do as a doctor. You should have turned me in to the authorities, but you didn't. I can't put you in this position anymore. I won't do it."

I am clutching him, trying to make him listen to me, to reason. But he won't. He is stoic now, hard. His face grows impassive, once more the Luca Minaldi that I used to see before I grew to know him. The softness and sadness are gone, replaced by power and authority. He is unwavering and he won't listen to me.

He touches my shoulder and leans in to murmur in my ear.

"I love you, Eva. I do. Please do this for me. Please have a happy and glorious life. It will make me happy. I'll send Adrian to retrieve your bags and take you to your cottage. You'll be safe there now that you know that the danger is me."

"No, Luca!" I clutch at him but he pulls away and walks out and there isn't anything I can do but watch him through my watery eyes.

He's gone. And it feels like he took my heart with him.

I sit still for a while, soaking in his scent from the room around me, absorbing him as much as I can. I look at the walls, at the priceless pieces of art that I know he chose himself. At the silver cufflinks that I have seen him wear a hundred times. They are laying on his heavy mahogany desk. A pair of soft leather loafers peek from under the desk. Bits of him are scattered throughout this room and I try to memorize every bit of it before I finally get up and leave, turning only once to look behind me before I close the door.

I make it to my room before I fall to pieces. I collapse onto my bed and cry until I can't cry anymore. I don't have any more tears left, and my eyes are red and hot and burning. I picture Luca here, in this room with me. I remember him smiling over me, his smile white against the dark shadows of his eyes. I remember him laughing as we rolled in the bed, twisted in the sheets.

I remember him squeezing my throat. I remember his eyes as he looked into mine. I remember the look on his face when I found him in the stables, so shattered and alone. And I don't want to leave him here. He'll be alone, with no one close to him but Adrian.

But I have no choice. As I sit up and wipe at my eyes, I know that I have no choice. He has decided and I will not be able to change his mind. It's done.

I get up and fold my clothing and place them into my bags. I gather my research and my notes and my laptop and put everything into a pile to load into the car. With each thing that I place on the pile, I feel my heart breaking just a little bit more. I don't know how much more it can take until it shatters into a million jagged shards.

There is a knock at my door and I open it, hoping to see Luca, but knowing that it will be Adrian. And it is.

Adrian is apologetic and sympathetic as he carries my things to the Mercedes. I look behind me as we get into the car and I think that I might have seen a movement at a window, that Luca might have been watching, but I can't be certain. As quickly as I see it, it is gone. I close my eyes, fighting the hot wetness that I feel building there.

We are silent on the way to my cottage and I force myself to not cry. Not in front of Adrian. I am stoic like a stone as I look out the window, watching the greens and blues blur past. We pull into the drive and Adrian unloads my things from the car, carrying them into the house. We are still silent.

As he leaves, I walk him to the door, standing silently, willing myself not to break down.

He pauses, touching my cheek for a brief moment. "Eva, please let me know if you need anything at all. Luca is not abandoning you. He just can't be with you. It's for your own good."

A lump forms in my throat and my eyes fill with tears and I nod.

I know what's good for me, damn it. But I don't say that. I just nod. I can't open my mouth and speak or I will collapse into tears. Adrian nods and leaves.

And I am alone.

Utterly alone.

I look around the tiny cottage and for the first time, it seems enormous in its solitude. It seems enormous because anywhere where Luca *isn't* seems so very lonely. I open the back doors to allow fresh air to blow through, then curl up on the couch. I don't feel like doing anything else today but wallowing in my own misery. I decide that I have earned a day of doing exactly that, so I cover up with a blanket and close my eyes.

Chapter Thirty-One

Days pass.

Each day seems cold and empty without Luca. On the fourth day, there is a knock on my door and I open it quickly, hoping to see that Luca has relented. It isn't him.

A courier waits on my porch with a slim package in his hands. I sign for it and take it inside. After I cut the top open, I find a CD and a note inside, written in Luca's scrawling handwriting.

Dear Evangeline,

I want you to know that I miss you. I never expected to meet someone like you, and now that I have and you are gone, your absence is almost too much to bear. Yet I know it is necessary, as I am certain that you know, as well. I cannot bear the thought of something happening to you, something by my very own hand. It would be the death of me. I know that much is true.

I have recorded a few things for you on this CD to help you sleep. It makes me happy to envision you safe in your bed listening to my music. When I play now, it will always be for you.

I will always picture you happy and safe, Evangeline. Please endeavor to remain that way.

All my love,
Luca

My eyes are burning and hot and I close them, feeling the warm wetness slide down my cheeks and onto the linen stationery in my hands. I shakily put the CD into a player and the sounds of Luca's hands, the music that he makes with them, fills my house. It is haunting and beautiful, just like the man who is created it.

I spend hours listening to it, surrounded by memories of him. The fourth day is a sad day.

More days pass. They are empty and difficult and I find that I am numb, that I simply move through the motions of life without feeling them. I know now why I created the barrier around my heart so long ago. It hurts so very much when something breaks it down and I feel something.

I cannot bring myself to leave Malta, not yet. Even though I have finished my dissertation. I don't feel anything at all as I push the 'send' button and email it to my mentor, the head of the Psychiatry program. I know I will have to return to the states to defend it at some point, but I don't think of that now.

I also fill my days trying to find answers for Luca. There have been no more killings in Valletta, so I have to assume that he has been secluded in the cave, which makes me want to weep. I throw myself into trying to help him, even though it must be from afar.

There are so many things that his affliction could be, so many things that it could be part of. Mental illness is fluid, it can bend and morph until one disorder can actually be components of several others. Without having Luca in front of me, it is hard to diagnose him with anything. I still refer to his problem as the Dr. Jekyll/Mr. Hyde disorder.

I finally hear back from my mentor concerning it and he doesn't have much insight on the subject as he's never seen such a thing before. Although he is fascinated as well and cannot wait to read my research, which is not really any help at all. He suggests, as I already suspected, that the disorder is something comprised of components of several other disorders. I begin researching them yet again, trying to patch together what it might be.

I eat with Marianne several times, although I am not hungry. I feel pathetic, like a lovesick schoolgirl who cannot come to terms with a breakup. But this thing that Luca and I had was so much more than a relationship. I can't even define it, yet I grieve the loss of it.

Marianne force feeds me. She comes to my cottage and demands that I eat, bringing with her pasta and wine and bread. She sits with me sometimes, having coffee on my patio and chatting with me, filling the silence. She is a good friend.

It is she who makes the deduction that I am pregnant.

I had been nauseas and emotional for a week or two and I attributed it to stress and nerves, which is completely plausible in this situation. But as I struggle to eat pasta without vomiting, Marianne looks at me in concern.

"When was your last period?" she asks me gently.

Her words stun me.

"I don't know," I stutter. And I feel foolish because I am a physician and I didn't see this. My hand automatically grazes my flat belly, shielding whatever might be inside. I feel something for the first time in weeks besides grief and sadness.

Wonderment.

"It's not possible," I say without conviction.

Because I know that it is.

That first night, the night that Luca came into my room when he wasn't himself, I wasn't on birth control and he didn't use anything either. He wasn't himself. He didn't even think to use it. I went into town shortly after that and filled a prescription, but that first and second time, we didn't use anything at all.

Two times.

My hand rests against my belly, against what might be my unborn child. And Luca's. That realization brings with it so many thoughts. Happiness, although it is bittersweet. I am strangely happy that I might have a piece of Luca. Which brings with it the darker thoughts, the realization that the child within me might inherit the dark affliction that is born in the Minaldi men.

I don't focus on that, however. I can't. I will deal with that when the time comes because that is all that I can do. In the meantime, I revel in the idea that I will bear Luca's child. It is a sense of wonder, a sense of awe.

Marianne becomes a mother hen and her sense of protection where I am concerned kicks in to overdrive. She comes over almost every day, bringing with her fresh food and conversation, making sure that I am okay. Every day, I am. Every day, she tells me that I must tell Luca. Every day, I balk. I know what his answer will be. He will want me to terminate the pregnancy. He won't want to risk having the affliction pass to yet another person.

The idea of terminating this pregnancy leaves me feeling sick with horror and sadness. I would never do it, no matter how much Luca begged. So it seems easier to not tell him, for now. And to hear his voice might be my undoing, anyway. I have become stronger in these past few weeks, but it's a tenuous strength. I don't know how long it would last if I were once again face to face with that which I cannot have.

Luca.

I sigh as I turn to Marianne today.

"I know," I answer her familiar plea. "I'll tell him."

"When, bella mia?" she asks, her attractive face concerned. "It has been six weeks already. In another month or two, you will be showing because you are so thin. It will be difficult to hide. If you remain here in Malta, it will come to his attention. Someone will see you and rumors will fly. He will hear of it and it should be from you."

"I know," I tell her. And I do.

That night, I write him a letter. I can't bear to do it in person or to tell him over the phone. That seems inhumane. He shouldn't hear it on the phone. If I can't do it in person, he should be able to read it, instead, which allows him the privacy to absorb the words alone before he has to process them and discuss it with me.

I drop it into the mail the next morning and butterflies surround my heart. I can't imagine what he will feel like when he reads it. He feels guilty enough already for involving me, for becoming close to me. I pass the day nervously, doing anything that keeps my mind off of Luca's reaction.

Because I'm too anxious and filled with nervous energy to do anything else, I sit on the patio in the fresh air and sift through baby name websites. I don't see anything I like, however. I finally decide that it is a boy. And that I will name him Luca after his father. I don't even look at girl names, even though I know that Luca will probably pray that it is a girl.

I am exhausted and go to bed early. I lie awake and concentrate on the life that grows within me. I hope that it is strong and thriving. I meant what I said in the letter. This baby is part of Luca and part of me and I just know that it will inherit the very best parts of each of us. And now that Luca will know, I am free to go into town and find a physician. No more hiding. I need regular check-ups from someone other than myself.

I fall asleep with my arms wrapped around my stomach.

* * *

I am walking on the beach the next day when I see him.

He is so beautiful. He is striding toward me on the beach, the sun bathing his perfect face in golden light. Grendel is with him, but I don't focus on the dog. I can only see Luca. His face is drawn and tight and I start to run, my feet sinking deep in the sand with each step. Before I know it, I am in his arms. He smells of woods and musk and Luca. I inhale him, as though I have been holding my breath for the past few weeks and am only just now able to breathe again.

It might as well be true.

Luca's strong arms encircle my back, pulling me to him, kissing me fiercely. He has missed me too. I can feel it. Just as I can feel the sadness within him. It surrounds us now, ever present.

"What have we done?" he asks, his voice steeped in angst. He scoops me into his arms, carefully as though I am so very fragile. He carries me gently back to my cottage and into the house, sitting me on the sofa. He situates himself with my feet in his lap. His eyes are so tortured, so stormy as he watches me.

"Eva, we can't bring a child into the world," he tells me painfully. Each word rasps from his lips like broken glass, like it is painful for him to even think it, much less say. And it is. "We cannot bring *my* child into the world."

I stare at him, the pain welling in me like a cresting wave, even though this is exactly what I knew he would say. I was expecting it, but suddenly I realize that it doesn't make it any easier to hear.

"Luca," my voice breaks, so I try again. "Luca, I cannot harm our baby. I can't. Perhaps it is a girl and so it won't matter." He is already shaking his head.

"Even if it is a girl, she can carry the anomaly," he says. "She can pass it on to her male children who would pass it onto theirs. Eva...."

He drops his head into his hands and I grab one, pulling it from his face and forcing him to look at me.

"Luca, you haven't given me a chance to help you. You simply sent me away. I've been doing research and there are so many things that this might be. They are all treatable with medication. You can be

238

helped, if you will just give someone a chance to try. If you give *me* the chance to try. *Please* let me try."

He looks at me, his face contorted with his angst.

"Eva, I belong in prison. I don't deserve to walk free or to sit here with you. Or to have a life with you. I don't deserve it. Don't you see that?"

His fingers are so long and slender and strong. I focus on them, holding them tightly in my lap as I gulp.

"These are not the hands of a killer," I tell him softly. "Luca, whatever you have done, it wasn't you who did them. You didn't. Your affliction did. Not you. You would never consciously hurt anyone. I know that. Let me find a way to help you. Let me discover what is wrong. We can treat it and pretend that nothing ever happened. We can be happy, Luca. No one will ever know."

He stares at me calmly, his dark eyes shining.

"*I* would know," he says softly. "And *you* would know."

I'm crying now, my shoulders shaking as I sob into my hands. Luca pulls me to him and I cry against his chest. He is so strong and warm, but his warmth doesn't pass into me. I am chilled to the bone with the realization that he will never let me help him. He is condemning himself to a life alone, an empty life without me.

"I'm so sorry," he murmurs into my hair. "I'm so sorry to have hurt you this way. I never should have come near you. It's my fault. Everything is my fault."

"No." I am fierce now. "I will never be sorry. You have changed me, Luca. And I am not accepting this as an answer. I never want to be without you. I won't let you do this."

He grabs my hands and holds them, clutching them to his chest, pulling the rest of me there as well.

"Shh," he whispers into my hair. It is now that I realize that I am crying yet again. I fall limply against him and allow him to hold me. The hormones from this pregnancy are wreaking havoc with my emotions. I hate that I feel so weak and weepy.

"Let me take care of it," Luca says. "I'll set up everything up and you won't have to even think about it. I'll do it."

I pull away and stare at him incredulously as I realize that he is speaking of our child.

"I won't have to even think about it? You think I can abort my child, *your child*, and not even think about it? Are you insane?"

I get up and stalk backward, my heart frozen as I stare at his expression. He is quite convinced that we will be aborting our baby. And suddenly, I feel as though I need to get away from him. I don't know why, I only know that the maternal instincts inside of me are telling me to run.

Luca follows me as I back away from him, watching me carefully.

"Eva, that's not what I meant. But I'm trying to be frank with you. We can't have this baby. Trust me, no child would want to live the life that I've lived. I would never wish that on anyone. There's no way that you can understand. But *I* understand. I've lived it. I'm still living it. And I would never put a child through it."

His voice hardens toward the end, growing even more determined.

I stare at him again in disbelief. "You are telling me that you would rather be *dead* than the person that you are?"

Luca says nothing, but his silence says everything. And suddenly, I can't take it anymore. I have to listen to my instincts. They are screaming at me and I can no longer tune them out.

Run.

I whirl and race from the cottage, down the paths leading to the beach. The trail is uneven, filled with rocks and pebbles and roots. I stumble, then right myself. I don't know where I'm going, but I can't stay there with him. I hear him behind me, calling for me, but I don't stop. I reach the rocky incline that slopes steeply to the shore before Luca catches up with me and grabs my arm.

"Eva! What are you trying to do? Get yourself killed?"

The sea is crashing below us and I turn, staring Luca in the eye.

He is desperate and anxious, two things that I have never seen on his face before. I don't know his motives. Is he scared that I will hurt myself or scared that I will get away and he can't force me to abort our baby? The wind whips my hair around my face and I impatiently push it out of the way.

"No," I answer. "But that almost sounds more appealing than the alternative at this point. Now let go of me!"

I wrench my arm out of his grip, but as I do, as I yank backward, my foot slips free of my tenuous foothold. The rocks and dirt give way and there is nothing holding me up anymore. I scream as I skid downward at an unnatural angle. I flail and struggle to regain my balance, but I can't. Everything is happening too quickly. Luca grabs for me, but it's too late.

I tumble down the rocks, down the steep incline, flipping over several times before I finally land with my cheek resting in the watery sand below. The jarring blow knocks the wind out of me and I struggle to breathe as I gather my wits. It happened so quickly that it seems like a blur.

Luca is beside me in an instant.

"Eva! Can you hear me!"

I nod without lifting my head. I can't seem to breathe well yet. I don't have enough air to move or speak. Long seconds pass before I can urge any sound from my lips.

"Go away, Luca," I finally rasp. "Just go away."

"Not a chance," he says. He bends and picks me up from the shallow water and rocks. As he lifts me from the water, my scraped feet sting in the breeze. I have no idea if I am injured. I feel completely numb. I am dirty and muddy and wet as he wordlessly carries me back to my cottage.

He carries me into my bathroom where he runs a bath and strips off my wet clothes. He holds my hand as he settles me into the tub, then kneels next to me, washing my arms and legs carefully. I'm scraped all over and it burns as the hot water seeps into the cuts. But I don't care. I draw my knees up to my chest and lean my cheek against them, closing my eyes.

I'm too numb to cry.

"It will all be okay," Luca says carefully as he washes my muddy face. "I promise, Eva. You will be okay, no matter what. I will make sure of it."

I don't answer, but I allow him to help me back out of the tub and wrap me in a towel. I feel so empty and alone, even though he is right here. Because I know what he wants and it is very different from what I want.

I feel utterly alone.

I pull a t-shirt over my head and then collapse back onto the couch.

Luca settles me in with a blanket and a pillow and sits at my feet, stroking my legs soothingly.

"Rest, Eva," he tells me. "I know you are exhausted. You aren't taking care of yourself. I can see it. Please sleep. I'll be right here."

I stare at him wordlessly for a moment, then grasp his hand and close my eyes. He might be against what I want, but I still love him. I can't help it. And his presence comforts me. I sleep more quickly and deeply than I have in weeks because even in sleep, my body knows that he is here.

I wake several hours later in horrible pain, my body wrenching and twisting as my abdominal muscles contract. I double over, clutching my stomach, trying to breathe. The pain takes my breath away. As I look up, Luca is watching me in horror, in pain. And I see something in his eyes that I don't wish to see.

"What is happening?" I ask him limply. "Luca."

He turns away, but not before I see the terrible answer in his eyes.

And I know, even while I am asking him, what is wrong. I am miscarrying.

It isn't long before the sticky wetness between my legs lets me know that I am correct. I cry as I clean the blood from my legs. I use washcloth after washcloth to wipe my unborn child's remains from my skin. With each ragged breath, with each cloth filled with tissue and blood, I cry a little more.

"Don't touch me!" I screech at Luca as he tries to help me. "This was our child. If you hadn't tried to grab me, I wouldn't have fallen. This is your fault. *Your fault!* You did this to me on purpose. You wanted the baby gone and now it is. I hate you for this, Luca."

And at this moment, I do.

Luca stops moving and stares at me sadly, quietly.

"I know you do," he answers finally. "But that's the way it should be. It will make it easier on you."

I collapse into my bed, crying once again even though I didn't think I had any tears left. I am empty inside; completely, soul-shatteringly empty.

"You did this," I whimper. "You killed our child."

Luca takes a shuddering breath and kneels next to me, his forehead pressed against my arm. I move away from him. I can't bear his touch. He takes another ragged breath as he pulls the blanket up around me.

"Eva, I wanted to terminate this pregnancy for the good of the child, because I know what it is to be a monster. I would never purposely hurt you. I didn't grab you hoping that you would fall. I grabbed you so that you *wouldn't*. I promise you that. I would never knowingly hurt you. Even I am not that much of a monster."

I cry. Tears fall onto my nose and drip onto the sheets and Luca wipes them away. I look up at him and the sadness in his eyes convinces me that he is telling the truth. He didn't want me to fall. How could I have thought that? Why did I run?

I did this.

I know that much is true.

Luca didn't run, *I did.*

I whimper with that knowledge and Luca stares down at me in concern. I don't object when he folds in behind me and wraps his arms around me. Deep down, I long for him even now.

"I'm so sorry, Eva," he whispers into my ear with his husky voice. "I am so sorry."

And I know that he is which is why I can't truly hate him for this. I close my eyes and sink into sleep. I am awakened several times in the night by pinching cramps in my abdomen. Luca finds a heating pad and drapes it over me. He gives me painkillers and wipes me clean as I continue to bleed.

At one point, I stare up at him. "I love you, Luca," I whisper.

"I know," he sighs. "I love you, too."

When I wake in the morning, he is gone.

Chapter Thirty Two

Luca

I have never hated myself more than I do at this moment.

As I walk back toward Chessarae, the sun peeks over the horizon and I know that I don't deserve to stand in it. I should never see light of day again.

I may not have physically caused Eva to fall, but deep down, I know that I am relieved that she miscarried. It is a terrible, heinous thought, but it is true.

If I were normal, I would welcome a child with Eva with open arms. I would welcome a *life* with her with open arms. But I'm not normal. And no child of mine could ever possibly be normal. My own mother has told me many times that she wished she had never carried me to term, that she wished I hadn't been born. If my own mother feels so strongly about me, if I am that much of a monster, then why would I ever want to bring a child just like me into the world?

It is for the best that Eva miscarried. But the fact that I even think that, especially after seeing her pain throughout the night, only cements my knowledge that I am a monster. Who else would think such a thing? My mother is right about me.

I am damaged in unfixable ways.

I am tempted to wade into the sea, to walk into the deep depths and refuse to swim, but I know that my body's subconscious need to survive would propel me to the surface and nothing will have changed. I would still be what I am.

I continue walking, knowing that the person who I love most in the world has been utterly crushed by an event that I am almost thankful for.

She is the only thing I love.

She is in pain right now and I can't fix it.

It is a knowledge that I can hardly bear.

Chapter Thirty-Three

Eva

I have no purpose here now, no reason to stay in Malta.

So, I make preparations to return home, to defend my dissertation and begin my life in Portland. Or perhaps I will move to somewhere sunnier, like Phoenix or Santa Fe or maybe even Honolulu. Somewhere like Malta. I gulp. I can't be reminded of this place, of Luca. It would be my undoing.

I'll probably just stay in Portland.

I want to hate Luca for what happened and I try very hard because it would be easier than blaming myself. But I can't. I know that he didn't mean for me to fall. He was out there trying to keep me from harm and if I hadn't run, then we would never have been out there on those rocks at all.

Luca sent a doctor to look at me. The doctor thinks that I miscarried partly due to stress, in addition to the fall. He said, and I know that it is true, that a woman's body is more durable than one would think. That normally a fall wouldn't cause a woman to miscarry by itself. So, truly, I'm even more to blame for not managing my stress better.

It's a thought that does nothing to ease my guilt.

I feel like a failure as a strong woman. All my life, I've been the strong one in any given situation. And now, I feel like I've allowed myself to get sucked so far into emotional situations that I handled them weakly. And I hate that thought more than I can even admit. I am not *that girl*, the one who falls to pieces. But here lately, that's exactly who I am. I make a concentrated effort to pull myself together, to focus on moving forward.

I am packing when a knock raps on my door and as always, I turn towards it with a sharp pang of hope. Is it Luca? But I know that it isn't and when I answer the door, I find that it is not. I try not to feel disappointment as I greet Marianne.

Her face is grave however.

"What's wrong?" I ask her.

"Melina Minaldi died in the night," she tells me solemnly. "I thought you would want to know."

"She died?" I am stunned. "But she was in perfect health. How did it happen?"

Marianne shakes her head. "I don't know. But I thought you would want to know, that maybe you would want to go to Luca. I know he will be devastated."

I'm not sure that he is devastated, but I do want to go to him.

However, I restrain that urge.

"When is the funeral?" I ask her. Again, she shakes her head.

"I don't know, bella. Probably in a couple of days."

"Thank you for telling me," I murmur.

"Of course, sweet one," she says.

After she leaves, I pick up the phone and dial Luca's cell phone. He answers on the first ring.

"Eva," he says. He is surprised that I have called. "I thought that I would never hear your voice again."

My heart breaks with his words. I can imagine that is what he thought.

"I'm still angry," I tell him. "I'll probably never get over the fact that you wanted to abort our baby. But I know it wasn't your fault that I fell. I said some terrible things to you in anger. And I'm sorry for them. But that's not why I'm calling. I want to give you my condolences. I'm so sorry about your mother. What happened?"

Luca is silent for a moment.

"Thank you," he says. "It has been difficult. The official cause of death is listed as a heart attack. But I know you probably know better. My mother overdosed on her own sedatives. She did it herself."

I am not surprised. I remember her chilling voice as she begged me to do it. I nod even though he can't see me.

"I knew she would try," I admit to him. "I told Adrian."

"I knew, as well," Luca tells me. "We tried to prevent it, to watch her around the clock, but Sophia isn't a machine and mother wouldn't allow anyone else near her."

"Sophia must feel horrible," I say.

"She does," Luca answers. "But it wasn't her fault."

I don't voice the unspeakable; that Melina is at peace now, that she can no longer torture herself, that she can no longer torment Luca. Instead, I simply agree with him.

"No," I answer. "It is certainly not Sophia's fault. When is the funeral?"

"Day after tomorrow, at the cathedral in town. But you don't have to come."

Pain shoots through me at his words; it feels like yet another rejection.

"Of course I'll come," I tell him. "I'd like to say goodbye to you in person, anyway. I'm leaving for home next week."

There is silence, painful and empty.

Finally he speaks.

"That is how it should be," he says, his voice smooth and devoid of emotion.

"I'll see you in a couple of days," I tell him, trying not to cry.

"Until then," he answers and then the phone goes dead. I hold it in my hands for the longest time before I lay it down.

The next day passes woodenly, as though I am simply treading water until I see him again. I'm both looking forward to it and dreading it, because I know it will be for the last time.

The morning of the funeral, I dress in a simple black sheath dress and pull my hair into a knot at my neck. I carry with me a bouquet of flowers from my own garden. I take the bus into town and arrive to find that the cathedral is packed full of people from Valletta. Apparently, because the Minaldis are so prominent in this town, everyone wanted to show their respect. Marianne waves to me and I make my way to sit at her side.

The mass is a normal funeral service. I spend most of it staring at the family pew. Luca is there in a somber black suit, along with his brothers. I still would have known they were brothers even if I hadn't seen them together. They look very much alike. Damien and Luca could practically pass as twins, while Christoph looks like them, but is just an inch or two shorter.

When the service is over, the priest announces that there will be no public interment and that everyone is free to mingle in the community rooms beneath the church. I swallow hard. It is time to say goodbye to Luca.

I steel myself. I can do this. I've done everything on my own in this life. I can do this.

I wait for a while until Luca appears to be done chatting with well-wishers. He retreats to a back corner and sits, comfortable in the shadows. He meets my eyes and I walk to him, my legs shaky.

"Hi," he greets me softly. I long to reach out and hold his hand, but he doesn't move toward me, so I don't. I sit next to him instead. We are alone over here, alone in a crowded room. There is no one near.

"I'm sorry," I tell him. "I'm sorry for everything. For your mom, that I couldn't help her, that I couldn't help you...."

My voice trails off and he stares at me.

"After everything, you're apologizing to me?" He's incredulous now. "What have I done to you? Have I truly taken a strong, independent woman and turned her into someone who apologizes for things that she hasn't done? This isn't you, Eva."

I sniff, fighting back tears once again.

"My hormones have been crazy," I admit to him. "Because of the pregnancy and losing the pregnancy. It seems like all I can do is cry lately. I'm sorry."

His eyes soften now and he looks away.

"I'm the one who is sorry," he finally says, turning to meet my gaze once again. "I never meant to hurt you. I never want that."

"What will you do now?" I ask. "I hope that you let someone try to help, even if it can't be me."

The words are difficult to say, because I so much want to be the one who helps him.

He studies me for a moment, then looks at his hands.

"I'm going on an extended trip," he says quietly. "I love to sail and it's been a long time since I've been. Adrian and I are leaving tonight. I can't hurt anyone on the water, away from the civilized world."

"So, you're just going to run?" I ask bitterly. "You're going to hide away from the world, isolating yourself again?"

He shrugs, his shoulders elegant. "I don't know what else to do."

Let me help! I want to scream. But I don't. It would be a waste of time and dignity. He's made up his mind.

"I wish things had been different," I whisper instead. He nods.

"I do, too."

He reaches out now and grasps my hand, enveloping mine with his larger one. He is warm and strong and I ache to melt into his body. I know, from the way he is staring at me with such stormy, dark eyes that he wishes nothing but the same.

"Please, Luca," I whisper.

I don't know exactly what I'm begging for.

Everything, I guess. Everything and nothing.

Luca stares at me for a moment longer, then gets to his feet, still holding my hand. He leads me through the crowds of people, ignoring the curious stares. He winds up the back staircases of the church, and through a hallway to a room upstairs. It's a side room and I can tell that it isn't used very often. I look at Luca questioningly. How did he even know it was here? He senses my question.

"I was an altar boy," he says as he closes the door. "I know this church like the back of my hand."

He turns to me and lifts me up, his mouth closing in on mine. It's hot and needy and electric.

"I can't stay away from you," he growls into my neck. "Even though I know I should."

"I know," I whisper. My hands are in his hair, driving his head into my chest, into my neck. I want him everywhere, I want his taste, his touch, his tongue. I just want him. All around us, there is a lingering, overwhelming sense of sadness. We know that this will be the last time and it makes us ache.

He lifts me against the wall, pushing into me. There is no foreplay, because we don't need it. We only need each other.

When I whimper, he gently covers my mouth with his hand and stares into my eyes. He rocks with me until I feel him explode. He quivers against me and then stills, still clutching me to his chest.

After a moment, he slides me to the ground.

"I love you." His words are soft and quiet in this reverent place.

For the first time, I acknowledge that we just had sex in a church. I should feel guilty, but I don't. I doubt that God cares.

"I love you, too," I answer, grasping his hand as if I can make him stay with me. But I can't. Finality is in the air between us. We are over and we both know it. All that is left is the goodbye. The very worst part.

Luca fastens his pants and adjusts his suit jacket.

"Please be happy," he says and his voice is choked. He bends and brushes a soft kiss on my forehead. I fight back tears as I nod, unable to speak and he wrenches his gaze from mine. He leaves and doesn't look back.

Chapter Thirty-Four

I don't remember walking through the church or the bus ride home. Everything is a blur as my emotions numb my body and my heart. I feel like I'm in shock and I probably am.

I get off the bus down the road from my house and walk the rest of the way, one foot in front of the other. When I get to the house, I find that I don't want to go in.

But I also don't want to go to Marianne's. I don't really want company. Instead, I walk along the beach for a while, my shoes in my hand. I sit on the sand and stare at the water, burying my toes in the white beach, trying to ignore the pain in my heart.

No one dies from heartbreak, I remind myself. I should know. I lived through it years ago.

I honestly don't know how long I sit like this, zoned out and staring at the water. But eventually, after an hour or two, I grow cold. I walk back to my cottage and make my way up the path to my door. As I do, I see something propped against it.

An envelope.

Curiously, I pick it up and take it inside so I can see it in the light.

It's from the lab where I sent Luca's blood-work.

I rip it open and pull it out, my hands shaking in anticipation. And then I almost drop the paper.

The chemical components of his blood are all normal. But that's not the interesting part.

On a whim, I had decided to have his blood tested for drugs. And it is positive for several things. Enough things, actually, that the lab manager compiled a letter to accompany the results, explaining what the poisonous components likely are.

There is heavy evidence of recent use of Rohypnol, more commonly known as the Date Rape drug. Trace components of Angel's Trumpet are there too, a strong hallucinogen that is known to put a person in a zombie-like state, able to function but unable to remember it afterward.

He was drugged.

My breathing is coming in pants now as I finish reading.

There is a presence of several other naturally growing herbs, all of which are known to cause violence and aggression when used in excess. I stare at the incriminating words on the white page, so astounded that they practically blur together.

Luca has been poisoned.

I sink to the floor as I ponder what this means. Is he not cursed at all? There is no strange, dark affliction, only drugging? I know that he didn't do this to himself. He wouldn't. These poisons are very, very dangerous and in fact, Angel's Trumpet is highly fatal. Since only a trace is found in his blood, whoever has been drugging him is skilled. They know what to give him to produce exactly the reactions that they want to see without lethally overdosing him.

Who has access to him? Who would do this to him?

Adrian.

My heart pounds heavily in my chest as his name and face spill into my mind, although I don't know why he would do it. He's the only one who has round the clock access to Luca. He's the only one that Luca trusts completely and absolutely.

He's like a brother to me, Adrian had said. I fell for it. Luca fell for it. Everyone fell for it because Adrian carries it off perfectly. He is perfectly charming, perfectly friendly. He's very skilled at portraying that image.

I can't breathe now.

Luca is about to leave on an isolated trip with Adrian.

Tonight.

I pull out my cell phone with shaking hands and dial his number.

No answer.

I leave a voicemail and try again.

No answer, so I leave another frantic voicemail.

Oh my god.

Oh my god.

Oh my god.

Without thinking, I run out the back doors and down the path to the beach and then I'm flying as fast as my legs will take me toward Chessarae.

I am not a runner, so I don't know how I even make it without hyperventilating, but I do. I keep going because I know that since Luca runs this route, it is possible. I keep going because I have to. I race along the beaches, trails and roads until I reach the front doors of

Chessarae. I ring the bell, then double over, trying to catch my breath.

Christoph answers and he studies me curiously as I struggle to breathe.

"Luca," I manage to get out. "Can I see Luca?"

Christoph smiles apologetically.

"I'm so sorry, miss," he tells me. "Luca has left for a trip. Can I help you with something?"

It is several more minutes before I am able to breathe well enough to partially explain who I am, who I am to Luca, and why I am here right now. By the time I am finished, Christoph's tanned face has leached of color and he is as pale as paper.

"Come in," he tells me, ushering me through the house to Luca's study. He settles me into a chair, hands me a bottle of water and then leaves.

"I'll be right back," he tells me over his shoulder. He returns scant moments later with Damien, his older brother.

Damien looks so much like Luca that it takes my breath away when he walks through the door. He introduces himself and I re-tell everything that I've just explained to Christoph. When I am finished, Damien is the same pale shade of white.

"This can't be," he mumbles. He shakes his head and pours himself a Scotch, then one for Christoph and me.

"Why would he do it?" I ask as I gulp at it. I can hear Christoph on his phone. I don't know who he is talking to, but he's requesting boats. Fast ones.

A search expedition.

"We can't call the police," I tell Damien. "We can't."

Because we can't have them investigating Luca's involvement in the girls' murders.

Even though I don't want to think that way, I have to protect Luca. He wasn't himself when he blacked out, but I'm not sure that a court would believe that. I'm not familiar with Maltese law at all. I don't know if they have a temporary insanity plea and I don't want to chance it right now.

"Don't worry," Damien tells me. "We have extensive resources. We'll handle it ourselves. We'll find him."

"Why would Adrian do this?" I ask, my heart still numb.

"I don't know," Damien admits. "I just don't know."

"Luca told me that the Leopoldos have always worked for your family," I say. "How far back?"

Damien thinks on that and Christoph pipes up from behind him.

"Generations," he says. "Generations ago, our great-great-great grandfathers started our shipping business together. It was known as Leopoldo-Minaldi Shipping back then. But apparently, Enzo Leopoldo had a really bad gambling problem. He lost everything he had and Lucien Minaldi- which incidentally, is who Luca is named for, bought out his shares. That's the story, anyway. Apparently, they had a deal that the Minaldis would always employ the Leopoldos. As the years passed, they began to work for us here at Chessarae rather than at the business."

"But if you've always taken care of them, why would Adrian turn on you?" I ask, still confused. "But more importantly, the curse didn't begin with Luca. Luca told me that it has gone on for generations."

"Yes," Damien said. "It began with Lucien."

Christoph looks at Damien and I. "Did it begin before or after we bought out the Leopoldos?"

Damien is quiet. "I believe it was after, if the stories are correct. When Lucien was younger, it never happened to him. That's why it was such a mystery. The doctors could not figure it out."

We all suck in our breath.

Can it be a coincidence? Or has this been an elaborate, horrible act of revenge that has spanned generations?

"If that's the reason, the Leopoldos have some issues of their own," I point out unnecessarily. "Perhaps bi-polarism runs in their family or schizophrenia. Either way, this is almost too elaborate to be real."

Damien looks at me.

"This isn't America, Dr. Talbot. Here in Malta, our pride is very valuable. It's completely plausible that Enzo Leopoldo was so humiliated by the whole affair that he plotted out ways to lash out at us because he blamed us for his shame. I can see it happening, actually. There have been a few times over the years, when I've heard Adrian and even his father, slip and say something derogatory about our family. And as you've said, we've never done anything but take care of them. Enzo Leopoldo's gambling problem was his own. Did Lucien take advantage of the situation by buying them out? Perhaps, but if he hadn't, someone outside of the family would have and that was not an option for us."

"Adrian has always seemed so happy to me," I say absently. "I certainly misjudged him." And that doesn't say a lot for my thesis project which I've already sent to America...but that is not important right now.

"How long will it take for your boats to find them?" I ask Damien. He shakes his head.

"I don't know. We don't really even know where they were going. But we know how long they've been gone, so we're sending boats into every conceivable direction."

"Do you mind if I stay?" I ask. "I'm never going to sleep until he's found and safe, anyway."

"Of course," Damien answers cordially. He hands me another Scotch. "I assumed that you would. It will be nice to have you here when Luca returns anyway. It will be helpful to have a professional explain what we think has happened."

That's a good thought. After a lifetime of believing he is a monster, it is hard to say how Luca will process the revelation that he isn't. That none of the Minaldis have ever been... that his best friend in the world has betrayed him his entire life.

It's an inconceivable thought and it would be difficult for anyone to handle.

I settle into a leather chair and cover up with a blanket that Christoph brings me. The only thing we can do now is wait. I take another sip of Scotch, allowing it to burn my throat on the way down. Grendel pads quietly into the room and sits at my side. I'm surprised, but it seems fitting. Luca's dog is waiting for him, too.

Chapter Thirty-Five

Luca

The sea is a lonely place. I had forgotten how much so and we've only been sailing for three hours. My melancholy is already laughable.

"I don't know how you talked me into this," Adrian calls from where he is sprawled on the starboard side. "Being out here indefinitely without any female company whatsoever? It's inhumane, Luca. I deserve a raise." He laughs and props his feet on cushioned seat. "But it *is* beautiful out here. That's a plus."

"You're a good friend, Adrian," I tell him. "You do deserve a raise. Think of how many women you can charm when you have more money to spend." I smile even though my heart isn't in it. My heart is with a beautiful red-headed doctor. I push the thoughts away.

"True," he answers good-naturedly. "And we've got a nice supply of Scotch, and that's what is really important, no?"

I nod. "If only we had a cell signal, it would be perfect," I tell him.

Adrian agrees. "The satellite phone should be up and running soon. I spoke with the company right before we set sail. They assured me that they were working on the problem."

263

"It makes me slightly uncomfortable being out here without a phone," I admit to him. "I know we have a radio and I realize that sailors have sailed for hundreds of years without cell phones, but still."

Adrian laughs. "Pansy."

"If by pansy, you mean that I'm accustomed to the comforts that the twenty-first century has to offer, then yes. I guess I am," I banter back. Idle conversation with him is helpful for me. It keeps my mind off of *her*. Off of my heart, which vacillates between being numb and broken.

Jesus. My own thoughts are making me sick. Maybe I *am* a pansy.

And I have a fucking headache.

"I'm going below for more Scotch," I tell him. "Do you need anything?"

"Not unless you find a gorgeous blonde down there," he answers back lazily, his eyes already closing. "If you do, send her my way."

I shake my head as I walk down the steps that lead to the living quarters below. This sailboat is large, and it houses two small bedrooms, a galley area and a bathroom below. I poke through the bathroom cabinet to find aspirin and come up empty-handed. I don't have any in my bags either.

Son of a bitch. My head is throbbing. I blame it on the emotional toll of the day, which would have given anyone a headache.

I duck into Adrian's room. He's always prepared. I know he will have painkillers in here. He's very accustomed to hangovers.

His room is neat, almost Spartan. He has already put away his things and I quickly rifle through his toiletries, hunting for what I need.

What I find, though, is not aspirin.

My fingers stumble upon a leather bag. It looks like a toiletry bag, so I open it. And inside, I find several clear bottles. One contains a black thick liquid and is capped with a dropper. The other two contain clear liquid. They also are topped with droppers.

Interesting.

But not surprising. I've long suspected Adrian of using recreational drugs. It's just something that goes along with his carefree and adventurous personality. But to bring them on the boat when it might incriminate me in case of a border check is annoying and I'll have to speak to him about it.

"What the fuck are you doing in my room?" Adrian snaps.

I look up, his bag still in my hands.

His face is hard and rigid and I am surprised by the tone of his voice.

"I'm hunting for aspirin," I snap back. "But this is my boat, so technically, *all* of the rooms are mine. What's with the attitude? Afraid I'll find your little stash here? What are you thinking? I don't want the kind of bad press that would come from a drug sting."

I toss the bag back onto his bed. "You need to get rid of it. In fact, I'll get rid of it."

I snatch it up again, then push past Adrian to go up on deck. He clenches his jaw so tightly that I can practically hear his teeth grind as I pass.

I am halfway up the stairs before there is a sharp pain in the back of my head and everything goes black.

* * *

"Why did you have to snoop?"

I hear Adrian's voice, but it is as though it is through a fog.

Did I black out again? I think harder, trying to focus.

I did. But it wasn't from my curse. I was hit in the head. And there was only one other person on this boat.

I open my eyes and the light in the room is blinding. Unnaturally blinding.

I've got a concussion. That much is clear. My wrists are bound to the back of a chair. I wiggle them, but the knots are tight.

"What happened?" I ask, even though I already know. For some confusing reason, Adrian hit me and bound me while I was unconscious. The problem is, I don't know why. Has he sold me out to someone? Has he kidnapped me for ransom? Nothing makes sense.

"You were being rude," Adrian snaps. "You were going through someone else's things. We were taught better than that, Luca."

"Adrian, I don't understand what is happening," I tell him. And I don't. He laughs, finding my confusion funny.

"I'm a fuck up, that's what," he says, his face growing serious. "I'm the first one in my family to fuck this up. My father would be so fucking proud." He's sarcastic now and I still don't know what he is saying.

"You fucked what up?"

I struggle to keep my eyes open, but the light is so bright that it hurts.

"This, you fucking idiot." Adrian shoves my shoulder hard, hard enough that the chair I'm sitting in flips over on its side. Since I am bound, I can't right it. I struggle with it for a moment, then lie still. Adrian laughs.

"Look at you now," he sneers. "The great Luca Minaldi tied on the floor like a trussed up hog for slaughter. *Your* father would be so proud."

I am silent now, my confusion growing by the second, but I know that Adrian isn't going to enlighten me. I'll simply have to wait. My silence annoys him and he tries to bait me, but I ignore it. He kicks my chair in agitation.

"You've always thought you were better than me," he snaps. "And you never were. It was all in your head. And the funny thing is, Mr. So Fucking Holier Than Thou, is that everything else in your head, I put there. *I put there.* So where's your fucking arrogance now?"

My eyes open.

"What do you mean you put things in my head?"

Adrian eyes me. "Exactly what I said. I put everything in your head that is there right now. You've been tormented for years... by thoughts that I've planted there. By things that I've told you that you've done. By things that I've made it appear that you've done. But it was always me, Luca. *Always. Me.*"

He sees the confusion on my face and laughs.

"You always thought you were so smart," he snickers. "You thought you had to tutor poor dumb Adrian so that he didn't fail Algebra. Yet poor dumb Adrian was making you think you were a monster, that you were trying to kill innocent things, that you were *cursed*... and you never were. You never were, Luca! Who's dumb now?"

His words stun me but his maniacal laughter shocks me even more. Adrian has lost it.

"That can't be true," I argue. "My entire family is cursed. My father, my grandfather..."

Adrian looks at me patronizingly. "And who has always worked for your family? *My* father? *My* grandfather?" He laughs again. "I have poisoned you and lied to you, Luca. Just as my father and grandfather before me. And theirs before them. It was the poison that made you violent. It was the poison that took your memory. It was *me* who fed you lies. Poor, dumb Luca."

Shock slams into my chest and fury turns my vision red.

"You did this to me? YOU??" I roar like an animal but it only causes Adrian to laugh harder.

"Yes, me," he laughs. "Always me. And your mother... your poor demented mother? That was me, as well. The tea that she just had to have shipped in from Italy like the spoiled bitch that she was? I drugged it. Your mother would have been right as rain if it weren't for me. And the funny thing is that she thought it was you. She told me once, in a lucid moment, that she thought *you* were poisoning her. But it was me all along."

"Why?" I rasp, still unable to wrap my head around it. "Why would you do this to me...to my family?"

He looks at me like I'm a fool.

"Because we hate you," he says simply. "We fucking hate you. You ruined us so long ago and your family has used us as servants ever since. Why the fuck wouldn't we hate you, Luca? We're not fucking servants. We're *men*. And I'm so much more of a man than you are," he snaps. "Do you think you had the balls to kill those girls? Do you really think that? You're too much of a pussy. You had all the balls in the world to fuck them, *to rape them*, but you left it like that... you left them alive. They would have gone straight to the police and reported you and then everything would be over. You would have been put in prison, away from my reach. Life in prison would have made your life easier and I couldn't have that."

He all but spits the words as he spins on his heel.

"So, I did what you couldn't because you're too weak. And now that you know, I'm sorry, but your battle has come to an end. Your family will be told that you couldn't bear to live with your curse any longer. They'll believe that, you know. You're such a pathetic excuse for a human being. So fucking weak. The public will be told that you drowned. All will be well."

"Except for me," I answer bitterly. "And for those girls. You killed them. It was you...all along."

He smiles down at me.

"It wasn't only me. You were there, Luca. I may have killed them, but you raped them. And then, of course, I raped them, too. It would have been wasteful not to, don't you think?"

I feel nauseous at his words. "I can't believe this," I mutter. "I raped them because *you drugged me*. I trusted you. You were supposed to be my closest friend."

Adrian smiles sardonically in a way that I've never seen him smile before. It is in this moment that I realize that I never really knew him at all. He's insane.

"Oh, you can trust me when I say this: I will put you out of your misery, *friend*."

Adrian starts to walk up the steps when I hear something loud.

Chopper blades.

Adrian freezes.

Lights are flashing all around us and then I hear a loud-speaker.

"Luca Minaldi, if you are on board, come out where we can see you."

I've never been more relieved in my life.

That is, until Adrian returns with a large knife in his hand. He cuts my ropes and yanks me to my feet, sticking the knife against my spine.

"Go," he says. "Don't try anything or this knife gets buried in your back. Don't doubt it."

"I don't," I say calmly, walking slowly up the steps.

We step on deck and there are helicopters circling low and boats surrounding us.

"Luca Minaldi? Are you alright?" the loud speaker calls out.

I shake my head no.

"Adrian Leopoldo! Step away from Mr. Minaldi. Be advised that there are rifles trained on you at this moment."

"Fucking son of a bitch," Adrian mutters. "You're a fucking son of a bitch, Minaldi. You always think you will come out ahead. But not this time."

Before I can think, breathe or move, he has yanked me overboard with him. On the way over, his knife sinks into my shoulder but I don't even feel it.

The water is choppy because of an impending storm and I fight to get back to the surface. I choke in water as the waves roll over my head and I am washed under again, slammed into the side of the boat. I grapple with a line that I feel there, and pull myself to the surface, clinging to the boat. When I push my head above water, I don't see Adrian anywhere.

I hold fast to the side of the boat with one arm, the uninjured one, until help arrives. I'm hauled back on board and friendly faces surround me, wrapping a blanket around my shoulders while a medic examines my shoulder.

"Mr. Minaldi, this is your lucky day," one of them tells me. "The knife missed your artery. You're going to be fine."

"Did you get Adrian?" I ask, searching behind them. Adrian isn't there and the medic shakes his head.

"No. We haven't found him yet. The current is bad today. He can't survive out there."

It doesn't matter. There's only one thing that matters. One *person* that matters.

"Do any of you have a satellite phone?" I ask. "I need to make a call."

Chapter Thirty-Six

Eva

My cell phone buzzes in my pocket and I pull it out. I don't recognize the number, but I answer it anyway.

"Eva?"

I would know that voice anywhere, that husky, rich voice.

"Luca," I cry in relief. My knees feel like they will collapse and I sink back into the chair, my fingers trembling as I clutch the phone. "Are you alright?"

"Yes," he tells me. "I am now. I'm coming home. Will you meet me at Chessarae? There's so much to explain."

"I'm already here waiting for you," I tell him happily. I feel the tears streaming down my cheeks. "Hurry home."

And he does.

A couple of anxious hours later, Luca is walking through the door. Tall and strong, he strides directly through the room, stopping for no one until he reaches me. He is wet and as he bends in front of me, his dark hair falls across his forehead and droplets of rain drip into my lap. He stares at me and it is like we are the only two people in the room, as though his brothers aren't even here.

Looking into my eyes, he whispers, "I'm not a monster, Eva."

My heart seems to split into two at the vulnerable look on his face. At this moment, he is a little boy who wants acceptance. He is the little boy whose mother hated him, who grew up thinking he wasn't fit to be alive. I picture Luca as a scared five-year old, tied to his bed in the dark and my eyes fill with tears.

"No, you aren't. You never were."

He buries his head in my chest, his arms wrapped tightly around me.

"But I've done terrible things. Can you forgive me?"

My heart cramps and a lump forms in my throat. "It wasn't you, Luca. It was never you. There's nothing to forgive."

He draws me to him, then pulls me from the chair. Holding my hand, he leads me from the room. Christoph and Damien speak to him as we pass, telling him they are glad he's safe. He speaks to them, but we don't stop. We pass through the large house, winding through the halls until we reach his bedroom. We tumble into his bed and Luca wraps his arms around me.

We stay awake for the longest time. We don't speak, we just exist together. My head rests against his chest and I listen to his heartbeat. It is that comforting, strong sound that lulls me to sleep and we stay wrapped together all night.

When I open my eyes, Luca is staring into them. He is lying on his side watching me, ever beautiful in the morning sun. He has a bandage on one bare shoulder.

He watches me wake and smiles.

"Good morning."

I smile back. "Good morning."

"We have a lot to talk about," he says. I nod.

"I know. But everything will be alright now, Luca. We're going to be fine. *You're* going to be fine."

"I know," he agrees. He bends and kisses me and everything really does feel like it will be fine.

We get up and shower, then have breakfast with his brothers in the formal dining room.

Christoph is leaving today, but Damien will stay for another day or two to take care of some loose ends. I don't ask what his loose ends are, but the following afternoon, a group of hunters come across a pack of wild wolves. A news story intimates that these wolves might be the very same ones that were responsible for the vicious killings that have happened of late.

Hearing that, I look up into Damien's intense eyes. I suddenly know what his 'loose ends' were. He was ensuring that his brother was protected. I'm sure that someone, somewhere, is getting paid so that the DNA test results on those girls is suppressed, so that there is no evidence that they were sexually violated.

I should feel guilty about being thankful for that. But I tell myself that the girls are dead anyway. There's no reason why Luca should have to further pay for a crime that he didn't want to commit. He was drugged. It wasn't really him committing those acts. And I know that Damien will also ensure that Adrian, the one who should truly pay, is found and privately punished.

I am more grateful than I can express to Damien.

"You don't have to thank me," he says when I try to talk to him about it. "Luca is my brother, but more than that, he is a good man. He doesn't deserve what has happened to him."

"None of you have," I tell him. "This thing hasn't just affected Luca. It's affected all of you, for so very long."

I stop talking and think about Melina and Nicolas and all of the Minaldis before them, all of them believing that they carry some sort of evil genetic anomaly. All of them believing that they were monsters. It's heartbreaking. I glance at Damien, and I know he's thinking the same thing. He shakes his head, as though to free his head of troubling thoughts.

"It's over now, though," he points out. "And Luca has you. And I know you will help him through this. My brother is strong and so are you."

I smile and hug him, and he even feels like Luca. Strong, powerful and lithe. He leaves to return to London with instructions to call him if he is needed.

Luca and I are once again alone.

We attempt to return to normalcy, taking it one day at a time. I stay at Chessarae with him and put things in motion to get my license to practice medicine in Malta. I can't imagine returning to the States right now. I can't imagine leaving Luca. I know that he can't, either.

"Stay with me," he said to me the day after everything happened. "Don't leave."

And I promised him that I wouldn't.

Chessarae is a beautiful place, filled with dark memories and beautiful scenery. I spend my days walking through the gardens, taking trips to town and revising my thesis with my mentor from the hospital in Portland. When it is finally ready, Luca and I take a week and travel to the States while I defend my dissertation in front of a panel at the University.

I pass with flying colors and I am approved to specialize in Psychiatric medicine.

Luca and I spend the weekend celebrating in Portland, strolling down the scenic walks beside the Willamette River which flows through the center of the city. Luca laughs about the near constant rain, but I remind him that that is why the Pacific Northwest is so beautiful and green. He laughs and reminds me that Malta is beautiful, too, and it doesn't need to rain constantly to stay that way. I have to concede that point.

We return to Malta and life continues, seemingly idyllic.

I pester Luca, insisting that at some point, he will have to talk about everything that happened with me. And if not with me, then with someone. He agrees.

"Adrian is still out there," I remind him. "I know that Damien has hired people to find him, but he's still out there. That must weigh heavily on your mind. You need to talk about it."

"But I'm not ready yet," he tells me. "I have to process it first myself. Then I'll discuss it with you." I agree with that. It's perfectly understandable.

"We're completely safe at the house," he assures me. "We've hired extra security. Adrian can't hurt us." I believe him. Damien told me himself that the Minaldis have extensive resources. I know that we are safe. Chessarae is a virtual fortress.

I know he is troubled, however. I wake many times in the night to find that he isn't in bed. I always know where to find him. He plays the piano because the music soothes him. Each time I wake and he is gone, I sit with him while he plays for a while before I lead him back to bed.

One night, I find him alone on the terrace at 2:00 a.m., staring at the moon in the darkness.

"I should turn myself in," he tells me quietly. When he turns to me, I can see the angst on his face. "It's the right thing to do."

"No," I am firm. "How is that the right thing to do? Adrian is at fault for everything. You didn't rape those girls. The drugs that Adrian gave you raped those girls. Then Adrian killed them. Why should you turn yourself in for that? Because of Adrian, you've hated yourself your entire life. Because of what he did, you will feel guilty for the rest of your life. I know you. You will carry this guilt forever and that is quite enough punishment for something that you had no control over. You didn't do this, Luca. Adrian did."

He nods, but I can see that his heart isn't in his words. "I know that. But my body forced those girls against their will. It was my body, even if I wasn't in control of it. Every once in a while, I get memory flashes, just little bits and pieces. There are times when I see their faces and it makes me sick."

I turn his chin so that he is looking at me. "It wasn't you, Luca. It was Adrian. You have been a victim in this, too. And Damien's men will find him and he will be punished. The *rightful* person will be punished and that is not you. Those girls will be vindicated. I promise."

He nods, but mumbles, "Still, I have to do something."

Soon after, I hear from Marianne that an anonymous benefactor has set up very large memorial funds for the girls' families. I know it was Luca, although he never mentions it.

Time passes; weeks, then a month.

One night at dinner, several weeks after we return, we are eating a formal six-course meal when Luca pushes away from the table during the second course.

"I'm in the mood for a ride. Are you?"

I smile. "On a horse?"

Luca nods. "On the beach."

He doesn't have to ask me twice.

We share a horse, like we did the last time, so many weeks ago. I lean against his chest and he wraps his warm arms around me, keeping me safe and secure in the night. I watch the sea lap gently at the sandy beach. It's soothing. Being here with Luca is soothing.

Luca draws the horse to a stop and slides to the ground. I stare at him in confusion.

"I'm in the mood for a swim now," he tells me with a wolfish grin.

"In the dark?" I quirk an eyebrow. "I didn't bring a suit."

"Neither did I," he says wickedly. He strips off his clothes, then helps me strip off mine. We run into the waves, laughing like children. The moon hangs overhead, romantic and full. The magic of it is too much to resist and I grab Luca, pulling him to me. I cover his lips with mine, kissing him with everything that I have.

He makes love to me in the water, as my legs wrap around his hips. When we are finished and spent, we lay in the sand on the beach, staring up at the stars.

"You've saved me," Luca says quietly. I turn to him in surprise.

"I didn't save you," I tell him firmly. "You didn't need saving, Luca. Your entire life as you know it was a lie. Even if I hadn't been here, you would have come through it just fine."

He shakes his head.

"You have been my saving grace from the moment I met you, before you even knew it. It sounds silly to say, but it is the truth. You offered me hope when I didn't have any. I've clung to that notion from the beginning, even when I knew that I shouldn't endanger you, that I shouldn't chance it. I knew, even then, that there was something different about you. I can't imagine ever being without you."

"You never have to be without me," I assure him, my voice catching. "Luca, this has been difficult, I know. But I'm here to stay. You'll never have to be without me and I'll never have to be without you."

"Promise me," he says, picking up my hand and staring into my eyes. His are a stormy black. "Marry me. Stay with me forever."

I look at him, at his beautiful chiseled features, at his handsome grin, his perfect smile. "Yes," I tell him. "I will stay with you forever."

He kisses me softly, pulling me to him and we make love on the beach.

"I don't have a ring," he tells me as we ride back to Chessarae, tired and spent. "I don't want to use my mother's or my grandmother's. I want something new, something that isn't associated with anything dark or ugly. We'll go to town tomorrow and you can pick anything you'd like."

I smile in the dark. "I'm not worried about the ring," I tell him sleepily. "If I could wear *you* on my finger, I would."

"I'm wrapped around it already," he says drily. "Does that count?"

We laugh and return the horse to the stable, then find our way upstairs to Luca's bedroom. To *our* bedroom. We fall asleep immediately with our arms wrapped around each other and the moon shining in our room through the open balcony doors. Life is perfect.

Or at least, it is until Luca wakes me in the night.

I startle awake, taking a moment to realize that Luca is perched above me, drenched in sweat. As the moon shines in and my eyes adjust to being awake, I see the same empty expression in his eyes that I've seen so many times before.

The empty, *dark* expression.

My heart seems to freeze in my chest, afraid to even beat.

"Luca?" I ask, my voice hesitant. "Are you alright?"

He doesn't answer. Instead, he mumbles something that I can't understand. I shake his shoulder.

"Luca, wake up." But he doesn't respond and I realize, with a sinking heart, that he isn't asleep.

"Luca," I say again, more firmly this time. He looks at me, but doesn't see me.

"I'm sorry," he mutters over and over. "So sorry. Forgive me. There was so much blood. Forgive me."

He's repeating himself over and over, and wipes at his hands as if to wipe the blood away.

He's not himself.

How many times have I heard him say those words? *I'm not myself.*

But he's not.

Again.

My heart drops into my stomach as he climbs from the bed and walks naked from the room. I jump up and chase him, calling for him to come back. But he doesn't stop. My voice doesn't sway him, my fear doesn't move him. He's immersed in something that only he can see.

Finally, as I scream at him to stop, he turns to me and the empty, dark expression in his eyes, so devoid of anything but torment, terrifies me.

And I know that it isn't over.

Part two:

Darkness and Demons

By Courtney Cole

It is better to conquer yourself than to win a thousand
battles. Then the victory is yours. It cannot be taken
from you, not by angels or by demons, heaven or hell.
-Buddha

Prologue

At night, I walk alone.

Amid the dark and the shadows, I sink my feet into damp sand and continue on my way. The salty sea water laps at my ankles, washing over the bare skin of my feet. It can't wash me clean, however. Nothing can.

But that doesn't matter here in the night. No one can see me for what I've done, for what I might still do. The demons can't chase me. They can't find me in the dark although it wouldn't matter if they could. I'm worse than all of them, yet I'm one of them all the same.

The dark, the demons... I belong to them.

My will doesn't matter, my intentions don't matter, my thoughts don't even matter.

They aren't my own anymore.

I am a child of demons and darkness.

The sooner I reconcile myself with that fact, the sooner I will no longer be tormented.

As if that time will ever come.

The moon hangs heavy on the horizon, like a pregnant star, its yellowed belly grazing the sea. I gaze at it for a moment, chasing all other thoughts from my mind, until I finally acknowledge that I have to go back. I have to face that which is too nightmarish to face.

Too inconceivable.

Too horrible.

I turn, and step by step, my feet carry me back to Chessarae.

My home.

My prison.

Chapter One

Eva

Sunlight slants through the balcony and shines onto the gleaming mahogany floors of our bedroom. The light illuminates Luca's face in an almost ethereal way and I have to smile. When he sleeps, Luca is innocent and free from torment.

But only when he sleeps.

I hesitate to wake him, but we have an appointment to keep. It's important and we can't be late.

I slide into the bed next to him, shaking his shoulder lightly, before I run my fingers along the chiseled length of his jaw. Even now, his masculine beauty astounds me. I should be used to it, but I am not. His dark hair, his even darker eyes, his lithe and muscular body. He's strikingly refined, absolutely beautiful.

"It's time to wake up, sweet," I whisper into his ear. "I've already showered. It's your turn."

He stirs, then turns to me, automatically opening his strong arms for me to fold into.

"Good morning," he mumbles into my neck. I smile.

"Good morning."

He pulls me closer to him, kissing me softly.

"Did you sleep well?" He stares at me, worry hidden in the depths of his eyes. What he's really asking is, *did he do anything to keep me awake?*

"I did," I assure him, not telling him that he tossed and turned with nightmares all night, which did keep me awake. He can't help it and he feels bad enough already. "And while I'd like to stay here in bed with you all day, we have an appointment to keep."

"Ah, yes," Luca stretches. "An appointment to fix me."

"Don't make fun of it," I grumble as I attempt to pull him from the bed. "We *can* fix you. We just need the proper help."

Luca shakes his head. "I love that you are so optimistic. It is one of the many things I adore about you. But I fear that we have been outmatched. It has been two months since Adrian stopped drugging me. Yet I still have black-outs that I can't remember. The drugs should be long gone from my system. But they're not."

As he speaks, Luca sits up, staring at me pointedly.

"The doctor already told us that Adrian's herbal cocktail was unique," I argue. "Even the best doctors can't determine how long the effects will last because a drug made with these exact components has never been tested. The components themselves should have killed you, but they didn't. It's mystifying. But Luca, you'll be fine. You just need time."

"You're a psychiatrist, Eva," Luca says softly. "Have you ever seen such a thing as this?"

I'm silent. He knows that I haven't. We've had this conversation before.

His eyes meet mine. "You know that you haven't."

I refuse to answer him. Instead, I throw the covers off of him, laughing when he howls from the cold air.

"You should have gotten up," I tell him, giggling as I roll from the bed and stand above him.

He stares at me, cocks an eyebrow and then before I can even think he leaps from the bed and drags me back onto it with him. I am tangled in his arms and legs as his fingers tickle the bony recesses of my ribs. I squeal and thrash about, but it does no good. He's much stronger than me.

He pins me down and hovers above me, his face inches above mine.

"Do you give?" he asks playfully, his fingers curling into my ribs. I cackle wildly and squirm, but he doesn't release me. "Do you?"

"I give," I shriek. "I give." I'm wildly ticklish and always have been. The mere movement of his fingers on my skin causes me to howl. Luca laughs, all signs of worry gone from his face as the laughter reaches his dark eyes.

It's the first time I've seen him worry free in months.

I lay still, staring into his eyes. Reaching up with my fingers, I brush his hair away from his face.

"It's going to be ok, you know," I tell him softly. "I promise."

The shadows pass back across his face and I wish I hadn't mentioned it. He looks away from me, out the balcony doors, staring at the sea.

"You shouldn't make promises you can't keep, Eva," he murmurs, as he climbs from the bed, leaving me alone. "I thought we'd already established that."

I sigh, watching as he disappears into the stone shower. He's been pulling away from me lately, as though he's afraid to be near me. He's afraid he'll hurt me. He hasn't said it, but I know it's true. There's been no talk of our wedding.

I stare down at my naked ring finger.

He had proposed to me before he realized that he was still afflicted. Once the darkness settled into his eyes again however, once the strange periods of unconsciousness came back to him, Luca didn't speak of marriage anymore. He hasn't uttered another word about a ring, or a ceremony or a life with me.

He loves me. I know that.

But I'm beginning to come to the realization that love might not be enough. Not anymore.

Not for Luca.

It's a thought that sends terror racing through me, causing my heart to pound.

I'd walk through hell and high water for him.

But only if he'll let me. Sighing, I watch the sea as I wait for Luca. The blue water pounds the shore almost angrily, but each time, relents and slides back into the sea, settling into the rippling mass. Time after time.

Watching it mesmerizes me, and before I even know it, it's time to go.

As we glide along a Valetta highway in Luca's sleek Jaguar, he's quiet behind the wheel, pensive. Finally he glances over at me.

"Evangeline, I don't want you to get your hopes up. I'm seeing this doctor because you want me to, not because I think it will help."

I nod. "I know. But just because you don't think it will help, doesn't mean that you're right."

Luca stares at me for a second, before returning his attention to the road.

"Just don't set your hopes too high," he murmurs, not looking at me again. I reach over and rest my hand on his leg, but he doesn't react. He doesn't cover my hand with his own as he once would've.

I sigh. "I won't. If you won't set yours too low."

Luca shakes his head now, the corners of his lips tilted just slightly.

"You're so stubborn," he remarks as he noses the car into a parking space.

I smile. "I know," I acknowledge. "But you like it."

He doesn't answer. Instead, he gets out and walks around to get my car door, ever the gentleman. My heart twinges as I get out and pause in front of him, my fingers on his chest.

"I love you. And I'll make everything all right," I tell him. I kiss him softly and quickly. "That's a promise."

Luca's dark eyes are stormy as he stares down at me.

He turns and walks away, but as he does, he grabs my hand.

The smallest exhibition of hope.

I smile as I trail behind him, my fingers entwined with his.

When we reach the building, he drops my hand so that he can open the door for me. I notice that he doesn't pick it back up but I don't say anything.

It was significant that he picked it up once. He still wants to touch me, to draw comfort from me. It's very telling.

We don't have to wait. The receptionist ushers us directly back to Dr. Bianchi's office. He's waiting for us, his fingers templed in front of him as he stares quietly at the wall. When we enter, he glances up, his forehead furrowed.

But he smiles warmly as he stands to shake Luca's hand.

"Luca," he greets us. "Eva. How are you?"

He has the casual demeanor of someone who has known Luca a long time, because he has. He's been the Minaldi family physician for years, and in fact, was Luca's mother's doctor until the end.

"We're fine, Stefano," Luca answers, settling into a leather armchair. "A bit anxious, perhaps, to hear what you have to say, but other than that, we're well."

I sit next to him, my feet crossed at the ankles. *A bit anxious* is an understatement.

Dr. Bianchi stares at us from behind his desk and his expression is somber.

"I'm afraid I don't have good news," he says bluntly, his thick Maltese accent coloring his words, making them more beautiful than they are. "I don't necessarily have bad news, but I simply don't have answers."

Luca's head drops almost imperceptibly, but I see it.

"So you can't help me," he replies with a sigh. "The night terrors, the blackouts…. There's nothing to be done."

Dr. Bianchi looks away. "Not nothing," he clarifies. "The blackouts, I'm afraid, are something we will have to wait out. They could fade away on their own. You will need to stay with someone who can monitor you when you can't monitor yourself. But the night terrors…. I think those are related to suppressed memories. Things you might've done when you were not yourself."

He pauses and I look at Luca, startled. It's too close to the truth for comfort. We haven't told anyone, including Dr. Bianchi, what Luca did when he was drugged, when his mind was not his own.

We haven't told anyone that he raped several women, that he sees glimpses of these women's faces when he sleeps and he wakes in cold sweats.

There's not a point to telling someone.

Luca wasn't himself. He would never have hurt anyone if he'd been in his right mind. It was Adrian's drugs that tapped into a dark and dangerous side of him. It wasn't Luca.

It's something that's taken him a while to come to terms with. He wanted to turn himself in for a long time. But I wouldn't let him. He doesn't deserve to rot in prison for something that he didn't do. It was Adrian. It might've been Luca's body, but it was Adrian pulling the strings and directing his actions.

And so help me, if I ever find Adrian, I might kill him myself.

"Perhaps you're right," Luca agrees with the doctor. "I can't remember what I do or where I go when I black out. Perhaps I have bad memories suppressed."

I suck in a breath, waiting for him to say something, but praying he doesn't. I grip his knee tightly, willing him to say nothing.

"What do you suggest?" he asks simply. The doctor nods.

"I suggest that you see a psychiatrist. Not Eva," he amends quickly. "She's too close to you and the situation. I think I might be, as well. You could talk to a colleague of mine. She might be able to help you deal with the issues that are causing the night terrors."

As he looks at Luca with his dark eyes, it almost seems like Dr. Bianchi knows something… that he suspects. But then the look is gone and he is simply waiting for an answer.

Luca shakes his head. "Not right now," he answers quietly. "I don't wish to talk with a stranger. I'll continue to confide in Eva."

Dr. Bianchi sighs. "I had a feeling you would say that. I'd like for you to stop by the lab and give more blood for analyzing. The life of the poisons in your blood stream is astounding. It's like nothing I've ever seen. I'd like for you to come in on a weekly basis and give blood samples so that we can track the levels. Perhaps we can draw an accurate picture of how the toxins are degenerating in your system. I'll do some research in the interim. Hopefully, we'll have some answers for you soon."

Luca stands up and his face is a perfect impassive mask.

"Thank you, Stefano," he says politely, holding his hand out to grasp Dr. Bianchi's.

"You're most welcome," the kindly man answers. "Don't grow discouraged. We'll sort this puzzle out. And Luca, if you need anything at all, please don't hesitate to call me. You have my mobile number."

Luca nods and we move toward the door. As we walk quietly to the car, he never utters the phrase that I know he's thinking.

I told you so.

Chapter Two

Luca

Somehow, and I don't know exactly how, I am able to keep the hopelessness off of my face. I don't want Eva to see it. But she knows.

She knows in the way I move, in the way that I speak, in the way that I play the piano at night when I can't sleep. She knows because she knows me in a way that no one else does. It's something I wish I could spare her, but unfortunately, that's not something that I can change.

She's in my life and I am in hers.

If I were a better man, I'd convince her to leave me, to return to the United States and start a healthy life there, a life away from all of this darkness. But I'm not a better man. I'm simply a man who is clinging to an idea of something he'll never have.

A man devoid of hope.

But despite that, I'm very good at going through the motions.

I conduct all of my Minaldi Shipping business from Chessarae, from the privacy of the mahogany paneled conference room and my den. I participate in satellite conference calls, answer emails, approve expenditures, and do all the tedious things that come with my job as Senior Vice President of Operations. Luckily, it's a job I can do from this remote location. Thank god my brother handles the role of CEO. That wouldn't be something I could manage from home for very long.

My cellphone buzzes in my pocket and I pull it out, glancing at the name on the screen. Speak of the devil.

"Damien," I answer. "How are you?"

"I'm good, brother," he answers. "And you?"

His words are formal, because that's how my family is. Formal, well-mannered, refined. Well, everyone but Christoph. My younger brother is far more relaxed than Damien or I.

In my head, I picture Damien, and what he's probably doing right now.

Since he is headquartered in London, he's probably standing in his penthouse condo, drinking Scotch while he stares out over the wet, gray city, his glass in one hand, his phone in the other. Physically, he looks almost exactly like me, but he's a year older. He's adept, good at everything he attempts, and calm in the face of chaos.

Much like me.

"I'm fine," I answer. "For the most part. Have you located Adrian yet?"

There's a pregnant pause, then Damien clears his throat. "No. I think we have to examine the fact that he might've perished at sea."

I think back to the night my best friend had tried to kill me on my boat, the night that his craziness had emerged from behind his perfect façade. His body wasn't recovered from the sea and Damien had employed search missions to find him. Each search mission has returned empty handed.

"He's alive," I say simply. "I can feel it, Damien. He's out there."

"I know you believe that," my brother says carefully. "But perhaps you feel that way because the events of that night were so traumatic. Luca, you trusted him. We've trusted his family for decades... they fooled us all. It's no wonder that you're having issues dealing with it."

My blood boils and I count to ten before I answer.

"Damien, I'm not having issues *dealing with it*. I've handled the fact that the Leopoldos have secretly betrayed our family for generations...and that there was never anything wrong with me other than the poisons that they fed me. Trust me, I've come to terms with that.

"What I haven't been able to overcome is the fucking drugs that are still in my system. You have no idea what it's like because I was the one drugged, not you. It's me who is still a danger to everyone around me. So please don't patronize me with your sympathetic platitudes. Just find Adrian. Until we find him, I'll never know how to overcome this. I'm sure that's part of his fucked up plan."

There's quiet on the line, then a sigh.

"I'm sorry, Luca. You're right. I don't know what it's like and if you have a gut feeling that Adrian is still out there, then we'll continue the search. We'll behave as if we know for a fact that he's alive. Keep the enhanced security at Chessarae and watch what you're doing."

"I seldom leave the property," I answer in resignation. "And I'm sorry if I seem short. My patience is wearing thin."

"I understand," Damien says graciously, his perfect manners carrying every word. "You have a right to feel weary. How's Eva? Have you set a new date for the wedding?"

It's a thought that causes my gut to constrict and a knot to form in my throat. As I think of Eva and her perfect faith in me…. It makes me almost cringe.

"She's doing well," I reply. "No, we've not set a new date yet. I can hardly think of chaining the poor girl to me now, can I? She deserves far more than that."

Damien attempts to protest, but I cut him off. "She's in bed now and I should join her. Come to think of it, why aren't you sleeping?"

I can almost see my brother shrug. "No rest for the wicked," he answers, then chuckles. "Or the overworked. I'll come home soon and we'll catch up."

"Do that," I tell him. "I'll look forward to it."

We hang up and I glance around my study. The dark wood panels on the walls reflect a rich sheen and the spines of a thousand books face me from the shelves. I've been spending too much time secluded in here. And if I'm not in here, then I'm down the hall playing the piano.

I stare out the window, past the manicured English maze that sits behind the house directly in front of the jagged cliffs that lead to the ocean below. In the center of that maze, beneath the surface of the earth, my hideout lurks. The hidden room that used to keep me confined when I couldn't control myself. But that was back when I trusted Adrian to help keep me safe.

I haven't stepped one foot in that room since he betrayed me.

Now, I linger here, either within the walls of Chessarae, or out on the grounds. I don't leave this place. I can't trust myself around innocent people any longer.

With a weary sigh, I take one last drink of water. I would rather have scotch, but it's grown much later than I thought and I know Eva will wait on me to go to sleep. She always does. She wants to know that I'm safely in bed before she closes her eyes. I look down at the massive wolfhound resting by my feet.

"Come on, Grendel. Time for bed." My loyal dog stands and stretches, then accompanies me as I make my way through the darkened halls of the large estate.

Pausing, I place a hand on the wall, envisioning the tunnel that hides behind the hallway. Chessarae is filled with hidden tunnels since it was built hundreds of years ago and used by the Knights of Malta before it became my family home. I know all of them like the back of my hand. A part of me longs to enter one, to keep walking and never come back. To leave who I am here... and all of the darkness that accompanies that behind. One thing stops me though. One person.

Eva.

It's Eva who keeps me sane, who keeps me from leaving or doing something foolish. It's Eva who gives me a reason to keep trying.

Outside of the doors to our suite, I stop and glance at Grendel.

"Guard us while we sleep," I instruct him. He stares at me so intently, I can almost see the understanding in his eyes. He immediately sits and watches down the hall alertly. The idea that he is guarding us brings me a certain comfort. I know he would die defending us.

As I enter our bedroom, Eva looks up from the massive bed and smiles. Her long dark red hair is draped over her shoulder, her grayish green eyes clear and bright.

"Hey," she greets me softly, laying her book down on the bed. "I was wondering where you were. I couldn't hear the piano."

"I wasn't playing," I tell her as I sit to take off my shoes. "I was talking to Damien."

Eva freezes in anticipation. "And?"

"And there is still no sign of Adrian," I tell her softly. "Don't worry, Eva. We're safe here. We've got a full staff of trained guards patrolling the perimeter of Chessarae. He might know these grounds, but he can't breach our walls without us knowing about it ahead of time. You're safe."

"It's not me I'm worried about," she says firmly as she tucks a tendril of stray hair behind her ear.

I strip my clothes off and she watches, her eyes filling with a familiar hunger. It's the same hunger I feel whenever I look at her, touch her, or listen to her. God, how I want her. Something in me has retreated from her though. It's as though a part of me thinks to shield her, to protect her from me. Or against losing me. Because something ominous hangs over our heads and I know that it will drop upon us any day.

But tonight, I shake those ugly thoughts away as I walk to the bed and slip in next to the woman I love. Whatever else we have or don't have, we do have this moment.

"I've missed you," I admit hoarsely as I fold in next to her. She looks at me in surprise, then pulls me to her.

"I've missed you too," she murmurs, her hands sliding along my back, pulling me closer. "I've missed you so much, Luca. You're here, but you're not really here. You're gone from me. I know it sounds stupid to say, but that's how I feel."

I nod, but don't acknowledge that she's right. She already knows.

"Be with me tonight," she breathes, her hands fluttering down over my chest, down to my groin, where my manhood pulses and waits. Her fingers find it and I suck in my breath before I crush my lips to hers.

"Yes," I say simply. I push her into the mattress and her legs wrap around my waist, her tongue in my mouth, her breath warm and sweet.

"Luca," she moans softly. "Touch me."

So I do. I touch her everywhere. My fingers slip into her and she arches up toward my hand. My fingers are cool as I slide them in and out, slow then fast. I know this woman. I know her scent, the way she moves, what she enjoys. There's comfort in that, a blessed familiarity. I bring her to orgasm within minutes, her breath quickening as she whispers my name.

I slide into her wetness and I groan as her warmth surrounds me, pulling me into her. I grip her hips, pulling her closer, as I delve further inside of her. My hardness contrasts with her softness, and the friction is exquisite. It isn't long until I orgasm as well, shaking as I hover above her, pulsing into her.

When I collapse onto her, she pulls me tight.

"You're staying with me tonight."

Lately, I've made a habit out of sleeping on a lounger in our sitting area. I hate to disturb Eva when I can't sleep, or when I wake with nightmares. But I don't argue tonight. I need her, too.

"Yes," I agree. I hold her until she falls asleep, her breathing soft and even. I watch the shadows on the wall move and sway, I listen to the sea crash against the shore, I stare at the moonlight slanting in on the floor.

I still can't sleep.

For hours, I can't sleep.

When I finally do, my dreams are filled with darkness.

But that is nothing new.

Chapter Three

Eva

When I wake, Luca is gone.

Unfortunately, that's not unusual. He sleeps so little now. I worry about the toll it takes on him, on his body and on his mind, but it doesn't show on the outside. The only indication is the haunted look I see in his eyes.

I swing my legs out of bed and dress quickly, pulling my hair into a low ponytail and making my way down the stairs. I pass Luca's study and peek inside the half closed door.

He's bent over his desk, intently studying something. His dark hair falls onto his brow and every once in a while, he brushes it out of the way. His hands are slender and graceful and I can't help but remember the way they moved across my body last night, fluidly, sensually, perfectly.

Only Luca knows exactly how to touch me.

Warmth floods through me at the mere memory and I squeeze my eyes closed, remembering every moment. My memories are what will sustain me, because I know Luca. I know that it will be awhile before he touches me again. He's trying to distance himself from me. I can tell. I hate it, but I know that I can't change his mind. It's something he'll have to work through on his own.

I continue on my way before he sees me, into the kitchens to grab a piece of fruit and through the back veranda to the gardens.

"Dr. Talbot, would you like coffee or juice?" A young maid, Alessa, calls to me from the doorway. As part of the new staff we hired after Adrian's treachery, she tries very hard to do a good job, to cater to our every need. I turn and smile at her.

"Not yet, Alessa. I'm going for a walk, but I'll be back. Please let Mr. Minaldi know if he asks."

She nods and hurries away and I continue about my morning walk.

Breathing deeply, I inhale the morning Malta air. Something about this place is serene and tranquil and if I didn't already know what darkness Chessarae has hidden for so long, I'd never believe it.

But I do know and so I tread lightly here.

As I walk along a cobbled path, past the stables and toward the sea, I catch a glimpse of a uniformed guard walking along the fenced perimeter. High above his head, the stone fence guards us from the outside, keeping intruders out and at times, keeping Luca in.

It is at the same time comforting and intimidating.

It makes me wary of passing over the perimeter and so instead of continuing to the beach as I had planned, I stop in an unlikely place. A dark place, a lonely place. A place I've never yet been.

The Minaldi family mausoleum.

A hundred yards or so from the trail leading down to the beach, the mausoleum is beautiful in a haunting way, nestled in a grove of trees and secluded from the rest of the estate. Stone walls stand forbiddingly, tall and dark, while ivy grows over the top. A large stone angel weeps on a boulder just outside of the door, lending a beautifully eerie feel to the entrance. I've glanced in this direction every time I walk to the sea, but I've never once stopped. I've never felt the need. But today, my mood suits it.

As I step through the doors, the air temperature immediately drops, and it picks up an earthy, mossy smell. It's cool and dark in here, and it takes a minute for my eyes to adjust to the darkness. But when they do, I glance around, breathing in the dampness and absorbing the history surrounding me.

The walls are lined with crypts, dating back a couple hundred years. Plaques with names on them are scrolled above each hinged door, each door containing the remains of a Minaldi family member, each door locked tight. I'm sure Luca has the keys somewhere, although I can't imagine why we would need them.

There is a long row of empty doors left and I imagine that someday, Luca and I, along with his brothers, will rest for eternity in here, too. The thought sends chills down my spine for some reason. Death is inevitable, but thinking of it is never pleasant.

I glance at the names. Lucien and Alessa Minaldi. Luca's namesake and the co-founder of Minaldi Shipping. It was he who bought out the Leopoldos and in doing so, brought out their need for revenge that has spanned centuries. I finger his name, wondering if he had any idea what consequences his actions would bring. I pause as I read his wife's name, recognizing that our maid shares the same traditional Maltese name.

I move on to the other names. Albert and Angelina. Alexander and Alice. Stefan and Angela. And Luca's parents, Nicolas and Melina.

I pause here, staring at the elaborate scrolling of the names. Everyone else is entombed together with their spouses. Nicolas and Melina are not.

Interesting. I know for a fact that Melina loved Nicolas long after he died, to her own dying day, actually.

And while Melina wasn't a nice person, I have to imagine the fact that she had been drugged for years had something to do with it. Still, Nicolas is entombed in a wall crypt, and Melina's is in the middle of the room, in a stone crypt that rises out of the floor. She seems vulnerable out there, alone and exposed, all by herself.

It's very curious and I run my hand along the cool stone, staring at her name.

Why would the boys have done this? Had it been Melina's last wish? I can't imagine that. But then again, it's not my business. I'm simply curious.

Alcoves in between the crypts offer lighting, so I flip a switch and the gas wall torches ignite. It's very old-world in here, very ancient. Very eerie. The illumination only serves to expose every nook and cranny of the spooky building, giving me chills. I turn the switches off and hurry back out the doors.

As I pause on the path out front, standing in front of the weeping angel, the hair lifts on the back of my neck. Every instinct in my body tells me that someone is watching me. I can feel eyes on my skin. I whirl around, looking in every direction, but no one is there.

Adrian isn't here, I tell myself. *There's no way. We're too closely guarded.*

Even still, I abandon my plans to walk on the beach, opting instead to return to the gardens. Every few steps, I look behind me, and every few steps, I see that no one is there. But the goose bumps still stand at attention on my arms and a leaden feeling still rests in my stomach.

No one was there, I insist to myself. But no amount of comforting thoughts soothe me, or ease the unsettling thought that my every move was being watched.

At lunchtime, as I push the soup to and fro in my bowl, I play with the idea of telling Luca... but when I look at his drawn face, at the way he is withdrawn and quiet, I decide against it. I'm being paranoid, imagining dark things where there were none. I don't need to add to Luca's worry.

"How's work today?" I ask politely, taking a cooled bite of bisque. Luca glances at me, smiling slightly.

"Same as always. Mountains of it, never ending piles. How was your morning? Did you contact the clinic in town?"

I stare at my food silently. How do I tell him that I don't want to start a Psychiatry practice just yet? That I'm afraid to leave him alone?

He stares at me, his eyes dark and knowing.

"It's okay," he tells me quietly. "You don't need to babysit me, Eva. I don't leave the property for a reason. I'm fine here at Chessarae."

I swallow hard. "I'm sorry," I tell him simply. "Was I so transparent? I just hate the thought of you being alone. If you need me, I want to be here."

"And so you are," he acknowledges, warmth spreading to his eyes. "I'm lucky to have you. But there is no need for you to put your life on hold for me. You have interests outside of me. Pursue those, my love. I'll still be here in the evenings when you come home."

Home. I stare at him, a myriad of feelings welling up in me.

"*You* are my home. You know that, right?"

Luca smiles, the candlelight flickering around us. "I know," he answers. "As you are mine." He stands and outstretches his hand.

"I'm not hungry any more. Would you like to walk with me?"

More than anything.

I take his hand and relish his touch as we walk the grounds, over the paths, through the flowers and by the sea. When Luca is with me, all seems right with the world. All of my worry fades away and all that matters is him. He's become my sun and I am his moon. Separate, we are strong and bright, but together, we are breathtaking.

I smile at the thought and Luca notices.

"What?"

I shake my head. "I'm just a romantic fool sometimes."

Luca raises an eyebrow as he takes my elbow to guide me around a jagged rock on the trail. This far away from the house, the grounds are not as manicured, and it would be easy to turn an ankle on the uneven trails.

"You're many things, Eva, but a fool is not one of them."

He stops by a garden of roses, blood-red and lush. Pulling a small knife from his pocket, he unfolds it and cuts a rose, slicing off the thorns before he hands it to me.

"This is the Chessarae rose. My mother grew them. She used to enter them in floral contests. They won a great deal of the time."

I bury my nose in it, inhaling the sweetness. "Thank you," I tell him. "I can see why. They're beautiful. But since when do you carry a pocket knife?"

He sniffs. "Since always. I'm as your American Boy Scouts would say…always prepared."

The idea of that makes me laugh. Luca is so refined, distinguished and beautiful. Prepared to build bonfires and pitch tents… it's just not something I can easily picture.

"Luca, you are many things, but a boy scout, you are not."

Luca shoots me an indignant gaze as I throw his words back at him. I laugh again and pick up his hand and hold it as we continue on our way, breathing in the sea air and flowers.

As we pass the mausoleum, I pause.

"I went in there today," I mention hesitatingly. "I've never been in there before and I wanted to see it."

Luca glances at me. "And what did you think?"

"I think it's a lovely final resting place," I answer carefully. "But I was surprised to see that your mom is buried separately from your father, away from the rest of the family, in fact. Is there a reason?"

Luca stills, his mouth tightening just a bit. "My brothers, Damien in particular, thought it would be appropriate. She's fortunate we allowed her in the family crypt at all. As you know, my mother wasn't the kindest person in the world. I'm not sure my father would've continued to love her had he known... had he been in his right mind."

I put my hand on Luca's arm. "But your mother wasn't in *her* right mind," I remind him. "She should be given the benefit of the doubt, don't you think? You yourself did things that you would never have done otherwise."

Luca stares at me, his gaze hard and stormy. "My mother used to tie me to my bed at night," he says harshly. "Forgive me if I can't forget that. Somewhere in me, I feel like a mother's love for her child should overcome any drug or any curse. She left me alone when I needed her the most."

Pain floods my heart at the mere thought of little boy Luca alone in the night, waiting for someone to save him, to rescue him from himself, from the dark, from the curse...from the unthinkable. But no one ever did.

"I know," I answer softly. "I know."

Luca walks away from me, toward the mausoleum with long strides and I follow him, tripping along at his heels. I don't know what he's doing and I don't ask. I do know he hasn't been here since his mother died. Before he enters, he stoops and grabs a handful of wildflowers from nearby.

He's finally going to say his goodbye to her, I decide. He steps inside, and freezes in his tracks. The horror on his face freezes me to my core and I'm afraid to look, afraid to see what put that expression there.

But I do. I nudge beside him, slipping through the door and I halt in my place, as well, my blood turning to ice in my veins.

Atop his mother's tomb, a cat has been impaled with a long switchblade. Stabbed through the heart, the little animal is lying on its back, its legs broken and hanging limply to the side, its eyes gouged out. Fresh blood drips down the stone tomb, onto the stones of the floor.

I can't seem to catch my breath and I stare up at Luca.

Someone had been here after all.

Adrian had been watching me.

He's here at Chessarae.

And this is a warning.

Chapter Four

Luca

I should be horrified. I should be alarmed. I should probably even be afraid. But I'm not. I simply feel cold inside, and I go through the motions calmly, ushering Eva back to the house and directly into my Jaguar.

"Go to Marianne's," I instruct her. "Stay there while we do a complete sweep of the property. I'll tell you when it's safe to come home."

"I'm not leaving you," she insists, her voice firm as she tries to get out of the car, her leg blocking me from closing the door. I lean down and stare into her eyes.

"Evangeline. Adrian could be here right now. He could even be in this garage. I can't have him hurt one hair on your beautiful head. I'd never forgive myself. Please do this for me."

Eva stares at me, her gaze uncertain.

"Marianne's is just down the road. Adrian is very familiar with her restaurant, as you know. He could just as easily have guessed that you would send me there and he could be there waiting."

Her theory sends my heart thumping against my ribs because she's right. It's just the kind of plan that Adrian would make. He'd target Eva to get to me.

Eva can see my hesitation and pounces on it.

"Just come with me," she pleads. "We'll leave here together while they search the property. Please."

Eva never begs and to see her do it now completely does me in.

I nod curtly and she quickly climbs over the center console, allowing me to sit in the driver's seat. I rev the engine and we are barreling down the road within a minute. As I drive, I call the head of my security.

"Oliver, Chessarae has been breached."

I quickly explain what we found and that Adrian must be on property.

"I'm taking Eva to a secure location until Chessarae has been searched. Don't call the police. As Damien explained to you, we're handling this situation ourselves. You know what to do if you find Adrian."

Oliver assures me that everything will be taken care of and we hang up.

Eva stares at me from the passenger seat.

"What is he supposed to do with him?"

I stare at the road, concentrating very hard on the blurs of the trees as we race past them.

"Nothing you want to know about," I finally answer.

She doesn't say anything, but continues to stare at me. I ignore it for a minute or two, but finally have to address it.

"What?" I ask. "You feel badly for Adrian?"

She shakes her head.

"Of course not. I just didn't expect you to acquiesce so easily back at the house. I'm happy you did, but I'm surprised that you agreed to leave with me."

I shrug. "I didn't want to. But I've dragged you into a bad situation. The least I can do is honor your wishes. You had an excellent point- Adrian is probably counting on me to send you away alone. And he might very well be waiting for you. He'll use you against me if he can."

I feel oddly detached from life right now, as the trees and the road and my life at Chessarae blur behind me. I'm not worried or afraid or even angry that Adrian has chased me from my home. I'm numb and I'm tired. The one and only emotion I have is a worry for Eva.

"The only thing that matters is keeping you safe," I continue. "If I must personally carry you off to safety, I'll do it. I'll have to trust Oliver to manage Chessarae."

"Where are we going?" Eva changes the subject, turning to stare out the window. "This isn't the way to the airport."

"No," I agree. "It's not. Adrian could just as easily be waiting for us there. Or at the ferry. We're going someplace else, someplace that no one would guess we would go."

Eva doesn't even ask where. She simply settles into her seat and leans her head against my shoulder. She doesn't complain, she doesn't whine. She simply waits to see where I'm taking her. Her trust in me is implicit. It's a knowledge that guts me because I'm quite sure I don't deserve it.

Ten minutes later, I pull into the isolated driveway of Fort St. Elmo. The abandoned stone walls fold in around us, providing an air of mystery and a haunting feeling of solitude.

Eva glances up at me. "Um. Is it wise to come someplace so isolated?"

"How do we know what's wise anymore?" I answer tiredly. "We're in a situation where we can't enlist the help of the polizia. We can't involve anyone we know because we don't want to endanger them. The only thing we can do tonight is to try and keep ourselves safe. When Adrian isn't expecting us to leave the island, we'll leave. Or we'll return to Chessarae with more security. Either way, we can't do either or those things tonight. So we'll come here. I'm an investor in the campaign to refurbish the fort as a tourist venue. Even if someone discovers us here, they won't question our presence. There are a few quarters finished. We'll stay in one."

I pull the car into a stone tunnel where we glide out of sight, down a passageway that is truly meant for pedestrians. The Jaguar doesn't hesitate, however, it just rolls over the uneven cobblestones like it was made for it.

I pull into a darkened area in front of the finished living quarters. From here, we can see tips of the granaries and the bastions in the distance, but there's a feeling of security here. We're surrounded by solid stone in a place that was built to withstand attack. If we're not safe here, I can't imagine where we would be.

As we get out of the car, Eva looks around. "What exactly is this place?"

I help her into the building, through a heavy wooden door. "The knights of Malta built this fort in the sixteenth century. It sits on twenty-eight acres and has withstood the forces of time... even with no refurbishment whatsoever. They're planning to fix it for tourist reasons."

"Adrian doesn't know you're investing in this?" Eva glances at me as we walk down an ancient corridor. With each step, the new lights come on, sensing our motion.

"No, he doesn't. This is a new project for me. I just signed on a month ago. I hadn't even mentioned it to you."

She nods, satisfied by this and I lead her into an office with an attached bedroom. The lights come on and we look around.

"This is where the foreman of the project will live," I tell her. "The project will take a couple of years to finish, so the project manager needs to stay onsite. I promise you that we'll be safe here tonight."

"I'm not worried," Eva tells me solemnly. I stop and raise an eyebrow.

"Why not?"

"Because I'm with you. Although, I do wish we'd thought to bring Grendel."

Me too. Knowing that he was here, patrolling these dark halls would be a welcome comfort.

"We'll be fine," I assure her.

The foreman's quarters are sparse because he hasn't taken residence yet, but there's a bed with linens, a kitchenette that looks like it has been recently stocked with water and non-perishables, and a desk with writing supplies.

"What shall we do to kill the time?" Eva asks as she settles into a chair at the small table. "I see some wine on the counter."

"Well, you know Valetta. We wouldn't be caught dead without wine," I joke weakly as I stride across the room to get it. "There aren't any glasses though."

Eva shrugs. "We'll share the bottle. We can pretend we're hobos."

I chuckle at the thought, then open the bottle and hand it to her. She sniffs at it.

"A very good year," she announces, waving it around. I raise my eyebrow again.

"Oh?"

She nods seriously. "Yes. Last year. The year I met you."

A lump forms in my throat but I ignore it. I should argue that meeting me might've ruined her life, but I don't. Eva takes a gulp, hands me the bottle and I take a swig as well.

"What are we going to do, Luca?" she murmurs, grabbing my fingers from across the table. "We need to make a plan. We can't live in fear any longer. We can see now that even Chessarae isn't impenetrable. We have to be proactive. We can travel to the States and get you in a clinic... we'll figure out the poisons in your bloodstream and get you de-toxed from them... we'll—"

"No."

My voice sounds cold and harsh in the quiet little room and Eva's head snaps up, her hair very red in the darkness.

"No?" She sounds stricken.

I shake my head as I stare at her, as I soak in her beauty. Even here, in this dimly lit room and ravaged by the effects of stress and little-to-no sleep, she's stunning. Her skin is luminescent, her eyes wide and clear. A decision forms itself in my gut, a hard and painful decision. I speak the words before I can talk myself out of it.

"Eva, you have such promise. You're so bright and ambitious, so full of hope and optimism. You will go on to do great things, amazing things. But you won't be able to do those with me. You can't be tied to me any longer. I'm releasing you now—and you have to go. Tomorrow, at first light, I'll take you to the airport and send you home. You have to go. You must."

Each word carves itself from my throat like a scalpel, the pain of each one etching into my flesh as though I'm cutting them with a blade. Eva is frozen, horrified. Silent.

Her pink mouth opens in a perfect O and she shakes her head back and forth, unable to even reply.

"No," she finally manages, her voice caught in her throat. "No. I'm not leaving and you don't mean it. Luca, you are my home. I already told you that. I don't want to be anywhere where you are not. Come to the States with me. We'll be safe there. We'll live happily and we'll be together. That's all that matters."

I wish I could listen to her, to believe that what she says is true, but I know that it isn't possible. For me, living happily ever after will never be a possibility.

I stare at her, meeting her gaze unflinchingly.

"Eva, you know it isn't possible, not without endangering you. Adrian is insane. He'll follow me to the ends of the earth to cause me pain and misery. The easiest way for him to do so is to target you. I know him. I know him better than anyone, and I know that's what he'll do. I'll never endanger you in such a way. I should've been less selfish and made this decision before... but I couldn't bear the thought. But now that he's breached Chessarae... what if... instead of a cat, it had been you in that mausoleum? I can't take that chance. We were lucky once. We can't tempt fate again."

Eva stands up and flutters around the room, nervously pacing.

"I can't let you make this decision unilaterally, Luca," she protests. "If I'm in so much danger, the decision should be mine. And I choose you. I will always choose you."

She looks at me in such desperation that my heart wants to voluntarily stop beating at the pain in her eyes. But it only serves to steel my determination. I must stop causing her pain. It's the only thing that is still in my control.

"That's why I'm taking the decision away from you, my love," I tell her softly. "Even now, you are in danger. Not from Adrian, but because you are isolated with me. What if I have an episode tonight... here, far from my safe room? You would be vulnerable. I could hurt you. And for that, I'd never forgive myself. We both know what the answer must be. You know it and I know it."

Eva reaches for me, her fingers cold and shaking.

"No."

"Yes."

She collapses into my lap, molding herself to me, pulling my face to hers.

"Luca, I mean it when I say that you are my life. I can't imagine living without you and I don't want to. You are my home. I'd face hell with you. I'd walk through it and fight against it... as long as you are with me. Nothing else matters. Only you. And me. Together. I haven't stayed with you through all of this only to leave you now."

She beseeches me with wet eyes, pulling my lips to hers. Hers are trembling and soft and the very idea of being away from her kills me. But the idea of keeping her in danger is equally painful.

I hold her close, allowing her to cry against my chest as I stroke her back.

"Don't cry," I murmur into her hair. "We'll sort this out. Let's not talk of it any longer tonight. Go to sleep and I'll hold you. You need the rest."

She clutches my shirt in her fingers, as though she's afraid I'll leave her while she sleeps.

"I'm here," I tell her firmly. "I promise. I won't leave you. Sleep now. Before you know it, it will be tomorrow and we'll decide what to do."

"There is no *deciding*," she insists, her voice muffled against my chest. "I know what we'll do. We'll fight through this together, like we always do."

I stay silent, but I tighten my hold on her.

Can we? Can we continue on as we are? Constantly looking over our shoulder, constantly worried that Adrian will breach our home?

I don't know that I can.

Even after Eva finally falls asleep, I stay alert, watching the door. I'll never allow him to hurt her.

Whatever it takes to keep her safe, I'll do it.

Without question.

Chapter Five

Eva

When I wake, I find Luca still holding me. His body is tense and he is alert, although his eyes are tired.

"You didn't sleep," I observe. He brushes the hair from my face with a slender hand but doesn't admit that I'm right.

"Oliver called while you were sleeping," he says instead. "There's no sign of Adrian. We can go home."

"How did he get in?" I ask as I pull away and stretch. Luca shakes his head.

"It looks like the fence might've been climbed at the front. How he got in without being noticed is beyond me. But we're installing more cameras and Oliver is hiring five more guards. It's all we can do. You and I must decide if we'll stay... or if we'll go."

"We?" I can hear the hope in my own voice. "You can see that we need to stay together?"

Luca's gaze is dark and stormy and fathomless.

"I can see that I can't bear to let you go. But I *will* keep you safe, Eva. We'll settle on a plan once we get back to Chessarae. Damien is there waiting for us. As you know, he's been hunting for Adrian. He came because I wasn't sure how long I'd need to stay away with you, and now he'll stay to help us decide what to do."

My heart leaps as I hear the resignation in his voice. He listened to me. Despite our situation, it buoys me. The sheer knowledge that he isn't giving up fills me with hope.

The ride to Chessarae is quiet and when we arrive, we find Damien in Luca's study, waiting for us.

Damien stands up and like always, I am slightly shocked at how much they look alike. Tall and lithe, dark and handsome. They could pass as twins, and they look very like their mother, with their dark eyes and hair. Damien's eyes are serious now as he kisses both of my cheeks and examines me.

"You are both fine?" he asks anxiously, looking from Luca back to me. Luca nods as he takes Damien's glass of scotch and downs it in a gulp. I sigh as I glance at the clock. It's barely 9am.

"We're fine," I tell him. "Shaken up, but unhurt. How did this happen? Where do you think he is? You see now that he's alive, right? Luca was right all along."

Damien nods, turning to stare out the balcony at the sea. "I see that Luca was right. I'm sorry I doubted you, brother."

Luca shakes his head. "I would've doubted you, if it were me. I don't know how he survived the sea that night. All I know is that he did. What matters now is what we'll do about it."

"Well, I'm here to help," Damien announces, staring at both of us. "Three heads are better than two.

Christoph can pick up our slack at work, while we're dealing with this."

Luca shakes his head. "No. I can't allow that. It's already too much that Eva is involved. I can't have you in danger, too. Go back to London. I think perhaps Eva and I will go someone else, as well. Just for now. Until we can find Adrian and put an end to this."

Damien is already shaking his head, his hand on Luca's arm. "No. The Minaldis don't run, Luca. We aren't going to let him chase us from our home. We'll face him now and finish this."

Luca stares at him, then at me. "I want nothing more. I just can't risk Eva. I could send her away alone, but I'm worried he'd follow her. He knows that to hurt her would cause me the most pain. I've got to keep her with me."

Damien nods thoughtfully. "No harm will come to Eva. Between the two of us, we'll protect her. I promise you."

I stand at the veranda doors and stare out at the property as they discuss weapons and strategy and protecting me. I feel as though I'm in a different time and place, a time in ancient history when matters had to be taken into one's own hands.

Being born and raised in the West, with all the modern conveniences of the United States, it's hard to believe that this situation is even possible. But at the same time, sequestered behind Chessarae's stone walls, it's just as easy to pretend that I live in that ancient time, back when knights still protected Malta and there was no polizia to turn to.

"Eva."

Luca's voice brings me back to the present and I turn, facing him and his brother. They stare at me with identical dark eyes.

"You can't leave the house alone," Luca continues. "You'll have to walk with a guard, or with Damien or me. Until Adrian is dealt with, none of us can ever be alone."

I nod.

Luca watches me. "If you choose to stay with me, I'm afraid you'll have to put your plans to open a practice in town on hold for now," he says hesitantly. "I don't like it, but it won't be safe for you to travel to and fro right now."

I nod instantly. "There is no *if* I stay with you," I tell him firmly. "I'm here and I'm not going anywhere."

I see the brief flash of satisfaction on his face before he hides it.

"Very well," he says finally. "We've got a plan."

We do. We have a plan to stay and hold our ground, to try and draw Adrian out, to take back our lives. A plan that will hopefully save us all.

But as I'm escorted to our bedroom so that I can take a shower, the reality of it hits me...the reality that I'm now confined to these grounds and can never have a moment alone.

Chessarae might be our home, but it's also our prison.

* * *

Chessarae might be a prison, but it's a beautiful one. I have to give it that.

I stare out from my tiny table on the balcony of my bedroom, out at the tossing sea to where the horizon just grazes the water. From further in the house, the haunting melody of the piano drifts down the halls and envelops me, calming me.

I close my eyes, letting the music surround me. With my eyes closed, I can pretend that everything is well, that my life is normal.

Just for a moment.

"You look beautiful."

Luca's voice surprises me and I snap my eyes open to find him entering our rooms.

"I thought it was you playing the piano," I say uncertainly because the piano is still playing while Luca is standing here, running his hands over my arms and up to my shoulders, rubbing my tense muscles.

"It's Damien," he answers. "All three of us play. Mother insisted on it."

I nod. Of course. Why hadn't I thought of that?

"I just spoke with Christoph," he continues. "He's joining us here as well. I wish that neither of them would come, but they're both stubborn."

"It must run in your family," I point out with a small smile. Luca glances at me, then grins.

"Perhaps," he acknowledges. "But you'd know something about being stubborn, wouldn't you?"

I shrug. Perhaps I do, but I'm not committing to it.

"Do you really think that we can beat him at his own game?" I ask quietly. "Without involving the polizia?"

Luca stares out at the water, away from me.

"I would rather just call the polizia," he admits. "I don't care if I'm punished for my part in Adrian's crimes. I just want to make sure you're safe. But Damien is adamant that we keep our name clean, that there's a way to bring Adrian down without implicating me. The selfish man in me wants that.... I want to believe that I can have you all to myself forever. That there's still a way."

I reach up and grasp his neck, pulling him down to me, breathing in the spicy scent of his aftershave.

"There *is* a way," I tell him firmly. "And we'll find it. Adrian is just a man, Luca. There will be three of you here, as well as me. He can't outsmart us all."

Luca doesn't speak, he simply pulls me to my feet and lowers his lips to mine. His are soft, yet firm, crushing mine, taking my breath, causing my heart to race.

My hands flutter up to grip him, to pull him to me.

Everything about him causes my head to spin...his scent, his strength, his piercing dark eyes, his touch.

He picks me up and carries me to the bed, laying me down gently and covering my body with his own.

"Do you love me?" he asks huskily against my neck. He pulls away and looks into my eyes. His own are such deep and bottomless wells of darkness. I feel I might tumble into them and drown.

"Yes," I tell him simply. "With everything that I am. You know that."

"Then all of this is worth it," he decides simply, pulling my back into an arch and kissing the curve of my neck, worshipping my skin with his mouth. "All of it."

He makes love to me several times, one after the other, time after time, as though he can't get enough. As though he can't breathe enough of me in, or taste enough of my mouth.

"You're everything, Eva," he murmurs to me before he finally sleeps, his body tangled with mine. "You're worth anything."

I sleep with a calm sense of well-being, filled with the love I have for this tortured and beautiful man.

I have to believe that everything really will work out for us. It's the only acceptable scenario. Luca doesn't deserve anything less, and neither do I.

Chapter Six

The small schooner bounces atop the waves, and with each harsh landing, my teeth jar. I look to Luca, who is seated with Oliver and Damien, examining the shore. He's unfazed by the rough sea, the waves don't bother him. He was born here and practically lived on the water. The roughness causes my stomach to roll, however, and I swallow hard to suppress it.

"Look there," Oliver points, his thick finger gesturing towards an inlet, his face shiny from the sun. We're a mile or so away from Chessarae now, examining ways that Adrian could penetrate Chessarae's borders. "There's a possible weakness. He could shore a boat there, and that inlet is hidden from our perimeter above. Guards wouldn't see him until he climbed over the cliffs. We can't monitor this area with cameras here."

Damien nods. "We'll need a guard patrolling this shore by boat, then. If we did it that way, the entire shore would be secure."

Luca agrees. "I think that's best," he tells Oliver. "Hire one more man."

Oliver shakes his head as he takes notes in a small tablet. He's old school and hard-headed, firm in his convictions and steadfast in his own abilities. I can see on his face that he believes we're over reacting.

"With all due respect, this is one man we're talking about," Oliver tells Luca. "One. I've already got a staff of ten. They patrol the estate like a grid, making sure that no area is left unturned."

"Yet this area is vulnerable," Luca points out. "You said so yourself."

"I only meant that we could move one of my existing men to this area. We don't really need to hire more. You want to keep your situation quiet, but the more men we hire, the more vulnerable you are to an information leak. You know how the people in town love to hear about the Minaldis."

"That's a good point," I agree. "He's right."

Damien shrugs. "Maybe so. But we don't particularly care what the townspeople gossip about. We want another man, Oliver. Just explain to them that we've recently increased security. We don't have to explain why."

Oliver doesn't agree, but he nods anyway, making a note on his pad.

"Very well," he mutters.

I tune out their conversation and turn my attention to the cliffs in front of me. Rugged and beautiful, they rise out of the sea, jagged stone that stretches toward the clouds.

The water pummels the rocks at the base, then slides back out over the sandy beach. Ebb and flow, to and fro. There isn't a trail leading up to the estate for a mile, and I don't see how anyone could climb the cliffs. I mention as much to Luca.

He glances down the beach, then pats my leg.

"Don't fret about it, Eva. While Adrian could climb the rocks if he wished, we'll get this area guarded."

"I'm not worried about it," I grumble. "And I'm not a child, Luca. You don't need to protect me from reality. I was just curious about how someone could climb these rocks."

Damien chuckles, looking at Luca, then back to me. "This one gives you a run for your money, brother. I like it."

Luca rolls his eyes. "This one would give anyone a run for their money."

They chuckle together, then Damien turns to me. "It would be easy for anyone skilled in rock-climbing to climb these cliffs. All they would need is the proper equipment and they could scale the rocks, then emerge onto our property. As you know, there is no fence on this side of the estate."

"Let me guess. Adrian is skilled at rock-climbing," I venture. Luca and Damien nod in unison.

"Adrian always liked extreme sports," Luca tells me. "Rock-climbing, sky-diving, hiking mountain trails, river rafting. He did all of it when we were younger."

"Of course he did," I answer wryly.

It takes me a minute, but I think of something else.

"If he can easily scale this cliff, then he could easily climb over the fence at any point around the estate. It is only ten feet tall."

Luca and Damien glance at each other. Oliver is the one who answers me.

"That is true, miss. But I have ten guards patrolling the property, and keeping a constant eye on the fence-line. No one will get over that fence."

"But someone did already," I remind him. "And left a nice bloody gift in the mausoleum for us."

Oliver looks away. "That won't happen again. I've increased my staff from five to ten. And I'll add another guard on the shore. You'll be safe, m'am. I promise."

"All of these promises are making me hungry," I announce to the men. "Can we call it a day and get some lunch?"

My announcement seems to lighten the mood, and Damien turns the boat back toward land, toward Chessarae's dock.

We have a light lunch on the veranda, with only Alessa serving us.

"Will that be all, miss?" she asks me as I finally push away my salad plate. I nod.

"Yes, that will be fine. I'm exhausted today. I think I'll take a nap."

Luca presses a kiss to my cheek. "I'll walk you to our rooms," he tells me. "I'm going for a jog, so I need to change."

Damien bids us a good afternoon, then turns to Alessa. "Sit," he tells her, pushing out the seat next to him. "I'm in the mood for conversation, and my brother doesn't seem to be in the mood to humor me."

Alessa flushes, but sits and as Luca and I walk away, I have to laugh.

"Even now, in the midst of all this turmoil, Damien is flirting with the maid," I tell him. Luca shakes his head.

"Damien has a woman in every country, I think," he replies. "He travels a lot, by choice. He could conduct a great deal of our business from headquarters, but he likes new places. And new women."

I glance over my shoulder, and see that Alessa appears relaxed now, as she twirls a piece of her hair and laughs at something Damien said. He's engaged, relaxed, and appears at ease for the first time since he's been here.

I'm glad. Chessarae shouldn't be filled with only anxiety and fear. It's refreshing to see laughter and flirtation within these walls.

Luca changes into jogging clothes, and after getting me settled into our large bed, he ducks back out of the room. From our bed, I can see him through the open balcony doors as he strides away from the house, then starts to jog toward the beach. Several paces behind him, two security guards follow, guarding his every move.

I find their presence both reassuring and intrusive. I hate that they're necessary, but I'm glad that someone is watching Luca's back when I cannot. With a sigh, I close my eyes and take a much needed nap.

When I sleep, and only when I sleep, the anxiety fades away.

Chapter Seven

Luca

Days seem long now.

This is something I ponder over dinner, as I look down the length of the table at Eva and Damien, as we all push our food around on our plates.

Eventually, I shove away from the table. "I'm restless," I tell them. "I'm going to the atrium."

"I'll come too," Eva tells me, immediately rising to follow. Damien glances in the direction that Alessa had just disappeared into, toward the kitchens.

"I think I'll stay a while," he replies with a small smile. I roll my eyes.

"Men," Eva mutters beneath her breath. Damien hears her and grins.

I take Eva's arm and together, we stroll the halls. I watch Eva gazing about, watching the dark corners, skirting the edges of the hall, and finally, when we reach the atrium, I set her down on a lounge and face her.

"Eva, I know this is stressful, but everything will be fine. Please don't worry. We're doing everything we can to protect you. I know you're not sleeping. I know you worry. You're not eating. You're going to make yourself sick."

She nods. "I know. It's just hard not to think about...everything."

"I know," I tell her softly. "But we'll be fine. I feel as though perhaps I've added to your burden by trying to keep things from you. I've felt all along that if I don't discuss it with you, it will shield you from the stress, but maybe it's had the exact opposite effect."

Eva looks up at me, her eyes wide. "What have you hidden from me?" she asks curiously. "I thought you'd told me everything."

"I've told you almost everything," I reassure her. "But there are a few things I left out. One thing in particular is the reason we are so diligent about the guards that patrol the grounds. We need increased security because there's more to Chessarae than meets the eye."

Eva pulls away from me now, her eyes still wide.

"Meaning?"

"Come with me and I'll show you," I answer. "You'll just have to see it to understand."

I lead her to a panel in the atrium wall and pull a small lever that is hidden by books. As the panel pops away from the wall and slides heavily to the side, Eva breathes in sharply.

"You've got to be kidding me," she exclaims as she pokes her head into the tunnel and looks around. "Seriously?"

I flip a switch just inside the doorway and the long stone hall lights up with the electric torches hanging along the way. The lights are dim, but adequate. Taking

Eva's hand, I lead her along. Grendel follows behind, his toenails clicking on the stones.

"As you know, the Knights of Malta built Chessarae," I tell her. "The torches used to be real torches, but years ago, one of my ancestors ran electricity through all the tunnels. The Knights built the tunnels as escape routes and a secret means of travel beneath the entire estate. There are more tunnels here than you could ever memorize."

Eva stares at me in shock. "It's like something from a movie," she murmurs, running her hand along the rough stone wall as we walk. "I can hardly wrap my mind around it. Where do all the tunnels come out?"

"Well, that's what I wanted to show you," I tell her. "Today, when you asked why we were more concerned about the cliffs rather than the fence... these tunnels are why. The tunnels themselves are a labyrinth. But one of them opens in the little inlet on the coast. It was an escape route that the Knights devised."

"So Adrian could, in theory, figure out how to open the tunnel door from the outside and make his way in from the base of the cliffs?" Eva's face is appalled and I can't blame her.

"In theory," I stress the word. "But in reality, it would be quite difficult. The entrance doors are very heavy, made from solid stone and concealed in the cliffs. I don't even know if he realizes it is there. But just in case, we need that area patrolled."

"Of course we do," Eva agrees. "Your insistence makes sense now. Does Oliver know?"

I nod. "We had to explain to Oliver, but not the rest of the security team. Very few people know of these tunnels."

"But Adrian knows," Eva points out as we pause in a central hub, in a place where the tunnels break apart into six separate routes. I nod again.

"Yes, he does. But he doesn't have them memorized and he hasn't been down here much. There was never a need. The only one he's quite familiar with is the one leading from my safe room in the center of the maze to my study."

Eva gasps. "We need to close that off."

"Already done," I tell her. "The entrance in my study has been barricaded with steel beams."

She nods slowly, satisfied by that. "And the rest?"

"We can't barricade them all," I tell her with a sigh. "But you'll be safe. In fact, I want to show you a place... a very safe place."

We continue walking down one of the tunnels, a narrower tunnel than the rest, and one that splits apart four times before it comes to a dead end. In the end, a small circular room waits for us.

"Did you notice how every time the tunnel split, we took the left side?" I ask. Eva nods.

"Yes. Do I need to remember that?"

"Yes," I tell her. "I don't think anyone else has found this little spot. I used to come here to be alone."

I flip a switch inside the room, revealing that it completely encircled by shelves of books. "I used to read down here, away from the rest of the world, when I needed a few minutes of solitude...when I didn't even want to be bothered by Adrian. He always knew where to find me otherwise."

Eva sits on a nearby chair and fingers the cover of an old book.

"Why did you bring me here?" she asks quietly.

I sit next to her, picking up her hand.

"In case you ever need to run, I want you to come here. I'll show you the entrances throughout the house. Each one is hidden and each tunnel leads to a center hub, which then branch out to other destinations on the property. I'll show you which tunnel to take once you reach the hub. No one can find you here but me. So if you need to run, run here. I'll always know where to find you."

Eva sighs slowly.

"As you wish," she answers softly. "But I'll never run. Not without you."

Gripping her hand tight, I stare into her eyes.

"You must promise me, Eva, that if there is a situation in which you are at risk, you *will* run. And you will *not* worry about me. I'll take care of myself, then I'll come and find you here. But if I'm distracted by worrying that you aren't fleeing the danger, that puts me at greater risk. So do you promise you'll run?"

I see the wheels turning in her head as she thinks the situation through and finally she agrees.

"Fine," she sighs. "But hopefully, it will never come to that."

"Hopefully not," I agree. "But if it does, we're prepared."

Eva is patient as I show her the tunnels that lead beneath the house, and how to find my secret library from any of the hub's tunnels. When we finally retreat to our bedroom, she curls onto her side watching me undress.

"I hate this," she tells me. "I hate worrying about you. I hate knowing that Adrian is out there and we just have to sit here and wait for him to make a move. I hate knowing that we can't do anything other than that. That we're at his mercy."

I climb into bed with her and hold her hands, clasping them next to my chest. "We're not at his mercy," I disagree. "We just have to wait for him to make a move. He's not patient. I can't imagine that we'll have to wait long."

"That makes me worry more," Eva announces, brushing the hair away from my eyes. "I wish it would just happen so that we can deal with it. I hate having it hang over our heads."

"I'm sure that's part of his game," I tell her. "He wants to make us worry. He wants us to look over our shoulders and wonder when he'll appear. He wants to make us afraid."

"This isn't a game," Eva mutters, closing her eyes and folding in against me. I wrap my arms around her, pulling her close.

"No," I agree. "It isn't. But Adrian thinks it is. Sleep now, bella. Put all thoughts of this ugliness out of your head.

"I love you," she whispers, without opening her eyes.

"I know," I answer, kissing her forehead.

I hold her until I fall asleep.

At some point, the crash of the sea against the shore wakes me and I stir, carefully pulling my arms and legs from Eva's and watching her for a moment.

In sleep, she's innocent and peaceful.

When she wakes, she'll be consumed once again with our new reality, so I'm careful not to disturb her as I slip from the bed. Since I know I won't sleep again tonight, I don't want to wake her with my restlessness.

I stand on the balcony, watching the sea for a little while, for an undetermined amount of time. Staring at it doesn't make me sleepy though, so I finally sigh and head back inside. A nightcap might do the trick, so I pull on my trousers and pad barefoot through my bedroom doors, toward my study, without bothering with a shirt. Grendel snaps his head up as I enter the hall and immediately stands.

"Stay, boy," I murmur. "Stay here and guard Eva."

He instantly drops back to his haunches, watching me nervously as I walk away. Because he is so loyal, it makes him anxious to be away from me. But I can't leave Eva unprotected.

My study is quiet and massive, empty in the middle of the night. I head straight toward the bar, and gulping down the scotch, I enjoy it as the familiar warmth spreads into my chest, warming my gut. I empty the crystal decanter, pouring a second portion into a glass. Three fingers of the amber liquid should do it and soon, I should be ready to sleep.

I settle into a wingbacked chair, closing my eyes, waiting for sleep to come. But instead of the welcome sleep, I feel the stirrings of an unwelcome sensation....the dark twinges of a drug-induced episode.

Fuck.

My eyes pop open and I lunge from the chair, determined to make it to my brother's room before I lose consciousness. Damien can keep me from hurting anyone…from hurting Eva. I have faith in that.

But the darkness comes quickly and before I reach the door, it is already overwhelming me, turning the crisp and clean lines of the room into wavy blurs and contortions of color. My sensations turn visceral and everything turns into scents and feelings.

As I sink onto the floor, I feel as though hands are on me, on my shoulders, pulling me up. I twist to look, but my vision is black. Except for one thing. Before my sight goes, my vision tunnels on one thing.

The crystal scotch decanter glimmers in the moonlight. It's empty now because I just drank the scotch it contained… mere moments before this episode's onset. A dark realization slams into me.

It was the scotch that was poisoned. It was always the scotch. As I quickly think back, I always drank it before an episode emerged. How did I not put this together before?

Even though I scramble to hold onto the last vestiges of consciousness, to get to Eva and warn her, I can't. The drugs are too powerful and they take my mind prisoner, rushing in like clouds of ink. Hands are on my shoulders, but I can't fight them off. I'm no longer in control of my limbs. All I can do is succumb.

Within a moment, all is black and lost.

Chapter Eight

Eva

The sunlight is warm as it tickles my shoulder, and I open my eyes, content in the warmth, and in the memories of last night...the memories of Luca. I remember how earnest he was when he showed me the tunnels, how concerned for my safety, and then I remember how tender he was when he held me until I fell asleep.

I stretch out my arm to find him, but his side of the bed is empty and cold. I sigh, but it's nothing new. He was probably up at dawn, not wanting to wake me with his restlessness.

I take my time getting ready, soaking in a hot bath, pulling my hair into a low chignon and dressing casually in capris and a white button-up. As I make my way into the house, various servants greet me, and as I look at all of their faces, something in me stirs and tenses.

Could one of them have assisted Adrian, allowing him onto the grounds?

The mere thought sends a chill down my spine and I would normally feel silly for being suspicious, but after Adrian betrayed Luca the way he did, I know that anything is possible. Loyalty is a hard trait to come by.

I fight to subdue the suspicion. I can't let it consume me. I can't get to the point where I trust no one.

When I enter Luca's study, I expect to find him bent over his large desk. I don't. Instead, I find Damien there, on the phone, scrawling his name on a stack of documents.

When he sees me, he hangs up immediately, smiling a greeting.

"Eva," he greets me, standing to hug me good morning. "You slept well, I trust?"

I'm not sure if he's kidding. Why would he assume I slept well, when our lives are under attack by a madman? I smile back hesitantly.

"Not as well as I once would have, but well enough, under the circumstances."

"Is Luca still sleeping?" Damien asks, pouring a glass of fresh orange juice and handing it to me. I startle, glancing up at him.

"No. He's not in our room. I thought he'd be in here. I was surprised to find you instead."

Damien shakes his head. "I couldn't sleep so I thought I'd borrow Luca's desk and catch up on some work. I haven't seen him yet. I imagine he couldn't sleep either and got up early to walk the grounds. We'll have to remind him not to go out alone. That rule doesn't only apply to you, my dear."

He holds out his arm. "We should see if he's at breakfast. And you should eat."

"I'm not very hungry," I murmur quietly. "I'd like to find Luca."

Damien nods. "Let's check in the dining room first. It stands to reason that he might want breakfast."

The dining room is empty, but for the heavily laden sideboard filled with breakfast foods and juices.

"I guess the kitchen staff got excited that you're here," I tell Damien. "They made enough for an army."

Damien smiles a bit. "Well, we should probably eat some of it so it doesn't go to waste. Why don't you text Luca and see where he is, and we'll sit here and wait for him?"

Staring at the mountains of food, I have to agree. I don't want it to go to waste and I'll have to speak to the kitchen staff about preparing such large amounts in the future. It simply isn't necessary. Even after Christoph arrives, we won't eat so much.

After loading a plate with fruit, a bagel and yogurt, I pull out my phone to text Luca. Setting my phone beside my plate, I give Damien a wry look.

"We'll have to see if he answers. He's not much of a texter."

"I know," he agrees. "It drives me insane."

I have to admit that it does me, too, so we spend the next minute or two complaining about Luca's aversion to technology. But after we've finished discussing that bad habit, and after we finish eating, Luca still hasn't appeared and he still hasn't answered my text.

Alessa comes in to clear my plate and as she does, I put my hand on her arm.

"Have you seen Mr. Minaldi this morning?"

She shakes her head. "I don't think so, miss. I might've seen him first thing this morning, walking out toward the cliffs, but I can't be sure. It was foggy."

My head snaps up. "You saw someone walking toward the cliffs? A man?"

Alessa nods.

"And did you tell Oliver about this?" I snap, instantly annoyed with the girl. I know she tries to be helpful, but honestly. It's only common sense to report such things with the situation such as it is.

She looks stricken. "I...uh. No. It didn't seem out of the ordinary. I thought it was either Luca or Damien and I didn't think twice. I'm sorry, miss. I'll make sure to not make that judgment call again."

I stare at her. "Alessa, I know it seems severe, but I also know that Oliver has discussed our situation with you. There is a man out there who is targeting Luca. Chessarae might seem secure and it *is* secure, but we have to take every precaution. If you see anything that might be unusual, report it immediately."

She nods quickly, her cheeks flushed. "Yes, m'am. I'm sorry."

I relent now, feeling bad for her. "No harm done. But if you see Luca this morning, please tell him I'm looking for him."

"Yes, m'am," she murmur quietly before she hurries off.

Damien stares at me. "Eva, I'm sure everything is fine. You need to stay calm. We'll be under stress until Adrian is found. You can't stay in a state of distress until then. Put it out of your mind and continue about your life as normal."

I return his stare incredulously. "Normal?"

He nods. "As normal as possible. You must."

I'm absolutely confounded by his ability to detach from the situation, but I shouldn't be surprised. Luca shares the same ability.

I push away from the table.

"I'm going to find Luca. Enjoy the rest of your breakfast."

I hear him sighing as walk from the room. But it doesn't matter. Nothing matters but finding Luca because deep down, I feel like something is wrong. Even though nothing is amiss around the house, the hairs on the back of my neck are at attention, chills racing down my arms. My instincts are on high alert.

The question now is why.

I search high and low. I search the house, I search the manicured lawns and the paths leading to the sea. I search the stables and the beach. It isn't until I search the garage that I find that his car is missing from its slot.

I stand still, staring at the yawning emptiness, startled and annoyed.

Luca left and didn't tell me where he was going? Now, of all times? When we're not supposed to leave the property and if we do, certainly not alone?

I'm furious.

I whip out my phone and try to call, but his phone only goes to voicemail. I try again, and once again, reach his voicemail.

"Luca," I grit between my teeth after the beep. "You can't just leave when you feel like it and definitely not without telling me. You need to call me back. Right away."

I march back to the house, fueled by indignation, and in a huff, set out poring through books in the library to fill my time. An hour passes, then two, then three. I attempt to call Luca several more times, and leave several more messages, each one more frantic than the last.

Grendel paces with me, his massive head cocking at every noise, waiting with me to see Luca come striding in the doors with a good excuse for his absence.

The problem is, he never does.

Night falls and Luca is still gone.

That's when I know that something is terribly wrong.

Chapter Nine

Luca

A buzzing sound brings me to, awakening me from a foggy sleep. I lift my head and find that my hands are restrained above me, bound in manacles attached to chains in the wall.

A wall. A stone wall, covered in damp moss. That explains the dank smell.

I force my eyes open wider and try to determine where I am. It doesn't take long.

A crypt sits on one side, a stone tomb that rises from the ground... the name scrolled across it reads Melina Minaldi. My mother.

But I'm not in the mausoleum.

I'm in the secret room beneath the crypts... the room where the gateway is my mother's crypt above. Very few people know that. No one knows that her true crypt is in this room, a room that has been secret since the Knights of Malta built this estate. A room that houses treasures that we don't wish to put in vaults at local banks. A room that currently imprisons me....along with my dead mother.

Because the existence of this room is such a secret, like so many others here at Chessarae, the likelihood of me being found is slim.

As my eyes adjust to being open, I can see my cellphone buzzing on a nearby stone, its screen lighting up and showing Eva's name. Before long, the ringing stops.

How did my cell phone get here?

How did *I* get here?

"Would you like to hear what Eva said?"

A voice comes from the shadows, a voice I've been both dreading and anticipating that I'd hear soon.

Adrian.

He steps from the darkness, his blonde hair glinting in the dim light, his blue eyes sharp and hard. His arms are thickly muscled and his footsteps fall heavily on the stones.

I don't answer him. I press my lips tightly together so I don't succumb to the temptation. I don't want to give him the satisfaction.

He picks up my phone and puts it on speaker, laying it down once again. Eva's frantic voice fills the crypt.

"Luca, where are you? You're scaring me. I love you. Call me. Please."

The desperation in her voice turns my blood to ice and I grit my teeth, trying as hard as I can to remain silent.

He studies me, his eyes gleaming with the light from the wall sconces.

"Isn't that sweet? Eva is worried about you. With good reason."

348

His tone turns icy and he towers above me. With a lightning quick hand, he coils back like a snake and backhands my face with all his strength. My head snaps back and I taste blood as pain explodes in my mouth.

But still I remain silent.

"I'll bet you're wondering why I didn't just kill you," Adrian muses aloud. "Because I could've, you know. I've watched you sleep, I've watched you jog, I've watched you living... when you should've died already. I'll rectify that oversight... but not yet. First, you need to pay for what you've done to me. Eventually, you'll beg me to die... and only then will I allow you that escape."

My heart thuds hard in my chest as I look at the expression in Adrian's eyes... the insane expression. He's not in his right mind. To him, I've wronged his family. To him, he's completely justified in exacting revenge on me for the perceived wrongdoings of my ancestors.

As I dangle from chains in this damp crypt, confined and entombed, I have no doubt that he will get it.

Chapter Ten

Eva

A full search of the property turned up nothing. I even ran through the underground tunnels, flinching at the shadows, but still I ran on, hunting everywhere I could think of. When Luca wasn't even in his secret library, I knew I wasn't going to find him. There was only one thing left for me to do.

Beseech Damien.

But now, as I face him in Luca's study, I know it's useless.

"You don't believe me," I utter helplessly, twisting my hands around in my lap as I stare at Luca's brother. Damien stares back sympathetically, but unmoved.

"Eva..." His voice trails off and he stares out the windows, away from me. "It isn't that I don't believe you. It's that I know my brother. I think he wanted to spare you the pain of this situation. He wanted to draw Adrian away from Chessarae, away from you. Surely you can imagine that of Luca. Just last night he was telling me how he felt selfish for allowing you to be a part of this."

He stares at me earnestly, willing me to believe that Luca would've left me on his own accord. I can't believe that of him. If I don't want my heart to shatter into a million jagged pieces, I can't believe that of him.

But still, I can't help but remember the night in the fort, the night he told me that he was taking me to the airport, that he was sending me home to America to keep me safe from Adrian. I'd refused. *Adamantly refused.* What if... instead of arguing with me about it, he'd chosen to leave instead?

Would he really have gone to such lengths to keep me safe?

At my feet, Grendel whines just a bit before he gets up to once again pace the perimeter of the room, his toenails clicking on the mahogany floors. He's been restless since Luca left, disturbed, and something abruptly occurs to me.

"Luca wouldn't have left Grendel," I blurt out. "I can see where you'd believe that he'd leave to keep me safe, but he'd never have left Grendel. He knows Grendel is miserable without him."

Damien's expression grows even more sympathetic and I resist the urge to punch him.

"I'm serious," I insist. "Luca wouldn't have left him."

Damien shakes his head. "Luca would do anything to keep you safe. If it wasn't convenient to take Grendel, then he'd leave him. Grendel might be a loyal pet, but he's still but a dog, Eva."

A lump forms in my throat, a hard knot that I can't seem to swallow.

"He wouldn't," I whisper limply. But to be honest, I'm not so sure.

"There's no sign of a struggle," Damien says calmly. "Trust me, we've looked. Oliver's teams have searched everywhere for any sign. They've found nothing but an empty garage stall. It appears he left on his own free will, Eva. Knowing that Adrian breached Chessarae probably drove him to this decision. My heart tells me that he left to protect you. He's my brother. If I had any inkling that there was foul play here, I'd take immediate action. But there is no sign of that. We can't overreact and bring in the polizia. We have to protect Luca's secret."

My heart breaks again at his words and I press my lips together to keep from crying. *Luca's secret.* God, I'm tired of being held hostage by *Luca's secret.* The secret that was thrust upon him through no fault of his own.

"What do we do now, then?" I finally manage to ask.

"We wait," Damien answers softly, reaching over to grip my shoulder. "I'll get Oliver hunting for him, but I'm guessing he doesn't want to be found until Adrian has been dealt with."

"But what if Adrian finds him first?" Even I can hear the panic in my voice. Damien hears it too and almost visibly flinches. I can tell he's not used to being around devastated females.

"We have to have faith that that won't happen," he answers firmly. "Eva, you should go rest. This has all been so much. You've had a shock."

A shock. That's what he calls Luca leaving me? I shake my head as I walk from the study and pad toward my bedroom. Apparently, Damien doesn't think I'm in as much danger now, now that Luca is trying to draw the danger to himself like a magnet, because he lets me walk alone.

But as I close my bedroom doors behind me, doubt floods me.

I know Luca and he would've thought this through from every angle. He would be worried that his plan wouldn't work, that Adrian would target me simply to cause more pain to Luca. If something happened to me, it would hurt him far worse than if something happened to himself. For that reason, it's hard to fathom that he would leave me here, defenseless.

Then again, he knows I'm not defenseless. I'm smart, I'm hidden behind the walls of Chessarae and his two brothers will be here to protect me if I need it.

I fall into a chair and stare at the fire in the fireplace, watching the flames flicker and spit.

I don't know what to think. The only thing I'm sure of is that Luca is gone and he took part of me with him.

* * *

One day without Luca turns into two, two into four and so on.

Each day that passes without him is empty and barren. It's as much because of the fact that I simply miss him as it is the fact that I'm afraid for him. I don't know where he is and I'm afraid for the things that I don't know... for the things that he could be facing this very minute without me.

"Eva?"

Marianne's voice is questioning and I can tell that she's said my name more than once. I bring myself back to the present and focus again on my only friend in Malta.

"I'm sorry," I tell her, reaching to fill her tea cup. "I was thinking of something else, I'm afraid."

Marianne nods, her lined face concerned. "I can see that," she says gently. "What were you thinking of? Is everything all right, little dove?"

Her endearment causes my insides to clench, aching to crumble and tell her everything, to ask for her sage advice. But I can't. Luca's very life could depend on me keeping the secret... so that Damien's men can find him, unhindered by police questioning and involvement.

"I'm fine," I answer. "Just tired. I haven't been sleeping well. But I'm very glad you have come to visit me today. I could use your good company."

She smiles. "You know I love seeing you. And I love seeing your beautiful home. It's not many people who are fortunate enough to be granted access. You've given me a golden ticket with your friendship, my dear."

She laughs and I laugh and I pretend that all is well. It's a pretense that I've gotten good at.

"How is that man of yours?" Marianne asks as she takes a bite of biscotti. "And when will the wedding be? I haven't heard you speaking of in a while."

I sigh. "I don't know when the wedding will be," I tell her honestly, skipping over her inquiry about Luca. "Soon maybe. Or maybe not. Things are rather in the air right now."

Marianne's wise eyes sharpen on my face. "Is there a reason why?" she asks quietly. "Has something happened?"

I quickly shake my head, already regretting my words. "No. Luca is just... busy. Very busy. And it's hard to carve out the time."

Marianne stares at me, studying my face, before she finally nods slowly. "Well, a wedding is important," she replies. "You'll have to get him to take the time. Chessarae will be beautiful for a wedding. And you'll be a beautiful bride."

My throat squeezes tight at her words because in my head, I'd had it all planned out. There would've been white flowers everywhere... gardenias, lilies, roses... the heady scents would carry down the beach for miles. There would've been candles in every corner and my dress would've been stunning. Luca and I would've been happier than any two people on earth.

Would've been.

Those thoughts are distant memories, however. Trite, inconsequential things in the face of what my reality is now.

"Yes," I agree with her tightly. "Chessarae will be beautiful for a wedding." For Damien's or Christoph's. Probably not for mine.

I am numb throughout the rest of our visit, going through the motions, smiling, chatting, laughing. All of it is fake and half-hearted, but I pray that Marianne doesn't know it. She's the kindest soul I've known and I'd hate to hurt her feelings.

After she leaves, I stroll the halls of Chessarae, restless and alone. And since I'm not really thinking, I find myself in the unlikeliest of places.

Melina's wing of the house.

I hesitate at the mouth of the dark hallway, staring into the dark abyss. No one has entered it since Melina's death, since her caretaker Sophia moved out and into Valetta. I'd wanted to offer her a job elsewhere in the house, but Luca had been hesitant. I think it hurt him to have someone so close to his mother near, and I could see that Sophia didn't want anything more to do with Chessarae anyway.

I can hardly blame her. She'd tolerated so much during her time here. Of course she'd want to leave as quickly as she could.

I take a step, then another, and before I know it, I'm standing in the middle of Melina's abandoned suite.

The silence is deafening. Not a thing has been moved and Melina's things are strewn about here and there. A cashmere throw is folded over the back of a leather chaise. Her slippers still sit next to her bed. Her perfumes are lined up on her mirrored vanity and I lift one to my nose, inhaling the expensive flowery scent.

I close my eyes, remembering how interesting Melina could be in her few lucid moments. But I also remember how vicious she could be otherwise.

My son is evil. He is the devil's, not mine. I should've had his nurse drown him when he was an infant.

I squeeze my eyes tighter at the memory of those words, remembering how Luca had refused to react, how his eyes had hardened... because he was accustomed to his mother's horrible claims and her vitriol toward him.

I open my eyes again. How had Luca managed to come out of his childhood as normal as he is? I don't know. It fascinates the Psychiatrist in me. With his drug-induced episodes aside, Luca has remarkably few emotional scars. At least so far as I have seen. The human mind's ability to shield itself from injury is remarkable.

Moving through her rooms, I come across a small writing desk that faces the sea. Sitting, I stare at her papers and books, my eye falling on a thick leather bound journal, embossed with Melina's monogram. Picking it up, I find myself reading the demented ramblings of a dead woman.

But it begins when she is not demented. It begins years ago, when the boys were small.

Dear Mother,

I'll never give you these letters. I want you to continue to believe that your little Melina has a happy, perfect life. But the truth is, I do not. I have no one to talk to, because I can't speak to you of this. You'd just tell me to square my shoulders and do my duty. And I will, mother. But I hate it here. I love Nicolas with all of my heart, but Chessarae is stifling. The walls close in on me, mother. And the boys. I watch them like a hawk, to see if and when one of them will develop Nicolas's curse. None of them have shown signs yet, but little Lukey was sleep-walking the other night. I had him confined to his room. I don't know what else to do. Nicolas does terrible things in the night, Mother. He can't help it and he tells me it will get worse. I wish he'd told me of it before we married.

The first entry ends abruptly here, as though Melina was interrupted. My heart pounds as I read her most innermost thoughts.

Little Lukey was sleepwalking.

Adrian, of course, wasn't old enough at that point to poison Luca. Which means that his father had not only poisoned Nicolas, but he'd also begun poisoning a little boy… setting Luca on a course that was meant to eventually destroy him. The monsters here are not the Minaldis, but most certainly the Leopoldos.

And one Leopoldo is still living, intent on finishing what he started.

The lump that has been in my throat for days returns and I swallow hard, trying to dislodge it. Closing the book, I take it with me as I hurry from Melina's haunted rooms. Her ghost might not be here, but her presence is as strong as when she was still living.

Even her presence is chilling.

Chapter Eleven

Luca

Eva's voice floats through the crypt again, through the speakers that Adrian has rigged in the corners. He plays her voicemails to me periodically, from a remote location. It's a mechanism designed to torture.

"Luca, please. Just come home. Or pick up the phone. You didn't help me by leaving. Everything is worse with you gone... I don't know if you've found Adrian, if you're safe. I love you. Please call me."

I squeeze my eyes shut, trying to will away the sound of her frustration and pain. She thinks I left her. Adrian has made sure of that.

I shift in the chair he moved me to, the metal chair that is cold against my bare back. Clad only in my trousers, the cold emanates from everywhere around me, from the very walls. It keeps me in a constant state of shivering. My arms are tied behind me, my fingers impotent after falling asleep from lack of circulation.

But a thought occurs to me. I have a pocketknife in my trousers.

If I could just tip my chair over, I could maybe knock the knife from my pocket and I could grab it. It's a long shot. But I have no other choice.

Rocking back and forth, I ignore the way the ropes cut into my hands and with a last hard shove, I sprawl onto my side.

Lying still, I listen for Adrian. The stone floor is cold against as I listen, but there is only silence.

I wriggle about, trying as hard as I can to jar the knife loose from my pocket. I strain my ears, listening for the metallic clink it would make against the floor.

It doesn't come.

But Adrian does.

His voice emerges from the dark in a roar, and before I even know where he is, he stomps on my hands, which are still bound to the chair.

I flinch, but otherwise don't acknowledge the debilitating pain. Behind the blindfold, bright shoots of light explode from my eyes, a reaction to the pain, and I squeeze my eyelids closed. Broken fingers won't kill me.

Adrian pulls my chair upright, and when he speaks again, his mouth is very close to my ear.

"If you try to escape again, I swear to God above that I will bring Eva here and kill her in front you. But I'll rape her first, and I'll make you watch. She'll scream your name and beg for your help, but you'll be helpless. Weak. She'll die knowing that you failed her."

I know he'll do it. So I won't do anything to escape. I'll sit here and I'll take whatever Adrian gives me.

For her.

Chapter Twelve

Eva

Dear Mother,

The wind that comes in from the cliffs calls to me. It beckons me. I want to end it. I want to end it all. Only Nicolas's promise that all will be well keeps me from it. Even though I know he lies.

The same wind that Melina speaks of blows across my balcony now and rustles the pages of her journal and I lay it down in my lap, looking across the lawns to the rocky ledge that leads to the beach below.

I'm only halfway through Melina's journal and it's only now that she begins to sound disturbed, the way she did when I knew her. At this point in her journal, it's still years before she died.

I don't know why I continue reading, only that I hope to learn something about her... about her motives, her mind. Perhaps even something about the Minaldi family that I don't already know. People tend to be more truthful in their journals, when they rest assured that no one will read it.

A hint of nausea wells up in me and I swallow hard, taking a drink of chamomile tea to try and soothe it. With all of the stress, my stomach hasn't handled it well. As I glance at the clock and see that it is almost three in the afternoon, I realize that I haven't eaten today.

No wonder I feel sick. Tucking the journal into my desk, I hurry down to the kitchen to find something to eat.

As I stand staring at the massive kitchen, with its huge expanse of counters, the walls suddenly do close in on me, much as Melina describes in her journal. Being confined to Chessarae does grow stifling.

On a whim, I decide to leave. Damien is gone for a few days to see to some business and Christoph is here in his place. He's out riding right now, so there's no one to report to. I slip out the back doors and head down to the beach before anyone sees me. With quick steps, I hurry toward Marianne's.

When I burst through the restaurant door, her face lights up.

"Bella mia!" she exclaims, dropping the stack of paper she was looking at. "I'm so happy to see you." She kisses both of my cheeks and motions for a waiter to bring some wine and bread.

"Come and sit," she instructs, pulling me with her to a secluded table by the windows. "What has brought you here, bella? Why do you look so sad?"

"Is it that apparent?" I murmur, grasping her wrinkled hand tightly. "I wish I could tell you. I really do. But I've been carrying around a secret and it's eating me from the inside."

Just saying that much brings me such a sense of relief, as if I'm not alone in the world any longer. With Luca gone and Damien closed away in Luca's study much of the time, I'm almost always alone. Only the burdens of the secret keep me company.

Marianne raises an eyebrow. "You can trust me with any secret, bella," she chides me. "Haven't you known me long enough to know that?"

I want to. God, how I want to. It's all become so much to bear.

My hand shakes as I take a sip of wine, then another. I look at Marianne.

"If I tell you, you have to promise to not ever breathe a word."

She glances at my face, then nods solemnly. "What is it, Eva?" she asks softly. "What has you so troubled?"

So I tell her. I don't go into the details of what Luca did and that he was involved with the girls who were murdered, but I tell her that the Minaldi's have a secret and because of the secret, Luca has left to protect me... and that I feel so alone.

"You're not alone, bella," she says simply, after I'm finished speaking. "You're never alone. I'm here for you."

She gathers me into her arms and gives me a warm hug. "You're always welcome here. If it becomes too much to bear at Chessarae, you can always come here. You can stay here until you find a place of your own, or until you want to return home to America."

I stare at her. "But see, that's the problem. Chessarae is my home now. I can't leave. I have to wait for Luca."

She shakes her head, troubled on my behalf. "But you don't know when he'll return."

She doesn't utter the word I know she's thinking.

If.

If Luca returns.

"When he does, I have to be there," I insist. "I shouldn't even be here today. Apparently, I could still be in danger, even though Luca is trying to lead the danger away."

"But who are you in danger from?" Marianna asks hesitantly. "And why can't you just go to the polizia?"

I can't tell her. "I know it sounds strange," I answer slowly. "But I can't tell you. I shouldn't have told you this much."

Marianne shakes her head. "It's fine, my dear. I'll never speak a word of this. I'm only concerned for you. You must promise me that if it becomes too much, you'll come to me."

I nod and promise, then decide I have to be getting back.

"Come see me again soon, Eva," Marianne tells me as she hugs me goodbye. "I'm going to worry about you."

"Don't," I assure her. "I'll be fine."

I set off down the beach, watching the sea, clearing my mind of troubling thoughts. What I don't know, as I walk back to the stone walls of Chessarae, is that it shouldn't have been Marianne worrying about me.

It should've been *me* worrying about Marianne.

Her body is found the next morning, washed up on the shore outside of her restaurant, her throat ripped out.

* * *

It's Christoph who tells me, and I know from the second that he steps into my suite that something is terribly wrong. His dark eyes normally twinkle, shining with a lightness that neither of his brothers have the luxury of having.

But this morning, Christoph is somber, his eyes flat, and as I look up from where I'm sitting, my heart thuds heavily against my ribs.

"Is it Luca?" I whisper, certain that the grave expression could only mean that something had happened to Luca. Christoph quickly shakes his head.

"No, there's still no word from Luca," he answers. "But... it's Marianne, Eva. She's dead. They found her body this morning, outside of her restaurant."

The shock that floods me is overwhelming and my stomach rolls in reaction. Grabbing the wastebasket next to my desk, I retch into it, not once, but twice. When my belly stops quaking, I wipe my mouth with my hand and stare up at Christoph.

"But I... It's not possible. I just saw her yesterday. She was fine." My voice sounds limp, but it's because of the shock. I feel like I've just been hit with a truck. "How?"

Christoph looks away, walking away to run a washcloth under the water in my bathroom before he returns and hands it to me. His hand is shaking a bit. That tiny thing alarms me and I press the wet cloth to my mouth.

"How?" I insist.

"Her throat was torn." His voice is low and quiet in my room and I have to strain to hear him. "She bled to death."

I suck in a breath. "Like those girls…" Christoph nods.

"But that would mean Adrian is close. He never left this area. How is that possible? Luca drew him away."

Christoph falls silent again, looking at the floor, at the wall, at his hands. "Perhaps Luca wasn't successful in drawing him away. Perhaps they're still close."

I stare at Christoph's face, at the grave expression that lingers there, the apprehension, the horror.

"You're afraid that Luca is involved," I realize slowly. "You think he might've done this."

Christoph closes his eyes, then slowly opens them. As he stares at me, complete pain floods his face, so much so that it causes me pain to look at it.

"I don't know what to think anymore. The brother that I grew up with wouldn't do any such thing. But what if Luca isn't Luca anymore? He's been poisoned for years. The doctors can't figure out how to get it out of his system. He's not in control of his behavior, Eva. I…I can't overlook the idea that he could be involved. Perhaps he's even the one who sacrificed the cat in the crypts. Maybe he's gone crazy like my mother. We have no way of knowing."

I'm already shaking my head. "No. There's no way. He didn't kill those girls before. Adrian did. And the drugs that Adrian gave him rendered him unconscious, but sexually aroused and aggressive. Adrian set him up to rape those girls. Luca didn't kill them. He wouldn't.

Adrian is still alive. It's Adrian doing this. Not Luca. Luca's not crazy."

I believe that with every fiber of my being. Thinking back to the night that we first had sex, the night Luca came into my bedroom in the midst of an episode, Luca had acted wooden and drunk. He didn't act violent. He was abrupt, he was insistent. He wasn't murderous and he certainly wasn't crazy.

"It wasn't him." I say it again, more firmly this time. "I'll never believe it and I can't believe that you would, either."

Christoph sighs tiredly. "I didn't say that I believe it. I said that it's a possibility that we have to examine. I love my brother, Eva. I would never condemn him without cause. I'm just worried that perhaps Luca knew his episodes were changing or growing worse. Maybe that's one of the reasons he left. He didn't want to expose you to danger. Since he didn't tell us his reasons, we're left guessing, and wondering the worst."

I shake my head. "Not me. I'm not wondering the worst. I know Luca. I know his heart, I know his mind. He didn't say anything to me about his episodes worsening. He simply said he was worried about the danger Adrian poses. Christoph, you have to believe me. If you don't, then no one will."

He nods slowly, his eyes ever so serious. "Damien's on his way home, Eva. We'll re-evaluate what to do."

He steps back out into the hall and I hear his footsteps as he walks away. I collapse into a heap on the bed, staring at the ceiling, still shivering with shock. And then the tears come.

I cry for Luca… because his brothers think he's gone crazy. I cry for Marianne. I cry because I know that somehow, she was killed because I went to see her. I told her a brief version of the truth and for that, she lost her life.

It was my fault.

Chapter Thirteen

Luca

Water drips somewhere, off in a darkened corner where I can't see. Adrian has blindfolded me now, cutting off my optical sensory, so I can't see anything at all.

As I sit in complete darkness, I ponder his plan.

He brought me here to the crypts, to a place where only he and I, and my brothers know about. My brothers would never think to look here for me, so Adrian knew it was a safe place.

I'm sure he chose this place specifically... knowing that it would torture me to know that I'm so close to Eva, to home, but I might as well be a million miles away.

So far, he's restrained me, broken my fingers, and blindfolded me in a room where my dead mother is entombed. He's threatened Eva if I try to escape, and he plays her frantic voicemails to emotionally torture me.

But as of yet, nothing else.

What is his end game? Why hasn't he just killed me and been done with it? I don't even know how long I've been here. Time has ceased to exist.

But perhaps that's part of his game, too. He wants me to think about it, to try and figure it out, to cut off all of my senses until I'm left hopeless and half insane. He wants me to dread my death so much that when it finally comes, it will be a relief.

I'm not going to play into his hands.

I force myself to stop thinking of it, and instead, I focus on Eva. In my head I picture her smiling at me, stretching out her hand to hold mine. I can't help but remember how often I've distanced myself from her these past weeks, to try and shield her from an inevitable bad end. If I could take it all back, I would.

I'd spend every minute I could with her, soaking in her bright smile and hopeful spirit. Every minute. Because all those other minutes were just wasted.

Something crawls over my bare foot, a spider perhaps, or a mouse. I don't even flinch. At this point, nothing matters.

Chapter Fourteen

Eva

"Three weeks, four days, seven hours. That's how long he's been gone," I tell Damien and Christoph.

They sit across from me in Luca's study, their faces drawn, their eyes troubled.

"You keep saying that he hasn't been gone long enough to panic, that we shouldn't call the polizia because we have no basis, that it could've been Luca who killed Marianne and we don't want to implicate him…. But I disagree."

Damien swirls the scotch around in his glass, a motion that pains me because it's so like Luca. And Damien looks so like Luca. Every time I look at him, a throb of pain slices through me. The way he stands, the way he walks, the way he moves.

So I've been avoiding him.

"Eva, I know you disagree. But you're distraught. We absolutely cannot call the polizia. I promise you that I'm doing all that is possible to find him. The polizia couldn't possibly do any more. Our resources are far more extensive than theirs. We will find my brother. When we do, we will find some way to help him. And because of the way we're handling it, we won't have to deal with any legal implications at that time. You'll thank me then. I promise you that."

I sigh heavily. "I understand what you're saying. I understand what you're doing and why. But what you don't understand is that you're wrong. I know Luca didn't leave me on his own. I know it. And I know that every minute that we don't act as though he was abducted rather than simply left on his own, is a minute that he could be in very serious trouble. You're still treating this as though Luca is in control. He's not. Adrian is. I feel it."

Damien blinks hard, staring at me. "I can't change our plans because of your *feeling*, Eva. As much as I respect you, we need more than that to go on. I'm sorry. I know my brother, too, and the man that I know is different than the man that you know. I feel certain that Luca is taking matters into his own hands."

"If that's the case," I attempt again, "Then why didn't he tell you before he left? If you know him so well, wouldn't he have told you his plans?"

Damien stares at me, sympathetic once again. "He knew that I would try and stop him, just as *you* would've tried to stop him. Our odds were far better when we were together than they are with him being alone."

I didn't need to hear that. My stomach churns and I press my hand on it. The stress has taken a huge toll on me. I'm constantly nauseous, unable to eat much. I'm always woozy, physically drained. Something has to change soon.

"I'm sorry," Damien adds, his voice gentler now. "I don't mean to upset you. I just need you to understand that I do care about my brother. I'm doing what I think he wants us to do."

I look away, at the wall, at the floor, at my hands. I don't know what to say now to get him to hear me.

"Eva, you look tired," Christoph points out kindly. "You really must rest. Come with me. You can lie down on a sofa in the atrium and I'll play you to sleep."

Woodenly, I accompany him to the grand and luxurious atrium and after I'm settled on a couch under a cozy blanket, Christoph seats himself at the piano and softly plays.

The music that flows from the keyboard isn't what Luca usually plays, but it's soft and melodic all the same. It reminds me of him and if I just barely stare through my eyelashes, Christoph looks like Luca playing. As his hands sweep across the keys, I pretend that they are Luca's. That all is right with the world, that Luca is here, playing me to sleep, keeping all the dangers of the world at bay.

I close my eyes, letting the music surround me, cocoon me like a soft blanket. I'm so very weary, it does feel good to rest. And in my head, Luca is here. The delusion makes me feel so good, I decide that I might just keep my eyes closed until Luca returns.

But then something occurs to me, something startling.

As my hand brushes my belly, a vague sick feeling continues to plague me. It's always there, some days worse than others. I've been attributing it to stress, but as I'd just pointed out to Damien and Christoph, Luca has been gone for almost a month.

The last time I'd had my period was two weeks before he left.

Six weeks ago.

I sit straight up on the sofa, my heart pounding as I try and think this through.

I'm on the pill, but after we realized that Luca was still having episodes, I grew distracted. I forgot to take the pill on several different occasions, and so I took two the next day.

But as a physician, I know that isn't always effective.

My hand cups my stomach and I realize that the thought that I could be pregnant makes me happy. Luca and I lost a baby before... and he'd thought that was for the best. But that was back when he still thought he had a genetic anomaly, a wretched curse that he would pass on to a child.

That isn't the case now. Any baby we have together will be beautiful and strong. I know that much. And it will be a blessing, particularly now when he's gone. I have this part of him to cling to, to dwell on. A healthy thing to focus on.

First thing in the morning, I'll go into town and get a test. But for now, I revel in the possibility. I lay back down, listening to the soft music and concentrating on the idea that I could even now be carrying Luca's child. I fall asleep with my hand splayed across my belly, protecting a child that may or may not be there.

* * *

There are two pink lines.

I stare at the fuzzy lines, my hand shaking as I sit on the side of my bath tub.

I'm pregnant. It's certain.

A particular joy wells up in me, causing tears to fill my eyes and my heart to leap. I'm carrying Luca's baby. We made a baby...a baby that will have the best of both of us.

I'm consumed with wanting to tell him, with wanting to hear his voice. So, for the hundredth time, I call his cell phone. For the hundredth time, he doesn't answer, but when his voicemail picks up, I revel in the husky sound of his voice. I memorize the sound of each word and when the phone beeps, I can't help but spill the news, my words so excited that they fall over each other.

"Luca, I don't know where you are. I don't know if you're listening to your messages. But I'm pregnant. You're going to be a father. And you don't have to worry about your baby carrying your curse...because there is no curse. This is a blessing, Luca. I only wish you were here to share this day with me. Please come home. I need you."

I hang up with shaking fingers and I stand, examining my body in the mirror. My belly is still flat, my breasts still smallish. Very soon, those things will change. But until then, I feel the need to keep it a secret, something that I can relish myself for a while.

My tiny secret.

I smile as I palm my belly, imagining the child who rests inside.

No matter what I do, I have to keep it safe. That's my responsibility and I'll take that very seriously. For now, this child is all I have of Luca.

Chapter Fifteen

Luca

Eva's pregnant.

Her words fill the tomb and despite everything, happiness leaps inside of me, regardless of my confinement and my doomed fate.

I don't know how it happened, but I'll consider it a blessing.

She's pregnant. No matter how it ends here between me and Adrian, my child will live on.

"Clever," Adrian says, stepping from somewhere in the tomb. I have no way of knowing how long he's been here since I'm still blindfolded. "Very clever. Your girlfriend is pregnant. Too bad your child will be born a bastard and will never know his father, isn't it?"

There's a satisfaction in his voice and I can feel him moving behind me, close enough to smell his aftershave.

"You know we can't let this stand, right?" Adrian asks icily. "Your line will die with you. That I promise you."

My heart stops.

"No," I say raspily. The first word I've spoken since I've been here. My throat rebels, and I cough, clearing it, then trying again. "No. Don't hurt her. She's done nothing to you."

Adrian laughs. "He speaks! The great Luca Minaldi speaks. What, pray tell, do you want to say? What could you possibly offer me to get me to leave her alone? Tell me that!"

I shake my head. "I'll give you anything. I'll do anything you ask. Just leave her be. Please."

Adrian's acidic laughter echoes through the stone room. "I love hearing you beg, Luca. Perhaps Eva has given me a gift. She's given me the one thing I can use against you. I should thank her in person."

"No!" I protest sharply. But Adrian only laughs in response.

"Eva was wrong," he utters in the dark. "The Minaldi curse is real. Your curse is *me*."

Then there's silence and I can no longer feel Adrian's presence near. He's gone.

All I can do at this point is pray that God will keep Eva and my child safe from harm. Since I'm not a monster anymore, maybe he'll listen.

Chapter Sixteen

Eva

Grendel and I walk the property, and I inhale the sea air. The saltiness of it fills my lungs and I lift my face to the sun.

Despite Luca not returning, I can't help but be filled with hope. I'm carrying a child, tucked deep inside my body, safe from harm.

Luca's child.

Every day, I make sure to walk for exercise and to breathe in the fresh air. Today, like every other, I take careful steps on the path leading to the cliffs, stopping long before I reach the jagged edge and turning back for the house. Grendel pauses at my side, his nose lifted high in the air as he sniffs.

Whimpering, he looks at me, pleading.

"He's out there somewhere, isn't he, boy?" I ask quietly, stooping to scratch the massive dog's chin. "I know he is. And so do you."

Grendel scans the perimeter, the cliffs, the trees, the English maze, the mausoleum, before he whimpers again and starts to lope down the path.

"No," I call out to him, suddenly afraid. All of a sudden, I feel like there are eyes on me, watching me. The wind swirls around me, whipping at my clothes and hair, all the while a presence lingers near. I can feel it. The hair lifts on my arms and I spin around, searching the trees, but nothing is there.

Ever obedient, Grendel returns to my side, but he still whimpers as he stands alertly, staring into the distance.

"What do you see?" I ask him quickly. "Who's there?"

Of course he doesn't answer, and I feel the need to get to the safety of the house. The last time I felt a presence, a cat was killed in my stead. Grendel stays by my side, although one time he does stop in his tracks and turn around, staring behind us.

I look too, but nothing is there.

"Come, Grendel," I urge him and he does, accompanying me into the stone walls of the house, feeling as though every step of the way someone unseen is behind me.

My feet unconsciously carry me to the atrium, where I slide back the hidden door and enter the tunnels. I pause only to close the door behind me before I run for Luca's secret room.

If ever you need to run, run here.

My feet barely touch the floor as I fly down the stone halls with Grendel at my side. I break to the left every time the tunnel splits and Grendel runs ahead, as if he knows exactly where I'm going. With a start, I realize he probably does. He's been here a hundred times before with Luca.

When I arrive, Grendel is already inside, waiting for me on his haunches as I burst out of breath through the door.

Beside Grendel, a single red rose lays on a chair, standing out starkly against the drab background of sandstone.

I suck in a breath and whirl around, but no one is there.

"Luca?" I whisper. "Are you here?"

Only silence answers me. Goosebumps raise on my arms as I stare at the blood red petals of the flower in front of me. Luca cut roses for me before he disappeared and only Luca knows of this room.

"Has he been here, boy?" I ask Grendel, absently patting his head as I pivot, looking around the room. Everything looks untouched since I was here with Luca last.

None of this makes any sense. If Luca were here, he'd come to me, especially after I'd left him the message about the baby. He wouldn't leave a flower in an unused room in the tunnels.

But what other answer is there?

I snatch up the rose and walk quickly back toward the atrium door.

When I emerge inside the house, the utter silence is startling. There is no hustle and bustle of staff, there is no noise at all. It's unsettling. Each step I take seems to echo, to carry loudly through the halls and before I know it, Damien is standing in front of me. He looks relieved to see me.

"Eva," he says, placing his hand on my elbow and turning me around. "We need to speak to you in the study."

Luca's study, I want to tell him. It's *Luca's* study. Not *the* study. But it's a childish thought, a tiny detail and so of course, I don't voice it. Instead, I follow him obediently and sit in a chair. Damien thrusts a glass of scotch at me, which of course I don't drink. I simply hold it in my hands along with the flower that I still carry.

"What's wrong?" I ask slowly, looking from Damien's grave face to Christoph's. Christoph's is filled with pain, his eyes giving him away. Something has hurt him. "What happened?"

Damien motions to my glass. "You might want to drink that."

I shake my head, alarm flooding me, causing my hands to shake so much that my drink sloshes against the sides of the glass. They are both so somber and grave, so pale and quiet.

"Just tell me," I whisper, clutching the crystal.

Damien moves to the chair next to me, reaching over and grasping my hand.

"This is hard to say," he says slowly, his eyes trained on my face. "But you need to know. Luca's car was found in the sea this morning. It washed up on the rocks down the road."

My blood runs cold as it thrums through my veins, throbbing into my temples and blurring my vision.

"No," I breathe. But that's the only thing I can say before I can't see anything more. It's too much for my body to handle and blackness overtakes me.

I don't know how long the black fog surrounds me, keeping my mind safe from overload. The human body is magnificent in the way it is self-protects. I find myself counting internally, unconsciously, as I try and swim out of the murkiness.

One.

Two.

Three.

Four.

What I'm counting toward, I don't know. But I continue to count, continue to swim. Out of the darkness, toward the light.

"Eva?"

Five.

A voice comes through the tunnel, making its way into my ears. A squeeze of my hand, a hand on my brow. Cold skin. Warm skin. Strong fingers.

"Eva?"

Six.

My eyelids are heavy, but I open them anyway. Groggy. Blurry. Pain. Luca.

"No," I say. The first word that comes from lips, wrenched from my heart by the news. "No. It can't be because he was here. He left me a rose. It had to be him."

Damien is cradling me to his chest, my legs looped over his arms. He stares down at me, as Christoph grasps my hand.

"Are you all right?" he asks quietly. "Can I set you down now?"

No, I'm not all right. Yes, he can set me down. But I can't seem to make my lips work.

Damien sets me in the chair anyway, and Christoph hovers by my knee. I sway woozily, trying to focus.

This can't be happening.

"It was only his car," Christoph says softly. "There was no body."

No body. No Luca.

My mind is a chunk of wood. Driftwood brought in by the sea and bleached by the sun. It doesn't work, it simply splinters, the thoughts that I have falling apart and lying limply in the sand.

I close my eyes.

Luca's not dead. I'd know it if he was dead. Grendel would know it.

I freeze, remembering Grendel and how he had whimpered at the wind, toward the sea.

Had he known?

I open my eyes and stare down at him, into his large golden eyes. There's an expression there that I can't read, because he's a dog and I'm not, but it seems to be pained, tortured even.

I slide from the chair onto the ground, and cling to Grendel's neck, my face buried in his fur. I don't cry because I'm numb now, numb to the devastation, to the loss.

Hands pull me away and arms carry me to my bed, placing me within the softness and pulling the blankets over me, the same hands pull the rose from my fingers. A minute later, they place it on my nightstand in a glass of water.

"Luca couldn't have left this," Damien tells me gently. "His car... Eva, it was totaled. There's just no way that he....survived. I'm so sorry."

I don't answer and Damien eventually walks away, closing my bedroom door behind him.

I'll stay here forever, I decide, as I close my eyes. I don't have to face a world without Luca in it. No one can make me.

Chapter Seventeen

Luca

"Don't be dead," Eva whispers, each painful word grating into my heart through the voicemail that she leaves. "They're telling me you're dead. But you were here. You left me a rose. And I don't feel it, Luca. Wouldn't I know if you were dead? Wouldn't my heart know? Please don't be dead. I love you. I love you."

She cries before she hangs up, haunting sobs that impale my heart, like a knife that twists and twists. I can feel her pain as if it's my own, it breathes with its own life. It is that tangible.

"You're a fucking monster," I say to the darkness.

I don't know if Adrian is here, but I sense that he is. I know for certain that I didn't leave Eva any flowers. But one person would know what strings to pull to manipulate Eva's strained emotions. One person would know what to do to extract every ounce of pain that he could, every ounce of hope so that he could eventually crush it. I know he's here, because he'd want to see my face for this particular brand of torture.

A low chuckle answers from somewhere behind me. Or in front of me. I no longer have any sense of direction, which is what happens when you're kept blindfolded for so long.

"Isn't this better than a simple death for you?" Adrian asks sharply. Out of nowhere, something brushes my face. His hand, or his arm, then it is gone. "Isn't this so much more fun?"

"For you, because you're a monster," I tell him again. "You might have the upper hand now, but someday, you'll get yours. If you think you'll get away with this, you're mistaken. My brothers will hunt you down and kill you slowly."

Adrian laughs again, a sound filled with true pleasure. "I'm not worried," he answers cockily. "If I can bring down the great Luca Minaldi, I won't worry about his brothers."

Coldness floods through me, even more so than I was before.

Eva thinks I'm dead. She's devastated and feels alone.

"I'm not dead," I whisper to her, knowing full well that she can't hear me. "I'm not dead."

Adrian laughs.

Chapter Eighteen

Eva

I lay on my side, staring from my bed at the sea... the sea that might've taken Luca from me. The moon shines on the water and I find myself taking comfort that somewhere, Luca might be staring at the same night, at the same sky, at the same stars and moon.

Damien feels sure that Luca is dead, that there can be no other explanation now for his prolonged absence, that there's no way Luca could've survived an accident like that.

Christoph would like to hope otherwise, but even he, the eternal optimist, can't dismiss the likelihood that Luca didn't live.

I can't bear the thought of a world without Luca in it.

The Polizia have been here. Something I once wanted, but now it makes everything seem so final, as the detective seemed to agree with Damien.

"I'm sorry for your loss, m'am," he'd told me. As though they had a body.

"You don't know I lost him," I answered him simply, lifting my chin into the air. Everyone looked at me sympathetically, as though I'm a grief-crazed woman with no hold on reality.

Perhaps I am.

I don't know anymore.

The rose that even now wilts in the glass next to me…I don't know where it came from. But I know that Grendel thought something was out at the cliffs, and I felt someone watching me, and then this rose appeared. Did Luca leave it as a sign that he was gone now, but that everything was going to be all right?

Is that possible?

I sigh, realizing how insane I must be.

They talked to Damien about the process to have Luca declared legally dead, a discussion that got a swift reaction from me.

"No!" I'd cried out, shocking them all with my insistence. "You can't do that yet. You don't know for sure."

And even though he didn't have to, because I have no legal say in the matter since Luca and I haven't gotten married, Damien agreed.

"We'll not talk of this right now," he'd told the detective. "It's too soon."

"When you're ready then," the detective had answered.

I'll never be ready.

I look again toward the water, the water that had supposedly taken my Love from me. It looks so innocuous, so innocent and beautiful as it laps peacefully against the shore.

I curl onto my side, my arms wrapped around my waist, shielding the baby within. I haven't yet spoken of it yet, not to Damien or Christoph. I desperately miss Marianne. She was my confidante. And because of that she had died.

My life is a vortex of pain.

Chapter Nineteen

Sunlight has the audacity to shine upon my face and I squint before covering my head with the pillow. The light is persistent however, and I can still see it from the corners, from the spaces the pillow doesn't cover. With a sigh, I throw it across the room.

Grendel snaps his head up from where he's resting the foot of my bed.

"It's okay, boy," I assure him.

He lowers his head again, resting it on his paws and I can't help but remember when I first saw him. He'd been suspicious of me. Luca didn't leave Chessarae much, so Grendel was suspicious of everyone. I've apparently won him over now, though. Or perhaps I'm just the closest thing he has to Luca... although I'm still curious that he doesn't attach himself to Damien or Christoph rather than me. They're family and I am not.

He must feel that I'm the closest to Luca. I'm certainly the only one who hasn't given up on his life.

I tighten my arms around my waist, curling onto my side, reveling in how I no longer feel nauseous.

My new doctor in town estimates that I'm sixteen weeks pregnant. I've been hiding my tiny baby bump with baggy shirts, but soon, it will become apparent. For some reason unbeknownst to me, I feel reluctant to share my news, even with Luca's brothers.

I like my little secret. I like not answering to anyone about it. Once I share the news, they'll press me for answers... for my plans. And I don't want to think about that yet.

Luca would want me to be strong. He'd also probably want me to leave this place and return to America. But I can't do that yet. Not when I'm not convinced that he's gone. Perhaps I'm in the denial stage of grief... but until I'm convinced that he's coming back to me, I'm staying at Chessarae. I feel Luca here... I feel him all around me. I feel him in the trees, in the cliffs, in the walls of his study, in our bedroom.

Pulling one of his shirts from his closet, I pull it on and button it up, remembering how he looked in it. How the chambray complemented his skin and dark eyes, how he usually wore this one out to the sea, so when he came in, I could taste the salt on his skin. I picture how his hair always fell into his eyes, how he brushed it away like it was a bother.

I open my eyes and look into the mirror. I look ridiculous. His shirt hangs to my knees. But in addition to feeling close to Luca in it, it will also help me hide my belly. And Damien and Christoph will simply think I'm being sentimental.

I pull on a pair of leggings and make my way to the kitchen for fresh juice. I don't feel like eating at all, but I make sure I do for the baby. Everything I do lately is for the baby.

Eating a bagel, I stare out the windows at the sea. Here in Malta, staring at the sea is practically a national pastime. But I have another reason for doing it. I always pray that I'll see Luca walking from it.

I know it's irrational. If Luca is still alive, it's because someone, somewhere, pulled him from the water and kept him safe. Perhaps he doesn't even know who he is. Maybe he hit his head and has amnesia. I've seen that tired storyline in a hundred different movies. It could happen.

And I could be delusional.

I know this, too.

But maybe my delusions are keeping me sane. They're all I have right now.

When I return to my room, I catch a glimpse of Melina's leather journal lying on my desk, and an idea comes to me. I need to keep my baby a secret until I've decided what I will do.

I quickly set out to find Damien... and quickly find him in Luca's study.

I quell the sense of annoyance I feel when I see Damien sitting behind Luca's desk. It isn't Damien's fault that Luca is gone. And of course he needs to step in here, to take care of things in Luca's absence. He needs to sit in Luca's chair to do it.

"Eva," Damien says in surprise, rising quickly to kiss my cheek. I turn my body so that he doesn't feel my burgeoning bump. "How nice to see you."

How nice to see you come out of your room, I'm sure he means. I shake that off and smile in return. A tight, small smile.

"Hi Damien. I'm sorry that I haven't been very social of late."

Damien shakes his head. "There is no need to apologize. This is a difficult time for us all."

"Have you found Adrian yet?" I can't help but ask. I'm prepared for the disappointment when Damien shakes his head. I'm used to that answer.

"He's like a ghost," Damien answers softly. "We'll keep looking, but... my guess is that with Luca gone, Adrian will be gone too. He has no interest in the rest of us."

"But why?" I ask suddenly. "His entire premise for revenge was based on the Minaldi family, not simply Luca. He focused on Luca for years, but now that we all know that Luca wasn't cursed, and now that Luca is...gone, what will prevent Adrian from targeting you or Christoph? Why would you think he wouldn't?"

Damien looks surprised by the question. "I don't know," he answers slowly. "That's a good question and you have a good point. It's just that we haven't seen any sign of Adrian. We still don't have any proof that he didn't die at sea. But you're right. Christoph and I should most definitely use caution. It's better to be safe than sorry."

I can see on his face that he doesn't consider Adrian a threat because he most certainly believes that Adrian is dead, too. He believes that Adrian has always been dead. That Luca went crazy and killed the cat, before he drove his own car into the sea to escape his drug-addled reality.

I blink hard to keep away the tears.

"I came to see you to ask for a favor," I change the subject. "As you know, I'm having a hard time dealing with... everything. I'd like to move into your mother's wing, at least for a while. It provides more privacy. I'd like to immerse myself in memories… in the solitude, so that I can come to terms with everything that has happened, so that I can decide how I'll move forward."

Damien stares at me, his eyes widening just slightly, before he masks his surprise. "Are you sure that's wise?" he asks hesitantly. "To seclude yourself like that… it doesn't seem healthy."

I shake my head. "I'm a psychiatrist," I remind him. "And everyone handles grief in their own way. I'll be fine, Damien. I just… my future as I thought it would be isn't going to happen. I need time to wrap my mind around that, time to think in private, to decide what I'll do instead."

Damien nods thoughtfully. "Of course," he answers quietly. "You may do whatever you like. Please consider Chessarae your home for as long as you wish."

"Thank you," I whisper.

He turns away, before he looks back at me, an uncomfortable expression in his eyes.

"Eva… we have to discuss having Luca declared legally dead. There are business implications that I must address. I know it's difficult---"

I cut him off, my heart pounding. "Please not yet," I plead. "I can't… just not yet. Please just let me pull my thoughts together. I have to come to terms with it, Damien. Please."

He nods silently. "Of course. We can discuss it again at a later date."

I am grateful that he's heeding my wishes. He doesn't have to.

I enlist the aid of a couple of maids to help me move my things (and some of Luca's shirts) into Melina's wing. When they leave, I close the double doors behind them and turn, surveying the vast quiet space that surrounds me.

It is here, surrounded by Melina's memories, that I must either come to terms with the fact that Luca is gone... or maintain hope that he isn't.

Chapter Twenty

Luca

I'm hanging again, my feet barely able to touch the floor. Every couple of days or so Adrian injects me with something to induce unconsciousness, and then he moves me to another position.

A few minutes ago, Eva's whispers filled the crypt once again.

"I call to hear your voice," she said quietly, her voice broken. "I know you aren't going to answer, but I don't want to forget what your voice sounded like. I know you're gone, Luca. Whether you simply left and wanted it to appear that you're dead, or if you're actually....*gone.* I know you're not coming back. It kills me. Every day it kills me a little more. But I have to get stronger. I have to get stronger for the baby. *Your baby*, Luca. It's a part of you. And I'll take good care of it. I promise. I love you."

Leave, I silently will Eva. *Leave Chessarae and don't come back.*

I hate the mere thought. Knowing that she's close to me brings me a small amount of comfort. But I know that sometime soon, Adrian will grow weary of his games and he'll kill me.

When he finally does, I want Eva far from here.

Chapter Twenty-One

Eva

Dear Mother,

I have a secret too. Nicolas isn't the only one. I wish I could tell you, but I can't. I can't tell anyone. I'm all alone with no one to talk to. Sophia judges me, but I'm not concerned with that. She's a servant. Her judgment doesn't matter.

Nicolas doesn't see me anymore. He comes to visit me in my rooms, but he doesn't really see me. He's consumed with his own troubles. He cares not about mine.

I suck in my breath, appalled at this newest passage in the journal, sad for her desolate state of mind. Curled up on Melina's chaise lounge, covered up with one of her cashmere throws, I shiver with the implications.

What could her secret be? And is it real? Her drug-induced dementia wavered in and out for years. It's hard to say if there was ever a secret at all. Even if there was, the fact that she secluded herself might've skewed her sense of what was important and what was not.

Looking around her quarters, where I've secluded myself as well, I can't help but ponder the similarities between Melina and I. We both loved a man tormented by demons. Those demons chased Melina, just as they chase me. But she and I handle things differently. I can earnestly say that I would never tie my child to his bed. Not ever.

But even though I know I wouldn't handle my angst and fear the way she did, I do appear to be going down Melina's road of becoming a recluse... of dwelling in my misery. As miserable as I feel, I can't do that. I can't become Melina. I deserve more than that, as does my baby.

So I rise from the couch and get dressed. Today, I'll go into town. And maybe I'll get answers about her secret. Why I care, I don't know. But it's something to focus on besides my own pain. That has to be a good thing.

An hour later, I find myself outside of Sophia's house. As Melina's personal maid for so long, I'm sure she knows far more about Melina than she's ever said.

She's surprised to see me when she answers the door.

"Dr. Talbot," she exclaims. She looks just the same. Small and slight. "It's so nice to see you."

She ushers me into her small, but pin-tidy home and situates me in a cozy chair.

"What brings you into town?"

I take the cup of tea that she offers. "You do," I tell her simply. Her eyes widen.

"I do? How is that?"

So I explain the journal that I found and the most recent entry. Sophia is clearly uncomfortable, her foot bouncing against the edge of the seat.

"You were there," I observe. "All along, you were there with Melina. Do you know what she's speaking of? Do you know her secret?"

A red flush stains Sophia's paper thin skin and she stares at me with age-clouded eyes. "Yes. I believe I do. But I'm bound by ethics not to discuss it, Dr. Talbot. I hope you understand."

I calmly take a sip of tea, nodding. "I do understand. I'm a doctor, I do understand ethics. It's just that Melina is gone. And the way she spent her last years are so interesting to me, particularly since I find myself at Chessarae, alone, like she was. I feel a certain kinship to her. I can't explain it."

Sophia's head snaps up, her eyes filled with instant concern. "You're alone at Chessarae? Where's Mr. Minaldi?"

"He's away right now," I answer quietly, ignoring the wave of pain that spreads through me at the mere thought of Luca. "And while he's away, the solitude of Chessarae is a bit overwhelming. Damien has come to stay for a while, but I don't see him much."

Sophia is puzzled now, I can see it on her face. "Damien? I don't understand. Not that it is my place to understand. Forgive my curiosity. I was a part of the household for so long that it's hard to not wonder about the family."

"I'm sure," I nod. "That's understandable. And you need not worry. The family is well. But going back to Melina. Are you sure you can't tell me anything about her secret? Was it something substantial? Or had her poor tortured mind manufactured something that wasn't there?"

Sophia looks away, twisting her bony hands in her lap. "Oh, it was there, all right. Melina's mind was tortured for good reason. Some of it was of her own making, I can assure you. But I can't tell you of her troubles. I simply cannot. It wouldn't do anyone any good at this point. Dr. Talbot, all secrets can bring are devastation. And Chessarae is filled with secrets."

That is something I already know.

As I finish my tea and prepare to leave, Sophia pauses hesitantly.

"Dr. Talbot, don't linger too long at Chessarae without Mr. Minaldi. I know it is simply a place, but Chessarae has a way of eroding a person. It is lovely, I know. But the secrets it is has kept... I've grown to believe that the secrets have tainted the very ground that Chessarae is built on. If you stay there, there's no escaping that."

Her warning causes chills to run up and down my spine.

But then Sophia chuckles. "Listen to me. I sound like a crazy old woman. Forget my words, child. Pay them no heed. Living out there with Melina has affected me more than I'd like to admit and my superstitions have gotten the best of me. Please feel free to come and visit me whenever you feel lonely. I'm an old woman and I don't get enough company. And if you visit, could you be so kind to bring me some of Melina's roses? I've grown attached to them over the years. Melina used to cut me fresh blooms every week."

I smile and hug her goodbye, but I don't forget what she said about Chessarae. How can I?

I pause at the door.

"Sophia, this might sound like *I'm* a crazy woman, but please be careful. The last person I spoke with about Chessarae died. I barely spoke of it to Marianne, and the next day, her body was found in the sea. I don't know if it was a coincidence, but just be careful. I'm sorry if coming here has endangered you in any way. I should've thought it through better."

Sophia waves her hand. "Don't worry about me, child. I lived at Chessarae for years. If it wanted me dead, I'd be dead already."

If *it* wanted her dead.

The way Sophia speaks of Chessarae, as though it is a living, breathing entity, unsettles me. Chessarae is a home, built of stone and sitting in the dirt. *It* can't hurt anyone.

But I do agree with one thing she said.

Chessarae is cursed by secrets.

Chapter Twenty-Two

The night wraps itself around me from the open window, the full moon beckoning me. The silvery light shines onto my skin and I run my fingers over my arm, playing with the shadows.

I've never heard a silence so loud as the quiet in Melina's quarters. It rings in my ears, echoes through the corners. From the window seat that Melina used to perch in, I stare down at the water, listening to the crash of waves.

Perhaps the water is what echoes through these walls, not the silence.

I'm going insane.

I worry about that.

As I stare down, a glint of red catches my eye and I focus harder on the stone pathways below. In the moonlight I see them, a lush carpet of red petals, sweeping along the stones, carried by the wind.

Where did they come from?

My heart pounds as I rise from my seat, clad only in a nightgown. I pull a wrap from the chair and open the door, padding lightly down the hall and out the back doors toward the gardens.

When I arrive on the paths beneath my windows, the stones are bare, although I can smell the distinct scent of roses in the air.

What is happening?

I look around me in confusion, but nothing is here. The breeze rustles the shrubbery, but nothing else moves. I'm losing my mind.

I must be.

The grief and confusion overwhelm me in a way I can't explain and a sudden and overwhelming compulsion to walk to the sea comes over me.

Grendel follows, his large paws padding next to me, but I barely notice. I can only focus on the moon, on the water… and the way it pulls me to it.

Making my way carefully down the trail leading to the sea, I find myself standing in front of the water, my bare feet sinking in the cool sand. The night breeze brushes my hair from my face and I breathe it in.

Looking over my shoulder, I stare up over the cliffs at the way the spires of Chessarae loom on the horizon. I can't help but shudder. I'm not sure I can face it anymore without Luca.

Mesmerized by the movement of the water, I strip off my nightgown and let it fall to the sand. Standing naked in the moonlight, I step into the water, one foot after the other. Behind me, Grendel whines, but I ignore it.

Luca has been here, in this water. It was here that his car washed ashore. If I stay here long enough, perhaps he'll come back.

I'm not lucid. I know that. The emotional stress and solitude has gotten to me. I'm still cognizant enough to know that. But I don't care. I don't care about any of it.

I sink into the tepid water, flipping onto my back and staring at the moon as the water carries me away from the shore. It's gentle, like fingers lapping at my skin.

What would it be like to float away? To simply let the sea carry me far from here, far from the secrets and pain? Is this what Luca faced? Did he give in to it? Did he simply float away from me?

I close my eyes and let the water splash gently against my face, buoying me up as the waves swell and recede.

Through the mist and waves, I hear something and I hesitate, lifting my face. My name, called from the direction of the cliffs.

"Eva!"

Sitting up, I paddle the water and look toward the shore.

It's Luca.

Striding to me, his face grave with concern, he calls to me.

My heart leaps and I swim toward shore, splashing through the shallows and pulling myself onto the sand, before I stand and run toward him, oblivious of my naked, pregnant form.

Luca stops, his face bathed in astonishment as his gaze drops to my protruding belly.

It's now that I see something I should've seen before and I stop as well, my face falling, my heart sinking.

It's not Luca.

It's Damien.

* * *

"Why didn't you tell us?" Damien asks as he holds my elbow while we climb the trail back to Chessarae.

I've dressed now, in my damp nightgown, and I stare longingly over my shoulder at the sea. I feel as though I'm walking away from Luca.

"Why didn't you tell us?" Damien asks again. I glance at him, my teeth shivering with the damp cold of the night.

"I don't know," I murmur. "It's a piece of Luca and I wanted to keep it only to myself for a while. I can't let go of Luca, Damien. I can't."

I start to cry because I can't help it and Damien stops in his tracks, his eyes wavering with a soft kindness. He pulls me to him, into his arms and holds me close, my face pressed to his shoulder.

With strong movements, he strokes my back, up and down, and lets me cry as we stand in the moonlight.

When I'm finished, he stares down at me.

"We'll take care of you, Eva," he assures me. "If that was what you were worried about, don't. Your baby is a Minaldi and we'll take care of you both."

"I wasn't worried about that," I answer honestly. "I hadn't thought of it. All I can think of is Luca. Every day, every minute."

Damien nods, sadness flitting over his features. "I know it's hard. But you have the baby to think of now. You must be strong for it, if not for yourself. Luca used to tell me that you were the strongest woman he'd ever met. You need to be that woman now, bella."

Bella.

Beautiful.

The endearment twists my heart, for it is one that Luca used to murmur to me in the night.

I put that out of my mind and nod. "I know. I will."

Damien walks me to my rooms, then pauses at the door. "You'll be fine now?" he asks, his brow wrinkled in concern. "Luca would want me to care for you. I'll send a doctor first thing in the morning."

"I've been seeing one in town already," I tell him quickly. "Dr. De Barro."

"I'll send for him first thing in the morning," Damien says firmly. "Luca would want that. You have to take care of yourself, Eva. You're too thin. You must eat. You're carrying the only thing we have left of Luca."

I nod shakily. I know he's right.

I bid him goodnight, then close the doors. My secret is out now. By morning, when my OB/GYN arrives here at Chessarae, everyone will know and my little baby will cease to be my own. It will be everyone's last tie to Luca. Perhaps that's the real reason I kept it a secret. I wanted it for myself for as long as possible.

I strip off my damp nightgown and change into one of Luca's shirts, wrapping my arms around myself as I pretend that it is Luca holding me. Burrowing into covers of the bed, I try to sleep, but I'm tormented by dreams.

By Luca's dark eyes, by his grin, by his face.

How can I let go of him, when he still dwells in my every thought, in my every action?

I don't think I can.

As I twist and turn, trying to lose myself in the oblivion of sleep, something stirs within me, a flutter. I freeze, remaining still, hoping to feel it again. A few minutes later, I do. A sensation akin to twenty butterfly wings fluttering in my belly.

My baby's first movements.

Luca's baby.

Despite everything, it flourishes within me, rising out of the sadness and grief to remind me of the world's goodness. Of Luca's love.

It's almost like a sign from Luca. *Pull yourself together for our baby, my love.* I can almost hear his voice, carried in from the sea.

I don't know if I can. But I know I have to try.

Chapter Twenty-Three

Eva

The doctor pokes and prods, then finally nods.

"All seems to be well, Dr. Talbot," he tells me in approval. "You're underweight, however. You need to make sure you eat, even when you feel nauseous."

He begins putting his things away, tucking them into his black bag. "Do you have any questions?"

I shake my head as I button my shirt. "No."

The doctor gazes at me. "You've got bags under your eyes. You're clearly not sleeping. You've got to make sure you rest, as well as eat."

I sigh, my hands dropping limply into my lap.

"They're saying Luca is dead. I feel like he isn't. It's all I can think about. I lie awake at night and all I can see is his face. What if he's somewhere and he needs me?"

My voice is small in my large bedroom and Dr. De Barro looks at me, then sits on the bed next to me.

"You can't think like that," he says gently, picking up my hand and patting it kindly. "All indications point toward the very sad fact that Mr. Minaldi perished in a car accident. There is no explanation why he wouldn't return otherwise, is there? I know it's hard, but for the good of your health, you have to stop torturing yourself. I've seen these cases before... it's very difficult to wrap your mind around a death when there is no body. It makes closure very difficult. Concentrate on whatever thoughts you need to in order to pull through this."

My voice cracks. "I feel like I'm crazy, Dr. De Barro. I see things that aren't there."

My head drops to my chest and the doctor pats my back. "You're grieving," he says simply. "It's normal for your mind to play tricks on you, for you to see things that you simply want to see. It will get better, I promise you. Day by day. Time heals all wounds, Eva."

Time heals all wounds.

Does it?

I thank the doctor and promise that I will come see him at his office later this week for a sonogram, and he leaves. Once again I am alone, with only Grendel to keep me company.

Time is my enemy now, because every day that passes is one day more since the last time I saw Luca.

Chapter Twenty-Four

"Do you want to know the sex of the baby?" Dr. De Barro asks five days later, his kindly eyes searching mine as he rolls the sonogram wand over my belly.

Do I? I'm not sure. But I nod anyway.

He smiles.

"It's a girl."

Relief floods through me, for a reason I don't understand. We don't have to worry about a boy carrying the curse anymore. But I can't deny that the relief is still there. Perhaps because I won't have a son that will likely grow up to look like his father... because every time I look at him, it would cause me pain.

It's selfish, but true.

I smile back, then get dressed when he leaves me alone.

On the way home, I stop at Sophia's to deliver an armful of roses. She's not home, so I leave them on her step. It'll be a nice surprise for her.

After dinner, I relax in the atrium, resting my hand on my belly as Damien plays for me.

"The baby enjoys the music," I tell him. "She stops moving whenever you play. I think she likes it. It puts her to sleep."

Damien pauses, his hands still on the keys. "She?"

I smile. "It's a girl. I found out today."

Joy shines on Damien's face. "A niece. She'll be a blessing. Luca would be so happy."

The mention of Luca's name brings a pain to my heart, but I promised myself, and him, the other night that I would be strong. That I would move forward for our child.

For our daughter.

Damien begins playing again and I close my eyes.

Aria. A melody, a song.

That will be her name.

I fall asleep and when I wake, I find that Damien had covered me with a blanket. That mere action causes me pain, because it's something that Luca isn't here to do.

* * *

My days are empty, and each day seems like a week. Each week brings such changes.

As I examine myself in the mirror, the shape of my body fascinates me. I run my fingers over my belly, which protrudes straight out in front of me. Although the rest of me is still slender, I can't feel my ribs anymore. Pregnancy has made my hair shiny and lush, and my skin does seem vibrant. My breasts are swollen now.

I sit with a sigh on the edge of my bed, naked, as I think about my life.

Luca isn't coming back. Everyone is right.

The pain of it is too much to bear, too much to think about, and so I've tried to block it from my mind. I've tried to pretend that it's not happening, that it's a horrible dream.

But it's not.

I'm here and he's not and soon, I'll have our baby without him.

The sea breeze kicks up and flutters the curtains, blowing them hard. I get up to close the doors, and as I do, I glance down and find Damien standing in the windows of the study, staring out at the gardens.

Before I can move, he looks up and sees me. His eyes brush over my nakedness, his face a perfect mask. I can't read it. I close the doors quickly, blocking him and everything else out.

Perhaps it's time, but I simply can't bring myself to face it...the real world.

Not yet.

Chapter Twenty-Five

Luca

How long have I been here?

I don't know.   Hours and days and weeks run together, the blackness folding in and containing me.

Once, I knew I was a child of darkness, and now that I exist in it, it makes all the more sense.

I was born for this.   Fair or not, it's been my lot in life.

Thoughts of Eva fill my mind and I focus on that. How has the pregnancy changed her? Does it make her sick? Can she eat? Has she felt the baby move?

I don't know any of these things because she hasn't called. Or if she has, Adrian hasn't played the messages.

My hope for her is that she's gone... that she has flown back to America, where she will raise my child in safety.

The thought, while it is something that I want and hope for, is at the same time something that makes me feel so alone.

Suddenly, the room seems to still, and I think I hear a voice. My mother's voice.

Semper perstant, Luca.

The words are Latin, and they are emblazoned on the Minaldi crest.

Always persist.   My mother used to whisper those words to me from time to time, in rare moments of decency.

Her crypt is in here. So of course my mind is playing tricks on me and I'm imaging things that aren't there. My mother can't be whispering to me. She's dead. It's all part of Adrian's plan, I'm sure, to drive me to the brink of insanity.

Always persist.

I hang my head and wait for whatever Adrian has in store for me next.

Chapter Twenty-Six

Eva

I'm in the atrium when he approaches, quietly and hesitantly, clearly not sure if he should disturb me.

I smile. "Hi Damien."

I've not mentioned the day that he stared up and saw me naked on my balcony. There doesn't seem to be a need.

"Hi," he answers. "May I speak with you a moment?"

His face is so serious, so grave, that I'm instantly on edge, and even though I pat the seat next to me, my arms feel like wood.

"Of course," I manage to answer. "Do you have news?"

Damien shakes his head. "No. But I do have to discuss a few things with you. I've been waiting for the right time, but there doesn't ever seem to be one."

I stare at him nervously. "Now is fine," I assure him. Although I'm sure it's not.

He sighs. "Eva, we have to talk about the future and what we will do. I know that Luca intended on marrying you, but unfortunately, you didn't wed before

417

he... died. There is no legal paperwork declaring you his heir, and so Minaldi Shipping will pass to Christoph and myself."

The way he phrases this as new information surprises me and I raise an eyebrow, closing my book.

"Doesn't it already belong to you? All three of you?"

Damien shakes his head. "Luca didn't tell you? He owned Minaldi Shipping, solely and completely. Our father, believing that he'd passed a curse to Luca, felt consumed with guilt, and to assuage that guilt, he willed the company to Luca. It carried the stipulation that Christoph and I should be granted permanent executive positions. Luca didn't want to run the company and he knew that I did, so he named me CEO."

Shock covers me in waves.

"All of this is his?" I ask softly, staring around the room. "I thought he shared it with the two of you."

"And he did," Damien agrees. "Luca felt that our father was wrong to solely will everything to him."

"So, he left everything to you?" I ask curiously.

Damien shakes his head. "Luca didn't have a will," he admits. "My father's will specifies that if something happened to Luca, the company would then go to Christoph and me."

"That makes sense," I nod. "You deserve it."

Damien smiles a tight smile. "I don't know about that. It's simply a birth right. But the birth right I'm concerned with now, is that of your daughter. She's a Minaldi, Eva. And she deserves her place in the family."

I'm confused and I tell him so.

"Eva, I've thought a lot on this lately. And I think this is the right thing to do. Marry me. Let me raise Luca's baby as my own. It will solve many things... she won't be born a bastard, she'll be taken care of by her rightful family. Luca would want it, Eva. He's been gone for months. He wouldn't want you to face the world alone."

He stares at me intently, seriously. And I'm bowled over by shock. And I'm appalled.

"No," I breathe. "I can't. Luca."

Damien's face softens and he takes one of my hands.

"Luca's gone, Eva," he says gently. "You have to think of the future. You could go back to America and raise the baby there, but is that fair to her? To deny her the rightful place in her family? Her culture? Her heritage? Just think on it. Many people get married for reasons such as this, and eventually, they even come to love each other. I respect you as a sister. And someday, perhaps that will develop into more. I would venture to say that a mutual respect is not a weak cornerstone for a relationship."

I literally feel sick to my stomach, but I desperately try to conceal it as I flounder, as I stutter to find my words.

"Damien... I....this is unexpected. I think that you've taken your role of caretaker for the family very seriously for so long that you think you need to be *my* caretaker. That isn't the case. I'm more than capable of taking care of myself."

"I know you are," he agrees. "But if you choose to leave Chessarae, you'll have to face reality and go back to work... and it might be too soon for you to do that. If you remain here with our family, you can re-enter the world at your own leisure, after you have come to terms with everything that has happened. I won't expect you to be a true wife to me... not yet. I simply want to provide for my family, which you and your baby are part of. Let my family take care of you, Eva. It's what Luca would've wanted."

"I can't," I whisper, trying to ignore the rushing sound in my ears. All I can see in my head is Luca's face. I can't get past it. I know that I never will.

"Just think on it," Damien tells me firmly. "Christoph and I spoke this morning. We agree that the time has come to declare Luca officially gone. We must do this for business reasons, as well as personal. We truly must find some sense of closure, Eva. And so must you."

For some time after Damien leaves, I stare blankly at the windows, trying to formulate thought, to gather my emotional strength to process this. I can't.

Instead, I get to my feet, a feat that is becoming more and more difficult with each passing day as my stomach grows. I slip inside the secret tunnels and wind my way around to Luca's room.

When I enter the damp solitude, I collapse into a chair.

"I can't do this, Luca," I whisper to the silence. "I can't. I can't stay without you here. I can't marry Damien."

The thought makes me sick to my stomach. The very idea of saying wedding vows to anyone other than Luca makes my heart rip into two.

But what about Aria? Is it selfish of me to flee to America? To raise her alone, without knowing her Minaldi family?

I am limp as I think of my options.

"Give me a sign, Luca," I plead. "Wherever you are, please. If you're really gone, give me a sign. Anything. Leave a rose in my room. Just let me know, somehow, that I should give up on you. That you're really gone. Please."

The air around me seems to still, and the hair raises on my neck. "Luca?" I ask softly. Of course there is no answer.

There's no one there. I'm alone.

Yet even still, later in the evening, after I retire to my rooms after dinner, I almost expect to see a dark red rose on my bed.

I don't.

My bed has been turned down by a maid, the crisp white sheets bright. There isn't a red rose in sight.

Chapter Twenty-Seven

Luca

I open my noise to a sound, although why I bother, I don't know. I still wear a blindfold.

"Are you ready to see, Luca?"

I remain silent, refusing to answer Adrian. His taunts and tortures have grown tiresome.

I hear a rustle, then feel pulling against my blindfold. A second later, it falls away and I squeeze my eyes shut. Even the dim light in the crypt is too much for my sensitive eyes to bear.

"Go ahead. Take your time," Adrian taunts. "When you're ready, look in front of you."

I don't want to. But I know that regardless of whether I do or don't, Adrian will make sure I know what he wants me to know. After a minute, I open my eyes, allowing them to adjust to the light.

In front of me, hanging on the stone, are two things.

A clock, and a dry-erase board with a large number three drawn on it.

I stare at it for a moment, then look away.

"Do you want to know what it means?" Adrian asks, barely containing the glee in his voice.

"No," I answer. "It doesn't matter."

"Oh, but it does," Adrian sneers. His expression makes his face ugly. "It's a countdown to your death, old friend."

I startle, staring at him for a minute, before I look away yet again. "Like I said, it doesn't matter."

Adrian chuckles, a hoarse sound. "If it really doesn't matter to you, then I was right to do it this way. I was supposed to kill you immediately. But I thought it would be so much more gratifying to do it this way. And I was right, like always."

His words echo through the crypt and I focus on them, on a handful of them. I stare up at him one more time. "You were *supposed* to kill me?"

Adrian stills, then refocuses. "That was my plan," he clarifies. "But I changed it. That's my prerogative."

"I guess it is," I answer slowly, but his phrasing still bothers me. *I was supposed to kill you immediately.*

Adrian watches me, a knowing expression on his face. "Fine. I have a secret. You have three days to figure it out before I kill you. But don't worry. Even if you don't guess it, I'll tell you. It'll be fun."

I try to deaden my heart, to stop the curiosity that runs rampant through me. I don't want to know. It doesn't matter.

"I've done as you asked," I point out. "I haven't tried to escape. Do I have your word that you will leave Eva alone?"

He laughs once again. "I don't think it's me that you should worry about." With a flourish, he pulls out a photo and holds it in front of my face.

At first, I think it's a photo of me and Eva embracing, and fury runs through me that Adrian got so close to us. But then I realize that the photo isn't of me. It's of Damien and Eva. Eva's in her nightgown, her face buried in Damien's chest, his arms wrapped around her.

"He's comforting her," I manage to say, although I can't ignore the hurt that shreds through my heart. Adrian smirks.

"If that's what you want to believe."

He knows that I don't know what to believe, that I've been entombed in this crypt for weeks, that I have no idea what is going on above me. He's counting on that to bring me pain.

"You're a monster," I remind him. He smirks again.

"Thank you."

"It's not a compliment."

"If that's what you choose to believe," he shrugs. "Either way, you've got three days, friend. Do what you need to do. Say your prayers, count your blessings, whatever you want. Just prepare yourself."

He walks away, up the stairs that lead out of the crypt and I stare at the whiteboard in front of me. The number three mocks me.

Once upon a time, the number was innocuous. It meant a long three-day weekend. Or half of a half-dozen. Or a lucky number.

Now that it means I have seventy two hours left to live, it has new meaning.

But I'm still numb. And oddly, all I can think of is the picture in my head of Eva in Damien's arms. Given my surroundings and my circumstances, it shouldn't hurt me. Yet it does.

She's better off with him, I tell myself. *He won't hurt her like you will.*

My jaw clenches at my own thoughts. In three days, this will all be over and Eva will be free to live a life that doesn't involve pain. Damien can raise my child and it will grow up happy and strong.

In the darkness of the crypt, I try to convince myself that that's all that matters.

In the darkness of the crypt, the large number three mocks me.

I close my eyes, wishing for the blindfold.

Chapter Twenty-Eight

Eva

I walk with Grendel again. It seems as though that's all I do nowadays. I can't begin a practice in town when I'd just have to take a maternity leave when the baby is born. That doesn't make sense.

But the walls of Chessarae close in on me, so I walk outdoors, in the flowers, in the sun, toward the sea.

Grendel stays right by my side, night and day. He refuses to leave it. Even when I take long baths at night, with flickering candles surrounding me, he sleeps by the bathroom door, waiting for me to emerge.

It seems as though he's worried about me, as well. Everyone is worried. Damien, Christoph, my doctor. They needn't be. My baby is my priority. I'll do anything to keep her healthy, even if that means moving forward when I don't want to.

I've told Damien that I'll give him an answer by the end of the week, and although everything in me says that the answer should be a resounding no, I've promised to weigh it from every angle and to think of the baby's wellbeing.

Aria's wellbeing is my foremost thought, always.

Grendel suddenly takes off running, down the paths, toward the cliffs, but instead of continuing on the

THE MINALDI LEGACY

current trail, he veers to the right, down the path leading to the mausoleum.

Rushing toward it, he pauses at the door, staring back at me, beckoning me to join him. Shaking my head, I follow his steps, reaching him after a few minutes.

"What's wrong, boy?" I ask quietly, trying to avoid looking at the building. I hate it. I hate the building, hate the walls, hate knowing what it is, when I know that Luca should be resting within. But we have no body. Until we do, he can't rest in his rightful place.

Grendel just whimpers, his eyes sad. It's as if he knows that Luca belongs here. The knowledge tears at my heart.

I don't have a pocketknife like Luca did, so I can't cut roses. Instead, I pull a handful of wildflowers from the ground and enter the building, ignoring the way the chilled air lifts the hair from my arms. Carrying the flowers, I set them down on top of Melina's crypt, directly above her name.

As I do, I catch sight of the empty crypts along the wall. With wooden steps, I walk to the one next to Nicholas, trailing my hand along the cool metal of the door. There is no plaque on this one, for as of yet, it is empty.

But it belongs to Luca.

Sliding to the stone floor, I close my eyes. I've got to move forward. I have to let go of him. It's been months. If he were alive, he'd come back to me. Damien and Christoph are right.

He's gone.

I pull out my phone.

There's one thing left for me to do.

Say goodbye.

Chapter Twenty-Nine

Luca

I stare numbly at the number two in front of me as I listen to her beautiful voice.

"I love you, Luca," Eva tells me through the phone. "I'll always love you. Every day, every hour. But I know now that you aren't coming back to me. If you could, you would. I have to wrap my mind around the fact that you're gone and allow you the peaceful rest that you deserve. Wherever you are, whatever comes after death, I hope my unrest hasn't disturbed you. I hope that you haven't been tormented by my grief, that it hasn't somehow held you to this place when you should be somewhere beautiful and empty of pain."

She pauses, and I hear her sniff. When she speaks again, the tears are evident in her voice. I grip my fists tight as I listen, unable to do anything else.

"Our baby is a girl, Luca. I'm going to name her Aria, because when I think of you, besides your beautiful face, I think of the music that you used to play for me. Back when you played me to sleep, you allowed me to think that nothing would ever harm me... that you would always keep me safe. I know that wherever you

429

are, you'll keep me safe, Luca. You'll watch over Aria and me.

"Rest easy, my love. You'll have no more torment, no more tears, no more curse. You can walk easily and lightly. I know that I promised you once that I would save you. And I really tried, Luca. I tried so hard. But there comes a time when a person has to let go... and I am. I know you would want that.

"I'm here in the mausoleum now, leaning against what will be your final resting place. When I get back to the house, I'll talk to Damien about getting your name put on it. Even though we don't have your beautiful body, you deserve a place of your own, a place where I can bring Aria to talk to you. I feel you here, Luca. I know I'm imagining it, but I feel you here. It's almost as if you can hear me. If you can, know this.

"I love you. I'll always love you. And I'll make sure Aria knows what a wonderful man her father was. You'll live on forever in her, I promise. I won't call you anymore. I'll let you rest in peace. You deserve it. Peace at last, my love."

She hangs up, and finally, I'm not numb. The tears streak down my face, falling onto my bare chest. Eva is above my head right now, so close, yet so far away. I could scream out her name, and it's possible that she might hear me, but to do so would endanger her life. Because my hands and feet are still bound and I'd be unable to protect her. Adrian would run upstairs and effortlessly kill her. And with her, my daughter. There's nothing I can do but let her walk away.

So I do.

The pain.

God, I can't take the pain. The pain in her voice, the pain I've put her through, the pain that threatens to rip me apart.

"Just kill me now," I tell Adrian. "Today."

He laughs. I knew he was here, hidden in the shadows.

"Not yet, friend," he replies. "My fun isn't over yet. You've got two days remaining to guess my last secret."

"I don't care about your secret," I tell him harshly, through gritted teeth. "Last or otherwise."

"Oh, but you will," Adrian says knowingly. "Chessarae is a house of secrets. And this is the best kept of them all."

Chapter Thirty

Eva

My soul feels so wounded, so numb.

Acknowledging that Luca is truly gone was harder than I ever thought possible. Damien and Christoph had hugged me and cried with me, but I know they were relieved. Since I'm choosing to move on, it gives them permission to move on, as well.

I haven't told Damien no yet. But I will. When the week ends, I'll tell him no and I'll pack my things and leave for America. If I can't have a life with Luca, I don't want a life with anyone.

For now, I balance Melina's journal on my knees. I've been so preoccupied with my own pain, that I've forgotten to explore her secret. It grew unimportant to me. But today, I need a distraction. So I'll finish her journal. Surely, it will finally give me an answer.

I read page after page.

Her lunacy is apparent by three-fourths of the way through. Much of her writing doesn't make sense. But one entry gives me instant pause.

He still doesn't know, mother. He'll never know now. He came to me last night, saying such terrible things about Benjamin. Benjamin, the only one who has been kind to me. I

*couldn't let him continue, so I told him the truth. He exploded
in a rage that he couldn't control. I couldn't let him hurt my
boys. So I killed him, Mother. And now he'll never know.*

My breath leaves my body and my blood runs cold.

So I killed him, Mother. And now he'll never know.

Melina killed Nicolas to protect her sons? Why?
What could the secret possibly be that it would incite
Nicolas to hurt his own sons?

I've got to know.

And there's only one person who can tell me.

Thirty-five minutes later, Sophia twists her
handkerchief around and around in her hands as I
question her.

She's uncomfortable with my questions, but I'm not
merely curious now. Melina admitted to killing Nicolas,
and Sophia knew about it and concealed it. That's a
criminal action.

"I didn't have a choice," she insists to me, her voice
small. "It was already done. Exposing the truth
wouldn't have made a difference. So Benjamin and I
moved Nicolas out to the secret room, the one under the
English Garden, and made it look like a suicide. It was
for the best."

"You knew the Benjamin that she speaks of?" I'm
startled by this. Sophia nods.

"Of course. Benjamin worked for Nicolas—his
personal assistant."

Realization slams into me.

"Benjamin Leopoldo? Adrian's father?"

Sophia nods again. "He was a very nice man. He
spent a lot of time with Melina throughout the years. I

433

was grateful for that. Nicolas kept to himself and neglected her. Benjamin was kind to her."

Something about her tone causes my eyes to narrow. "How kind?"

Sophia looks away.

"How kind?" I press again.

"It's not really polite to talk about," she tries to hedge. But I don't allow it.

"Did Melina and Benjamin have an affair?" I ask incredulously. "She wasn't in her right mind half of the time. He was taking advantage of her. That wasn't kind, Sophia. That was predatory."

Sophia shakes her head. "It wasn't like that, Dr. Talbot. He cared for her. He came and saw her when no one else did. Half of the time, she thought he was Nicolas, and the other half, she didn't care. All she cared about was that someone could see her. She felt so invisible most of the time. Benjamin gave her that gift... the gift of someone *knowing* her."

I stare at Sophia, astounded and in total shock. "I can't believe this. When I saw Melina, all she ever talked about was how much she missed Nicolas. I would never have guessed she was unfaithful."

Sophia turns away, her slender shoulders hunched. "Things are not black and white, Dr. Talbot. Melina did love Nicolas. But he betrayed her, too, you know. He betrayed her by leaving her alone, by letting her shoulder the darkness that the Minaldi name brings. Surely you can see that."

"What I can see is that the Minaldi curse is real," I announce quietly. "It seems that the Minaldis always end in pain and treachery. I didn't believe Luca when he insisted that it was true, but he was right all along."

Sophia nods, smiling a small smile. "I'm glad you realize it, dear. Too often, westerners don't believe in such things. And that is exactly when the very things that they sneered at will turn up and bite them."

Her tone gives me pause and I set my tea cup down.

"You almost sound as though you admire it, Sophia. This horrible string of luck that the Minaldis seem to have. It's nothing to admire."

"Everything is a matter of perspective," she shrugs. "What *you* fear, I admire as a way that karma triumphs."

"Karma?" I lift an eyebrow, uneasy at the turn this conversation has taken. "What does karma have to do with Melina's secret? She betrayed her husband. The secret ends there. Karma has little to do with that."

Sophia laughs. "I don't know what is funnier, Dr. Talbot. The fact that you don't believe karma had anything to do with Melina's pathetic life, or that you think the secret ends there. My dear, that's where the secret *began.*"

Sophia's face turns dark and chills once again run up my back, lifting the hair on my neck at her eerie expression.

"What do you mean?" I ask slowly, keeping my eyes trained on her face. It's hard, because my vision has turned a bit blurry. The lines fade in and out. My cheeks feel flushed and hot, my palms sweaty.

What the hell? I struggle to focus as she continues.

"It means that her secret begat secrets, doctor. Her indiscretions with my husband bore fruit...two sons.

435

Sons that even now bear the Minaldi name, but they are certainly not Minaldis."

I can barely stay conscious now, the blurry lines of her face blending together and I sway into her, unable to stay upright.

I've been drugged.

"Your husband?" I say stupidly. "Two sons?"

"For a doctor, you haven't been that smart," Sophia says acidly. "For instance, you've never once asked my last name. It's Leopoldo. Benjamin was my husband. Melina bore two of his sons, Christoph and Damien. When Nicolas found out, he flew into a rage and he was disposed of. Luca was the only true Minaldi. He's been taken care of and my dear, his line must die with him."

Shock is the only thing I'm conscious of as I slump into her, as I breath the scent of her jasmine perfume, so like the scent Melina wore, perhaps even the very same.

I curl my hands around my belly, impotently trying to protect my daughter from Sophia's evil intentions. She laughs.

"That won't help, my dear. But truly, this isn't personal. I rather liked you."

I try to stay conscious, but I feel myself fade. Amid the blackness, I hear her voice as she speaks to someone, presumably on the phone.

Adrian.

Words.

Fuzzy sounds.

The thoughts that I focus on before I slip away are terrible ones. Adrian isn't dead after all. And Damien and Christoph are Leopoldos.

Chapter Thirty-One

Luca

As I'm staring at the number one on the dry-erase board in front of me and listening to the clock tick, a rustling noise snags my attention. Footsteps, a muffled voice, a scraping noise on the stone.

It's strange, because Adrian is always silent when he approaches the crypt.

The door slides to the side and Adrian enters, along with Sophia. Behind him, Damien carries Eva, her legs dangling limply from his arms. I'm at first ecstatic. My brother has found me.

But then I notice the strange expression on his face. He's not surprised to see me here. And he doesn't look happy.

"What the..." Words escape me, but I'm flooded with emotion. But then I'm furious and I find my tongue. "Why did you bring Eva here? Why didn't you call the polizia?"

Damien looks away and I try to wiggle my hands free from the restraints, but months of being confined has made me weak.

Adrian laughs. "He thinks you're here for him," he says to Damien. "How sweet."

I'm confused as I look from Adrian, to Damien, to Eva, who is even now dangling from his arms, her belly swollen with my child, her eyes closed.

"What's going on?" I ask slowly, when Damien doesn't respond to Adrian. "Damien? What's wrong with Eva? Is she all right?"

Sophia motions to the top of my mother's crypt. "Put her here," she tells Damien. My brother does as instructed and doesn't answer my question, and no one finds it strange that Sophia is directing my brother.

"What are you doing here?" I ask Sophia acidly. "You were told never to return to Chessarae."

"Oh, I know," she answers. "But I don't answer to you anymore, Luca."

I stare at her harshly.

"So who *do* you answer to?"

She glances at Damien. "Him. We all answer to him."

Her words slam into me like a concrete wall, her implication clear.

My brother betrayed me.

Chapter Thirty-Two

Eva

I open my eyes at the sound of voices, and my sight is still blurry. I feel drunk. It's hard to move, my limbs heavily affected by whatever drug Sophia gave me in my tea.

Struggling to focus, I look around a dark room. I'm lying on a large stone rectangle, surrounded by dark and blurry faces.

"Eva?"

The familiar voice breaks through my fog.

It isn't possible.

I blink my eyes hard and re-open them, refocusing.

I see Sophia's slight form. Next to her, I see Adrian. Then Damien. And seated to the side, a shadowed form is seated in a chair. It looks like his feet are tied. And his arms are pulled behind his back.

But the face... the face that turns up toward me in the dim light of the room is unmistakable, even though it's impossible, the chiseled jaw and the dark eyes.

"Luca."

The word escapes my lips in a rush and he smiles, gently, beautifully, sadly.

439

"You're alive."

The words are limp, not reflective of my happiness at all. My heart thuds against my ribs. This can't be happening, but it is.

Luca is here. He's alive.

But Adrian is here. And Damien. And Sophia drugged my tea.

"What's going on?" I manage to ask, trying to sit up. The dizziness won't let me though, it holds me down with chemically induced restraints. "What you are doing?"

Adrian laughs, glancing at Damien. "I can't believe you brought me this prize, brother."

"Brother?" Luca repeats hesitantly. But Damien cuts him off, glaring at Adrian.

"And I can't believe you defied me, *brother*. Your instructions were quite clear. Get rid of Luca and drive his car into the sea. You weren't supposed to keep him alive for your own pleasure."

"Damien," Luca says slowly. "What is this?"

"Your mother... she betrayed your father with Benjamin Leopoldo," I say simply. "Christoph and Damien are his, not your father's. You're only half brothers... and they are not Minaldis."

"But that... that's impossible," Luca breathes, staring at his brother. "You've planned this for so long? Why? What have I ever done to you?"

"You were born a Minaldi," Damien says bluntly. "And Nicolas willed controlling interest of Minaldi Shipping to you, instead of me as the first-born."

"But you weren't *his* first born," Luca says hesitantly, as if he's trying to comprehend the betrayal. "You weren't his."

"But he didn't know that," Damien answers coldly. "And he still willed the company to you."

"But I let you take over the CEO role," Luca replies. "Wasn't that enough? I never wanted it. Any of it."

"That's because you're weak," Adrian interjects. "Kill him, Damien. He deserves to die."

Damien turns, fixing a cold stare on Adrian. It's an expression that I've never seen on his face before, one of abject cruelty. It causes the breath to freeze on my lips.

"He deserved to die when I said he should die...months ago. I don't take to disobedience well, Adrian. When you told me of all of this... of how you were my half-brother, I agreed to participate, but my participation was contingent on one thing. I was to run the show. You were to obey me. And you haven't. You could've jeopardized everything that we worked for. That won't happen again."

Moving quickly in one deft move, Damien pulls a gleaming silver gun from his suit jacket, and without hesitation, shoots Adrian in the head, a silencer muffling the noise. Adrian falls to the ground with a perfect hole in the middle of his forehead.

I stare in shock as Sophia screams, and hurls herself at Damien. Things seem to happen in slow motion, a likely effect of the drugs they gave me. Things blur together in sounds and colors.

Sophia's screams split the air, long and shrill.

She slams into Damien, and he sprawls into his mother's crypt at my feet, arms and legs flying, head cracking against the stone. There's a struggle and I hear Sophia's wrist crack as Damien breaks it.

She cries out, then there's a shot.

Sophia crumples to the ground, blood flooding the area around her, pooling on the floor. Her hand is outstretched, mere inches away from Adrian's.

Mother and son are both dead and Damien lies limply, trying to regain his bearings. He touches the back of his head and his fingers come away bloody.

"I'm sorry you're here, Eva," Luca tells me earnestly, pulling my attention away from the scene in front of me. "I'm sorry you've been brought into any of this. It's my fault. I wanted to keep you safe from it. I tried."

"I know you did." My words are whisper soft in the crypt. "You weren't dead. You were never dead."

Slowly, I slide from the crypt I'm sitting on. My legs are wobbly beneath me, but I somehow make it to Luca. Collapsing to the floor, I hug his legs, staring up at him.

"I can't believe you're alive," I tell him weakly. "They wanted me to believe you were dead. I fought that off for so long, but I had to give in. I had to face reality... that you were gone. And all along, you weren't."

"Oh, he will be soon enough," Damien tells me, watching us with interest. "I can't let him live, Eva. Just as his baby can't live, either. I *am* sorry that you have to die, but surely you understand. You're just collateral damage, my dear. I was truly planning to marry you, to raise your child as my own. I didn't want more blood on my hands. You can thank Sophia for this."

"She's dead," I point out unnecessarily.

"And you shall join her soon enough," Damien says tiredly. "You can thank her then."

I grip Luca's legs, feeling his warmth. "I love you," I tell him. "No matter what. I was never going to marry Damien."

"I love you," Luca answers, his voice husky and sad. "Close your eyes, Eva. You don't need to see it."

See what? I turn to find Damien's gun pointed at Luca's head.

"No!" I scream, trying to get to my wobbly feet. "No!"

Just as I reach him, as I grab his arm, a snarling roar fills the chamber and a beast of an animal flies through the air, crashing into Damien.

Grendel.

Damien flies backward into the wall, but the loyal dog's snarls and growls are silenced by the muffled sound of the gun. The dog falls limply to the side, blood pooling around him on the stone.

I can't breathe as I see that Damien's throat is ripped from side to side, in a jagged dog bite. His eyes drain quickly of life, until they stare lifelessly at me, the darkness in them so like Luca's.

Grendel lies still, his chest shuddering slightly. I collapse next to him, oblivious of the blood that soaks into my clothes and saturates my skin.

"You're a good boy, Grendel," I tell him, stroking his head. "Such a good boy. How did you get in here?" His golden eyes are wide open, staring into mine, pleading with me as he whimpers.

He glances at Luca and whimpers again.

"He wants you," I tell Luca limply. But I know there's no way Luca will be able to walk, not after being tired to a chair for so long. So I gently pull Grendel's shoulders until he's resting next to Luca's legs.

"I'll find something to cut your rope," I tell Luca.

"My pocket," he tells me. "I have a pocketknife." I find it quickly and then cut through Luca's restraints. His arms fall limply to his sides while I cut the ropes holding his legs.

I pull him to the ground with me as he rubs at his arms, trying to get the circulation going.

Grendel whimpers and Luca rubs his head.

"You're a good boy," he tells him softly. "The best boy. Rest now. You've earned it."

Grendel closes his eyes and rests his massive head against Luca's knee, exactly where he loves to be.

After a few minutes, Grendel's chest stops shuddering and he breathes in tiny breaths, but Luca doesn't acknowledge it. He continues to stroke the dog's head.

"Rest now," he tells Grendel again.

Looking up, I notice that that a separate doorway is open behind us, a secret door. It's where Grendel came in.

"How did he open that door?" I ask in confusion. "It's solid stone. There's no way he could have."

Yet he did. Somehow. And if he hadn't, Luca and I would be dead this very minute. I drop my head onto Luca's shoulder, still in shock.

"I thought you were gone," I tell him simply, leaning into his side. "I thought you were gone."

I cry, in shock, in sadness over Grendel, and in happiness that Luca is still alive, as I slump into Luca. He pulls me close, his arms shaking with the effort.

"Everything is going to be all right," he tells me firmly. "It's over. We'll be okay now, I promise. I love you, Eva."

"I love you too," I tell him, my voice shaking.

Time falls away and we lie together for what seems like hours, surrounded by the treachery in Luca's life... and the loyalty. By his half-brothers, by his dog. Their blood blends together on the floor and still we remain, unable to recover from our shock enough to get up.

But we love each other. And we're both alive. At the moment, that's all that matters.

Chapter Thirty-Three

Eva

I don't know how long we lie together before a voice calls through the darkness, startling us.

Alessa timidly steps into the crypt from the open tunnel doorway.

"Eva!" she exclaims, running to my side, kneeling to help. When she sees Luca wrapped in my arms, her eyes widen.

"Oh my god," she cries. "Luca. I'll call for help."

She sprints from the room, and comes back a few minutes later.

"Help is on the way," she tells me, as she skirts around Sophia, Damien and Adrian, around the blood on the floor.

"What happened?" she asks in confusion. "Are we safe? Should we run?"

"We're safe now," Luca tells her. "There's no reason to run. Not anymore."

I hold his hand as we wait, and Alessa sits with us. A thought occurs to me and I turn to her.

"How did you know to look for us here?" I ask. "No one knew of that tunnel. No one except Adrian and Luca, I think."

Alessa's face is pale.

"If I tell you, you'll think I'm crazy," she answers hesitantly. I wait for her to continue, which she does with a sigh.

"It was rose petals," she tells me. "I've never seen anything like it. I was cleaning your rooms and I saw rose petals on the floor, blowing down the hall. I followed them, and they led me here. But when I ran back to call for help, they were gone."

She stares at me, her face pale.

"What's happening?"

Goosebumps form on my arms as I look at Melina's crypt, rising from the ground and sealed in stone. Luca and I look at each, and there is confusion in his eyes.

But he doesn't know about the roses I saw myself… the rose that gave me hope, and the roses on the path. The roses that I thought I'd imagined in my grief.

Melina's roses.

I look back at Alessa. "I don't know," I tell her honestly. "I think that sometimes, there are just things that we don't understand."

And sometimes the things that we don't understand, they understand more than we know. Perhaps a mother, even one who is dead and gone, knew that her son needed help and she found a way to bring it to him.

The thought gives me chills.

Luca's hand is warm and I hold it until help arrives, until my goosebumps have gone away, until they wheel us out on stretchers to help and safety.

Chapter Thirty-Four

Luca

"I don't want it," Christoph insists, staring out the windows toward the sea. "I'm not a Minaldi. I don't deserve it."

"You're my brother," I tell him firmly. "You didn't know what Damien was doing. You didn't know any of it. You're a Minaldi in every way that counts. Please. Trust me when I tell you that I don't want anything to change."

"How can you trust me?" Christoph asks hesitantly, turning to stare at me. "After all of the betrayal in our family, how can you trust that I knew nothing? That I don't even now plot against you?"

"Are you plotting against me?" I ask calmly, staring into my brother's innocent eyes.

"No," he says clearly. "I'm not. But how do you know?"

"Because I know you. I've known you since you were born and I used to carry you around Chessarae like a doll. You've always been the brother born of light, while Damien and I were born of darkness. I just didn't know it of him. But I know you. And I know that every thought you have is true."

Christoph's face crumples and he hugs me tight. "You're my brother," he tells me. "In every way. I'm loyal to you. I don't care who my true father was, I'll never be a Leopoldo."

"I know."

"What will we do about the polizia?" Christoph asks. "They've been here five times since the other night. They want answers. We can't hold them off very long."

"Seeing as how I just came home from the hospital today, I'm sure they'll be back tonight. But the answer is easy. Since Damien wanted so very much to be me, he can be me."

Christoph lifts his eyebrows. "Come again?"

"I'm finally going to tell the polizia the truth. Only instead of explaining how it was me that Adrian used as a pawn in his violent crimes, I'll simply explain that it was Damien. That they killed each other in a final fight. It will finally be over."

"Will the polizia accept that as truth?" Christoph asks, his face uncertain.

"I believe they will," I answer. "Damien was as involved in this as anyone. They will have no reason to doubt."

Christoph nods and I step back. "I'll talk more with you later. For now, I should find Eva. I want to make sure she's resting."

Christoph smiles and I stride from the room.

I find Eva exactly where she said she would be, resting in the atrium, waiting for me.

"Hi," I say softly, staring down at her. Even after her ordeal, she's beautiful. Her skin glows with her pregnancy, her eyes clear and bright.

"Hi," she answers, patting the seat next to her. "Can you sit with me?"

"I'd sit with you forever, if you wanted," I answer. She smiles.

"Words," she sighs.

I sit.

"Actions," I answer. She smiles again.

"I'm glad you're home," she tells me, snuggling into my shoulder. "I'm glad... about everything. But I'm so sorry about your brother. I'm so sorry that you've gone through what you have."

"Don't waste your energy on that," I tell her, picking up her hand. "It's over now. The doctors say the drugs have left my system. There won't be any more episodes. I'm finally free of it, Eva. We're free to be together, with our little family, without fear of what I might do. That's all we should focus on now."

I pull her close, gathering her into my chest. Her shoulders are so slight, even now when her belly is full with my child.

"Did you talk to the vet?" Worry hangs on her every word and I rub her back.

"Yes, this morning. Grendel is doing well from surgery and he's going to be fine, Eva. You can stop worrying over him."

She nods, settling against me, her body soft.

"Is everything all right with you and Christoph?" she asks quietly, her fingers laced with mine.

"Yes," I answer. "Everything is fine."

I mean more than just my relationship with Christoph and Eva knows it. She looks up at me.

"Will we stay here?" she asks hesitantly. "Chessarae has brought you so much pain. If you want to leave, I'll go anywhere you'd like...so long as we're together."

I smile down at her, tucking a red tendril behind her ear. "I'm never leaving you again," I tell her. "You can count on that. And as far as Chessarae... it's the people who have brought me pain. Chessarae is just stone, Eva. We'll air out its demons and all will be well. This is our home, and it will be Aria's home, as well. We'll make it a happy place."

As I stare over Eva's head, at the rolling green of the grounds and the gardens and stones and cliffs, I have no doubt that I'm right.

We'll make it a happy place.

Wherever we are will be happy, as long as we're together.

Chapter Thirty-Five

Eva

The halls are dark as I make my way from the kitchens, where I just ate three cookies and drank a glass of milk, to the atrium, where Luca is playing the piano while he waits for me.

I try not to shirk away from the shadows lurking in the halls. Adrian can't hurt us anymore. And Damien is gone. We're safe.

I repeat that as I walk around another shadow.

We're safe. We've been safe for two weeks now, as we've settled back into normal life, as Luca has regained his strength from being restrained in ropes for so long. He's resilient though, and he's strong. To look at him today, you'd never know that he'd been held captive.

A minute ago, I'd received a text from him, something that made me smile since he doesn't like to text.

Come to the atrium. I'm waiting for you.

When I walk in, he looks up and his fingers stop moving. The silence is tranquil as he smiles, and only then do I see a priest sitting on a chaise lounge next to Luca.

I'm confused as I smile. "Hello, father," I greet him. Then I turn to Luca.

"What's going on?"

He gets to his feet, slender and refined, and pulls me to him, staring into my eyes.

"Remember how you told me that you'd walk to Hell and back with me?"

I nod. "Of course."

"And so you did. You walked to hell and back. And we're still standing here today. Together. Only one thing could make my life more complete, Evangeline."

He stares down at me, his dark and stormy eyes so intent, so focused. So beautiful. With his finger, he brushes my cheekbone, tucking my ever-errant hair behind my ear.

"Marry me," he whispers into my ear, his voice warm as his lips graze my skin. "Marry me tonight."

I stare up at him in shock. Over the past two weeks, we've not said a word about a wedding. We've simply focused on resting, on healing, on being together quietly and happily.

Marry me.

His face is open, vulnerable. He's laying himself out there for me, offering himself to me. And I think about his life... how he's so beautiful and kind. And how the people closest to him have betrayed him, have rejected him. His own mother when he was a child, then Adrian and Damien.

He's used to devastation. He's used to treachery. I have to make him accustomed to beauty and truth and loyalty.

"Yes," I answer softly. Then more firmly. "Yes."

Luca smiles radiantly as he pulls me into his arms and hugs me, my belly pushing between us. He laughs, palming it with a large, slender hand.

"Aria will be born a Minaldi," he tells me. "All will be well and right. If you want a larger wedding after she's born, you can have it. You can have whatever you want."

I shake my head. "I don't need a larger wedding. I don't even want it. I just want you."

The priest smiles at us, approaching quietly.

"Would you like to say your vows in here?"

Luca looks at me, raising an eyebrow. I glance at the windows and see the magnificent full moon hanging in the sky.

"Let's do it outside, under the moon and stars. While you were gone, I used to stare at the windows, imagining that at the very least, we were staring at the same moon."

Luca flinches at the memory, at the thought that he left me, even if it was against his will.

But he recovers and smiles. "Very well. We need some witnesses anyway."

Witnesses? I don't ask and soon enough I realize what he's talking about as we make our way to the center of the English Maze. Statues of Greek gods and goddesses surround us in a circle, their stone faces looking down upon us.

I turn my back on the one in the middle, Hades, because he guards the secret entrance of Luca's safe room...the room that Luca used to contain himself during episodes. As soon as possible, I want that room destroyed.

But instead of focusing on ugliness, I focus on happiness. Grendel followed us out and now he sits to the side on his haunches, fully recovered from his gunshot wound.

"Do you, Evangeline Micah Talbot, take this man, Luca Alexander Minaldi, to be your lawfully wedded husband? To have and to hold, through sickness and health, through richer and poorer, for as long as you both shall live?"

The priest fades away, and all I can see is Luca.

The man standing before me is radiant and healthy and strong, and bathed in the moonlight. No more monsters lurk in his eyes, no more secrets. And I have no doubts.

"I do," I say firmly, clearly.

Luca smiles.

The priest repeats the vows for him, which Luca utters quickly and concisely. He slides a beautiful ring onto my finger, the large emerald diamond sparkling as bright as the stars.

"Then I now pronounce you husband and wife. You may kiss the bride."

Luca pulls me to him, careful not to crush my belly, and kisses me thoroughly.

The priest eyes the statues around us wryly. "Ladies and gentlemen, gods and goddesses, may you be the first to receive Mr. and Mrs. Luca Minaldi."

I giggle and Luca scoops me up, striding back to the house with long strides.

"Thank you, father," he calls over his shoulder.

"I'll just see myself back to the house," the priest answers limply. I giggle again.

Luca doesn't even falter as he carries my pregnant form up the grand staircase and down the hall to our suite. He deposits me carefully on the bed, then kneels in front of me, slowly unbuttoning my shirt.

When his fingers are finished moving, I'm naked.

Luca stares down at me, an expression of utter appreciation and love in his eyes.

"I've never seen anything more beautiful," he tells me softly and his voice is so sincere as he runs his fingers over the curve of my belly, over the sides of my swollen breasts, up to my face. He cups it, pulling my mouth to his and then he consumes me.

He consumes me.

Every bit of me. Gently, thoroughly, lovingly.

Perfectly.

He touches me as only Luca can, as only he knows how to do.

When we have stilled, and our legs and arms are entwined and damp with sweat, he rests his head on my shoulder.

"Mrs. Minaldi," he whispers. "You're mine. Finally. When I was closed away in my mother's crypt, I thought I'd never see you again. I knew it was for the best, that you should be safe, but it tore my heart to pieces. The mere thought of being apart was torture, but to actually experience it was the seventh ring of hell."

As always, whenever I picture Luca tied up in that dark, damp place, my heart rolls in my chest.

"I hate imagining you there," I tell him painfully, squeezing my eyes closed. "I hate it. I hate knowing that all along, you were on the property. I walked past that mausoleum every day, Luca. If only I'd listened to

Grendel whimper. He knew, I think. He whined every day, every time we passed. I didn't know."

"You didn't know," Luca answers firmly. "There's no way you could've. Adrian chose the place for that very reason. He wanted to torture me with your close proximity, in a place he knew no one would think about or even remember. But don't think of it. It's over. It's all over."

He holds me tight and I close my eyes, imagining our future instead of remembering our past.

Our past is tragic and ugly, but our future is beautiful.

Chapter Thirty-Six

Luca

"I just need your signature on these final copies of your statement," the detective tells me as he stands in front of my desk. As he speaks, his gaze roams over my things... over the heavy furniture, the thousands of books, the antiques that sit on the shelves.

"Of course," I say politely, accepting the file folder from him and opening it, glancing at the paragraphs on the page.

The black and white words sum everything up, the reality that the police now believe. Damien had conspired against me, Damien had worked with Adrian and had helped cover up Adrian's violent acts against the women in town. Then they had disagreed over money matters and had killed each other in a final conflict.

I sign my name boldly at the bottom in a scrawl. I don't even feel guilty. Damien and Adrian put me through hell. My part in their treachery was never my own. It was theirs. I finally believe that I don't deserve to pay for it.

"Will that be all?" I ask the detective. He nods silently.

"I hope so. Your family has certainly endured some rough times this year, with your mom's death, and now Damien's. I'm sure losing Adrian Leopoldo stung too."

"The only thing that stings is their betrayal," I tell him. "It seems that we can sometimes not trust those closest to us."

The detective nods again. "That's the truth. But I hope it will no longer be the truth for you. Good luck, Mr. Minaldi."

He pauses at the door. "And the families of those girls…. They really appreciate the memorial funds you set up. That was generous of you."

"It's the least I could do," I answer politely.

"It was very generous," he replies. "Have a good night, Mr. Minaldi."

"Thank you. You as well."

The detective leaves and I stare at the empty door frame.

It's truly over. The case has been closed. Damien has been repaid for his betrayal by taking my place in Adrian's crimes. It seems like poetic justice. He did so want to be me.

I start to pour a glass of scotch, but stop, watching the way the amber liquid sparkles in the crystal decanter. With one fluid movement, I throw the decanter out the balcony doors, into the gardens.

I'll not drink it again. That vice nearly cost me my life.

I take a gulp of water instead, before I hurry down the hall to my wife.

My wife.

The words make me smile.

Chapter Thirty-Seven

Eva

The pain threatens to rip me apart and I grab my knees, screaming, as sweat pours from my temples.

Luca sits at my head, holding my hand, even though I know I'm crushing his fingers. He doesn't complain.

"You're almost there," he tells me softly. "You're doing so well. You're so strong."

The doctor between my legs smiles up at us. "I see the head. Two more good pushes should do it."

The nurse on the other side of Luca leans into my face. "Take a deep breath and then bear down with all of your might."

I focus on the pain, on getting rid of the pain and I inhale as much as my tired lungs will allow before bellowing like a bull and pushing as hard as I can.

I feel a movement between my legs, a blessed relief from the ungodly pressure that had lingered there for hours, then hear a thin wail.

The doctor smiles again as he holds my dark-haired baby triumphantly in the air.

"I was wrong. It only took one good push."

He lays the squirming infant on my chest and despite her wet, red skin and her puffy eyes, I know she's the most beautiful thing I've ever seen in my life.

"She's beautiful," Luca breathes and I smile.

"She looks like you."

He shakes his head. "Not if she's lucky."

I chuckle and am filled with a tired joy. It took fifteen hours of labor, but Aria is finally here and I can hold her in my arms, safe and sound.

Luca doesn't leave my side. After the baby is cleaned up and resting comfortably in a bassinet next to my bed, he settles into the chair.

"You should go home and rest," I tell him tiredly. I can barely keep my eyes open and I yawn while I speak, covering my mouth sheepishly.

Luca smiles. "Go to sleep, love. I'll be here when you wake."

I have to admit that it brings me comfort to know he's near. Even though my head knows that we're safe now, my heart hasn't forgotten what happened. I nod.

"Then don't sleep there. Sleep here... with your arms around me."

Luca glances toward the door, where any minute my stern elderly nurse could re-emerge."

I laugh.

"Luca Minaldi is scared of a little old lady?"

He rolls his eyes as he gets to his feet and folds his tall form behind mine on the little hospital bed.

"This is cozy," he murmurs, minutes before we both fall asleep. Nowadays, we're only truly comfortable when we're together.

But after everything that's happened, I think that's understandable.

The last thing I see before sleep overtakes me is Luca's hand curled around mine, and my baby girl's peaceful face.

Chapter Thirty-Eight

Luca

I watch from the balcony as Eva strolls the gardens with tiny baby Aria. The baby's pink clad arms wave healthily in the air as Eva drapes her over her shoulder. Eva insists that the sea air is good for her, that she needs to walk with her every day.

Sometimes I join them, sometimes I don't.

Today, I sit with a battered leather journal on my lap, my fingers hesitant to open it.

Eva had given me the book weeks ago and had stared at me in concern as she told me what it contained.

"Your mom wasn't lucid sometimes," she reminded me. "Some of her words don't make sense. But some of them, you need to hear."

She looked at me so seriously, that I could no nothing but nod.

"Very well," I'd told her. "I'll read it when I'm ready."

I'm not sure if I'm ready today, but if I'm not now, I'll never be. So without another thought, I open it up and begin to read.

At times over the next hour, my fingers clench into fists over her words, or my stomach tightens, but I still read on. It's a side of my mother I never saw...an open and honest side, in a book she believed to be private.

When I'm almost done, when the book is almost completely read, one passage causes my eyes to burn.

I wish I'd miscarried Luca. His life will only bring him pain, and I can't bear the thought. I've brought him into a dark world, a world where he will be alone because I don't have the power to save him. Every day, I see the light in his eyes extinguish, replaced with a dark foreboding. He's tortured and I cannot save him. It would've been better had he not been born, then he would never have to live this nightmare.

A long ragged breath escapes me and I close my eyes, remembering the day on the cliffs when she'd screamed that she should've had my nurse drown me when I was an infant.

At the time, I thought she was simply being vicious... horrible words from a malicious person.

But now I think I understand.

Melina Minaldi wasn't a horrible person. She was tragic. A prisoner in this long and dark game between the Leopoldos and Minaldis. A victim of circumstance. She had no way out and between the drugs and her own dementia, she had suffered. She was never really given the chance to be a good person, or a decent mother.

I can't hold that against her. Deep down inside, I think she loved me in her own way. At the very least, she didn't want me to suffer. That has to say something.

I carry the journal with me through the gardens, down the trail and to the mausoleums. I can feel Eva staring at me from behind as she lingers near the house. She doesn't follow. She's so intuitive, she can probably sense that I need a moment alone to say this goodbye.

In the mausoleum, I pause.

The smell of the damp stone brings back instant memories of being confined here, beneath this room with the body of my mother. I blink the memory away. That time is past. This place will never confine me again.

I open the door to an unlocked, empty crypt and place the book inside. Laying my hand on the door, I picture my mother, in a rare lucid moment when she'd seemed happy for a minute.

"Mother, I'll have you moved up here, to your rightful place next to father," I murmur to the air. "I know you loved him, in your own way. I'm sorry for all that has happened. But I've made it right. Rest in peace."

The air around me is still and silent and the hair raises a bit on my neck. I feel as though a presence lingers near, listening to my every word. But I look, and nothing is there.

My imagination wanders away though, and I imagine that my mother is lingering in the shadows, listening to me. Watching me.

"I love you," I tell her. "I always did. Even when you didn't really deserve it. And I know you loved me, too."

I walk away.

I walk into the sunshine, back across the trails where the flowers sway in the breeze, back toward Chessarae, where the towers rise toward the sun. When I am almost there, I turn and look over my shoulder toward the mausoleum.

Rose petals blow across the path, swirling into the breeze. They weren't there a moment ago, and they quickly blow over the cliffs, drifting down into the sea, carried by the wind.

I pause, and I should be unnerved, but I'm not. It feels like closure, a closure that I've never had before. My mother and father are gone, both lives ended in so much pain.

But perhaps, just perhaps, they are finally at peace. I feel a certain stillness as I watch the flowers, my mother's roses, float in the water, out to sea in the current.

Chessarae used to house so many dark secrets, so much treachery and hate. But Eva and I will change that. Between us, we'll fill the rooms with laughter and love, open the doors and expose every secret.

Because secrets only breed more secrets and darkness and hate.

We have no need for that anymore. From this point on, we'll live our lives in the sun.

Eva smiles at me as I approach and I smile back, watching the way she cradles the baby near to her heart, sheltering Aria from the breeze, from anything that could harm her.

Eva is what a mother should be, loving and loyal and strong. She's my wife, my life, my best friend. I can't ask for anything more.

I take her hand, and together, we stroll through the halls of Chessarae, so I can play our daughter to sleep.

Epilogue

Eva

I lay on the beach, a floppy hat protecting my pale skin, as my daughter and Grendel splash in the shallow water of the sea.

"Mama, watch this!" Aria shouts, her dark curls bouncing on her shoulders. Her gray eyes, so like mine, sparkle with laughter as she takes a running leap and bounds over a tiny wave. Lifting her chin, she looks back at me proudly, as though she'd just hurdled the moon.

"Excellent job, sweetie!" I call back. She smiles and tackles Grendel and they roll around in the water.

It's been four years since everything happened, since Luca was held captive by Adrian, since Grendel was shot and Aria was born.

Grendel has grown old, his muzzle white and his joints tired. But he still guards Aria with the ferocity of a pup. He knows his job is to protect her and he does it very well. He never leaves her side.

"Are you getting too hot?"

Luca's voice breaks the silence around me and I turn, watching my beautiful husband tread lightly down the hill leading to the beach. He's dressed casually, in swim trunks and a t-shirt.

"You're joining us?" I ask happily. "I thought you had to work."

He shrugs. "What's the point in running your own company if you can't take a day off? I needed to make sure you didn't overheat. I've heard that's common in pregnancy."

I palm my belly, which is swollen with our son. I'm just weeks away from the delivery of our second child.

"I've come up with a name," I tell him hesitantly, because every name we've thought of lately hasn't been a match for us. He smiles patiently now.

"And what is it this time? Ronald? Archibald? Gilbert?" He rolls his eyes and I giggle.

"God, no. I thought of a traditional Maltese name. I think you'll like it."

He waits, his dark eyes sparkling.

"Michel Lucien," I tell him proudly. "Michel because I like it, and Lucien after your great-great-great grandfather and namesake."

Luca beams. "I love it," he announces. "It's perfect."

I sigh a breath of relief as I watch Aria splashing nearby. "Our son has a name."

"Our son has a name," Luca agrees. "And my wife is very smart. Speaking of that, your clinic has sent over the files that you wanted to see. Apparently, my wife isn't good at taking maternity leave."

I shrug. "The baby hasn't been born yet. It doesn't hurt to work a tiny bit."

"And they said that your patient will come out here at 4:00 for you to see him."

Luca stares at me now, humor filling his eyes.

"Before you say anything, I simply want to get his initial evaluation done. The baby will be born soon and—"

Luca shakes his head. "I love you. Of course I'm not going to say anything. It's why you turned my mother's wing into a lab and your offices.... So you could work from home when you wish to. You worked hard to get where you are, my love. And you put everything on hold for me for quite a while. I'm not going to get in your way now. I only ask that you don't overdo it. Don't wear yourself out."

I smile up at him. "How did I get so lucky?" I ask him. "Fate smiled on me when I met you."

Luca says nothing, but he reaches over and grabs my hand.

Slowly, over the last four years, he's come to terms with everything that happened, with his life, with the Minaldi legacy of lies and treachery... and with the idea that he can change the future of the Minaldi line.

His legacy will be one of beautiful things... of supporting the arts, of being active in the Valetta community, of helping those who need it, and of being a loyal and loving husband and father.

The Minaldi legacy has been forever changed.

"I love you," he tells me, leaning down to kiss my lips, his mouth soft against mine.

"I know," I answer.

Together, we turn and watch Grendel and Aria play in the sun, evidence of our beautiful life.

Peace has finally found us.

ABOUT THE AUTHOR

Courtney Cole is a New York Times and USA Today bestselling novelist. She love Greek mythology, cashmere socks and standing on the shore of Lake Michigan with her toes in the water. You can almost always find her staring dreamily out her office window.

To learn more about her, please visit
www.courtneycoleauthor.com or
www.courtneycolewrites.com

Preview of IF YOU STAY

Chapter One

"Pax."

I can't be sure that the girl said my name. Her voice is muffled and unintelligible and hard to understand, mostly because my dick is in her mouth.

Slumping against the black leather seat of my car, I push the girl's head down further, wordlessly urging her to bury more of me in her throat.

"Don't talk," I tell her. "Just suck."

I close my eyes and listen. I can hear the spit pooling in her mouth and sliding out the corners. Her cheek makes a soft sound as it grazes my open zipper. She moans periodically, although I don't understand it. She's not getting anything out of this. My hand is on her head, pushing, pushing. Guiding her movements and her speed. I grip the hair at the base of her neck, winding it in my fingers; pulling it, releasing it, then pulling it again.

She moans again.

I still don't know why.

I still don't care.

I'm high as fuck.

And I don't know her name.

Everything is a fog, except this moment. I tune out the crashing sounds of Lake Michigan to our right, and the sounds of the cars on the highway a few miles away. I block out the glowing lights from town. I tune out the roaring quiet and the occasional thought that someone might happen by and see us. No one is out here on the beach, not at 11:00 pm. Not that I would care anyway.

Right now, all I'm focused on is this blow job.

I already know that I'm not ready to come, but I don't tell her because I don't want her to stop yet, either. I let her go for a few minutes more before I push her away.

"Take a break," I tell her as I settle back into my seat.

I don't bother to put myself away, I just sigh loud and long as I relax in the breeze. The girl turns her attention to the visor mirror, trying to straighten her mess of a face.

"Wait," I instruct. "Hold on for a minute."

She looks at me in confusion, her lipstick smeared. I smile.

"I know you want some of this," I tell her, grabbing a little bottle from my jacket pocket. I dump a few coke pebbles onto a little mirror on my console and crush them with a razor, dragging the powder into two straight lines.

I offer her the little straw and now she's the one smiling with her distorted clown mouth.

She snorts at her line, coughs, then snorts it again.

Settling back into her seat, she tilts her face to the car roof as she lets the drug take effect. Her eyes are empty as she thrusts the straw at me and I hesitate for only a second.

I've hit it hard today and I've done more than I usually do.

Of everything.

But for some reason, the need to disappear into the black is strong today, stronger than usual. And it's on days like this that I hit the hard stuff. I grab the straw and do my line, breathing in the powder that never fails to take me away. Even when I can count on nothing else, I can always count on this.

The familiar burn immediately numbs my throat. The emptiness spreads throughout the rest of my body, dulling my senses, speeding up my heart. I can feel the blood pulsing through it, hard and pounding, carrying oxygen to my numb fingers.

I fucking love this shit.

I love the way it dulls everything but my attention. I love how it heightens my awareness while still turning everything else black and numb.

This is where I am comfortable. Drifting here into this nothingness, this obscurity.

Coke makes it easy to exist in the emptiness.

I run my fingers through the traces of the remaining powder and slide it along the skin of my erection before grabbing the girl by the back of the neck. I shove her head back down and she opens her mouth willingly. This is most definitely not against her will. She wants to be here.

Especially now that I have fed her habit.

Especially now that she can lick her habit from my dick. If she moans now I'll believe it because she's getting something out of it, too.

"Finish," I tell her. I stroke her back while she moves and I can't feel my fingers.

Her head bobs for a few more minutes and then without warning, I come in her mouth. Her eyes widen and she starts to pull away as my ejaculate seeps from the edges of her lips, but I hold her fast by the back of the neck until my dick stops throbbing.

"Swallow," I tell her politely.

Her blank eyes widen, but she swallows obediently.

I smile.

She gags, but she doesn't heave.

"Thank you," I say, still polite. And then I lean past her and shove open the passenger side door. It creaks as it swings wide, evidence that cars were still made from iron back in 1968. I pull out my wallet and hand her a dog-eared twenty.

"Get yourself something to eat," I tell her. "You're too skinny."

She's got the look that girls on nose candy get. The way-too-thin look. That's one downfall of the stuff. It's good for drifting away into oblivion, but it's hell on your appetite. If you don't make yourself eat, you'll waste away and start looking like shit.

This girl doesn't look like shit. Yet. She's not ugly. But she's not pretty either. She mostly looks hardened. Mousy brown hair, pale blue eyes. Bland, stick-thin body. I can take her or leave her.

And I'm leaving her.

She glares at me as she wipes her mouth.

"My car is in town. Aren't you at least going to take me back to it?"

I look at her and note how there are three of her that blur into one, then back into three, before I shake the blurriness from my head and try to focus again.

Nope. Still three of her.

"Can't," I tell her, dropping my head heavily against the headrest. "I'm too fucked up to drive. It's not that far, anyway. It's not my fault that you wore five-inch stripper shoes. Just take them off. It'll make it easier to walk."

"You're a fucking asshole, Pax Tate," she spits angrily. "You know that?"

She grabs her purse from the floor and slams my car door as hard as she can. My car, Danger, shakes from her efforts.

Yes, I named my car. A 1968 Dodge Charger in pristine condition deserves a name.

And no, I don't care that this coked up little bitch thinks I'm an asshole. I *am* an asshole. I'm not going to deny it.

As if to prove that point, I can't even think of her name right now even though it only took me one second to recall the name of my car. I might remember the girl's in the morning or I might not. That doesn't matter to me at this point. She'll come back. She always does.

I've got what she wants.

I strip off my jacket and lay it on the passenger seat, zipping my pants back up as I watch her stomp away. Then I open my own door, dangling one black boot over the doorsill, letting the cool breeze rustle over my flushed, overheated body.

The landscape up and down the coast is jagged and rolling and wild. It is so vast that it makes me feel small. The night is inky black and there are barely any stars. It's the kind of night where a guy can just disappear into the dark. My kind of night.

I rest my head against the seat and allow the car to spin around me. It feels as though the seat is the anchor that is holding me to the ground. Without it, I might drift off into space and no one will ever see me again.

It's not a bad notion.

But the car is spinning too fast. Even in this state, I know it's too fast. I'm not going to worry about it, though. I simply pull out my vial and take something to slow things down. My vial is like a magician's hat. It's got a little bit of everything in it. Everything I need; fast or slow, white or blue, capsule, pill or rock. I've got it.

I wash the pill down with a gulp of whiskey. I don't even feel the burn as it slides down my throat. I consider it for a minute, the speed that things are turning and blurring around me. I decide I should take another pill, maybe even two. I put them in my mouth and take another slog of Jack before I toss the bottle onto the passenger side floor. I realize that I don't know if I put the cap back on or not.

Then I realize that I don't care.

The drug-induced fog blurs my vision and all of the blacks and grays swirl together and I close my eyes against it. I still feel like I'm moving, like the car is spinning round and round.

The night swallows me and I am propelled into the darkness, far above the clouds and into the night sky, sailing through the stars, past the moon. Reaching out, I touch it with a finger.

I laugh.

Or I think I laugh.

It's hard to say at this point. I don't know what's real or not real. And that's just the way I like it.

* * *

If you have enjoyed this preview, the rest of the novel can be purchased at any major book retailer.